THE TEMPLE OF HYMEN

JACQUI LOFTHOUSE

THE TEMPLE OF HYMEN

HAMISH HAMILTON · LONDON

HAMISH HAMILTON LTD
Published by the Penguin Group
Penguin Books Ltd, 27 Wrights Lane, London w8 5tz, England
Penguin Books USA Inc., 375 Hudson Street, New York, New York 10014, USA
Penguin Books Australia Ltd, Ringwood, Victoria, Australia
Penguin Books Canada Ltd, 10 Alcorn Avenue, Toronto, Ontario, Canada m4v 3b2
Penguin Books (NZ) Ltd, 182–190 Wairau Road, Auckland 10, New Zealand

Penguin Books Ltd, Registered Offices: Harmondsworth, Middlesex, England

First published 1995
1 3 5 7 9 10 8 6 4 2

Filmset by Datix International Limited, Bungay, Suffolk
Printed in England by Clays Ltd, St Ives plc
Set in 11/13.5 pt Monophoto Garamond

A CIP catalogue record for this book is available from the British Library
ISBN 0–241–00308–3

For David Lewis

ACKNOWLEDGEMENTS

I would like to thank my agent, Caroline Dawnay, and my editor, Kate Jones, for their faith, advice and encouragement. Alexandra Pringle, Ravi Mirchandani and Antonia Till have all been instrumental in bringing this book to publication.

Dr Paula Johnson has advised me on specific medical questions. And Chris Norton, Stephanie Hale and Francis Mead have all made invaluable comments.

Thanks are also due to Pauline Savage, James Peries, Ian Diamond and Annie Lee. Also to my mother, Iris Lofthouse, and my late father, Jack Lofthouse. Most of all, of course, to David Lewis, who opened the door to the Temple.

I

VERMILION

I MUST BEGIN with a warning. A warning to the fair sex, to be precise, for if this narrative falls into the hands of a lady, she might be forgiven for thinking it a moral work, when indeed that would be far from the case. If I did not intervene in Emilia's tale, a person of modest disposition might imagine it to be a work of romance, believing that a female author can always be trusted to deliver an honourable tale of love and marriage, a story of a woman who faces great adversity, but never succumbs to the wiles of the rakish villain who pursues her. A heroine, you will know, by her very nature is beautiful and fair, chaste and virtuous. And when this tale begins, in 1780, the year that Dr Graham first opened his famed Adelphi Temple, so you will find Emilia. But, Reader, do not be deceived, and, if you are a lady, I advise you not to be curious, but rather to close this book immediately, and turn to another on your shelf, for this one will do you no good. I thank you for your interest, but I tell you, this story is not for you.

Good. Have they gone? I'll speak frankly then.

Gentlemen – what I am about to present to you is a document of unprecedented intrigue. A diary, in fact, unlike any you have read before. The story it tells is one in which I have a personal interest; indeed, I am a chief player in this drama, and though I may not agree with the author's version of events, it is to my credit, I hope, that I have not altered a word she has written. No, though Emilia suspected otherwise, let it be known that in these pages, her voice is her own. There is no tampering with the words, to titillate the reader. This is what she feared – that I would create falsehoods about her life – yet in truth, if she had not been so afraid, her story might never have been written. She would be forgotten now, by all but me.

Emilia will tell you differently of course. In her lifetime, it is true, I threatened to write her biography, yet I never truly believed that I had it in me. You will discover I am not much of a literary man, and if she had only realized this, perhaps she would not have taken the trouble to write the diaries in self-defence. Indeed, I would say that in her ignorance of my character, she brought the fate she feared upon herself, for had I never seen these documents, I am certain I would not have been stirred, as I am now, to tell her story. It is sheer chance, I would say, that I am embarking on this project at all, for though I was moved when first I read her scribblings ten years ago, it is only now that I desire to write. I have been absent in France these last years, and until recently was too caught up with pleasure to think about Emilia. Though one woman has gone to the grave, I told myself, there are thousands of others with flesh upon them.

Yet now I am home, and I find I think only of her. I imagined I would not be able to forget the unexpected horrors of these last months, but instead, I am plagued with more distant memories. Perhaps I am unwilling to think about the present. Carmine Hall has decayed somewhat in my absence, and I suspect it is the air of loneliness here that has provoked thoughts of the Temple. Though it is late June, I have never known so much rain. Each day it begins again, pouring from a granite sky on to absurdly green lawns. Only at night does it stop, and the silence echoes along the corridors. The servants sleep below, yet there is such a feeling of emptiness here that I believe myself alone in the house. Most of the furniture is still covered in sheets, the fires remain unlit. I am in a state of indecision, you understand, about the future of my home, and I am superstitious about fires. It goes back to my days in the Temple, and the teachings of the Doctor.

Even now it rains. From my window, I see far, along the rows of lime to the folly, and I am struck, once again, by the stagnant nature of this country. There is too much symmetry

2

here: the terms, the shadowless trees, the *patte d'oie*. This order will never be overturned. It is England's fate that it will always be the same. But I turn away from it. I find comfort in disorder, in the loose bundles in front of me, in the shapeless story that I have yet to weave. Weave! You see, I cannot help it. I desire the past, its lack of form, the luxury of warmth and colour and disarray that we experienced in the Adelphi, and yet I am an Englishman, in spite of all. I cannot accept untidiness. I must find a pattern. I must order it, so that I, Vermilion, can be at peace.

Bear with me then, Gentlemen, as I open the bundles. And if the Ladies have read thus far, I warn them once again to go no further. The packages have a deceptive appearance, for though they are wrapped in white silk and tied with a rose-coloured sash, I tell you, these garments are a sham. The contents of the parcels are not pure or decent as their clothing might imply. Emilia's diaries are full of lascivious thoughts, which, if spoken aloud, would offend the delicate ear. If you continue, Ladies, you must take the consequences.

Now, look again, as I remove the silk. I hold it high and its length tumbles to the ground. This is not just a piece of fabric that you see, but a dress, a white gown with rose girdle. And you will find that each sheaf of papers is wrapped in this way, in a robe that she wore for the Doctor. It pains me to see them like this, still beautiful, still intact when she is not. I remember when I was led to the diaries, shortly after her funeral. I was filled with a sense of loss to see these garments thus unchanged. So awed was I by the discovery that I did not dare open the parcels, but rather took one and held it to my nose, relishing its softness, breathing in the stale perfume and beneath that, the mousy odour of paper. I knew what lay within, I could feel each leaf that she had written on, each fibre of string, holding them together, but I was not ready for her words. And later, in my study, as I first fumbled with the knots she had so carefully tied, I was trembling, not in anticipation but with sorrow. Yes, Gentlemen. I, Vermilion, a libertine who has broken a thousand hearts. It is impossible, you might think, I should be moved,

3

and yet it happened. She was, you will discover, a creature of infinite charm.

Enough. For whatever my emotions at that moment, they have been tainted now by the words that she has written. I do not love Emilia, you understand. That notion is quite alien to my heart. But she had something. A thing I cannot define, for I believed I had forgotten her, yet here she is again, worming her way into my thoughts.

And so, as I have no choice but to think of her, I have decided to write this memoir. I will be her biographer, allowing her to speak for herself, intruding only where I feel she is not eloquent or rational. For though the female sex are wont to exaggerate, though they seldom speak with a knowledgeable voice, there are some who have a sensibility so exquisite that we are overcome and must bow down to their intuitive genius. Women, it is to be admitted, often have a superior talent in the realm of *feeling*, and though Emilia's work lacks modesty, she still retains some feminine graces. Often, when reading her words, I have been struck by a phrase, or an observation, that has no logical basis, but stems from this instinctive power.

These graces alone, however, are not enough – what is required is a balanced view, and it is with this in mind that I have decided to be your commentator. You will be glad, I am certain, to hear the voice of Reason once in a while. I would not wish you to be seduced by her words, as I was, but instead to see them for what they are. Her innocence, Gentlemen, is counterfeit. Do not be weakened by it. Do not pity her. I advise you to be sceptical.

Yet now, even before I open the first manuscript, I fear the outcome of this work. Already, I doubt if you will have the strength to resist her. When I found the papers, they were loose bundles, tied with string. So delicate, they were, each page such fragile parchment that I thought the paper was the product of some alchemy, fashioned from the wings of dragonflies perhaps, or beaten gold.

Words. Words. Words. They appear trapped upon the page, yet I am eager to preserve them, before they fade or flee. My

4

own book, this, when it is finished, will be printed and bound in leather. A book is superior to a pile of papers. It is much neater, I find: fully indexed for ease of reference.

My thoughts wander, Gentlemen, yet you will find there is a point to this rambling. When a thing has great potency, great force, one must try one's best to remain aloof. Objectivity is all. When you read Emilia's words, I tell you, remain at a distance from the page; remember that you are a man, and as such your element is earth. You must not be affected by aery substances if you wish to retain your strength.

And so, with the knowledge that you are prepared, I will present her words to you. Her pages will slip easily between my own. I too will read her journals once again, though I am afraid of what I will find here. Emilia has been silent these ten years; while I have been away, the journals have remained undisturbed, wrapped again in her white robes, which I had not the heart to discard. To delve now, into what is done, what is past, may not be wise or fruitful. Yet it is a compulsion. I have no choice but to hear her voice again.

It must be now, then. I cannot hesitate longer in this task. Though my hand trembles, I must let Emilia speak.

Yes. There, on yellowing pages, her script is still visible. A fine hand, with a slant to the right, but no flourishes, for, unlike me, she wrote quickly I think, knowing that death was upon her. You must judge for yourself, Gentlemen. You must form your own opinion. But read slowly, and read with care. I tell you, she is not to be trusted.

EMILIA

VERMILION HAS TOLD me that when I am dead, he will chronicle my life: my birth (of which he knows nothing), my youth (ditto), my days at the Temple (of which he knows much) and the unfortunate accident which forced me to leave that place. No doubt he means this as a kind of threat, for I cannot think of him now but as a sinister man, who means to do me harm. The very thought of his pen, scrawling black marks across a virgin page, marks that will tell a future generation about me and the events which have shaped me, fills me with fear. His story is not my story. His story, though it will no doubt be eloquent and amusing, will not be true. Yet it cannot be stopped. I know that when I die (which will be soon), Vermilion will live. He will scatter flowers on my grave and then he will retire to his room to defile my memory. Reader, if you believe him, you will betray me. Do not be charmed by him, as I was. Listen to my story.

VERMILION

NO! SHE KNOWS nothing! You must listen to me. For I am older than she, and she is rotting beneath the ground. I am obliged to remind you that our heroine is nothing but worm-food. If it were not for me, and my gracious act of saving her papers, even her words would have been lost.

I see you are shocked. You had not expected me to interrupt so soon. It is true, I find it difficult to stand back and allow you to be cajoled by her. The very act of reading these words is agonizing for me. I recoil from placing these pages between my own. For you see how she turns you against me? She suggests I will lie, but even I do not yet know what I shall write, so her statements cannot be justified. Even so – I feel I must repeat myself. She exists no longer. I am here, a live man, in my study. I am not, perhaps, in my prime, but I am more than she. She is a putrid mass of bones.

And so, continue. I will absent myself for a while. Like you, I will be a Reader. And if her words seem to bring her alive, if you feel sure you see her shadow pass beyond the window, remember it is not true. It is a simply a trick of the light.

EMILIA

IMAGINE A STORY with no beginning and no end. There is no beginning because the author fears beginnings and no end because the author is not yet dead. Is it possible that such a story could exist? And if it is, tell me, how can that story start?

I am faced, you see, with an impossible task; easier to spin straw into gold than weave a tale without form. I do not have the ingredients; the past is too painful to disturb. And yet I must disturb it; unearth my fears and let them breathe again. I must dig deep in the soil, and as I lever my shovel they will emerge, shaking the mud from their garments. I will watch them act out my story, these ghostly creatures of the dust that can do me no harm. For that is all they are now, faded shadows, dancing in my memory, waiting to be summoned. They are all there, and now, as night falls, I see them more clearly, spectres before my eyes. They are shadows of my self: the Babe, the Murderer, the Devil, the Goddess. Two step forward, hand in hand, their eyes fixed on mine. One wears yellow, the other black. Their purpose is clear.

'Begin with us,' they say. 'Begin with us.'

And at first I do not trust them. It is not right that I should start here, in the middle of the story. But no other spectre volunteers itself. The true beginning is indistinguishable from the crowd.

See me then in January 1780, more than three years ago now. A cold night in the Royal Terrace, Adelphi. My sleep is fitful and disturbed. Between bouts of dreaming, I raise my hands to scratch my head. I feel that there is something in my hair, though in truth it lies clean and undisturbed on my pillow.

In the next room I hear footsteps. They belong to my brother, who is still dazed by our father's death. But it is not this that prevents my rest. Nor is it a sense of loss that has prompted my recent illness, though my brother believes this to be the case. I have been suffering from hot flushes and fainting fits. Sometimes I feel as if I am burning alive, and even now I feel as if my scalp is being scalded, though I am shivering also. In my bedchamber the air is still, the mirrors are turned to the walls. The night seems interminable.

Outside, something is happening, though I am not yet aware of it. A change: winter metamorphoses the city. It will change me, also, but I do not know it yet. All I can do is drift between these two states, waking and sleeping, trying to banish the thoughts that run through my head. Thoughts of the Doctor.

But I cannot. His presence, though I have never met the man, will not leave me. I am trying, in my half-dreams, to find the cause of my obsession, but each thought only serves to fan the flames. I see his arrival, first of all, in the house next door to our own, and his erection of a huge golden star on the door of his house, which he calls his Temple. We have been at the Adelphi since last January; he arrived in August and opened his Temple in October, an event which caused my father great distress. I see his face, in front of me now, swelling with rage at the discovery.

'Nothing but a bawdy-house,' he says. 'If that little Scottish Macaroni wants to set up a seraglio, then he is very welcome to it, but I'll be damned if he'll do it in the Royal Terrace.'

8

My brother disagrees – an unusual step. It is rare that he contradicts my father.

'The Doctor is no Macaroni, sir,' he replies. 'And . . .'

I interrupt him.

'What is a Macaroni, Daniel?'

'One of those silly foppish long-haired fellows,' he replies, 'whose whole being is centred in his attire. And yet a Macaroni's dress is so womanish, I tell you, it is sometimes difficult to tell him apart from that sex.'

'Why do they have that name?'

'Because they are a much-travelled bunch, and delight in eating all the fancy titbits that they have discovered overseas. Macaroni is some Italian dish. But Emilia, you distract me. The point is, sir,' (he addresses my father again) 'that the Temple is not an indecent place. Have you not seen how many fine ladies visit it each evening? And do you not remember the great regard in which Dr Graham was held when he practised in Bristol?'

But already I have had enough. I throw the blankets from me. I want to banish this scene from my head; want to sleep. Again I put my hands to my hair, run my fingers through its length. I am on fire. Delirious.

'I remember it well, Daniel,' my father replies. 'Dr Graham – the man who claimed he could cure the blind and the deaf! You see my eyes, Daniel? You see my eyes?'

He grabs hold of Daniel; pulls him closer so they are face to face.

'Only half-blind! You see it? Only half-blind! But he could not cure me.'

Then my father vanishes, as quickly as he came, his fading voice crying out, 'Close your curtains, Emilia. Do not look from your window!'

But I do look, and I see the carriages arriving outside the Temple. And the Doctor, beyond my bedroom wall, passing his hand through the air, magically curing his visitors of their ills. I am there also, in black, my face raging red, my hair on fire. I am a black candle. But the Doctor gives me a pill and a potion

9

which I swallow, and the colour fades from me; the blaze is extinguished.

I pull the blankets close again; so cold now, and awake. I tell myself that mine are symptoms he cannot cure, symptoms of a greater malaise than a doctor might understand. And I must not go to him. My father forbade it. Though my limbs are numb with the insistent chill of this night, I remain still. What can I do but wait?

Dawn comes at last. Darkness is lifted from the room, and I see, once again, the shape of things. It is a stark light, a light I am not accustomed to, and I do not move. I watch the chink in the curtain from which the brightness emanates, anticipating the familiar morning sounds: the chatter of traders by the river, the clatter of horse-hooves on the pavement. But they do not begin. All is silent. Even the footsteps have stopped in the next room. And when, after an hour, there is still no noise, I get up and dress. I pull my stays tight, in the way that I have been taught, and fasten my cork rump on my behind, for today, my brother has told me, he may bring a visitor to meet me, and I must be fully dressed. I pull my black dress over my head, and button it up to the nape of my neck. Then I move to the window and tug at the curtain. At first I see nothing. I am confused a moment before I realize that the window is white with frost. I know now why I am so cold, but still the silence puzzles me, so I open the windows and, tripping over my skirt, step out on to the balcony.

I am astonished by what I see, almost disbelieving it. I close my eyes, then open them again to make sure I am not dreaming. But no. It is true. A miracle has occurred. The Thames has frozen.

I do not know how long I stood there, staring at the spectacle: the white sky above, the white ice below. Since we had lived in the Adelphi the ever-changing agitation of the scene, the river's flux, the passage of ships, had made me ill at ease. I cannot explain it, except by saying that perhaps I was jealous of these vessels that passed my window without acknowledging me. They came from far-off places that I would never know, yet they did not stop to tell their secrets. They passed in silence; they did not care for me. But now all had been stilled, frozen into immobility. Even the sails, which usually flapped in the wind, filling the air with a soft drumming sound, were held stiff, as if time had stopped for them. Trade had stopped, water had stopped, so perhaps the sun, also, would freeze in the sky and arrest the progress of the day.

The world had ceased its spinning, become still, like me, so that I might consider things anew. The world had stopped, for my pleasure: because I willed it. For the first time, I was the centre of things and I might regard this scene as a queen regards her dominion. There was no limit set upon the time. The world was ripe for observation.

And so I looked, first up at the sky (for perhaps, I thought, it held the secret of this change). It seemed low and heavy, all puffed up with snow that would not fall until I desired it. It was not white as I had thought at first, but yellowish, and thick, white only on the horizon, over the distant, snow-covered hills. But I could not long keep my eyes from the river. The dark green depths that held, I thought, secrets I could never know, had turned into a brilliant pavement, a creamy white surface that stretched to east and west as far as the eye could see, trapping barges and wherries, huge sail-boats and row-boats in its wake. It was like a carnival, I thought, that had not yet begun, for the colours of these vessels appeared so gay, and the vague sun, reflecting on the ice, made each flag, each sail, seem to light up with brilliance. All dullness had been drained from this place. London was held in a watery vice and had no choice but to submit to it.

I watched in a daze. The sun broke through the clouds, and tinted the ice pale gold, but it was not a strong sun, and I did not fear that it would melt the ice. I felt the chill still, right through me, and though I felt short of breath and extremely weak, I could not seem to draw myself away. Though I soon saw that the world had not stopped, that to think no person moved below had been a delusion, I remained convinced that this miracle was a kind of signal to me. And it was then, I believe, that I made my decision, the decision I had been delaying for many days. Before that moment, I myself had been frozen: immobile, unable to act. The freezing water altered everything. If water, I thought, whose very essence is movement, can be stilled, then I too can become something else. I too can be transformed. I decided to visit the Doctor.

3

VERMILION

SO, GENTLEMEN - HOW do you like my Emilia? She is a strange
one, I grant you that, but are you beginning to see her attractions? Now that you know her a little better, perhaps you might
understand why she haunts me still.

I am yearning, you see, for that winter of 1780. I have been
too long in France, and Emilia's words take me back to my
youth in London. There are moments, I believe, in each life,
that become symbolic of one's happiness. I had thought myself
happy in Paris, but I realize now that I never was. No. I see
myself, a young rake, still lean and agile, strolling along the Mall
from my lodgings in St James's towards the Adelphi. Emilia
might have seen me as she sat at her window, but at the time she
had no thoughts of men beside the Doctor. I close my eyes, and
see it all again – the ice, my easy stride, my sense of purpose.
And I see the Adelphi Terrace also, a kind of palace, rising from
the mud of the Thames; a building unlike any I had seen before.
But when I open my eyes, that moment when it all lay ahead of
me is elusive as ever. Going back is not an option.

This, then, is all I have. This house, Carmine Hall, and all its
contents, left to me by my beloved parents, whose untimely
death came shortly after Emilia's. That was the start of my
decline perhaps, for I sought to overcome my grief by a passion
for collecting: paintings, statues, furniture, and, of course,
women, but it did not take me long to realize that money breeds
boredom. A man, in fact a nobleman (for that is what I am, Lord
Vermilion), who has money in his purse, cannot long retain the
sense of purpose which he possessed when his purse was not his
own, but his father's. Once one has bought everything in sight,
when one has bought so much that one is sick of buying, there

is nothing much left to do (except buy more). That is why I went to France; not to recover my ambition, but to revel in my lack of it, as I was sick of revelling here.

And so, as I do not now wish to recount my time abroad (some things are not worth telling, much else is too close and too painful), you find me here. Lord Vermilion – portly, balding and full of gout. I am only forty, but I find, already, that my body is in decay. I am glad you cannot see me, for I am ashamed of my appearance. My swollen toe joints make it difficult for me to walk, my hands are unsightly: great bulging awkward things, the right one scarred from an accident I once had. Yes, a line of scar tissue crosses the flesh on the back of that hand, and not only are the joints disfigured by the swelling, but they are covered in small purplish marks, where the fingers also were badly cut. It is impossible to believe these hands were once as smooth and unblemished as white kid gloves. Indeed, it is unimaginable that in the course of a decade a man can change from a demi-god to a decrepit mortal, but this is what has occurred. Once, a woman had only to glance at me and I could be certain of a conquest. Today it seems the price of a fuck increases each day, as the severity of my condition advances.

But no more of this. Before we return to Emilia's diaries, the real business of this memoir, allow me to take you on a brief tour of Carmine Hall. It is, after all, the place where I grew up, and though I may complain about it, though today I feel a stranger here, I cannot, in truth, think of any other place which is more my home than this.

We'll begin outside, on a day without rain, by the folly, a smooth tower of white stone, standing alone, like a faery-tale castle: a love monument built by my father for my mother. When I was a child we would climb the spiral staircase inside, and from the top we could see beyond the house, across the fields of Chalk Farm. We could see the River Thames from there. The whole of London lay beneath us.

Since their death, I have kept the tower locked. I could not bear to climb those steps without them.

Let us stand instead, at the base of the tower, the focal point of the *patte d'oie*, the goose-foot avenues which spread before us. Ahead is the Hall, not red in colour as the name might suggest, but white, a Palladian mansion, designed by William Kent. We'll take this path (though in doing so, we miss the orange-tree garden by the lake and the grotto), for I am eager now that you see the house, suddenly proud of its grandeur. Look! What is your opinion of the portico? I am frequently stunned by its simplicity: the parallel lines of the columns, the perfect triangle of the pediment. Hear the gravel crunch underfoot as we approach closer, and at the foot of the stairs, beneath the columns, notice the stonework, all vermiculated, as if worms have burrowed beneath.

I am slow to ascend (have you forgotten – my gouty legs!), but wait, and allow me to open the door. I have asked the servants to lay a red carpet across the marble hall and stairway, especially for your visit. I have so few visitors these days.

And now, before I point out the main features of my home, I should make clear that it is not as it was in my parents' time. Though the structure of the building remains the same, and the surface decorations have not changed (the stucco mouldings, the cornices), most of the contents are my own, bought on my travels since their death. Note then, the statues in the recesses, originals from Rome, a Juno, an Athene, a Diana, a Bacchus. At the top of the stairs you'll see my sarcophagus and the porphyry urn at the door to the ballroom. But wait! Beyond that, dear Reader, we may not walk. No – we will not enter that room, but rather will pass it by. My house is yours! You may see it all – except for this. I tell you – do not open the ballroom door, for to do so would be to break my heart. The doors are locked and for good reason. What has passed in the room beyond, I cannot say. It is too painful to me. In my lifetime, I never wish for that door to be opened.

But let us not speak further of this. Come with me to the front of the house, to the room where I spend my days, the room I have not truly left, though you have never seen it. As I told you before, most of the house is beneath sheets, shielding my furniture from the dust; I barely have a use for it. Yet here, in the study, you can observe me, in what was once my element. It appears a cosy room, cluttered with furniture, though to me, since my return, it has been oppressive. There is an airless quality about the place, but in spite of this, I feel unable to leave it. The outside world is no longer my domain.

Instead, I remain here, not out of choice perhaps, but of necessity. It is true, I dream of the Adelphi, and the freedom of its ornamentation, yet I do not know how I should feel if I were to visit it today. I was thrilled, at the time, by the glamour of its design, the slim honeysuckle pilasters, the swags and the ribbons that decorated the walls – but all that novelty is too much for me now. I prefer the precision that I find in the old order; in Palladianism. There are no surprises for me in Carmine Hall. I have returned here with a sense of relief.

For you, however, there will be much that is unexpected. This room is stocked with treasures, and though I have now lost the appetite for collecting, I cannot find it in me to sell these things, for they are a kind of testament to what I was, perhaps to what I am. I think I might deceive myself when I say I do not care for them.

Observe then, the pictures I have crammed on to my walls. You might be surprised at their number, or impressed at their quality, yet though you may sigh about my Gainsboroughs and simper over my Watteaus, you will be further amazed as I reveal that the walls are but doors, which can be pulled back to reveal second walls, and these displaying my caricatures, my Hogarths and Rowlandsons, as well as others by lesser-known artists, of the Doctor and his Celestial Bed, or with his Goddesses in the earth-baths of Panton Street. Do not loiter here, however, for the best is yet to come. A third wall is hidden – it is impossible that the ladies should discover it – where I keep my lascivious paintings, more Venuses than you can imagine, more rapes of Lucretia, rapes of Europa, than you have dreamed of. And though now I do not often open these doors, it gives me pleasure to know that my lovelies are there. I sit, surrounded by decency, a Lady This, a Madame de That, each smiling demurely, absorbed in a book perhaps or gazing at her child. Yet this is a façade, my friends; my paintings prove it. Underneath they are carnal creatures all. Hogarth cracks the smile into a grimace, Boucher derobes them so they are all flesh and nothing more.

And so, without intention, I am brought again to thoughts of Emilia. She too appeared an innocent, and yet, I found, her appetite was equal to mine. Will you forgive me then, Gentle-men, if I stop short our tour? For I fear Emilia's story will not wait. I had intended that I, in my present incarnation, would not appear in this tale, and yet I find I am unable to suppress my rambling thoughts. No doubt I will interrupt Emilia more often than I had intended. I discover I cannot help but address myself to you. I cannot help but write the thoughts that occupy my mind.

But now I tell you. Forget my house, my paintings, my gardens, my words. I wish to be generous, I tell you. I do not wish to impose my views. Listen then, to Emilia.

4

EMILIA

YOU AND I are not acquainted. I have been at fault, for being led by spectres, creatures who know nothing of narrative, order and courtesy. Yet I knew no other way to proceed.

Now I see that you lack the simple facts. We are to travel a long way together, and it is essential that you understand me well. For if, before the river froze, my life was not extraordinary, after the thaw I experienced much which will astound you and make you doubt the truth of what I say. And though I too, one day, will be nothing but a phantom, a shadow, an absence in the history books, you must not doubt me. For I exist as well as Dr Graham. When you have heard my story, you will not question this.

And so I must attempt a beginning, though I will not delve too deeply; I am not ready for that. Let us begin, this time, with a simple introduction.

My name is Emilia Anne Beaumont. I was born in the village of Clifton, Bristol, in the year 1763, to John Henry Beaumont and Isabella Beaumont, who went to the grave soon after giving birth. This was the genesis of my distress, not the death itself, but the knowledge that it was I that killed my mother. Though I told nobody of my crime, I knew I was a murderer, the worst kind of murderer – one who kills what they love. As such, I thought, I did not deserve to live. And so, throughout my early years, though I had all the privileges of a child whose father is a wealthy merchant, I did not behave as I ought. I was an unsociable brat, who preferred to fade into the background.

Perhaps (if things had been different, that common refrain) I might have recovered from this feeling, had it not been for a strange and unfortunate event that marred my childhood further.

I had a nurse, Mrs Holland, who was to me my only comfort. My father was often away, and my older brother took no interest in me, so this woman, who bathed me and fed me, became the focus of my life. It is strange that, though she assumes magnificent importance in my early memories, I have never been able to conjure her face, nor, when I think of her, can I distinguish any true reason for the depth of my love. It was enough, I presume, that she was there. A vessel into which I could pour my affections; a warm bosom to embrace. Yes, that is what I remember – not her features or her manner, but the feel of her, the smell of her. Being in her arms was like burying oneself in hot dough.

It was spring, and Mrs Holland had a cold. Her eyes were smarting, she said, and her nose pouring like a tap. As she had never liked doctors, however (who would as soon look at you as put a leech on you), she decided that she would take a cure at the Bristol Hotwell, for though it was visited by those with much more serious disorders, the regime of the Hotwell could do wonders, she said, for all kinds of ailments. At the time I was eight years old, but still I clung to her skirts and would not have her visit any place without me. My father was reluctant that I should go, however, as he did not believe in the curative powers of the spa water. But he gave in, and the visit was arranged.

Together, then, Mrs Holland and I took a phaeton from our house on Clifton Hill to the Pump Room. She wore a new, emerald green dress, one I had not seen before, and I remember it made her smell different, like butter. We took a long route, across the Downs (all a part of the 'regime', I was told), and still I remember the exhilaration of that ride. As usual, I began snuggled against my nurse's side, so that half of my vision was taken up with the bulk of her legs and stomach and my cheek brushed against the coarse linen of her skirts. Soon, however, curiosity got the better of me, and I pulled myself up to watch the meadows flash by, the wild flowers – daisies, primroses and cowslips – streaks of white and yellow against the bright grass.

The driver, I remember, was hitting the horse to make it go faster, but I did not think of the animal, only of how happy I felt, to have the wind on my cheeks and the pale blue sky above me. We rode fast, Mrs Holland blowing her nose all the time, right up to the edge of the gorge, where we stopped to gaze at the cliffs, vanishing beneath us to the river far below. I had been here on several occasions before, but this was the first time that it truly impressed me, because, now I was older, I had acquired the power of conjecture. What if, I thought, I should step down from the phaeton and walk towards the edge? At first my nurse would not be suspicious, but I would know that each step I took would bring me closer and closer to the unthinkable. And yet each step in a sense would be quite innocent, until the last, one step too many, a plunge to my death: a fitting punishment for a murderer. Yes, I realized then how easy it was. I had killed one, I could kill another. But before I was able, Mrs Holland announced that she had no faith in the curative powers of the air, which, she was certain, was making her feel worse, and ordered the driver to take us down to the Well.

Shaking, then, I entered the Pump Room. It was an unfamiliar place, smelling of damp rock, and after my experience at the cliff's edge, I was in no mood for the jovial atmosphere that prevailed. I barely looked up as we entered. I was clinging once again to Mrs Holland's skirts. It was difficult for her, I knew, to manoeuvre herself between the tables; she did not need the added difficulty of a child appendage, yet still I remained there, as we wove our way across the room, between the many ladies and gentlemen who sat, drinking from glasses of cloudy water and listening to the music made by a small orchestra. The place was noisier than I had expected; much gossiping was in progress and some were even playing games of cards. There were very few places remaining, but eventually we found a table on the far side of the room, close to the window, which was occupied only by a large elderly woman. I looked up at this person with suspicion, and saw to my horror that she had huge red pimples on her face, and I began to tug Mrs Holland away from her. She took no notice of me, however, and asked the lady if she were expecting company. The lady said she was not, and would be pleased if we would join her, and Mrs Holland, glad, I believe, at the woman's friendliness, told me to wait at the table whilst she fetched the water. This I did not wish to do, but I found my fingers being pried from her petticoats and was told that if I did not sit, we would leave without tasting a drop.

And so I sat, by the window of the Pump Room, staring at the ships outside and the cliffs of the gorge, imagining myself toppling past the window and hitting the rocks below. I did not wish to speak to this ugly but finely dressed lady, and was sullen at first, but she was determined to enter into conversation with me.

'So, child,' she said, her fat fingers bulging around the glass which she raised to her lips; spa water fizzing lightly as she spoke. 'What brings a young one like you to the Wells?'

I did not speak, because the repulsion I felt for the welts on her face and the grey folds of skin beneath her chin, added to my general dislike of strangers, made it impossible for me. I merely looked back at her, and did not move, staring with morbid curiosity at the hair on her top lip.

'Have you lost your tongue, little one?' she said to me, when she realized I would not reply. But still I kept my mouth clamped tight shut, and continued to look at her.

'Come, come,' she said eventually, moving her chair towards mine, and putting her hand out to touch my face, 'I'm sure you are not a wicked child!'

This was too much. I lunged out towards her hand, then bit hard, so that the blood poured from the fleshy mound above her thumb. Then, without waiting to see her reaction, I ran to the side of my nurse, who was at the pump, watching while her glass of water was filled by the attendant. I smiled, sweetly, hoping she would not suspect my bad behaviour, but as I nuzzled her, she barely reacted. I looked up and saw she was staring at the water which poured out of the pump. I followed her gaze and saw something most strange, most terrifying. At first the water came out a pale, pinkish colour and the attendant put this glass aside. Then she took out a bucket, hoping no doubt that if she pumped longer, this discoloration would clear. Instead it got worse. The woman poured many pints of water, but with each movement of her hand the colour of the water deepened until it turned a turgid scarlet, the colour of blood.

I understood immediately what had happened; I did not wish to wait until they discovered me. Mrs Holland, I saw, had horror in her eyes, which increased as she saw the fat lady waddling towards us, holding up her hand, which also was pouring with blood.

'Look!' she was saying, 'look what the child has done to me. Give me a fresh glass of water!'

And then she saw the water, gushing from the tap, thick and red. Her eyes rolled in their sockets, as the realization hit her.

'She's a Devil Child!' she said. 'The daughter of the Devil!'

Then, across the room, I felt people's eyes were on me. There was a general alarm and panic as the word spread. All around, people began spitting out their (perfectly white) water. Water gushed from their mouths as from so many fountains, glasses smashed on the ground, and people stared at me in fear.

'The Hotwell has turned blood red!' one cried. 'It is the child that has caused it.'

'Volcano water!' I heard another say. 'It is a judgement on us.'

And slowly, like a rising tide, people began to stand up and to move towards us, crowding us, to see for themselves the dense ruby liquid pouring from the pump, and the fat lady, holding up her wounded hand as proof. I remember looking at the pump, wishing that somebody would turn it off, looking at the hand, hoping that the blood would dry up, but the two red streams continued to flow as the anger of the crowd increased. At that moment I was certain that the fate I had earlier contemplated was upon me, and all at once I no longer desired it, though it is true I would rather have been dashed against the rocks than torn apart by a mob of invalids. This, however, I am convinced, would have been my fate, had not Mrs Holland (who, to add to the chaos, had now begun to sneeze violently) had the presence of mind to whip me up in her arms and escape through a back door, shouting, 'For shame! Aaa-choo! For shame – a mere child!'

I do not know what happened inside the Pump Room after this, but a stubborn few, with flushed red faces, followed us outside, threatening the worst. After she had bundled me on to the phaeton, I saw Mrs Holland hesitate, wondering if she should climb up beside this Devil Child or stay to face the anger of the crowd. I was eager that she should join me, but too afraid to speak. She spoke to the phaeton driver and told him to take me straight home to Clifton Hill. He was to ensure that I was delivered into the arms of my father, and he should not stop, nor allow me to get down from the carriage. This was most important, she said, for to do so . . . But there she was inter-rupted, as the mob approached, waving sticks and fists. As the driver began to move, I saw her turn her bulk to face them and was afraid for her. I called her name and waved, but she did not turn to look at me again.

I never saw Mrs Holland after that date. She was replaced by another woman, Mrs Percival, who had a striking, thin face with a bent nose, but no smell that I remember. I did not warm to this woman, though she treated me well and tried to become my friend. What was the purpose, I thought, of liking my nurse, when I was sure to betray her and cause something terrible to happen to her? I had lost my bread-and-butter-scented nurse because I turned spa water, renowned for its health-giving properties, into blood. I was certain now that I was a Devil Child, who had killed her own mother. I even thought, at times, when I was lying in bed alone at night, that I could hear my mother screaming as she gave birth to me. Isabella Beaumont was crying aloud, was being torn apart as her child was delivered, covered in Satan's blood. Yet she loved it, even so, and when it was born, she held it to her. I saw her, looking with love into my eyes. She did not yet know that I would turn on her.

It was only later, when I was ten, that I learned the truth about the Hotwell water. I was in the music room. Daniel was playing the harpsichord and I was singing, but very badly. Miss Bright, our new music tutor, was not amused.

'What is the matter with you today, Emilia? Are you distracted?'

My brother stopped playing and laughed till he fell off his seat.

'Well, Daniel – what is it that you find so amusing?'

'It's the Devil,' he said, 'the Devil in her!'

And again, he could not speak for laughing.

After the lesson, Miss Bright took me aside and asked me what it was my brother meant. Though I did not know this woman well, I found myself pouring out the story of the bloody Hotwell. I told her about my nurse, about the fat lady and about the Devil. I did not tell her that I was a murderer, for fear that I would lose her. Miss Bright frowned as I spoke – I had never seen her pretty face crease so. She made me sit down beside her, took my hand and said, very gravely:

'Emilia, it was not you who caused this. No. The person who called the liquid "volcano water" was almost right, for the Hotwell has twice turned red, once before you were even born. My father is a man of science and he explained it to me at the time. The spa, he said, is influenced by the subterranean fire of the earth. The first time it happened was in 1755. I remember because it was the year that we first came to Bristol. We later learned that there was an earthquake in the Portuguese city of Lisbon on the very same day the waters turned.'

The relief I felt at this moment was enormous. I thought about her words for a short while, imagining the earth exploding on the other side of the world. But then I realized I might still be to blame.

'Perhaps my biting the fat lady made a volcano erupt some-where?' I ventured.

'No, Emilia,' said Miss Bright, 'you must banish that thought from your head. It was chance that turned the water red just as you bit her. An unfortunate coincidence, nothing more.'

I was satisfied with this, but one thing bothered me still.

'And who is it, Miss Bright, that causes the earthquakes and the volcanoes? Is it God or the Devil?'

Her frown deepened. She was silent a moment, and then she said, 'It is the Devil, Emilia. The Devil's work.'

But though I was now convinced that the Devil was in the volcano and not in me, still I knew that I was to blame for my mother's death. And my father knew it too. I saw it in the way he preferred my brother. Until I was a young lady and we came to London, I knew that for John Henry Beaumont I might as well have been invisible. I had a nurse, I had tutors, I had maids, but I never felt I had a parent. I spent my childhood sewing, reading, walking, learning a little. I did not speak much but I was always watching, always listening. Often, at dinner, my father would talk to Daniel as if I was not there; I truly believe he had forgotten me; or else he did not think my ears had life. He talked mainly of commerce, of money, of his frustration at not being taken seriously in London. He was a merchant, and merchants, he said, were the heart of Bristol. What business, he said, did the aristocrats from the capital have in judging him? He was as good a man as they. A businessman and not an idle dandy.

In spite of this, however, I loved my father. I listened hard to everything he said, hoping that if I listened long enough his words would mean something to me and I might understand him. I thought if I were simply quiet, I could learn about him. I hoped, perhaps, that just by looking, by watching his clear eyes, the way he sucked his lips when he spoke, waved his arms to prove a point, I would discover something about his nature and I might become like him.

And so I lived, an apparent empty vessel, a beautiful child with golden hair, a talented needlewoman, a good student. But nobody saw that though I seldom spoke, was often still, I was all the time absorbing what was around me. It was not just at home that I behaved in this way. When I went into town with Mrs Percival, we did not converse, but I saw everything. I did not look with pleasure, however, but with a sense of wanting to own things, to suck things in and store them inside me, in the hope that one day I might somehow benefit from this. I stored the glasshouse pyramids smoking on the hillside, the muddy, fishless river, the narrow, dirty streets. I stored the sledges that had worn the pavements to slippery tracks, the ladies in fine gowns, the paupers, and the strange men with black faces and bodies.

But most of all, I stored my favourite sight – the Quay by the Old Wall. There, at low tide, hundreds of ships, their masts bristling for space, were stuck, impotent, in the mud, in the middle of a long street with houses on either side. And it was the memory of this, I believe, which was awakened when the Thames froze over. The stasis of the vessels was what moved me; to see them caught there, trapped by forces that were beyond them, gave me a kind of illicit thrill. A feeling that my childlike hoarding of all I saw finally had a purpose. For the first time, I was making connections. Like the movement of the tides, I realized, the freezing water could not be controlled.

There were no choices when my father was alive. We were like ships.

5

EMILIA

IN 1774, WHEN I was eleven, my father entered a lottery. The Adam brothers, he told us, had begun a great development between the Strand and the River Thames. Indeed, he said, they had embanked the river, and the properties would have the finest views in the city. But though the terraces, called the Adelphi, were to be luxurious, the brothers found that not all those who could afford them wished to live so far from the West End. The splendid views, it seemed, were not enough. To save the project, the lottery was designed, each ticket costing fifty pounds. My father, at that time, was a lucky man, and when the draw was held at Jonathan's Coffee House, the Beaumont family gained a second home.

I did not ever visit London. My father and Daniel went, once a year, in the summer. I was not invited, and though I was curious about the metropolis, I was so fond of our home in Clifton (and so unaccustomed to the company of my father) that I did not mind being left at home with Mrs Percival and the other servants. The life I led there was by nature solitary, as I had never, to my father's chagrin, learned the art of making friends. I did miss Daniel, however. He had grown out of teasing me, and was becoming, now, an increasingly serious young man. Always large-boned, he grew into a kind of gentle giant. He was softly spoken, clumsy, and he walked with an ungainly saunter. Daniel's wide face could not be called handsome: the nose was very large, the teeth crooked, the flaxen brows too thick. His hair was the colour of straw, a great mound of it growing haphazardly on his head which he found almost impossible to curl. Always there were wild strands, flicking out from his coiffure, and as Daniel invariably missed sections when he powdered it, his hair always reminded me of a kind of elaborate, but badly made, cake.

And so, as I grew older, my longing for his presence increased. I was becoming tired of the dullness of things; I wanted the affection that he was beginning to show towards me. In spite of this, however, I was not ready for a great change in my life, so when, at the beginning of winter, in 1778, my father made an unexpected announcement, I was not sure how I should react.

'Daniel,' he said. 'Emilia. You are to pack your things. We are removing, permanently, to London.'

Neither my brother nor I dared question him but, as the days passed, I grew increasingly despairing. I knew that this would mean more time with them; I was aware that a whole new life was about to open for me, yet still I was unhappy. I realized that once we had left, we would never return to our home in Bristol. My father was selling it.

London changed everything. Though while *en route* from Clifton to our new home in the Adelphi I considered hurling open the carriage door and throwing myself on the ground in protest at this sudden change, in truth I lacked the courage. I was numb to everything and sat in silence for the most part. Yes, even when we crossed Hounslow Heath and saw the dead bodies of highwaymen hanging from the gibbets, I did not speak. I was waiting; imagining.

Nothing, however, could have prepared me for the metropolis. During the journey my brother, in an attempt to break my silence, had tried to describe the place where we would live, but his words seemed meaningless to me.

'The development was designed by the Adam brothers,' he said, 'and is based on the palace of Diocletian in Dalmatia. Our house is one of the most desirable, being situated in the Royal Terrace.'

Yet though his description failed to interest me in our new home, when I saw it I could not help but gasp in wonder. What my brother had failed to mention was that the Adelphi Terrace rose not from the pavement, but from the river. Though a road ran in front of it, beneath that road were arched cellars, cata-combs, which stood directly at the edge of the Thames. A terrible stench rose up from the water below, yet immediately I saw the Terrace, its elegance and simplicity, I knew there was no place I would rather be than here. Yes, standing by the railings, above the catacombs, it seemed as if all London was before me. To my right, I could see Westminster Bridge and Abbey and, nearer even, a strange tower made of wood, which my brother said was the York Water Tower. To my left, St Paul's Cathedral dominated the skyline. But more than all these, it was the river-life which fascinated me; the sail-boats, the skiffs, the opulent barges, the like of which I had never seen. I became fascinated by this new world which unfolded itself before my eyes.

It was not simply the exterior of the Adelphi, of course, that caught my attention. No, for in spite of the simplicity of the external design, the interior was so rich that I spent whole days examining the paintings and marvelling at the furniture. My brother told me names I had not heard before – Kauffmann, Cipriani, Zucchi. I loved to imagine these painters at work, creating fantasies especially for me. Indeed, I often felt as if the whole house was a kind of elaborate playground that had been invented with me in mind, and when there was nobody in the house, I would wander from room to room, admiring myself in the many gilt mirrors that covered the walls. I had not, before this time, given much attention to my appearance, but here it was a thing I could not ignore, for my reflection appeared so frequently to me that I came to feel that I must fit in with my environment; I must be as beautiful as the paintings if I were to be worthy of living here.

And, it is true, in this place I began to *feel* more beautiful, for my father began to take an interest in me. I have failed to mention that a great change had occurred in my father's life in the years before we moved to the Adelphi. Shortly before he entered the lottery, he had complained of a sore eye, which within a few days turned very red. At first he merely experienced a certain discomfort, but after a while his condition worsened and his vision became extremely blurred. He said it was as if he were looking through a thick, mist-covered pane of glass, and when he spoke of it, I detected his fear. As the days passed, I watched the once-clear irises of his eyes turn white and become opaque. It was plain to me, even before the doctors announced it, that he was suffering from a serious infection. Still, at first these very same doctors pointed to the spots of colour showing through, as signs of hope. Soon, however, it became clear that there was none. Though it was unlikely that he would lose his sight altogether, he was destined to remain half-blind.

Perhaps it was this infirmity and my realization of how it affected his temper and his daily life that made me warm more to my father once we moved to the Adelphi. Or it could have been that his new-found affection for me bred a parallel emotion in my heart. My life, indeed, was transformed. Within two weeks of my arrival, my solitary existence was ended. Suddenly I had invitations to attend balls and routs, charitable meetings and dinners. My father even employed a maid for me, Angeline, who was renowned for her knowledge of fashion and beauty. Angeline was not like any servant I had seen before. She was French, a Huguenot, and she swore allegiance to King George. Her knowledge of English could not be faulted. Indeed, she had adopted the way of speaking of an aristocrat. When first I saw her, I was daunted by her beauty and a touch appalled at the elaborate nature of her dress. She wore huge side hoops, which, she said, were the fashion at the French Court. Perhaps so, but to me they appeared quite ridiculous, impediments to freedom of movement, for she could not walk along a corridor without turning sideways, and it was impossible that she could wait on me dressed like that.

Angeline, though, I soon discovered, was not to wait on me at all. When I asked her to perform simple tasks she would raise her nose to the air and say, 'Madame. I am not dressed for it.'

Her only duty, I soon understood, was to ensure that I looked my best, at all times. She was to take me at least twice a week to the shops of Bond Street, a task for which, I soon discovered, she had a particular affection, not on account of the dresses, but rather because she was very partial to many of the young shop-men.

Everything, for me, was extremely strange, yet at first I did not question my new life. I was so dazed by each new event that I simply let it happen, believing that soon things would once again seem normal. And yet it was with difficulty that I accus-tomed myself to these new routines. Each day, without fail, Angeline attended to my toilette, praising in turn my fine, regular features, my light, graceful movements or my perfect figure. And yet, in spite of my so-called 'natural' beauty, I soon came to realize that it was not nature that was of importance in these matters, but art. For on an early trip to Bond Street Angeline had purchased stays for me, and before I could buy any dresses, it was necessary that I should learn to wear these new undergarments. On the day that I first tried them, Angeline pulled so tight that I felt I could not breathe. Regardless of my complaining, however, she would not let me loosen them. And though I was not to be seen in public that day, she insisted that I wear them in my chamber, to accustom myself to them.

By the end of the day, I was furious that she had put me through such agony. Though at first I had enjoyed the sight that greeted me in the myriad of mirrors around my room (for my room, my father had ensured, had more mirrors than any other, so that I might see my reflection, my beautiful reflection, he said, echoing back endlessly), I soon tired of the novelty of seeing such a perfectly straight back, such a tiny waist. All I could think of was the soreness from the rubbing of the whale-bone, and the way my sides were pinched beneath the fabric. I complained heartily to Angeline: I said I could barely breathe, but she had no sympathy.

'To be admired, madame,' she said, 'should be sufficient balsam.'

It was impossible that I could agree. Sitting upright in my room, I saw no purpose to this torture: these bones across my back, across my breasts and in my sides. The situation became worse when I was given a cork rump, or 'bum', which was fastened at the back of my waist and tied with tapes in front. Though Angeline pronounced that I was lucky I had avoided the hoop, I could not help but feel that the world was unjust to me, indeed to all women who were forced to wear these stupid contraptions.

Everything changed, though, once I had new dresses. In undergarments alone I had felt as if I wore a second skeleton, but once I had petticoats the skeleton had flesh, and when brocades and gauze were added, I acquired a second skin. It is true I remained uncomfortable, but the sight that greeted me in my mirrors was so astounding that it was indeed a balsam to my wounds. And when I ventured out with Angeline, I soon realized that in these garments it was I, not she, that was the subject of attention. Whilst Angeline lingered with the most handsome shop-men, discussing the merits of various coloured ribbons or the styles of shoes, I would look up from beneath my fan to take a glance at them. But theirs was more than a simple glance. Their eyes were a kind of liquid fire that burned into my own, and I experienced feelings that were entirely new to me. Though at times I was convinced that I would faint beneath the pressure of their eyes, though I was short of breath, and found myself so hot that I was inclined to rush from the shop and seek the air, in truth I was unable to move; I stood still, on the spot, looking down once more at the pattern on my fan, feeling my feet rooted to the floor.

Even so, there was a limit to my patience. Though I enjoyed the outings, they became over-long, and the physical discomfort I experienced began to outweigh the pleasure of the young men's interest. After a week or two I demanded of Angeline why I must so often endure these shopping trips. Surely I had acquired enough dresses by now?

'Madame,' she scolded, 'last week, Lady Simpson was criticized because her dress was more than a half hour out of fashion!'

My protests, then, were in vain. At first I had thought I could speak to my father about this, but soon I realized that Angeline only did as he requested. Though at first I had been unable to fathom the reasons for these new activities, had thought them simply an indulgence given to me by a newly loving father, it was not long before I realized their true purpose. My father was in search of a husband for me.

And thus I found that there was no answer but to accept my fate. I hoped that the situation would improve once a husband was found, and yet as each day passed there was no news of a husband and my only pastime was to endure the beauty treatments that Angeline arranged. When she had been with me for three weeks, I thought that the worst had passed, but it was not so. One morning she announced that I was to have a fashionable coiffure to set off the beauty of my dress. At first I was not alarmed, but soon I realized that this new hair-dressing was not a simple operation. I was to sit completely still for three hours whilst she hovered over me and transformed my appearance. She curled and teased, pinned and pasted sections into position, then applied a perfumed oil, a pomade (made, she said, of eels' fat), to moisten the remaining strands. I became nervous when she began piling wool and ostrich feathers on to the crown of my head, but she assured me that this was in the French manner, and these ingredients would not be seen once the work was completed. I became stiff and agitated, but she would not allow me to walk around the room, for fear her work would be disturbed. I was thankful, in a way, that I was not wearing my stays, but still I felt as sick as if I were, and my neck began to ache with the constant sitting in one position. As the hair began rising to a height of over two feet, the wool and feathers were indeed obscured as she had promised, but ribbons and lengths of false hair were added. When I thought she had finished, she stuffed a tiny vial of flowers in the centre, impressing on me the fact that this must be removed at night, and could be replaced each day with fresh flowers, or indeed with a small trinket such as a china coach or a piece of ornamental fruit. I thought I had misunderstood her, and said, 'But I cannot waste three hours each morning, Angeline!'

She smiled and stroked the coiffure.

'No, no,' she said, 'this arrangement will last at least a month, madame. You must sleep wearing a taffeta cap to protect it.'

I tried sleeping, the first night, but found it intolerably uncomfortable. I woke with a pounding headache and desired to rip the pins from my hair. Angeline, however, would hear nothing of it, so, after much consideration, I complained to my father that I did not wish to be a lady of fashion. It was agony to me, and I preferred myself as I was. At this he became furious.

'My fortune,' he said, 'is invested in your beauty, Emilia. Whilst I am deciding on the best husband for you, you will wear what Angeline dictates. When you are married, it will no longer concern me.'

And so (though on one occasion, during the drive to a ball, I was obliged to rest my head on my knees, so high was my head-dress) I had no choice but to continue this way of life.

Coiffure balanced precariously on my head, I waited. After a month my hair had become sticky, and Angeline renewed the coiffure, elaborating the design somewhat. My father promised it would not be long before a husband would be found, for (he said) news of my beauty was spreading fast, and where such a beauty was concerned, the size of her dowry was a matter of less importance. At the time this struck me as a strange remark, for I knew my father to be a wealthy merchant and assumed the dowry he would provide would be more than adequate, but I dismissed his words as carelessness and took them as a compliment to my charms, which (my brother assured me) were unrivalled. I was growing even more fond of my father at this time, for not only did he pay more attention to me than ever before, but also his eyesight was deteriorating, more than the doctors had predicted. He was a proud man and did not like to be given help, but he liked me to read poetry to him in the evenings, and, as I read, I would watch his fleeting expressions, seeing how he was moved by the words. He did not seem cold any more. Often, in the dim light of the library, I wanted to bend forward and kiss him, but I did not dare. Yet always I sat close to him, so that he could see my face, for I knew that the sight reassured him. Sometimes he would lift his tired eyes and do his best to focus on me; it was as if he was committing me to memory, so that if he did go blind, he might conjure me up the better.

'Beautiful,' he would say. 'You look beautiful, Emilia.'

There was one evening, however, when my father's reaction to my appearance caused me great distress. It was an evening in April, hot and balmy, despite the season, and I wore a yellow gown with half-sleeves and roses around the shoulders. My father could not see me well as I entered the room, but when I sat down, he appeared shocked. It was a momentary look which he soon corrected, but then he beckoned me closer still. I did as he asked so that my face was within a foot of his, and then a look of pure joy crossed his features, an expression I had not seen before. He gasped at first, and could not speak. Then, in a voice just above a whisper, he said, 'The image – the very image of your mother . . .'

This was too much for me. That I should be like the mother that I had killed! I turned and fled the room, without looking back at him. No wonder he had hated me as a child, when I had stolen such joy from his life. Safe in my chamber, I locked the door, and would let no one enter, refusing even to come down for dinner the next day. After that, I tried to come to my senses. I opened the door, but the very effort of getting up from my bed seemed too great. I developed a fever and was confined to my room for two weeks.

We came to London in January. In late April everything changed. Angeline was dismissed, the shopping trips ceased and I no longer received invitations. I questioned nothing. I knew that for some reason this was my fault, and resumed the quiet life with some relief. My father assured me that he was still searching for a husband, though as time passed I began to doubt that he would find one. Still he insisted I should not disturb the coiffure that Angeline had given me in March, and that I should continue to wear the undergarments and the dresses that he had recently purchased for me, for I should be prepared, at all times, to meet the man he would choose as my husband.

At first I was not unhappy with this situation, for I had grown quite fond of my reflection, and in donning my clothes each day, I felt I had a kind of purpose in my life. Sometimes I would walk out, along the Thames, admiring the prospect of the sail-boats and the Southwark spires over the river. Still I found myself amazed by the views of St Paul's to the east, and standing on my balcony, on a fine day, I could see the windmills, villas and hills of Surrey, receding in the distance. Always I was left alone in the house, wondering about the affairs of Daniel and my father. I reverted to the ways of my youth, but now I had the additional pleasure of more novels to read, and of the mirrors that surrounded me constantly, where I could turn and twirl and imagine myself something more than I truly was.

By July however, I was becoming unhappy. My head had started to itch and I became aware of a rancid smell emanating from my hair. The coiffure, I realized, had lost its beauty; I desperately needed to have it dressed once again, but my father (who could barely see it at all) refused and said it looked delightful, and I was an ungrateful child not to be thankful for it. I requested, if it could not be re-dressed, whether I might remove the pins and brush it free, but he insisted I should not disturb it, speaking so forcefully that I did not dare disobey. He was still searching for the right match, he said. When he found me a husband, I must look my best – the coiffure was to remain intact.

But though I had never been disobedient, I was certain that something strange was happening to my head. As July turned to August, August to September, I was often sick in the night, and I could not sleep, for I was certain that there was movement beneath my taffeta cap. When I told my brother of this, he laughed at me and said that my imagination was too active, but as each day passed, I knew that a transformation was taking place within the coiffure. The smell emanating from my head had become worse: a musty, unfamiliar odour. And the appearance of my hair was deteriorating – where once it had been smooth as satin, now it had the texture of coarse hessian, fraying at the edges. As each day passed, I began to feel weaker and my face appeared more pale, so I began turning mirrors to the wall, for I no longer wished to look at myself. The room had a duller appearance like this, the walls were dark and bare, but I allowed one mirror to remain, above my dressing-table, where each day I examined myself, in the hope that I had been dreaming. Always, however, I saw myself wan and fading, my dresses dirty, and with a dingy heap upon my head, which I powdered over and again in the hope that its appearance might be thus improved. Sometimes, exhausted, I was able to sleep, but then I dreamed only of the coiffure, of brushing my hair free of sharp ornaments and hard baubles, old pastes and fetid pomades. And when, one night, I awoke to feel an intense disturbance at the heart of the arrangement, I knew I must go against my father's wishes.

It was September, late in the month, and though others were complaining of the cold, I was hot and sweating and slept with the windows open. As I lay awake, once again I thought of my mother, and remembered what I had done to her. When I closed my eyes, I heard her speak to me. I heard her voice, clearer than stream water.

'Did you think that the Devil had left you, child?'

'Yes,' I replied. 'Yes.'

'You have been deceived, Emilia. The Devil never leaves his daughters.'

And I knew that she was right. I could feel him, fingering my hair in the night, and I placed my hands to my forehead to scratch, fearing that I would feel my horns. But there was nothing, though my temples were burning and swelling.

I lay still, silent, hoping that in the morning I would come to my senses. Surely this was not happening. Surely I was dreaming. A couple of flies buzzed about the room. The sound was insistent, though not loud. Occasionally it stopped and I hoped that they had gone, but then it began again, a soft hum, moving towards me, away from me, towards me again. I could not stand it, and sat up, then put my legs down over the bed, and in the light of the moon determined to kill them. I would sleep that night. I vowed I would sleep.

Once I was standing, however, the creatures were quiet again. I waited but no sound resumed. Even so, now that I was up, I realized that there would be no sleep. Hardly aware of my purpose, I moved towards the mirror. Small as it was, it reflected pale light across the room, and I sat before it and began pulling at my hair. I did not know why I was compelled to this act, I only knew that I must remove the ribbons and the false hair. I must stop the burning in my head and perhaps then the Devil might leave me. Slowly, barely able to think, I raised my hand to remove a pin. A section of powdered hair fell to my shoulder, and as it did so a tiny fly flew off. Again I removed a pin, and it was then that I realized my plight. I became transfixed; I could not move for fear. But though I did not believe it at first, and tried to find another explanation, soon I knew it to be true. As the second section of hair had fallen away, a small cloud of insects, black flies, had been released. They had not come from the window; nor were they figments of a dream. They were as material as I, and they buzzed around my head, settling on my face and shoulders.

Opening my mouth to scream, I found I did not have a voice. I wanted to faint, to wake up later, finding that a maid had washed me and removed the vermin. It should happen. That is what should happen. I waited. The buzzing sound intensified as more of the creatures escaped from the coiffure and hovered around my ears. I was patient. I stared at my reflection. But I did not fall.

Instead, I was forced to act. Each pin that I removed released another tiny swarm, yet knowing that I must discover the truth, I continued, until I reached the central pad of wool and feathers. They crawled over my fingers. They filled the air, and though I willed them to fly out of the window, they seemed enamoured of the room.

All the while, I knew my father was below stairs. I could call him; ask for assistance. Yet I was certain that, if he knew of this, it would kill him. So I continued, pin by pin, releasing the flies.

I moved into a kind of trance. It was as if the girl in the mirror was not me, but the child who had long ago turned water into blood. And when I reached the throbbing centre of my hair, though what I found was the worst yet, it seemed no worse than a mother-murderer deserved. At the heart of the coiffure I found a nest of maggots, little white wrigglers, soft to the touch. Almost without thinking I cupped them in my hands and threw them to the ground, peeling the stubborn ones from my fingers. In that light, beneath the moon, they seemed like little glow-worms, cascading across the room. I did not know what I was doing. I acted almost without awareness of the horror of it. And when I had finished, I could do nothing but continue to sit at my dressing-table, watching my night shadow as it moved across the floor. I do not know how long I sat there. I simply waited, until I had no shadow left.

6

EMILIA

MY FATHER DID not comment on the maggots. Though Daniel had told him what had happened, he remained silent, whilst I, alone, determined to understand his negligence.

Indeed, I had seen another change in him in recent weeks. He no longer ventured out alone, for now he was almost blind, and trusted nobody but Daniel. He became irritable (perhaps, I thought, because his daughter's head had become a breeding ground) and when I dared broach the subject of a husband, he would almost sneer, saying, 'Oh, you will get your husband, dear daughter. You will get your husband.'

I knew, however, from the tone in which he spoke, that I should give up all hopes of marriage. In any case, I could barely think of myself as material for wedlock. How could I please a husband, when I could no longer please myself? The maggots had poisoned me. I felt it, in my blood. And though I had washed my hair many times, I was sure I could still smell their odour. It overpowered the perfumed soap I used; nothing was strong enough to hide it, and so I knew I was contaminated. Each stroke of my hairbrush intensified the stink, so though I succeeded in untangling it, making it appear smooth to the touch, in truth I considered shaving it off, as Daniel shaved his beard; indeed I would have done this, had I not known that it was not the hair itself that was defiled, but something within me.

Mirror-watching, then, for me was over. When Daniel had discovered me, shivering and afraid in my room, the flies having flown, the maggots still squirming on the floor, he found me staring not in the mirror, but at a blackened glass. I had turned the last of my reflectors to the wall, for I knew the Devil was in me, and I did not wish to see him. After that day, I made a vow. When I was certain that the infestation was gone (from my blood, my nerves, my sinews), then I would look. And if people called me beautiful (Daniel did so, daily – he begged me to turn the mirrors back to see the evidence), then that was further proof of the evil that dwelled within me, for they say the Devil has many forms, and can prove himself quite charming.

And so it was that, for the space of nearly three months, I stayed in my room, not wishing that the world should see me, nor desiring to see the world outside my window. My father was happy with this arrangement, for he had news that Dr Graham had taken up residence in the house next door to our own. He still insisted that I dress formally each day, but beyond that he had little to do with me. He was frequently absent from the house, and seemed not to notice that my health was becoming weaker. I had terrible dreams, every night; I would tear my hair out with my bare hands; snails slithered across my naked scalp. I was weaker than I had ever been, finding it difficult to breathe and suffering from fainting fits. Sometimes I would wake up on the floor of my room, my novel by my side, barely remembering that I had fallen. When I looked at the clock I would see that several hours had passed. Even Daniel did not seem to see what was happening to me.

But it was my brother who told me me about Dr Graham. In spite of my father's opinion, Daniel could not hide his excitement at the event. My father had been raving about the 'charlatan' for several weeks, but Daniel convinced me that this was nothing but bitterness; the desperate ravings of a blind man, who could not be cured. Each evening I put my ear to the window, and though I did not dare to look, I heard the hollow clatter of the approaching carriages and the chatter of many voices, at least a hundred people, I guessed.

But soon listening was not enough. Though my father had gone so far as forbidding me to look from my window, I knew I must. Could the sight be so terrible as to merit denying me the night air? I pleaded with Daniel to tell me more about this Doctor, who stirred our father to such extremities, but he would say nothing. Still I persisted. What is it that is so unsavoury, Daniel? Who is this man my father calls a charlatan? Eventually, insisting first that I swear I would not tell, my brother replied, and it was his answer that captured my imagination.

'The Doctor, Emilia,' he said, 'has created a Temple next door to our house. A Temple of Health, they say, where, with the help of the Gods, fatal diseases can be completely cured. I cannot say more, Emilia,' he told me. 'I have said too much.'

A Temple of Health! A place where fatal diseases could be cured! I knew at once it was the deliverance I had prayed for. Yes, only the Gods could rid me of the curse I had been born with, for though the maggots had gone, I knew myself to be infected still. I was forced to disobey my father for the second time.

That night, when I heard the carriages arriving at the Temple, I silently drew my curtain aside, and was astounded. This was no indecency, no harlots' parade. Rather it was a conglomeration of all that is beautiful, a carnival, a masquerade. For it seemed to me that all society was collected, there, below, in the street. There were near twenty carriages, all spilling people of the first rank. And those not in carriages came in gilded chaise or sedan. In spite of the cold, these people were dressed in silks and brocades (the oil-lamps were lit, the moon was bright, I absorbed it all, like a sponge), but the most remarkable element of this was that every lady was incognito, hidden beneath a mask. There was one in particular who struck me. Once I saw her, I could not take my eyes from her, for though I could not see her face, she seemed, to me, the most beautiful thing I had ever seen. She seemed almost a foot taller than the other ladies and she held a jewelled peacock face against her own, covered in emeralds and sapphires, with glittering strands of silver about the eyes. Her hair was jet, an elaborate, puffed-up creation, and though it appeared clean and freshly dressed, I could not help but wonder what creatures it might harbour. But then I banished the thought. It was impossible, I thought, that this woman was like me. She wore a silver dress, finer than any that I possessed, and her gait was slow and deliberate, as if she wanted people to notice her. The severe straightness of her back, I thought, betrayed perhaps a pride that she shared with the bird whose identity hid her own. She was all, I believe, that I desired to be.

But I had seen enough. I knew that, at any moment, my father might enter. He would somehow sense my position, and he would explode, flinging his flimsy arms about, saying I would be the death of him. And so I went to draw the curtain, once again, but as I did so, I caught sight of two men, standing at Dr Graham's portal. Two giants rather, I should say, for I was sure these men were near seven foot tall, dressed in superb liveries, with large, gold-laced cocked hats. They held long staffs, with ornamented silver heads, and they acted with silent authority, nodding gravely at the guests who passed them, almost without observing them. I closed the curtain, and sat still for a moment. In the darkness, I fancied I saw my mother.

It happened again. I had imagined my father's words, 'you will be the death of me, Emilia,' and the next morning he was dead. When my brother told me, I was terrified. I waited for the tears to flow, and when they did not, Daniel stormed out of the room, saying he should have thought a sister of his might have a sensibility that would find a father's death worthy of wet eyes. When I did not cry, I knew that I had desired his death. I had conjured up the phantom of the mother that I had murdered, in order that she would take him also.

I heard Daniel go out of the front door (to fetch an undertaker, I presumed) and I sat, alone, unable to move. For more than an hour I was still, seeing nothing, until Daniel returned. He knocked on my door, and entered, struggling with a large box. He was ridiculous. The powder had been blown from his thick, orange-yellow hair, which now clashed with his ruddy cheeks. His large teeth protruded as he panted.

'Here you will find a thing to restore your sense of duty, Emilia,' he said, and threw the box down upon my bed, then stared at me from beneath his bushy brows, in such a way that my only response, if I had dared, could be to laugh. 'I hope you will wear your loss well,' he added, then turned and departed from the room and the house once again.

I knew immediately what this 'thing' was, yet was furious that he had felt it necessary to fetch this before any other action. In protest, I did not open it, but placed it in a corner. Only later did I don the mourning dress.

This was December. The river still flowed; my heart was still frozen. The pattern of our days was soon established. Daniel, whose foolish grin had once been a comfort to me, now seemed to vanish from my life. He left, early, each morning, and did not return until nightfall, and I remained in my room, tightly laced, dressed in black, each mirror turned to the wall. My only occupation was to watch. During the day, I observed the flow of paupers who flocked to the Temple for free treatment; at night, I waited for my Peacock Lady. But though I knew she might come in another guise, I became certain that I would not see her again. I tried to pull together the fragments of my memory, to build a picture of her, but all I could remember was her shape – her spine, a string of bone beads which hung from her neck.

The funeral took place shortly before Christmas, on a crisp, clear day, and was attended only by Daniel and myself. I was truly shocked by this, for I had expected us to return to Bristol so that my father could be buried in our family plot beside my mother, and I could not, at first, understand why there were not others to mourn him. Daniel would say nothing; I knew he was keeping the truth from me and I knew that the truth was a thing that I would not be glad to hear. I guessed, of course, that we were poor now. That somehow my father had lost his fortune and his place, but I could not then understand how, nor did I dare ask. My tears, that day, were crocodile, but served to placate Daniel, who himself wept copiously as the coffin was lowered into the ground. It was not that I did not care about my father, for indeed I had loved him dearly. But on that day, I could not feel my love. I felt I did not know how to grieve.

Afterwards, at the Adelphi, we ate biscuits together in silence. In truth, we did not know what to do.

After that, Daniel continued to avoid me, but I became aware, through hints that he dropped, that my fears had been well founded. With the exception of a certain small sum that was intended for my dowry, we were virtually penniless. Though we owned our house in the Adelphi, and had enough money for basic provisions, if we were not prudent we would have to leave our home. I was instructed not to question my brother any further, an easy task, because his presence in the Royal Terrace was rare. And so whole days passed where I did nothing but sit at my window, watching the visitors arriving at the Temple.

Perhaps it was not surprising, then, when one night a thought struck me which would not go away. I would go out into the street, I decided, and watch the guests arrive. Nobody, I was certain, would notice me.

I continued to watch, as the horses pulled up, the guests emerged, the paupers pointed. Eagerly, still watching for her whom I knew I would not see, I waited. I felt unable to move until the visitors to the Temple had gone inside and the spectators had dispersed. Though I knew I should not be thinking of this, my father's death being so recent, I could not help myself. All I could think of were the miracles taking place on the other side of my bedroom wall. The man who had been unable to cure my father of blindness was instead banishing Devils. He would banish the Devil in me, if only I could summon courage to go to him.

Outside it was quiet, but still the giant porters stood, as I had been, immobile. The moment I opened our door, I thought how furious Daniel would be, but the thrill of the fresh air was immense. I had been stifled; was slowly suffocating, without realizing it. I decided to take a short walk, but as I passed these giants, one of them caught my eye, and beckoned me towards him. I felt my cheeks burn. I had been so sure that none would notice me, but now I realized I was not invisible. He would see my shame and my pestilent head. Hesitating, uncertain even if it would be proper to speak to him, I moved nearer. But as I approached, I saw that their faces were as forbidding as their bodies. They were twins, I realized that now, waxen-faced, with huge eyelids that blinked slowly like the eyes of dolls. Even their huge lips were pale. I fancied they might speak in unison, but it was the one that beckoned me who spoke, though his lips barely moved in the effort, as if he, also, were wearing a mask.

'So,' he said, 'you are our little mourner, are you not?'

'I am in mourning, yes, sir,' I replied, 'but I am not your mourner, but my father's.'

His lips moved, as if to form a smile.

'We often see you, at the window,' he said, 'but my friend here thought you were a ghost.'

At this I was struck with fear and turned away. As I walked towards our door, I heard him speak.

'Little Goddess,' he said, 'little Aphrodite.'

That was the night before the river froze. When that happened, everything changed. That the Thames, whose very essence was movement, became still, meant that I, whose essence was stasis, should be able to flow. And on that January day, facing a sea of whiteness, I knew what I must do. Though exhausted after a night of bad dreams, I took out my dress of yellow roses, which I had not worn since the night I locked myself in my room. Then I went to the mirror above my dressing-table. I was afraid, remembering so clearly the sight I had last seen there. It all came back to me – the bluish moonlit face, the flies buzzing around my head, the little maggots burrowing in my hair. But though I knew the Devil was in me, the beauty of the ice made me determined to exorcize him, and to do that I was certain I must face him. It could be worse. I prepared myself for that. I wondered if it were my face that he had attacked this time; it must be something terrible, for Dr Graham's doormen had mocked me cruelly – it was not fair to call me Goddess when it was clear it was an evil spirit that infected me.

I did it suddenly. It was the only way – to act without thinking. Barely knowing what to expect, I turned the mirror to face me. But when I saw my face, I was startled. The Devil is devious. My face had never seemed so fair.

Cautiously, tenderly, I raised my hand to it, trying to find the point of difference; the feature that had changed since last I saw it. But there was no perceptible difference, no one alteration that made me see a beauty in the glass. It was astonishing: this sudden, unexpected burst of self-love. I wore black still, a dowdy dress, which threw no light on my face. And seeing this, I began to undo it, struggled out of the 'thing' my brother had bought me, until I wore only my stays and my cork rump. Then, pulling my stays yet tighter, in spite of the cold I dressed myself in the yellow robe, a dress fit only for the summer. I moved closer to the mirror, unable to believe that my hair shone gold, and appeared as it did before I had the coiffure. Though I had seen it about my shoulders, had felt my scalp to be clean, only now did I believe that it was true. I began to move about the room, turning first one glass and then another. Each time I turned I was afraid; one by the window – yes, in this one I am still fair – one above the fireplace – this one also pronounces it to be true – until, at last, the room was full of light and decorated with my reflection. I turned and smiled and posed for my own admiration, yet all the time was afraid that the images that greeted me would change. That I would see the façade crumble and find I was rotten beneath. But finally, convinced of my beauty, I left the room and walked again into the street, near deserted because of the frost. I looked down, beneath the Adelphi, and saw a thing that I will never forget. People were walking on the water.

I did not linger, however – I think I was afraid that all this would vanish if I dared to contemplate it, so I approached Dr Graham's door and saw that it was unattended. Above my head the Doctor's large, gold star hung, dripping with icicles, and beside it, I saw the words (which I did not understand): TEMPLUM AESCULAPIO SACRUM.

I knocked, and at first nothing happened. Then I knocked again, almost unaware of my actions. At that time, I believe I felt nothing. Nothing at all. I did not analyse. I did not ask myself why.

And then a man came to the door, a beautiful man.

'Are you Dr Graham?' I asked.

He laughed.

'No. I am his apothecary. Dr Graham is above stairs.'

Behind him I glimpsed the hallway, the mirrored walls.

'May I ask the reason for your visit, madam?'

How could I answer? I felt I was there without reason. Or rather, I had many reasons, but I could not put them into words.

'Come in,' the apothecary said, when it seemed I would not speak. 'You will freeze to death.'

Dazed, I entered the Temple. I was offered a seat, which I willingly took, and found I still could not speak, so astounded was I by the decoration of this room. I was dazzled by the many silver and gilt ornaments, the crystals and the flower garlands; all these things reflected in a hundred times more mirrors than adorned the walls of my bedchamber. Most astonishing of all, however, was this: about the base of the elaborate iron stairway, wooden crutches and walking-sticks were scattered. I knew the meaning of this and it disturbed me. Could it be true? That he cured the lame? Was he playing God, or was he indeed a miracle man?

'Your business with Dr Graham, madam?'

The apothecary's voice was sweet, like running water. I looked at him, noticing the clearness of his skin, the clipped perfection of his features, the dark hair, lightly powdered. And as I looked up at him, my eye was led to the staircase itself, at the top of which was a huge glass dome.

'I am possessed by the Devil,' I said, a little afraid of what his response might be. 'I wish to be cured.'

At this, the man seemed surprised, but not alarmed. He bowed low, flourishing his arm, and asked me to wait. He would see if the Doctor was available.

7

EMILIA

I SHALL NEVER forget the first time I saw Dr Graham. All was silent before his arrival: the apothecary had left me alone. But I had barely time to contemplate my surroundings further, before I heard soft strains of music, and I looked up to see that a flautist had appeared at the top of the staircase, beneath the dome. It startled me at first, but I was soon lulled by the sound his instrument produced. It was as if the music floated up to the glass dome which caught the sound and intensified it, before raining it down upon me.

And then it happened: a vision. First the sun came out, its bright, winter light pouring through the dome, almost blinding me, and suddenly, in the midst of the brilliance, I thought I saw an angel. He began descending the staircase towards me, with a majestic step, his glowing wings spread wide. As he came nearer, approaching the shade of the hallway, I saw that they were not wings but arms, held above his head as if in praise of God. With each step he seemed more and more like a man, but not a man in the ordinary sense. He wore a white linen tail-coat and white breeches with black silk stockings. His hair also glowed white, was thickly but finely powdered and curled perfectly at the sides, tied behind with a black silk ribbon, and as he came nearer I could smell his perfume, a sweet, intoxicating scent. His face was pale, and seemed almost a perfect oval, but as he approached, it was his eyes that moved me. They seemed to fix on me, in a way I had never known. It was not the usual kind of stare (I was familiar with the lascivious look, the stare of men trying to impress with their constant gaze). No, with Dr Graham, I swear it was different. It was a look that said I should adore him.

'So,' he said, his mouth curling agreeably at the corner. His voice was deep and soft. The 'o' of his first utterance reverberated. 'You wish to be my Hebe Vestina?' I realized it was a Scottish lilt.

'I'm sorry, sir?' I said.

'My Goddess of Youth and Health?'

'I don't know what you mean, sir,' I replied. 'I have come for a consultation with you.'

'Then follow me.'

Though I did not understand his words, in the instant of meeting him I had lost all powers of reasoning. And as he held out his hand, I, forgetting all sense of modesty and decorum, took it, and allowed myself to be led up the staircase. As I ascended, I felt myself enveloped by the bright glare of the sun. I felt totally cleansed by the light. Only – there was a moment, half-way up, when I felt a sudden chill. I could barely explain it. It was as if someone was watching me, someone very dear; someone with great sorrow in her heart. I shivered, but did not look up, for fear that I might see the thing I sensed. Instead, I continued walking, clinging tightly to the Doctor's hand. And with just one more step, the fear passed; the presence had vanished. No doubt it was nothing more than imagination. I felt at once radiant and weak. The light seemed to be burning through me.

Soon we reached the top of the staircase, bathed in light, and there I saw two doors, marked simply, No. I and No. II.

'Which will you choose?' the Doctor asked, infusing me suddenly with a sense of fear. I did not wish to make decisions.

'Number One – Sacred to Prudence and Resolution, Moderation and Tranquillity, Resignation and Hope? Or Number Two – Sacred to Early Hours, to Cleanliness and Exercise, of Body and Mind?'

I stood, for what seemed like an age, almost unaware of where I was. I realized I could feel the fever in me building again. And then I found the breath to say, simply, 'Number

One, if I may,' and he opened the door, to reveal for the first time the glories of his Temple.

It was too much. The sunlight through the dome was nothing compared to this. I was stunned by its lustre. The colour and the light seemed to engulf me; dazzle me. And after that I remember very little, because I fainted, there at the entrance. In a deep sleep, vivid imaginings once again passed through my head – I saw the face of my father, bent over a table beneath a dim lamp, his almost-blind eyes struggling to see the words he was writing.

'Go home, Emilia,' he wrote. 'Stay away from this fraud!' And then he raised his head and saw that he could speak to me. 'My eyes, Emilia,' he said, 'look at my eyes.' And I looked, to see the colour fade from his irises, so that his eyes were white flesh, completely blind. Then even this began to rot until he had empty sockets in an otherwise living head, and again he opened his mouth to speak. 'Do not be blind like me, dear daughter,' he said. 'Do not follow me.' And then there was blackness and a sense of great calm, which seemed to last several hours, though the Doctor told me afterwards I was asleep no more than ten minutes.

When I awoke, I found myself in the centre of the room. It was plunged into semi-darkness, and I was seated, uncomfortably, due to my cork rump, on a large, elevated, circular throne, with red velvet cushions about me. In front of me was a thick golden column, ornamented with white metal, and above my head was a silver globe, from which, when I craned my neck, I could see a bright flame emerge. I was afraid; desperately wished to leave the place; believed myself still to be in the realm of dream. My limbs, however, were too weak to move; a vaguely pleasant sensation drifted through them, but the relaxation of my body, in spite of the restrictions of my undergarments, could not quell the agitation of my mind. I attempted to lift myself, but, even if it had been possible, my movement was arrested by the voice of Dr Graham, which seemed to come from beyond the gloom that surrounded me.

'Rest, Hebe Vestina,' he said to me. 'My Goddess, rest.'

And there was something in his voice which made me obey; unclench my fists and close my eyes. Then, in the darkness, my limbs went weaker still. I felt my head loll to one side, and a pleasure I had never known coursed through me. Though at the time I could not place the feeling, nor give it a name, I know now that this was titillation; the closest I had ever come to sexual enjoyment. And the most marvellous thing was that it lasted. I kept my eyes tight shut, and the pleasure went on. I knew, for the first time, what it was like to throb between my legs.

Slowly, very slowly, the feeling subsided. And again I slept. When I awoke, I felt light flooding in, between my closed eyelids, and opened them to see, on the far side of the room, the apothecary, drawing a pair of curtains aside. I saw a great gilt fiery dragon that appeared to fly across the room, through the luminous atmosphere, towards a dark wooden frame which housed a highly polished glass cylinder. In front of this cylinder, in the centre of the room, were four metallic pillars, supporting a pedestal from which rose three columns of cut glass, containing spiral tubes of golden glass and lapis lazuli. There was more than this, far more, too much for the human brain to absorb. The room was at least thirty feet long, and it was full of ornaments, copper, silver, gold, rose, crimson and yellow. The windows were made of stained glass and they threw a rich dappled light across the room, in particular on two pale, carved female figures, both naked, on either side of the fireplace. There were machines, glowing glass jars, bronze rods, and an elevated platform, so high a man could walk beneath it. In short, it seemed a kind of earthly paradise, and I could hardly believe that my own bedroom lay just beyond these walls.

When the apothecary saw that I had woken, he moved to a space between the windows and rang a small bell which was placed upon a table there. Then, without warning, a hole sprang where the floor was, and Dr Graham (I could explain it, then, no other way) emerged from the ground, as if he were a growing plant or flower. I watched as he flourished his hand

and bowed to me, then, the smell of jasmine preceding him, came nearer, with a look of infinite concern on his fair face.

'My dear,' he said. 'It is clear you are a woman of great delicacy. I see you were not prepared for the wonders of my Temple.'

'No, indeed, sir,' I replied, my fear lessened somewhat by the sound of his voice. 'I must admit, I am somewhat confused.'

'Come,' he said, once again offering me his hand. 'Let us sit down together.'

And with this, he helped me from the throne, but as I struggled up, I realized immediately that my dress was unbuttoned, my stays unlaced. Yet the Doctor, as I moved, averted his eyes, and this calmed my fears, so I said nothing, and followed him to a seat between the windows.

'Child,' he said, as he took a chair opposite me, 'I understand you fear you are possessed.'

'Yes, Doctor,' I replied. 'The Devil has been in me for as long as I can remember.'

'Do not think of it any further,' he said simply. 'Believe me, child. The Devil does not reside in the likes of you.'

'But I have felt him there, Doctor. I know it to be true.'

'And how do you know this, child?' he asked.

'Flies and maggots in my hair,' I said, without thinking. 'Water turning to blood.'

And murder, I wanted to say. I murdered my mother.

'Maggots?' he said, nodding slowly, 'in a coiffure?'

'Yes.'

'And how long was it since this coiffure had been dressed?'

'Six months perhaps,' I said. 'I do not know.'

'I see.'

In the silence I became aware, once again, of my loose dress. Had the Doctor himself unbuttoned it?

'And the water,' he said at last. 'Tell me about that.'

'It was the Hotwell, sir,' I said.

'At Bristol?'

'Yes.'

'I see,' he repeated, and was silent for a moment. Then, he

seemed to come to some decision, a diagnosis, I hoped, but he simply said, 'You know little of the world, my sweet. And you have much to learn. Do you wish to learn from me?'

'Sir, I . . .'

'Call me "Doctor", child. And your name is?'

'Emilia. Emilia Anne Beaumont.'

'Beaumont?'

He said the word as if it had significance for him; for a moment he appeared to lose his composure. Then, almost immediately, it returned, and he spoke the name as if it meant nothing to him.

'Emilia Anne Beaumont. A pretty name. Tell me, Emilia. Is it you that my porters have spoken of? The girl who mourns.'

I blushed, for I had not imagined the Doctor would know of me.

'Yes,' I replied, 'but as you see, I am finished mourning now.'

Suddenly I felt angry, that this Doctor had not yet treated me. That he had undone my gown, made me sleep upon a pedestal, asked me questions, but had not given me a cure.

'I must go now,' I said, upon an impulse. 'For I fear my father was right when he said this place was no better than a seraglio.'

But at this Dr Graham frowned; his look expressed a true anxiety.

'No,' he said, most earnestly, 'oh no. Your father was very wrong. Is this what people are saying of me already? That will change. Oh, that will change. Prostitution, Emilia, is a grave sin. A grave sin indeed.'

'I am glad to hear you say it.'

'Emilia. I am a doctor. An unusual doctor, it is true. But none the less, my purpose is to cure. Let me explain – when you saw this room, a meagre room I should add, compared, say, to my Great Apollo Chamber, you fainted immediately.'

'The Devil,' I interrupted. 'It was he.'

'No,' the Doctor replied. 'Not the Devil. A simple combination of your being too tightly laced, and your extreme sensibility; an exquisite temperament. And though modesty dictates that I should not have loosed your stays, I have no time for modesty when it interferes with health. I was convinced, my sweet, that a dose of celestial fire would revivify you. And indeed, I see from the rosiness of your cheeks that your health has been restored.'

'Celestial fire, Doctor?' I said, remembering suddenly the words of my father in the dream.

He smiled.

'Electricity, child,' he said. 'The true quintessence of nature. The material soul of the universe!'

'Doctor!' I said, much alarmed. 'What have you done?'

I had heard Daniel speak of such things, of men who stole fire from the heavens, harnessed the thunderbolts and misused their power.

'Do not fret, Emilia. To be sure, in the hands of quacks and impostors, my machines could prove most fatal. But I have spent many years refining my art, and it is my policy never to use even the mildest electric shock on my patients, unless their case is extremely serious.'

'So what has happened to me?'

'You were treated on my Celestial Throne,' he said. 'What you received was not a shock, but merely partial frictions, sparks – brushings of electricity. In addition to this treatment, I would suggest you take daily my Electrical Aether, my Nervous Aetherial Balsam, and my Imperial Pills.'

'And will this banish the Devil?' I asked.

'Emilia,' he replied. His voice was low; he leaned towards me with a conspiratorial air. 'I tell you again, it is not the Devil that contaminates you. It is the world. You are now in the bloom of youth, but I see great sorrow in your eyes. A sorrow that will eat your soul, and rot your beauty if it is not prevented. Everywhere you go in this foul city,' he said, 'especially when you are indoors – you will be surrounded by bad air, exhaled by other people. Think how dangerous it must be, when, added to the internal parasite of unhappiness, you also draw into your lungs the foul and putrid exhalations of others, the stench of their dirty bodies and garments, not to mention the corrupted substances that may leak from hidden sores. You are young,

Emilia, and proud, but you are not safe from this. I tell you, there is but one answer.'

'And what is that, Doctor?' I asked, quite terrified of the fate he had predicted for me.

'You must stay here with me. You must be my Hebe Vestina!'

'I do not understand.'

'Do you sing?'

'Yes.'

'Play the harpsichord?'

'Yes.'

'Speak French?'

'Yes.'

'Then you are she. You will be my Goddess of Health! My Angel!'

8

VERMILION

TWO DAYS HAVE passed since last I wrote, for though I have had the conviction that I must contribute something more to this story, I find I do not know how. More and more I come to understand that the original documents, Emilia's diaries, are not enough. I, as her biographer, must make some impression. I must point out where she dissembles, make certain that you understand her reasons for writing as she does. And I must be objective in my analysis. I must not let that feminine thing, the heart, come in the way of truth.

Yet if truth be told, I have been shaken by the happenings in France, by the treatment I received there, and perhaps it is this that has disturbed me. Though at the end of Emilia's life I was disgusted by the thought of her and could not bear to see her, to read her words now reminds me of how she was, then, at the beginning. With this thought in my head, it is impossible for me to comment on her story, and yet it is necessary that I harden myself, or else my purpose will falter.

Against my will the servants have lit a fire in the bedroom; they say I'll catch my death without it, but I have thrown the windows open, and that, I hope, will lessen the damage the heat might otherwise inflict. It is somewhat pleasant, in fact, to feel the light rain blow across my face, as I lie here in my bed (an ordinary bed, solid, curtained, wooden – not the bed that haunts my dreams). A couple of moths have flown in, attracted by the candle-light, and whilst one stupidly pursues the flame, the other has settled on the breast of my statue, my Goddess of Health. This is not, however, Emilia that you see. It is the Doctor's second Goddess, one Emma Lyon. I try, as I look upon it, not to think of my spite, which inclined me to buy this object. Instead, I focus only on the movement of the moth, the flicker of the tawny wings against the stone.

Suddenly all becomes clear. It has been said that the art of the biographer lies in his ability to come to terms with his own invisibility. That is a notion I have often heard, and yet, I find, I cannot fully agree with it. For I am a biographer who plays an integral role in the story he is telling. How then can I possibly remain invisible?

The truth is, however intrusive I may appear, I am a man of principle. I try to abide by the rules as much as possible, and the rules of this game state that I am only important if the information I present to you has relevance to Emilia. This is history, after all. Emilia's history. When a man has lived as full a life as I, when he has seen the head of the French King roll into a basket, he is bound to have a story to tell, but this is not the place for it. I am your commentator, not your subject.

And yet there is a Vermilion, despair not, that I will tell you about. The Vermilion known to Emilia. France, the Revolution, my flight from Paris – these are fascinating stories, but they do not belong here. My recent life has changed me, and Emilia would not recognize me if she saw me now.

But I lived then, also, and I, like her, was a frequenter of Dr Graham's establishment. In the early days, before I grew bored of the distraction offered by the Temple, I was an eager disciple. Or at least, I pretended to be one. For to do so ensured many advantages for a young man of my means and position, not least of which was the free use of the Doctor's famed Celestial Bed, which he hired out for fifty pounds a night.

Yes, that Bed is one of the few things the unfortunate Doctor is remembered for. I have not heard word of him of late, but I believe that he is still alive, though he too has been transformed and is turned from a genius into a madman. But I remember him clearly. I remember what he was, not what he has become. His face, his words, his frustrations and his dreams. He thought of me as a believer in his cause, yet in truth I always thought his theories quite absurd. Regarding masturbation, for example. I could never have agreed with him on that subject, though I frequently pretended to support him when he spoke against the despicable practice of self-abuse. His theory was this, Gentlemen. A man's sperm is precious – a luminous principle! (I use his words, you understand, not my own.) It is the breath of beauty! The soul of the soul! The magnet of love! The essence of ages! The liquor of life!

And so, we have a liquid that is intended for the purpose of procreation (the Doctor believes our population is falling; degenerating – he is afraid), a liquid which, he says, once it is produced, is pumped around the body, blending and churning with our blood and animating us with its life-giving force. A man has this magnificent substance in his body, but what does he do? He sits in the dark and frigs himself, sending his luminous principle flying across the room. According to Dr Graham, this very act strikes off an irrecoverable chip from the staff of life, it enfeebles the body and cuts off many natural years from the term of the man's existence (the Doctor, incidentally, claims he will live till the age of one hundred and fifty). So harmful, in fact, is this practice of onanism, that the Doctor advises young people to fly to bagnio, to brothel or into the fiery and fetid gulf of certain disease, or even to put an end to his existence, rather than carry out this method of self-pollution. A man who thus abuses himself, he says, is as a poor, creeping, tremulous, pale, spindle-shanked, wretched creature, who crawls upon the earth, spurting, dribbling and draining off alone. I would say it is an unflattering portrait of ninety-nine per cent of mankind. And frankly, I do not accept it. How could I, indeed, when the Doctor – a man whose hand, we presume, never dared touch his private member when erect, unless it were to feed it into his wife – is now turned lunatic as the King, whereas I – who have had as many ejections prompted by my own hand as some have had hot dinners – am neither mad nor wretched.

I tell you, if you wish to live an exceptionally long life, then I recommend you frig yourself, frequently and without guilt. I have no proof of this theory, and yet I feel, Gentlemen, that it is a truth I must espouse.

And now would you excuse me? Perhaps Emilia's story will divert you. I watch the moth rouse itself, flutter across the surface of my Goddess, and land again on her mound of Venus. I am obliged to lay down my pen, for there is an urgent matter I must attend to.

9

EMILIA

I DID NOT at first know, of course, the meaning of Hebe Vestina. Or rather, though the Doctor went on to translate the name (the Goddess of Youth and Spring, she fed nectar to the Gods), I did not understand what he required of me. I find it hard, now, to explain why, throughout this meeting, I did not cry out, 'Stop! Explain yourself!' except to say that it was I who decided to enter the Temple, I who had cast aside my father's warnings from the grave, I who was embarking on an adventure. To be sure, I felt powerless to resist the pull of Dr Graham's great magnetism, and the allure of his electrical remedies. Even so, throughout our first encounter, I was aware that I also seemed to be the object of some fascination. The Doctor appeared unable to pull his gaze away from me – he complimented my fine features, my sweet voice, my clear eyes. And when he said I should be his Goddess, though I was not certain of the meaning of it, I nearly wept, so enchanted, so overwhelmed was I that I should be worthy of this.

'In short, Emilia,' he said simply, 'I wish to employ you. I wish to treat you with my medicines and teach you to live according to my regime. You will be an example to my visitors of the perfection one may achieve if one follows my advice.'

And so, entranced by this idea, knowing that my fate, if left in Daniel's hands, was uncertain, I allowed the Doctor to tie my stays loosely once again, so that I might appear decent to the world outside. He took me by the hand and led me back to the stairway, and I was all the while thinking that if this man could prevent me from breathing in the pollution of other people, then he could also ensure that never again would I have creatures multiplying in my hair. If I could be Dr Graham's Goddess, I thought, I could remain in the Adelphi, and experience daily the pleasures of the Celestial Throne.

It was not until we reached the entrance hall, with the Doctor bidding me return at eleven that night, by which time all his visitors would have left, that I first questioned his demands. This was an extremely indelicate request, and I knew my brother would not allow me to leave the house at that hour.

'Doctor,' I said, 'would it not be better if I were to return tomorrow morning?'

'Oh no, Emilia,' he said, 'for we must press on. There is much to explain, and I must teach you quickly.'

'Doctor, can you not teach me now?'

'No, for I must prepare for my evening lecture.'

'Sir, are you certain that this will not be an indecent employment?'

'Emilia,' he replied, 'those who wish for an indecent spectacle may go to Mrs Hayes's in Pall Mall. Your role will be to demonstrate the effectiveness of my remedies. To illustrate the perfection of body and mind which we all must strive for.'

'And may I not come tomorrow, Doctor? Eleven is a late hour for a young lady to be out, and my brother may not allow it.'

'Dear child,' he said, 'as your home is next door to my Temple, what harm can be done? This evening I wish for us to view the stars together. I find in the night skies ample illustration of my theories.'

'You seem to know much, Dr Graham,' I said. 'And I wish to learn from you.'

'Then I will see you this night, Emilia. At eleven.'

Outside in the street, the air was crisp, and I walked across the pavement towards the railings from where I could see the river. The afternoon sun, low in the sky, gave an amber glow to the surface of the ice. In the time that I had been inside the Temple, the light had faded, though the sky was now a clear, but muted, blue. London, it seemed, was spread out before me; that frozen river, the antithesis of my new life. It dawned on me suddenly how little I knew about this city. What was this place, Mrs Hayes's in Pall Mall? There were so many things I did not know. Where did my brother go each day? And the Peacock Lady – who was she? Where did she reside? Each of the workmen (I had not thought of it till then) loading goods into the warehouses beneath the Adelphi had a life of his own. Each coach-driver that passed behind me had a home, somewhere in this vast metropolis, and an existence that I could not begin to contemplate. Everywhere in this city, people were living their lives, and no life, I thought, was quite ordinary. Each happening in this place was in a sense miraculous.

And indeed, a miracle had happened for me that day. Somehow, though I had not believed it possible, I felt that the Devil had been exorcized from my soul. Though the Doctor suggested that I had never been possessed, I knew that I had. I also knew that the presence of evil within me was evaporating. The Celestial Throne had frightened it away. And now I was left with the possibility of a new beginning. At that moment, I did not fear the notion.

I shivered suddenly, and all at once realized that I was quite freezing. My lower arms and décolletage were bare; the yellow dress was a summer garment, intended for evening wear. I saw people in the street turning to look at me, horses trotting diagonally across the road because the drivers had their eyes on me. And the feeling of the air, caressing my body with its chill fingers, thrilled me. I leaned forward against the railing, feeling the rush of wind against my cheeks, my skirt billowing out behind. I breathed in the icy gusts and was exhilarated.

That was the true beginning of my vanity. Though it had surfaced earlier that day, it was born there, by the river.

And the nature of my vanity was this. Before meeting Dr Graham, I lived within myself, caring more for my own feelings, my own reactions, than what others should think (with the exception, of course, of my father and brother). But then, beside the Thames, I saw myself for the first time; truly had a consciousness of myself as an image in the eyes of others. I became one of the fine gentlemen taking an afternoon stroll by the river, and I saw a woman, or rather a girl, who had at that very moment, as I watched, blossomed into womanhood. The girl was dressed inappropriately for the weather; indeed, if she had not been in possession of such charms, she would have looked quite ridiculous, even quite indecent. But no, not this beauty. It was impossible that she should look anything other than dazzling, so alive was she with the bloom of youth. I moved closer to her. I was no longer the gentleman, but an invisible ghost, the wind. I rippled around her, sliding down her forearms, my descent eased by the fair, soft, down that coated them. I played about her throat, her breast, her lashes. I gazed into her eyes, the colour of cornflowers, I caressed her lips, blew on her cheeks and watched their rosy hue deepen. And then I tore away, playing about the surface of the river, admiring her from a distance, remembering my place. I flew high, above the Thames, above the city of London, until I could see the whole panorama, but still there was one bright spot that shone, no matter how high I flew: one yellow speck which was the centre of it all.

Where my musings would have led after this I do not know, but I was saved from further contemplation by the voice of my brother, who was walking quickly towards me from the corner of Adam Street.

'Emilia!' he was shouting, a smile on his large, freckled face. 'Emilia!'

And when he got closer, 'What are you doing out here – and in that dress? You'll catch a terrible cold. Come inside – I have wonderful news!'

The sight of Daniel, half trotting along the pavement, brought me immediately to my senses, and I felt quite guilty for allowing myself such indulgent thoughts. Still, I could not help comparing myself to him, and feeling, suddenly, a great chasm between us. His wonderful news was bound to be a trivial thing; he was so easily pleased. It was strange, but since my father's death it was as if Daniel's hold over me had evaporated. I could not respect him, though I knew I ought.

*

Once we were inside, Daniel lit a fire whilst I looked on. He was glad, he said as he blew the flames, that I seemed to have recovered my spirits, and he was certain my father would not mind that I had done with mourning. (I did not know what had provoked this change in him. I had thought he would be furious at me.)

'But Emilia,' he said, 'you should not expose yourself to the elements like that. You must not take risks with your health.'

'I am sorry,' I replied. 'I do not know what I was thinking of.'

'No, sister. It has not been easy for you since father died.'

'It has not been easy for either of us, Daniel.'

'True,' he said, 'but my first concern, in settling father's affairs, is that I arrange things in such a manner that he would have been pleased. I imagine you have thought me idle this last month – perhaps you have despaired of me? You see, Emilia, I did not like to tell you of my negotiations, for fear that you might be disappointed if I were unsuccessful.'

'Brother,' I said. 'Please come to the point. You make me curious with your rambling.'

'Emilia . . .'

He smiled, and blushed a little.

'Emilia – you will be pleased to know that I have found you a husband!'

Nothing – if he had told me that man had learned to fly, or a sea-monster had found its way into the streets of London – could have shocked me more than this news. If I had heard it from my father, just two months earlier, it would have seemed quite natural, and though I might have been nervous at the prospect of marrying a man I had not met, I would (providing the man himself had not seemed akin to the monster) no doubt have yielded to his fatherly will. But this was different. My brother had not told me of his plans. He had led me to believe that he was being idle, and this had influenced my acceptance of Dr Graham's proposal of employment. I knew I should have been pleased at the news; delighted that I would not have to succumb to the unknown indecencies of the Temple (for though the Doctor swore it was not indecent, I had suspicions to the contrary), yet somehow all I felt was the weight of a great chunk of lead upon my heart. Marriage would mean forsaking my new self, climbing back into the hardened husk which I had thrown off. And more than this – it was the idea of marrying a man chosen by Daniel that most revolted me. My brother – my ugly, clumsy brother – choosing a husband for me! It was not possible. I could not yield to his will.

'A husband!' I said, feigning high spirits. 'Why, Daniel! I do not know what to say.'

'Say you are pleased, Emilia,' he said, 'and I shall be a happy man.'

'It is a great surprise for me,' I replied, 'but I am of course filled with joy at the prospect.'

I had not lied to him before then, but I did not know what else to do.

'Are you not curious, dear sister,' he said, ruffling his hand across my hair, whilst I suppressed the shudder that this provoked, 'to know who this man is that I have chosen?'

(I am sure you have not chosen him, I thought. The dowry my father left was not great, so to find a willing husband must not have been an easy task.)

'Why yes, Daniel. Tell me his name.'

'His name, sister – and you must not judge him by his name, for he is a fine man and a rich one too – is Lord Smellie, Thomas Smellie. He has a great estate in Essex in addition to his house in Cavendish Square.'

I tried hard to crush my impulse to laugh, but found it truly was not possible. And each time I caught a glimpse of my brother's stern displeasure, I laughed the more. He waited, patiently, for it to subside, and he brought me a glass of water. Then he said, 'I did not realize how severely you had been affected, my dear, by the death of our father, but I see now it has rocked your senses.'

'No, Daniel! No,' I said. 'It's just so funny, surely you see that. To think that I could marry a man called Smelly.'

He looked down, and away from me, in an attempt perhaps to hide the emotion, but I saw it, etched across each feature; a sense of disappointment; a sense of his own failure. And I ignored it. I saw my brother's sorrow, but I disregarded it and thought only of myself.

'Lord Smellie is away on business for a few days, Emilia,' he said to me, when he had regathered his composure. 'When he returns, I will arrange for him to come to the Adelphi to meet you. I hope you will not be uncivil.'

'Brother, I will meet him,' I said, 'but I can make no promises.'

'You forget your place, sister,' he said. 'But I am sad to have to force the issue. I had expected to find you joyous at the news.'

'Perhaps you should have lied about his name,' I said.

'I did not think a sibling of mine were so shallow as to quibble over a name.'

'I did not think a sibling of mine were so deep he would arrange a marriage without telling me.'

At this, Daniel rose and turned to leave the room. He said nothing more. Alone, I realized that my arms had turned red with the heat of the fire. It was so easy, I thought, for one's beauty to be marred. Dr Graham had said sorrow would rot my bloom. I vowed I would not let that emotion enter my heart.

IO

EMILIA

BENEATH THE STARS I await Dr Graham. It is a cold evening, and I stand on the iron balcony, a cloak wrapped around me to shield me from the chill. Under the cloak I wear the yellow dress, but now I have removed my stays and I breathe easily.

The scene is familiar. One hundred feet above the river, on a clear night, yet I see very little. All I can think of is the prospect I am avoiding: the fate of becoming Lady Smellie. It must be prevented, I see that, at any cost. The danger, even of meeting him, going near him, seems too great. His stench would permeate me; spoil me.

As if in answer to my fears, I feel a hand upon my shoulder, which calms me; it is a fair, white hand. The hand of the Doctor.

'How is my Angel, this evening?' he says, his lilting voice deep and soft.

I smile, but I do not turn to him. Instead, I close my eyes. I want to savour the moment; breathe in his perfume, mingling with the crisp, night air. London has never smelt like this before. The frost has sanitized the city, the ice shielding us from the stink of the river. I am at ease; feeling that I belong in this world.

'Your Angel is well, Doctor,' I say, 'though she is afraid.'

'Afraid?' His voice is sand through an hourglass. 'There is no need to fear.'

In truth, I was about to confess to my planned marriage, but as the Doctor has assumed my fears stem from elsewhere, I know I should not contradict him. If I tell him of the marriage, he might not wish to employ me.

'No,' he continues, 'you should have no fears, for fear is a beast which will devour you. Here you shall know nothing but calm and serenity. In my Temple, your soul will be cleansed.'

He speaks a language I have longed to hear. I know that in this place I can hide from the world outside. I breathe deeply; feel the rush of ice through my nostrils, my rib-cage expanding freely to take it. I am full of air. The Devil has left me.

And I hear the voice of the Doctor.

'Are you going to open your eyes, Vestina?'

'Yes,' I reply. 'Yes.'

But I hesitate, fearing that what I will see might spoil my rapture.

'Open your eyes,' he says again.

And I obey.

Perhaps I had been sleep-walking when I came here; perhaps infected with my father's blindness. All I know is that the sight before me is more beautiful than anything I have ever seen. Stars speckle the midnight sky, bright points of light, shining down on the pale, solid Thames. The street below is empty, dully lit by the oil-lamps hanging along the Adelphi Terrace, and it is this emptiness that attracts me. London, the bustling capital, has come to a halt and is turned into an ice-desert.

The Doctor's hand rests on my own.

'What do you see, Angel?' he says.

'I see the stars blazing in the sky. I see . . .'

But then I flounder.

'No. I cannot describe it.'

'To be sure, Emilia,' he says. 'My soul struggles . . . it bursts with the immensity of what we see.'

And I turn, for the first time this evening, to face him. He is pale, like a phantom beside me, his hair freshly powdered, his suit white. He is not handsome, I see that now. There are slight bags beneath his heavily lidded eyes; his lips are too wide, his chin heavy. But he has the aura of a protector.

Can I ask him now, I wonder? Can I say the words that have been burning on my lips?

'Doctor,' I begin, trembling already, feeling faint again.

'Doctor – what is this place?'

He looks surprised.

'You do not know?' he says.

VERMILION

HERE I AM obliged to interrupt. Emilia's narrative, I find, grows lengthy at this point, so in *love* she is with the Doctor, so taken in by his mumbo-jumbo. It is not surprising, I suppose, that he had a great effect on her. I do not criticize her for falling for his charms, but for me, there is only so much *blazing* and *trembling* I can take. Though I cannot blame her for her language, surely I do not have to listen to her? And shall I be honest? The truth is, I find this story to be lacking something. It needs a new character in order to give it life. It needs a person of wit, in fact, to give it energy. A young man. A man about town. A man called Vermilion.

Yet this is not the only fault I find. Her manuscript is long. Too long, I think. It is a problem that I have been pondering this morning, whilst eating my breakfast, and I believe I have found the answer. It was not clear at first. My coffee, buttered toast and cake were brought on a tray, and John, who has been with us since I was a child, gave me a look of disgust as he observed the damp bedclothes and slammed the windows closed. In response I complained at the small portions he had made for me, and he replied that if I wished to die of obesity, he would have Hannah make a second breakfast, and a third, and for dinner he would bring me a full roasted pig. This is the treatment one receives from servants when they have tended one from a young age, but to get my revenge, I told him that yes, I was content to die, and he was required to bring me the second and the third repast, and ensure that a pig was put on a spit immediately and two bottles of port wine (or three, or four) fetched from the cellar, so that I would not have to wait too long for dinner.

And now, having eaten the last crumbs of cake, I have come to a conclusion. Food and drink are surely not simply intended to nourish the body, but to nourish the mind also. As my stomach has grown distended, so my brain appears to have enlarged and my capacity for thought has thus increased. I pay no heed to the Doctor's advice, for he would preach that it is not the quantity which one eats that is important, but the substance itself. He is against the luxury of meat, he denies the merit of over-indulgence; indeed, if he could have his way, we would all be starving, on a diet of nothing but vegetables! But I will ignore his maxims. Not only will I eat more than is necessary for mere survival, but I will eat such quantities as will swell my brain to the level of genius. In order to achieve such heights, I will have special plates made, special cups, five times the size of those that are now in my possession. A paltry, mincing, pigmy little cup, such as the ladies drink from with crooked little finger jutting out, is not fit to be filled with my morning coffee, for I must guzzle from a tankard, nay from a jug to ensure true clarity of thought. If I had not demanded a triple meal this morning, who knows what a muddle my mind might now be in. Instead, I am decided. I know what I shall do.

Allow me to explain. Emilia's sensibility, you understand, is a trait I have admired in her before, but I have come to realize that the result of this affliction is a tendency to write about herself, her delicate feelings, and not enough about what actually happens. I would venture to suggest that she has read too many novels, and, like the heroines she found there, she's trying to show you how *intensely* she experienced life, how truly *moved* she was by the stars. She doesn't understand that what we want are the facts! Indeed, so many pages has she written that, if I let you read them all, we would be publishing ten volumes.

Nevertheless, there is hope, and this is what I realized as soon as my stomach was full. If we cannot change her, we can at least be selective. Though I have promised not to alter her words, I have not said that I will include them all. If I did, there would be no room for me, and that, my friends, would be tragedy indeed. I do so hope that you are not attached to the idea of authenticity? There will be some, there always are, who create a fuss about such things. People who live in the past. But I shall not bother myself with them. If they don't like it, they, like the ladies, can find another book. I'll leave them in the manuscript library, poring over insignificant paragraphs. If you stay with me, however, your reading will be pleasurable, and easy as the butter that drips down my throat. What is interesting will not be denied you, but what is dull will be omitted. In other words, I will labour to make your experience enlightening and agreeable. Your role is to relax and to enjoy. I assure you, what you do not see, does not merit reading.

Travel then with Vermilion. Let us revisit that scene, beneath the stars – Emilia and the Doctor. We will not wade through unnecessary adjectives, but instead, experience it as it happens. For though I am, as yet, an absence in Emilia's diary, this is the night when I first caught sight of her. I was there, behind the curtain, watching, with the permission of the Doctor.

'You must tell me,' he had asked, before she arrived at the Temple, 'what you think of this beauty.'

Yet I knew, even then, that it was not my opinion required. The Doctor, I was certain, had made up his mind about Emilia. The way he spoke of her was proof that he was entranced. Yet he would not experience it fully until he had shared it, for he knew that I, like all men who encountered her, would be overcome with lust. Emilia, you must understand, embodied dreams.

But what of myself? How did I feel at that moment, as I watched, fearing she might smell a rat? I felt awed, immediately, by her presence. It was an inexplicable emotion; one I had not experienced before, and it came upon me so suddenly; it had no rational basis. I was saddened instantly that it should be this girl the Doctor had chosen to display. He had found the best there was – she was clearly perfect for his purpose – and yet I felt he should not use her. I made a silent, futile vow that I would prevent it. She would be mine, alone.

Stop! What am I saying? Stop! My tongue runs away with me. Vermilion's role is to record what he saw, what he heard, what he smelt, tasted, and touched. There are five senses only, not six. The heart is of no consequence.

So what did Vermilion hear that night that is worth repeating? The truth is that the Doctor was evasive. He did not lie, yet he told Emilia what suited him, not what she required to hear.

'The Temple, Emilia, as you know, is a Temple of Health. A place where the sick, those close to death, may be healed. But think of it also, Angel, as a Temple of Hymen.'

'Hymen, Doctor?' she replied, and I laughed to hear how shocked she seemed.

'This is not what you think, child,' he said. 'I can tell by the way you speak that you think I refer to a woman's most delicate part! But it is not so. Hymen, Emilia, is also the God of Marriage. A young Athenian he was, whose love was much above him in rank. Yet he won her hand through his bravery. And indeed, so much felicity did he experience in his married state, that the people of Athens instituted festivals in his honour and solemnly invoked him at their nuptials. Indeed, even now, it is said that no marriage will endure if he does not honour it by attending. And I invoke his presence here, for this is a place where the blessed state of marital harmony may be celebrated.'

'And how is it celebrated, Doctor?' the innocent asked, wide-eyed at his tale.

'In the usual manner, child,' he said. 'Only with a little help from myself.'

'What do you mean? That you are present while the couple . . . while they . . .'

'No, Emilia. Nothing of the kind.'

'Then what, sir? What are you telling me?'

'I cure barrenness, Angel,' he said. 'You remember Rachel's words, from the Bible?'

'Yes. She said, "Give me children, or else I die."'

'Exactly. For as we know, barrenness is almost always the fault of the female. Yet if this disease is not cured, our population will fall most terribly. Already the country is becoming populated with a race of sickly creatures, creatures barely worth the name of Man. And a sickly offspring weakens the bond between parent and child.'

'And do you know, Doctor, the cause of this sickness?'

'There are many causes, Emilia. And I know them all. But one thing I will tell you. The world will never be peopled with a race of true heroes if infants are begotten by rakish, debilitated men and women.'

And thus he continued, spouting generalities, never once mentioning the Celestial Bed. Meanwhile I slunk away, knowing that the Doctor would not talk frankly that night. He was breaking her in gradually, taking care not to use terms which would offend her. Soon she would hear his Lecture on Generation, and then all would become clear. She had so much to learn.

But I tire of them, don't you? All this skirting around the subject gets me down. Not that I am obsessed by the sexual act, you understand. Simply that if we must talk about it, let us discuss it in plain terms. Let us at least have a lesson in biology. Oh, how I dreamed of that. Lying awake in my room, I whiled away half a night, thinking how I would explain it to her, for I was certain that she knew nothing beyond the most elementary details. I imagined us both, naked on my bed in my lodgings in St James's. How she came there I do not know, but these details, courtship and the like, were irrelevant. Simply, she is there, but rather than copulating, I want to teach her the secrets of the human body. To make a schedule of its beauty. It would be inventoried, and every particle and utensil labelled to my will.

And so I see her, ivory-skinned, the curves of her breasts glowing in the candle-light, the soft line of her legs caressed by the sheets. No! That is not how I imagined it. That is how I think of her now. Then I had a different fantasy – she would lie in stark daylight, stripped of her allure.

'Item,' I would say, holding my erect penis in my hand, watching the confusion on her face. 'The Yard, or, because it hangs beneath the belly (though at this time, I admit, it rather *stands* beneath), the Penis or Pendendo (*pendere* – to hang). The Pendendo, as you see' (for she does indeed stare at it), 'is long

74

and roundish. It consists of skin, tendons, veins, arteries and sinews. And it has a miraculous quality. When the nerves are filled with animal spirits and the arteries with hot blood, the Yard quits its usual limber and flaggy state and becomes distended (as it is now).'

Next I grab my balls, rolling them beneath my fingers. She is a little intrigued by these, and leans closer to me.

'Item,' I continue. 'The Stones or Testicles, so called because they testify the person to be a man.'

Yes, indeed, I find that she admires them.

'Vermilion,' she says, 'how is it that they are so firm and resilient?'

'Dear Emilia,' I reply, 'have you not listened to the Doctor? Though without his remedies these Stones would be lank and pendulous, like the two eyes of a dead sheep (two grey eyes, with lids to them), dangling in a wet, empty, calf's bladder, having obeyed his doctrine of spraying them, daily, with ice-cold water, I now present them to you, two steel balls, enclosed in a firm purse of uncut Manchester velvet!'

But though she longs to touch the purse, I will not have it. We have not yet finished with our catalogue. I give her a mirror and instruct her to place it between her legs.

She is coy at first and does not wish to play this game (she wishes to hide herself away, to remain unknown) and yet I insist it will be an education, and so she capitulates. But it is with horror that she beholds these delicate parts of her body; with disgust even. This Vermilion, however, was a cruel man and he insists on continuing.

'Item. The woman's genitals, or Pudenda, from *pudere*, to be ashamed (for indeed, Emilia, I see you blush already to look at them). Item.' (She tries to please me by glancing at this sight.) 'The Outer Lips of this great orifice; as you see, covered with hair, and containing a pretty store of spongy fat. Their purpose is to protect the inner parts.' (And I reach between her legs, without mercy, holding the outer lips apart, letting my fingers brush the clitoris so she will be unable to resist.) 'Item. The Inner Lips, often named the Nymphae or Wings. These, also,

75

are made of soft spongy flesh, and in form and colour, being fresh and red, resemble the comb of a cock (two lips, indifferent red). In the act of coition (*coire* – to meet), the Wings receive the Yard between them. (Item. Vagina: a sheath. How my Sword longs for it, Emilia!)'

'Were you sent hither to praise me?' she says. She knows her part so well and is ready to perform.

'No,' I reply. 'I see you what you are: you are too proud.'

'Proud?' she says. 'Why is that?'

'Item,' I reply. 'The Hymen. Claustrum Virginale. A thin membrane, interwoven with fleshy fibres and endowed with many little arteries and veins, spread across the passage of the Vagina, behind the insertion of the neck of the bladder. It has a little hole in the middle for the menses to flow, so big that it will admit the top of one's little finger. This is that which is called the Zone or Girdle of Chastity. It is the bud of a Rose, half-blown, broken in the first act of copulation with Man. Hence, to deflower.'

'I will not be deflowered,' she says, 'until I know the measure of your love.' (Love! she says. How can she think of love?) 'How do you love me?'

'With adorations,' I say, recalling poor Orsino, 'with fertile tears, with groans that thunder love, with sighs of fire.'

And though I lie and though she knows I lie, she is overcome with lust. No Olivia she, she drops the mirror, opens her legs, and my Sword is sheathed, the Virgin Zone is ripped apart.

EMILIA

Hail! Vital Air – Ætherial! – Magnetic Magic – Hail!
Thine Iron Arm – thy bracing sinewy Arm! – is everlasting Strength!

My brother had joined Smellie for a few days, and I was free
to dedicate myself to the teachings of the Doctor.

And thou, celestial Fire! – Thou, FIRE ELECTRIC – GREAT
    RENOVATOR –
THE LIFE OF ALL THINGS! Hail!

I was given a light gown of white silk and a rose-coloured
girdle. I was forbidden from wearing stays or other undergarments, all of which were considered restrictive.

Come, then, ah come! O sacred HEALTH!
The Monarch's Bliss! – the Beggar's Wealth;

In the Great Apollo Chamber, where the Temple of Health
itself was situated, I was taught to sing this Ode, dedicated to
the essence of life – Electricity.

Root of the soft and rosy Face!
The vivid Puffe – each charm, each Grace!
The Spirits when they gayest shine;
Youth, Beauty, Pleasure – all are THINE!

I was free from the Devil.
    And I was learning quickly. Theories that I could never
have dreamed of were now lodged in my mind. My whole
way of life had changed, for I had begun to live according to
the Doctor's teachings and I was determined to serve him
well.

This then, was my new daily regime, which I wrote down, for fear I might forget it.

1. I am to rise, each morning, at five a.m. Six is too late for any person who values health and long life.

2. It is my duty, each morning and night, to bathe my whole body, but in particular my private parts and my fundament, with icy-cold water or milk. This is a most important key to health, beauty and desirableness.

3. Before noon, I must run about for fifteen minutes, wearing one of my loose silk gowns, in St James's Park, for exercise and fresh air are vital to well-being. (Tight lacing and high shoes, I must remember, are harmful to beauty.)

4. When I return from the park, I must inhale from my vial of Electrical Aether. This is essentially a preventative measure, for the substance is an enemy to diseases and corruption.

5. I must, at all times, abstain from animal food and all alcoholic substances. I may eat plentifully of green raw salads, succulent vegetables, ripe fruits, eggs and mild grains. Fish is permitted, especially shellfish and raw oysters.

6. At all times, the windows of the rooms that I inhabit must remain open, even on these winter nights, or in the coldest, stormiest weather. I must sleep on a hair-mattress or bed of wheat or oat straw, without removing the grain in the ear of the corn.

If I follow the above doctrines, the Doctor assures me, I will become glorious within, and outwardly streaked with celestial blue.

So much had changed. Impossible, it seemed, that so little time had passed. The world my brother inhabited now seemed to me nothing but a shadow, a vague remembering: the time before I saw the light. Now there were songs in my head and stories, so embedded in my mind, it seemed I had always known them.

The craze for all things electrical, I now realized, was sweeping

Europe. Safe within my father's home, I had not known the extent of my ignorance, for the electricity that Dr Graham possessed was the envy, he said, of Kings. This royal interest in the elementary fire began in France, when the old King, Louis XV, witnessed the administration of an electrical shock to a chain of monks, a mile long. He was convulsed with laughter at the sight, as each monk, one after the other, leapt several feet in the air. Our own monarch, George III, however, was a more serious observer of electrical phenomena. Indeed, he was known to have enjoyed demonstrations of the very Celestial Throne which Dr Graham consequently purchased, and only modesty prevented him from attending the Temple.

But if he had come . . . if he did come – how delighted he would be, I thought. Standing in the Great Apollo Chamber, he would have found an apparatus beyond his imaginings. The very Temple of Health.

A much larger version of the Celestial Throne, this Temple within the Temple was the seat of the Doctor's practice: his chief apparatus (with the exception, he said, of his Celestial Bed). Standing within it, six feet above the floor, you are surrounded by six glass pillars, beyond which a Chinese railing protects you from electrical fire. Silver and gold globes spin above your head, and sparks, like the aurora borealis, play between them. There is another dragon here, whose tail rests on the domes, and it is he that delivers electricity to the Temple. When you visit the Temple, the Doctor says, your diseases will be chased away, like clouds before the sun.

And I was overcome to be a part of this. When I was in that room, I felt there was no other place that I would rather be. More beautiful even than the first room I entered, the Great Apollo Chamber, near the very top of the Temple, was where the Doctor gave his lectures. On entering, you could not help but be seized by a sense of awful sublimity. For the light from the stained-glass windows, which reached from ceiling to floor, threw an incredible lustre across the room, a kind of celestial gloom. On entering, you were not only struck by the Temple itself, but by two smaller Celestial Thrones, and by the very figures on those magnificent windows. The Doctor had explained it all to me. On the central pane, Apollo himself sits, God of Music, leaning upon his harp. Victory crowns him, for he has slain the serpent: the winged python who is the devourer of the human race.

Even as I begin, I know it is near impossible to describe the Great Apollo Chamber. For had I many years ahead of me, then I could do it, but as my time is short, as death approaches, I must sweep over details that I should rather include here. Only, I will tell you of those elements of the room that I loved the most. The stuccoed ceiling, in the centre of which the Three Graces cavort; the fifty drums which can imitate the sounds of thunder; the table, loaded with near a hundred vessels for distilling and diffusing odoriferous essences throughout the room. There were Indian fumigators, also, full of oriental odours, and the figures of Sterility and Fecundity, painted on the dome of the Temple of Health. This Temple, as the Doctor has said, is not merely a Temple of Health, but a Temple of Hymen also: a place where the bliss of marriage and fruitfulness may be celebrated.

I had been in the Temple for three days, practising my role in the evening lecture, learning the Doctor's doctrines which seemed to have saved me from the Devil. I was determined to serve the Doctor well, for he had rescued me; he had clutched hold of me as I teetered on the edge of a precipice, about to lose my beauty. Neither Smellie nor my brother, I thought, would take me away from this.

I had not yet begun to perform but I had been told what would occur. I would work on the evenings when the Doctor gave his lecture, four evenings in each week. My duty was first to sing, accompanied by an organ and two flutes, and by the sweetness of my voice and the purity of my countenance I was to demonstrate the effectiveness of the Doctor's work. At all times, I was to wear a silk gown and girdle, the colours of which, I was told,

would sweetly modulate as the lighting in the Apollo Chamber
was dimmed. This would happen when I reached the line,

THE LIFE OF ALL THINGS! Hail!

and would be controlled by the apothecary, who would draw
the rose silk curtains. When we reached the Grand Chorus, the
windows would suddenly darken and then the Chamber would
be illuminated in a moment, with many thousands of electrical
stars and meteors of celestial brilliance.

That night, I was prepared. Tonight, I thought, before the
Doctor gives his celebrated lecture, I will perform, and then, at
last, I will hear him speak out. And I knew he feared it. When
he spoke of the Temple of Hymen, the ideal state of married
bliss, I saw him look at me askance, as if to say, 'You must be
ready for it, Emilia.' He was afraid that I would misinterpret his
words. And yet already he had let slip fragments of his thought,
and I was still certain that he was a moral man. Though the
thought of a man and woman, together in that way, was
distasteful to me (yes, this is how I felt; I lived in fear of it), I
saw that it was the future he was concerned with. Not the sexual
act for our own self-gratification, but to build a better human
race.

'Yet understand, Vestina,' he told me, 'there is no shame in
the joy of Venus. For the more pleasurable the encounter, the
greater the likelihood of a healthy child, providing of course,
that the couple are married. And it is to this future race of Man
that I dedicate my work. A thousand years hence, the benefits of
my work will be seen.'

And I imagined this race. A race of Heroes, he said. There
would be no cripples, no blind men, no immorality, no ugliness.
In the Doctor's new world, Health would reign supreme. By
crossing the breed of the human race in the correct way, he said,
a more enlightened and stronger generation would be born.

'Just compare it with breeding horses, Angel,' he said. 'All
Human Creatures will be as perfect as you.'

And so, in preparation, I sing, and my voice reverberates across the Chamber. For music itself can be a cure to many ills. It stimulates the imagination and when a man believes he is better, then he becomes so. The bite of a tarantula is not mortal, the Doctor said, but it is the fear which kills. The power of thought is greater than we once believed possible. And thus, by inspiring calm, I myself will play a part in the healing process.

Celestial Renovator! Thou Life of all things! – Hail!

But then I stop. Tom the flautist continues to play, but I can no longer sing, for I have the sudden feeling of being watched. I cannot quite understand it, but I am drawn to the far side of the room, and as I approach, I realize the reason for my unease. I am not watched by one pair of eyes, but rather a hundred. Nor are they ordinary eyes, but diseased ones, eyes with cataracts, with colourless irises, or thick red veins across their whites. They are not real, merely the product of an artist's pen, half on rose India paper, the rest on serene sky blue, but so finely detailed that they appear quite lifelike. And each of the hundred pairs is enclosed most perfectly in its own small, gilt frame.

Immediately I think of my father. The bright eyes, in a creased face, that I knew as a child, and the glassy stare, the crazed squint of his age. However many eyes the Doctor has collected, I know that the eyes I long for will not be here. He was unable to cure those I loved the most. Yet still I scan the images, trying hard to find a picture to match the near-blind eyes which were so familiar to me. Irises clouded white. Lids of parchment. Whites turned yellow; sour cream. And then I search for my father's other eyes – before the blindness. The pale blue of a duck's egg, speckled in brown. But I cannot find them. They are not here.

And I remember watching him, a man once full of vigour; one who had always insisted that the mind was more important than the body. Yet now his body was deteriorating, and without it his principles fell apart.

'Emilia! Emilia!'

I turn, roused from my dream, but though I know it is Tom who beckons me, I can take notice only of the man who stands by his side. I have not seen this creature before, but I am instantly drawn to him. I feel embarrassed, somehow, by his presence, yet I cannot help but look at him. He is not quite handsome, but he is tall and he holds his head to one side, his chin uptilted, his thin lips a pout. Though this unnatural angle of his head suggests he might be admiring the rather flattering portrait of our ugly Queen Charlotte (whose mouth is all pursed up, for fear we should see its truly shocking size), I know that he is eyeing me. Like a statue he stands to be admired, and against my will, as I move towards him, I am drawn into the role of observer. Look at the hook of his nose! How daring that his hair is unpowdered! (Thick, it hangs, dark curls about his nape.) But I cannot make out the colour of his eyes. The angle is too obtuse. I only see their glint.

'Emilia, this is Vermilion. A friend and pupil of the Doctor.'

He does not move. I see just a twitch of his mouth as if he is sucking on a cherry stone. Then a further twist of the head, away from me, and up, as if he would snap his neck to improve his profile.

I too look away, my posture echoing his, and then I hear him speak, not to me, but to Tom.

'So this is the Doctor's Angel, eh?' he mocks. 'I don't see any wings.'

'There are too many winged creatures on this earth, sir,' I say, though I know I have not been addressed. 'Too many moths and flies. An Angel would not wish to be akin to these.'

'And yet the butterfly, also, has wings,' he says, 'and when I have chased a butterfly, I have known its angel dust to scatter on my sleeve.'

'A butterfly is born of a caterpillar,' I say. 'A fearsome creature, whose dust can cause a nasty rash.'

'And yet it is the caterpillar who spins silk, and you do not object to wearing the worm's garments.'

'Nor you, sir, I see. For the feminine frill about your chest is made of no other material.'

He smiles. Only the centre of his mouth is tight now; the stone seems hidden beneath his tongue.

83

'If you wish, little Angel . . .'

He mocks me. I am certain of it.

'. . . I shall be the worm, for it is a role I am accustomed to.'

'Then I greet you, Worm,' I say, unable to suppress my smile. 'It is a pleasure to make your acquaintance.'

And at this, he turns to face me and bows low, flourishing his arm. He stands up and for the first time, fully meets my gaze. I see his eyes at last, their clear colour no longer distorted by the light. Perhaps I imagine it; I am much prone to imagining. Irises, duck-egg blue.

VERMILION

A STRANGE AND unexpected event has occurred, which I must relate, for though it sheds no light upon the past, yet I feel that it has significance, and I am quite shaken by it.

In all respects, I would say it was an ordinary morning. The rain continued and the prospect from my study seemed, to me, more gloomy than usual. Even the folly had an isolated air, and, I admit, I was in a melancholy way, unable to be comforted by the smell of roasting pig which drifted into my room from the kitchen. The prospect of eating alone, once again, gave me no pleasure. I felt, in truth, in need of company, for I was unable to fix my mind on anything other than the sight of Emilia, when first I spoke to her, clad in little more than a wisp of transparent silk, yet apparently unaware of the indecency of it. The Doctor, it must be said, had been right to choose her as his Goddess, for at that moment when we were introduced, she seemed, to me, not made of flesh and blood. I found myself wondering if she were indeed immortal; a thing conjured from the spirit world, to taunt me with her beauty.

You can imagine then, I think, my state of mind. Starved of company, I was conjuring up the most tender moments of my past. Whilst I was in Paris I never wallowed in such self-pity. In that place I was constantly entertained. I believe, looking back, I was never out of company. The noise of other people was always thronging in my ears. What was I doing now, spending my time poring over these pages, dwelling on the past, fragments of memory, when I could be spending time with the living? Vermilion should be a creature of the flesh, not a scholar who spends his life with his eyes so close to the page that he cannot see anything for the cloud of dust that surrounds his head and his craning neck.

There was I, alone, full of sorrow, railing inside against the world and its miseries, longing for company, longing for the past, when what should happen but John entered the room, carrying with him the scent of charred pig flesh and a silver plate, upon which was laid a letter. I was surprised, for I had told none of my return to England, and yet I was excited also, very desirous to know what lay inside the envelope. To John, however, I did not show my eagerness. Ensuring that my face did not betray a flicker of interest, I thanked him for bringing this letter and dismissed him instantly.

Once he had left the room, I did not delay in opening the letter. The seal seemed familiar to me, and the script also, yet I could not place them. This, however, is what I read:

My Lord,

If you have forgotten me, I will tell you now from whom this letter comes. It comes from Helena, Vermilion. Lady Quinton. She who was once a friend to you, and a friend to your Emilia. And if you wonder, sir, how it is that I have found you here, to that I will simply reply that I am aware of the events in France, and, having assumed that you have fled that country, expect to find you at home.

I am, sir, you are aware, not now naturally inclined to be a friend of yours, for I remember, do not doubt it, how you did treat my friend Emilia at the time of her greatest distress, and there are other things, best not spoken of, which I remember also. In spite of this, however, I feel that I must write to you, for I fear no other person will understand the nature of my recent experiences. I find myself, Vermilion, on the point of despair, for my husband, Lord Quinton, is recently deceased. Not only this, but I have been amazed at the manner in which he has bequeathed his fortune, for whilst I knew that he would leave most of it to his heir, Marcus (who is, as was apparent to all but Lord Quinton himself, no son of his at all), still I had thought that it would remain in trust with

86

me. Instead, however, he left it in trust with his sister and no portion of it has he bequeathed to me, his wife. How soon, then, have I discovered that all the friends I thought I had were not friends of mine, but friends only of my fortune! Indeed, they remember too well the indecencies to which I submitted myself in the Temple of Hymen and they have not forgiven me for this. Now, Vermilion, I find Lord Quinton's kinsfolk are invading my two homes, and it is clear that before long I will have no place in either of them.

Yet all this is nought but a precursor to the words I wish to write. The truth is, Vermilion, that I am plagued with thoughts of Emilia. I have no friends, sir, but you, who have been my enemy. And yet I hope (perhaps in vain) that you may have changed during your absence; that age may have mellowed your sometime callous nature and that you too may have regrets which you may desire to share.

I am a fool, sir, I think, to write in this manner, to one who, it has been said, is without a heart. But I have seen you, sir, in unguarded moments, seem to suffer for your cruelty. I have seen doubt cross your features, and (perhaps I have imagined it) love etched in your eyes.

If, like me, Vermilion, the Temple haunts you still, I would ask you to reply to me.

I am, sir, your servant,
Helena Quinton

I tell you, Gentlemen – to hear from that lady, after so many years, made me turn cold from head to toe. At the very moment that I find myself overwhelmed by my solitary state – that she should seem to know it and step forward, presenting her parallel situation! It is the thing I most had wished for perhaps. But though I may have wanted company, I question now if hers will be agreeable to me. It never was before.

But I forget myself. Surely, what you will wish to hear is the identity of this woman. You know her name now, that much is true, but you do not know her role in our history. All this, however, will be revealed, and, if you have read Emilia's diaries with care, you will remember her description of this lady. 'The most beautiful thing I had ever seen,' she said. 'She was all, I believe, that I desired to be.' Do you have it now? Yes, Lady Quinton is none other than Emilia's 'Peacock Lady'. The woman that she admired from afar, she with the jet-black hair and jewelled mask; she whose back was a string of bone beads. Emilia's darling, who, you will find, plays an essential role in our history.

Yet I must confess, though I was at first glad to receive her letter, I am beginning now to regret that she has turned up like this. For to my mind, the present is the present and the past is the past, and so they should remain. This is Emilia's history and the telling of it is mine. If Helena arrives and begins to give her version of the tale, I swear we will never finish. Already, I wish I had not replied to her. Yet it is too late. She will be arriving tomorrow evening for dinner. I shall be sharing the remains of my pig with a noblewoman!

And so – I feel it is my duty to inform you fully of the character you are about to meet. I tell you this woman bears no resemblance to my Emilia. She is of higher birth, it is true, and yet her nature is more base. You will discover that her manner is all sweetness or 'politesse', shall I say, and though most persons would not call such breeding base, I will explain my meaning. The Lady Quinton, I tell you, is so shallow that if she were a pool of water, and I were to attempt to bathe in her, I would find that her liquids would not reach to my ankles. Nay, I doubt if I would find my largest toe to be even half submerged. This, which is the acceptable depth, it seems, for most gentlewomen, I would call base, for lack of character, to me, is truly contemptible and I would rather converse with a beggar, I assure you, than most women of her class, for they can mouth nothing but niceties whilst all is rotten underneath.

Her letter, you will say, seems to contradict my judgement. Yes, indeed, I agree there is some semblance of feeling in it, but you must remember these ladies are taught to dissemble well. You think me harsh, perhaps? You think that she and I are two people at war with one another, with neither of us prepared to give ground. You may think, Gentlemen, what you will, for I, being fair, will ensure that you see this Peacock Lady through Emilia's eyes also. In her diaries she speaks much about the Bird, and I will not interfere with her descriptions. As always, you are not obliged to take my word alone.

No matter – I do not wish to spend more words upon her. I should be telling you that the true reason that I give you this particular extract is that here, in this fragment, you will be introduced to the Doctor's lecture, which he gave four times in a week, and in which Emilia played a vital role. A Lecture on Generation, he called it, a Genuine Libidinous Lecture.

Here, my friends – savour it. This is virtue in danger. The sweetest thing that ever this rake did experience was to see the shock on Emilia's face that evening, though it was not the Doctor's words, I assure you, which caused her alarm. I ask you, Gentlemen, to imagine it. A maiden in distress.

I 3

EMILIA

BEAUTIFUL! ON THE night when I was first to perform for the Doctor's guests, I saw a thing most beautiful. Indeed, so overcome was I that I barely knew how to describe it and though afterwards I returned to my antechamber in the Temple, I still felt the image of what I had seen burned on to my eyes. I longed to see it again.

And I knew I would, for finally the Doctor had agreed that I was ready. I had been waiting so long for this; all my life it seemed. But now I felt myself to be pure. I had never been so pure. After following the Doctor's regime for a whole week, I knew that the Devil had left me. I had moved closer to the Angels.

The time in the antechamber was supposed to be my quiet time, before the lecture began, when I was to gather my thoughts and meditate upon the wonders of electricity. But having seen what I had seen, it was almost impossible that I should stay calm. I was nervous, even before, about my performance, afraid that my voice might not reach the highest notes or that I might forget some vital action. Yet now I felt so much worse. Simply to look was ecstasy, and it had left me giddy and unbalanced. I could not sit still. I wanted to run about the park again like a colt.

But this was not allowed. Somehow I knew I must regain a sense of tranquillity, for that is what the Doctor desired for me. He wanted me to be true to my name, Hebe Vestina. Goddess of Youth and Health. The essence of serenity.

Why then, I asked myself, did he wait so long before showing me the Celestial Bed? Surely he must have known the agitation that such a vision would cause any person? In truth, I could not fathom it at all, for when I performed in front of the Bed, would I not be shaking all over, afraid of the magnificent power of that apparatus? I was beginning to realize that each time I thought I was getting to know the Doctor, he would surprise me again with his behaviour, and though I adored him, and it appeared that he adored me also, I sensed that I would never come close to understanding the workings of his mind. It was, I mused, as if he wore a wooden mask, and very often, when I believed that I was coming closer to perceiving his true nature, he would raise his hand to remove the mask. For a moment, then, I was full of joy and anticipation, until I realized that beneath the mask lay not his face but another mask, exactly the same. How many of these, I wondered, would he have to remove before he revealed his own flesh?

If ever this journal is read, in future times, I wonder – will it be in an age where there is nothing remarkable about that Bed? When a Celestial Bed is an essential requirement for any Grand Lady or Gentleman? In the nineteenth century, I predict that every couple not stricken by poverty will spend their nights cavorting on such a Bed, and so, it seems to me, that my own observations on the subject will not be of much interest. 'Why does she bother to describe such a commonplace object?' I hear the Lady exclaim.

And yet, already, the popularity of the Doctor and his electrical remedies has waned. In this year of 1783, as I write, the Doctor has already left his second Temple in Schömberg House, Pall Mall. That Temple (which he called, without shame, his Temple of Hymen) was cheaper to run than his first in the Adelphi, but the number of people visiting the Doctor had declined. Thus it was that at the end of last year, Schömberg House was seized for debt and advertised for sale. Even the Celestial Bed was sold to the highest bidder. Now the Doctor lectures in the chapels of Edinburgh, and I have read in the newspaper that he has been accused of indecency!

I do not know what has become of our Celestial Bed. Perhaps it thrives, even now. And yet, somehow, I doubt it. Rather, I suspect, it lies forgotten somewhere. And if this is so, then it will come to pass that the future generation, the generation spawned upon the Bed (and many others spawned on tables, in haystacks and upon grimy floors) will not remember the Temple. The Great Apollo Chamber and even the Celestial Bed itself will be completely forgotten, or if not forgotten, they will merit nothing more than a passing reference in a history book.

But this is not the worst of it. To be forgotten, I think, is not the worst fate. I myself would happily fade into oblivion, were it not for the fact that I am forced to tell my story, for fear of the alternative – that I should be a character in Vermilion's book.

If I am to speak of the Bed, as it was on the day that I first saw it, you must understand the way it seemed to me. My head was full of doctrines, do not forget that. I knew the purpose of the apparatus and, when I looked upon it, my mind was not sullied by lascivious thoughts. I knew that in spite of the high price the Doctor charged for a night on the Bed (fifty pounds, a sum I could not imagine), he would let it out to none but *married* couples: couples who had suffered for years, their hearts full of sorrow that their marriage had not produced children. Infertility, I understood, was one of the greatest miseries one might experience, yet here, in this bed, such misery could be cured. Just one night upon the Bed, the Doctor advised, and the woman would instantly conceive. The Electro-magnetic Celestial Bed was one of the greatest miracles Mankind had ever experienced.

All this I knew, before I even set foot inside the room where the Bed was housed. And yet it was impossible that I could have imagined its beauty; the hold that it would take over my imagination. For what I saw was not a bed at all, in the ordinary sense. For could you call a thing a bed, that was twelve feet long and nine feet wide? A thing supported by around forty pillars of brilliant coloured glass and topped by a dome panelled with mirrors? Could you call a thing a bed, when that dome is decorated with the figures of Cupid, Psyche and Hymen, whose torch sparks electrical fire? I tell you – this is but the beginning. For the brass pillars that supported the dome were in the form of musical instruments – golden pipes, flutes, violins, clarinets and trumpets, and each instrument seemed magically to breathe forth a genuine sound. The smells that emanated from the Bed also were the most delicious I had ever experienced – I recognized lavender and tuberose, but the other scents were unfamiliar to me. They came from the East, the Doctor told me, as he watched me sniff the air.

'Odoriferous, balmy, aetherial spices, Emilia,' he said. 'Rich gums and balsams from the Orient. They all have miraculous properties.'

I doubted nothing that he said. Though I had seen the orchestra rehearse, I did not imagine that the music came from any other source than the Bed itself. For to me, its very existence seemed a kind of miracle. I stood, aghast, each moment becoming aware of something new – the live turtle-doves perched on the dome, the organ at the head of the bed, sweetly toned, and above that an inscription, sparking fire: 'BE FRUITFUL, MULTIPLY AND REPLENISH THE EARTH.'

There was a painted landscape also, where moving figures, a priest and a bride's procession, entered the Temple of Hymen. This landscape was displayed to its best advantage for its colours contrasted perfectly with sheets of the richest, softest, sky-blue silk.

I moved forward then, and the Doctor, seeming to read my thoughts, said, 'Of course, Vestina. You may touch them. Though you must remember that I have sheets of many colours, to suit the complexions of the ladies who sleep there. Go on – sit down! You surely know by now the magnetism will not harm you.'

I did as he asked, and though I was afraid of the Bed's power, I could not help but love the feel of it.

'Such mattresses, Doctor,' I said. 'The Bed is so beautiful and yet so comfortable also.'

'My Vestina, you make me proud – for you have perceived that it is not just external design that makes my Bed unique, but the substance of the thing also. You sense the energy that flows from the mattress?'

'Yes. Yes, I believe I do.'

'Angel, you are right to do so, for these mattresses are filled with the strongest, most springy hair, produced at vast expense from the tails of English stallions which are elastic to the highest degree.'

'Stallions, Doctor?'

'I see you blush, child. But there is no need to be ashamed to hear this. The stallion's virility and fertility are to be revered. The properties of this mattress are essential to the workings of the Bed. It is not just the fire that aids conception. Each part of the Bed has a purpose and the stallions' hair is of the greatest potency.'

'Doctor,' I said, knowing that it was essential I tell him of my fears. 'I cannot help but be ashamed when you speak of such things. Though you have explained the joys of holy matrimony and the necessity of regenerating the species, why is it that I feel this is indecent? Why is it I cannot help but blush?'

As I spoke, I thought I saw a look of great respect cross the Doctor's features. He moved towards me, sat down on the bed, by my side, and took my hand.

'My Vestina,' he said. 'My dear Hebe Vestina. It is right that you should blush, for you are indeed young, and a virgin, as you should be. But as my Angel, as my Goddess, you will learn to transcend your fear of the joys of Hymen. You will learn to understand that a little knowledge will not harm your virtue. I will teach you, Vestina, all there is to know about the union of Man and Woman, and you, being more than mere Woman, will be able to speak of these things with dignity. You, being pure, can transcend shame. Only the guilty, sweet Emilia, are afraid to mention the act of love.'

And at this, I confess I was comforted. Who would not be, when told that she was more than mere Woman? Though I still knew little about the sexual act, I began, then, to think of it differently. I began to think of myself differently. Even when Dr Graham proceeded to demonstrate other properties of the Bed, I tried to listen with an Angel's ear.

'Should pregnancy at any time not happily ensue,' he was

saying, 'I have the most astonishing method to recommend which will infallibly produce a genial and a happy issue. The Bed, you understand, is constructed with a double frame, which moves on an axis or pivot which gives it its unique tilting mechanism.'

A tilt! (I thought) – why surely the couple would fall from the Bed! But though I said nothing of my doubts, again the Doctor perceived my thoughts.

'Child,' he said (one moment an Angel, the next a child – I did not know what to think). 'Child – when a man impregnates a woman, do you not think it foolish if she immediately *leaps* out of bed and starts parading the room?'

'From what you have told me, Doctor, his seed might fall from her body if she did so.'

'And what would you recommend, Vestina, to prevent this?'

'That she lie still for an hour whilst the seed penetrates the egg.'

(I could scarcely believe I was talking in this way, and yet, I comforted myself, I had no guilt. I was pure as cold air.)

'Exactly. And to take this further, imagine, if you will, that during the act of love . . .' (he paused, watching my face, to see if such imaginings would affect me) '. . . that during the act of love, the Bed should tilt, so that the man shoots his seed from a position of greater advantage.'

'And that afterwards,' I continued, proud that I could anticipate his words, 'the woman lies in the tilted position, with her legs higher than her head, so that the seed rushes all the quicker to its destination.' And at this the Doctor smiled, and took my head in his hands, bending it forward so that he could kiss my forehead.

'Spoken like an Angel,' he said. 'Spoken like an Angel.'

All this was no more than a precursor to the events of that evening. It is difficult for me now (so confused have I become about my feelings towards the Doctor) to remember my feelings then. So much was going through my mind that the events in

95

the Temple – my first sight of the Bed, the lecture I was about to hear – were like the new patina of frost that had formed outside on the river: crystalline, pure white flakes that settled precariously on the thick, glassy-grey slabs beneath. On the surface, I too was dazzling, dazzled, but beneath, I realized, when the initial shock of seeing the Bed had waned, that perhaps my heart had not fully thawed, as I had believed it to. I was living in a kind of dream, I thought. For the following day I knew my brother was returning to town, with Smellie.

As the thought occurred to me, I immediately tried to banish it. Surely this transformation *must* run deeper? Surely, if it did not, the Doctor would protect me from my brother – he would not be prepared to lose his Angel. Yet I was in truth afraid. Though since my father's death I had not seen that we had any friends in this metropolis, it was clear that my brother did have acquaintances. What if one of these had seen me as I ran through the park, half-naked? I knew nothing, after all, of this Smellie family, but it was possible that already the news had reached them. Their son's betrothed is nothing but a strumpet! And a mad strumpet at that! Have you seen the lunatic creature that runs barefoot across the frosty lawns each morning? The one who wears nothing but a silk shift, who is surely courting death to be out in the cold like that? A pretty little thing, she is – a rare sight for the gentlemen. But *she*, Countess, is the one to whom your son is to be married!

And though, if this were true, I knew I would be delivered from my fate, I was not thus comforted. Even if Smellie did forsake me, I still feared that my brother might take me away from the Doctor.

'You doubt, Angel!'

I was surprised to look up and find the Doctor at the door of the antechamber. I was ashamed that he caught me thus.

'I am afraid, Doctor.'

'Still afraid?'

'Not of the Temple, nor of our purpose. But of my brother.'

'Your brother?'

'He returns to the Adelphi tomorrow. With a husband for me.'

Immediately I regretted my words. I saw his eyes darken. His face changed in no other way, but this congealing of blackness I detected in those orbs made any other fears seem insignificant. His voice, when he spoke, was calm but his gaze did not waver.

'You did not tell me of this, Vestina.'

'No, Doctor.'

'My heart breaks that you should lie to me.'

In that instant I saw the end of all that I had grown to love. I felt he would withdraw his blessing. I would be made mortal again.

'I lied because I love you, Doctor,' I said. 'You have freed my soul and filled me with the essence of life. I was terrified lest I should lose this. That the aetherial influences within me would fade and I would be filthy again. The man who would be my husband is called Smellie . . .'

And at this, I broke down in tears, inconsolable. The Doctor instantly rushed to the windows and opened them wide so a chill air rushed in. He reached to a cabinet for a phial of Aetherial Balsam, which he opened and held beneath my nostrils. Between sobs, I inhaled deeply, and, slowly, in his arms, was calmed. So sweet it was to be there, a place of the greatest comfort. My anxieties seemed to fade, for I was overcome with sweetness and with electrical influence.

'Your father is dead, Angel?'

'Yes, Doctor,' I said, my voice weak. 'My brother is my only remaining relative.'

'Then I will protect you from him. You must move all your belongings into the Temple. There is a room here which will be yours. A plain and simple room, though the ceiling, dear Emilia, is adorned with nymphs, and Hymen also will dance above your head. I tell you, you will be safe in my Temple. *Never* will a Goddess of mine face marriage. It is a thing for mortals, Vestina. But you must have faith in my power to protect you. Without faith, you will not be worthy of your place.'

How could I ever have doubted him? His words soothed my every fear. And I smiled, feeling again the power of his voice. It was itself musical. It reverberated in my ear like the sound of the sea in a shell. There was something timeless about it; a sense that he, also, was not mortal, but a kind of sea-god. I was immersed in his voice, in the scents that surrounded me, and when I closed my eyes an instant, I fancied I saw him, emerging from the ocean, draped in weeds, a diadem upon his head.

'Come, Vestina,' he said, as still I reeled at the thought of making the Temple my home. 'It will soon be time for my lecture. You have an hour to bathe yourself and wash away your tears. I will leave you now. Have faith. Listen carefully to my words this evening. We have a great mission, Emilia. And when you sing tonight, and show your beauty, you will play your part in this grand design. You will be the living proof of my remedies. Our guests will adore you.'

'I have often seen those guests, Doctor. Before I knew you, I would watch them from my window, arriving at the Temple. All week I have been dreaming of these people – of who they might be. Who are they, Doctor, these ladies in masks? And who are the gentlemen that accompany them?'

'You are impatient, Angel. But I will say only this. Though by day I treat the sick, the poor, the needy – those who attend my evening lectures are the Adepts, Emilia – the Cognoscenti! So wealthy, Vestina, so well bred, so educated, yet they are, in matters of love, less knowledgeable than they ought to be. Have faith, my child. For you were born beneath a perfect star. Love is in your bones, Emilia. Love is in your bones.'

14

EMILIA

IT IS COLD. So cold, and yet exhilarating. Down my back, across my shoulders, my breasts, my arms, the water runs. Ice-cold like the river. Clean water, refracting candle-light across my flesh.

The windows still are open wide and I feel the chill air caress me, a cold breath against my skin. And I see myself like this, in the mirror above the fireplace. My nakedness seems the perfect complement to the gilt surround. I am like one of the nymphs that cavort above my head, so pale is my skin, so round my breasts. There was a time when I could not bear to look at myself, when my hair was full of worms. There was a time, before that, when simple modesty dictated that I should never see myself like this. I was ashamed. But now the Temple is my home. I have a room which is my own. I have removed all my belongings from my father's house, and now I feel as free as a man to stand and stare at myself. I have nothing to fear, for I know this body will never be defiled. My beautiful, most beautiful body will remain untouched. Vestina. Virgin Vestina.

And as I bathed between my legs, dashing the icy water again and again against my private parts, should I have known that the thrill I felt had nothing to do with aetherial influence? Should I have said – Stop, Emilia! You do not know what you do? It is impossible I should have thought this. For to be sure, I did nothing that could be called indecent – I merely bathed as I had been instructed. Following the Doctor's learned advice which I had read in a small treatise he had given me, written in his own hand.

BATHE YOUR PRIVATE PARTS WITH COLD WATER THOROUGHLY!
AND FOR A LONG WHILE, EVERY NIGHT AND MORNING, FROM
THIS DAY UNTIL THE LAST HOUR OF YOUR EXISTENCE. THIS IS
OF THE HIGHEST IMPORTANCE TO THE PRESERVATION OF
HEALTH AND STRENGTH, BEAUTY AND BRILLIANCY, BODILY
AND INTELLECTUAL.

No – though I felt a warmth that stemmed from between my legs and seemed to radiate outwards down my thighs, across my buttocks, in the small of my back, so that every nerve and fibre thrilled, I was certain that what I felt was the most chaste and virtuous sensation. Like the footsteps of Angels as they gathered around me, banishing all evil influence.

When the carriages arrived I was ready. Draped in white silk, I stood at the head of the staircase beneath the dome where I had first seen the Doctor. The Doctor himself was at the foot of the stairs, welcoming the guests, and though I desired to see them better, I knew I must be content to listen to the chatter, for I must not be seen to look towards them. Hebe Vestina should gaze only at the heavens.

Yet it was not the heavens that were then in my mind. It had been a long day, a remarkable day, but it was not the Celestial Bed which I thought of, as I stood posing for the crowd, nor was it the sight of myself in the mirror earlier. My mind was filled with thoughts of the Doctor's friend, the man named Vermilion. Knowing now how later he mistreated me, it pains me to remember how I then idealized him. He was a friend of the Doctor's after all – what higher recommendation could there be than that? Though I was more than mere Woman, and as such should not have thought of mortal men, I allowed myself this whim (or so I called it), for this was surely a most moral man – else the Doctor would not allow him as a pupil.

Vermilion, I thought, as my arm (held out at an angle so that I should seem more like a work of art than a woman) began to ache. Lord Vermilion! How beautiful a name, conjuring images of crushed red velvet and burgundy wine.

Where I should see the dome above the staircase, I see his face. It is imperfect, I am aware of that, and though I sense the danger of the vision (the mortal danger of dark curls, pale eyes, hawk nose, and thin lips, red as his name) I tell myself once again – he is a good man. He will be a friend to me. I am afraid of what lies ahead, of the necessity of this, my first performance, and this vision is not significant. My mind plays tricks on me.

All the time I see this face before me, I am waiting. There is an intense buzzing in the hall down below, so many voices, I would guess more than a hundred. But I hear one voice above them all, and I am awaiting my cue. Finally, the Doctor speaks.

'Let us ascend to the highest room in the Temple. The Great Apollo Chamber.'

And at this I am ready. My lungs fill with air and I begin my song with a long shrill note, so piercing that I believe I feel the air move as all faces below lift up to stare at me:

'Haaaaaaaaaaaaaaaaaaaaaaaaaaaaaaaaaaail!'

My mouth is open so wide I fear it will split, my brow is furrowed with intensity; the note I sing is a dagger that cuts the air. And then Tom begins to play on his flute as I ascend the staircase further, leading the guests, who are overcome not only with the music and the splendour of the Temple (for more music begins now, harmonious strains of wind instruments which reach the ear through hidden openings in the staircase), but also with the sweetest perfumes which flatter the sense of smell. They are awed by all this into a near silence, and when they speak to one another it is only in whispers. And I too am silent now. I feel my breast heave beneath my shift as I enter the Chamber.

'Hail! Vital Air – Ætherial! – Magnetic Magic – Hail!'

I was not distracted by the dimming of the lights, by the way my dress was tinted rose, nor by the sudden darkening of the room which was followed by an explosion of electrical fire – meteors and celestial brilliance, just as the Doctor had warned me. No. Instead, as I sang, I felt I was a part of this event. The guests sighed and marvelled at the dragon which seemed to fly across the room, they stared at the Temple, they screamed at the fire. The Doctor was indeed a great magician but I was no longer an observer of his magic. I was an element in his sorcery. I could not stand outside this wonderment again. I was an object, as marvellous to them as the lights that sparked around us. Only too soon I found my aria was over.

And it was then that everything changed. As the music ceased, as the brilliant sparkling fires died, and the Doctor stepped into the light of the Temple itself, a strange thing happened. I had been so caught up in my performance, so enamoured of myself, that it had seemed quite natural to dwell in this environment. Yet now, finally, my eyes were able to fix not on the lights or the apparatus, but on the audience. A roomful of mortals, they seemed suddenly, stinking of undistinguished perfume and roast dinners. The smell of them was so distasteful to me; the feeling of being amongst a crowd filled me with horror.

But this was not the worst of it. All of a sudden, I understood their looks: the haughty envy of the women, the undisguised lust on the faces of the men. Whatever the Doctor had told me, they did not see me as a Goddess. They saw me as one of them; more beautiful perhaps, with a finer voice, and cleaner. But I knew they did not see me as I had become. With dismay I saw the way the men craned their necks to stare at my breasts, clearly visible beneath the gauzy shift. The room seemed to burst with them – so many men and women, more than the hundred I had at first guessed at, more like two hundred. They were crammed into this room to hear the Doctor speak, and though I had dreamed this would be some kind of elevating, unearthly experience for them, this audience – notwithstanding their class, for they were surely aristocracy all – seemed as ill-mannered as if they were watching a spectacle upon the stage. They did not realize the hallowed nature of this particular performance, but rather they *gawped* at the Doctor and *leered* at me. So many faces were crammed into the Apollo Chamber, that it seemed to lose the sense of majesty which it had when empty. The richness of the costumes they wore was unsurpassed, yet it seemed to me there was something animal in their nature, something crude and unrefined. Most of the men wore powdered wigs and rouge upon their cheeks and lips, and there was a quality about the faces that was most abhorrent. Too many grimaces. Unkind faces. Even the women, when they removed their masks, though there were some beauties amongst them, seemed somehow jaded, and the extravagance of their gowns merely served to emphasize that what lay beneath the splendour was not comely. Plain faces they were on the whole, but topped with vile headpieces (that contained I knew not what) which were supposed to give a look of opulence, and their plump bodies were all contorted by their stays, so their bosoms puffed out above their dresses and their waists were squeezed like sausages into skins.

I moved from the light into the darkness, for I knew I was not needed now for some while, and as I moved, I glimpsed in the shadows, close to me, two faces that were an immense comfort to my ailing heart. In the glare of electrical brilliance I had not seen those standing nearest, and now I saw them to be Lord Vermilion and another that I had longed to see – the bespangled creation whose beauty had so inspired me, before I first entered the Temple – my Peacock Lady. I knew her at once from her figure, from her high, black coiffure and her silver dress. She was taller even than Vermilion (and his height was at least six feet) but this time it was not her stature that attracted me, but her face (which before had been hidden by the peacock mask) – such a face had I never seen.

Think now of eyes, like those of an Egyptian Queen. Almond eyes, dark enough to hold an infinite store of mystery, fringed by ebony lashes. They were large eyes, heavy-lidded eyes, framed to perfection by high, arched brows. As I watched her speaking to Vermilion, that other object of my fascination, I was drawn by the nobility of her visage. Her skin was a little too dark to be fashionable, but to me it lent her a touch of exoticism that is most rare amongst the English. She had a large nose, which on any other woman would appear unseemly, yet on her face it appeared regal, for it was balanced by a magnificent mouth, perfectly formed. Two red lips that did not pout or simper, but rather seemed a statement of her superiority. Both she and Vermilion appeared out of place in such a vulgar crowd.

And as I turned my eyes now to feast on him, feeling perhaps a small pang of jealousy that they should be together, he must have sensed my presence, for he turned and seemed to laugh that I should stand so close behind them yet not announce myself.

'Will you join us, Hebe Vestina?' he said softly.

I did so, and together we turned to watch the continuing spectacle, for at that moment the whole audience was all agape as a gigantic spectre, thin and haggard, appeared to rise from the ground (it was in truth another apothecary, dressed in white and painted pale, who emerged through a trap door). It was an illusion of genius, yet I was growing immune to such wonders. I was dazzled instead by the beauty of those who greeted me. Vermilion himself was all that I remembered him to be, and was dressed in the very fabric that I associated with his name – a dark red velvet, the colour of wild berries.

'Emilia,' he said (I remember the way he whispered my name, as if he found a ruby on the tip of his tongue and must mouth the word most carefully, so the gem would not break). 'I must apologize for my rudeness earlier. Now I have heard you sing, I know that you are indeed an Angel.'

'Why, thank you, my Lord,' I murmured (afraid, also, lest I should disturb the spectacle).

As he spoke, the Peacock Lady eyed me with some interest, yet I detected also some derision in her glance.

'I must introduce you, Emilia, to my friend . . .'

It seemed quite wrong that I should thus indulge in this hushed exchange, when I should be watching the Doctor. Still, I could not help myself.

'. . . the Lady Quinton.'

Quinton. That name, also, was jewel-like. An opal, perhaps, so smooth on his tongue that he did not notice it slip from his mouth.

The Lady Quinton nodded, blinking slowly as she did so. Then the corners of her mouth began to curl.

'I am pleased to meet one who has been blessed with such gifts,' she mouthed. I was just close enough to hear the sound of her breath and my reply was equally silent.

'Thank you, my Lady. I am truly honoured if my voice gave you pleasure.'

'Let us hold our tongues now,' Vermilion said. 'The Doctor is about to speak.'

And with that I looked to where the Doctor was standing, prompted also now by the gasps of those around me. The spectre was leaning towards the Doctor and now handed him a bottle of liquor, which I knew to be Electrical Aether. Then, as easily as he had appeared, he seemed to vanish. And at that moment Vermilion took my hand in his and I felt myself turn faint, as fire, hotter than anything celestial, coursed through me, and made the centre of my sex burn and my heart roar within my chest.

In the many months that I spent within the Temple, I heard the Doctor's Lecture on Generation many times. And though each time he delivered it, he made slight changes, certain phrases are etched indelibly in my mind. What is difficult for me, however, is to remember the effect those words had on me the first time that I heard them. For though I had heard him speak of his theories before that day, never had they been so clearly expressed. And never had I heard him speak with such frankness. If Vermilion had not been by my side, it might have been possible that I could have endured the lecture without experiencing shame, but the presence of this odious man (odious now, you understand, not odious to me then) gave the Doctor's words a strange resonance, for, as he spoke, Vermilion would whisper in my ear, seemingly in support of the teachings, yet somehow making me uneasy. Too afraid to remove my hand (my small, white hand) from his, I had allowed myself to be led to a small, hidden platform at the back of the room, where we could watch and hear the lecture, but could not be seen by others. I was sorry that the Lady Quinton did not follow us, and felt she must think it rude that our first acquaintance had been so brief. But though there was an air of secrecy about our movements (to hide, like that, in the dark, when I should be displaying my loveliness to all), I was no longer certain of what was proper or right. Was not this man, I reminded myself, a friend and pupil of the Doctor's? Who else should I obey if not him?

And then the Doctor began. And though, as I have remarked, I could tell you now the details of this lecture, the first time I heard it, I was immensely distracted. Never had I been so close to a man (who was no kin) as this. Never had I known the effects a large, strong hand (with hair upon it) could have.

Still, I did attempt to listen. A strange process was going on within my mind, whereby I would attempt immense concentration, knowing that it was vital for my role that I understand the Doctor's theories, yet often, almost without my being aware of it, I was transported elsewhere, by this constant, gentle pressure upon my hand. The darkness of this hidden platform, the brilliance of the room beyond, my sense of separation from the base mortals below – all contributed to this strange enchantment that I experienced.

But let me tell you, now, what I did hear – let me remember those words of the Doctor's that became imprinted upon my mind. For I was not entirely distracted. How could I be, for I was torn between the two men that I loved – the Doctor had not lost his magnetism – and I was Aether, suspended between these two poles.

The Doctor spoke first of the vital necessity for the further propagation of the species.

'No man can have felicity in the hymenal state,' he said, 'when his wife is barren . . .'

He raved against prostitution, which I admired him greatly for, and spoke in favour of the married state. And the Doctor was ardent about the importance of Life. He was passionate that the war with America must end, and spoke of the bloodshed in such a way that for the first time I came to see the true meaning of the word 'war'.

'O God!' he said, 'if the daemons of war are still to be let loose among mankind . . . let it not be recorded in the annals of heaven that they were Britons.'

Millions of gallons of innocent human blood, he said, had been wantonly shed. And at that moment, even Vermilion's presence could not distract me. I saw battlefields, across the ocean. I saw once-green fields, now flooded with blood. I knew nothing of this war we were engaged in, yet all at once I understood that there could be no true cause for this.

And then the Doctor seemed to soften, and speak of duller things – of who should marry and who should not. Those with congenital diseases should not marry, he said, and other things which I had heard before, and could not attend to, for Vermilion had begun stroking my hand.

'Listen now, Emilia. You will be much enlightened by what you hear.'

15

VERMILION

GENTLEMEN, I DISAPPOINT you. I interrupt your reading at the very moment when I am about to cause distress to this maiden. Is that not cruel of me? A little cruel perhaps, but remember, Vermilion does not act without reason. The fact is, it is plain Emilia does not do justice to the Doctor's lecture, and I cannot let the occasion pass without telling you more.

As I have told you before, your journey with Vermilion will be easy and pleasant. Thus, for your convenience and your pleasure, I will now set down the Doctor's five great maxims – I still have time before the Lady Quinton descends upon me, and I would not wish you to miss his wisdom. I shall call this 'A Short Treatise upon Dr Graham's Lecture on Generation'. And do not fret, Gentlemen. This diversion will be most entertaining, I assure you. And soon we will return to that dark corner, where Emilia trembles at a mere touch of the hand. You will see her virtue threatened before long.

16

A Short Treatise upon Dr Graham's Lecture on Generation

(THIS BEING DIVIDED INTO FIVE GREAT MAXIMS)

SINCE THE YEAR of 1782, when Dr James Graham was forced to leave his second Temple of Hymen in Pall Mall, many things have been said about him which are neither accurate nor true. Though in this year of 1793, it is clear (from what I have heard) that the man has become quite mad, whilst he resided in the Temple he was without doubt entirely sane. Rumours have spread, of course, even to my secluded residence of Carmine Hall, that the Doctor has now taken to religion, and calls himself the Servant of the Lord O.W.L. (Oh Wonderful Love), and that, more than this, he experiments in living without food or drink, sustaining his life merely by wearing mud-turfs against his body and rubbing his limbs with Aetherial Balsam. But I tell you again, in the years that I knew him, he was a kind of genius. Though his maxims which I shall set out below may be extreme and though I did not often believe in the benefits of his remedies – let it not be said that the Doctor was a charlatan. For he studied medicine at the University of Edinburgh under the great professors, Monro, Cullen, Black and Whytt, and I have no doubt that he truly believed in the virtues of his cures.

I spent several years in his presence and never once, in that time, did I hear him speak cynically of his purpose. And so, for those readers who wish to know the substance of his philosophy, I here set down the rudiments of his thought. True scholars may refer to the Doctor's full published work, which goes under the following title:

A Lecture on the Generation, Increase, and Improvement of the Human Species, Interspersed with receipts for the preservation and exaltation of personal beauty and loveliness and for prolonging Human Life, Healthily and Happily and to the very longest possible period of Human existence!

Other probationary mortals and wretches who prefer not to frequent the library would do better to study the basic principles, or five great maxims, which I here set down for your convenience (in a voice as near to the Doctor's own as I can muster, though it may prove somewhat lacking, for though some phrases of his adhere to my memory, others are lost to me). They are:

1. The Causes of Generation and Barrenness
2. Advice to Young Men, Regarding Virility
3. On Fertility
4. A Diversion on the Subject of Venereal Disease
5. How to Heighten and Prolong the Joys of Venus

THE FIVE GREAT MAXIMS

1. The Causes of Generation and Barrenness

As children are as necessary to happiness as health, it is essential that we understand the reasons why some married couples are cursed with barrenness. To achieve this understanding, we must first be familiar with the causes of Generation.

In my view, the complete future child lies, in a minute state, in the ovarium of the mother (like a plant with leaves, flowers, fruit and seeds wrapped up invisibly in the seed). Each egg, each ovum, contains a child in miniature and the sperm, when it arrives, merely animates this. During the connection of the sexes, the increased sensibility of the nerves of the womb communicate with the Fallopian tubes to facilitate the escape of the ovum. The exquisitely penetrating seminal liquor rouses life in the embryo and it is this we call conception.

This theory, then, is a perfect illustration of the reason for our decline. For if the germ and foetus of each child is sketched out in miniature whilst the mother is in a virgin state, then it follows that inside the first woman – Eve – all future men and women were contained. She was the outside pot or box, supremely decorated, within which a number of smaller boxes were contained, inferior boxes – galley pots or cheap pill-boxes. We, my friends, are these smaller boxes, which accounts, you understand, for the current degeneracy and diminution of the human race, which is leading (if we do not take care) to our extinction.

How then, you may ask, can we prevent this decline? And more than this – how can we ensure that our marriages will not be barren? I tell you – the source of the matrimonial connection should be love and mutual esteem. A union based on these precepts will seldom fail to prove fruitful. However, it is wise to remember that a sickly offspring is far worse than no offspring at all. It will render the parents miserable and weaken the bonds. And Gentlemen, know that barrenness is almost always the fault of the female. When seeking a wife, you must fix on an object that is healthful, well educated, and virtuous, these things being far more important than beauty, family and riches, for such women who have indulged in luxury are more likely to have a bad constitution. Marry a delicate woman at your peril and avoid those who have been debilitated by drinking strong, poisonous, foreign tea and coffee, spending their lives in close rooms, full of animal substances and feathers. Though such women may conceive, they are unlikely to bring forth a child at the full time, and it will be a puny, puling creature which will not deserve the name of Man.

But Ladies – do not despair if you are delicate and weak. You have seen the bright, rosy complexion of my Hebe Vestina, have you not? Come, Vestina – show yourself. (And at this, Emilia emerges from the shadows, leaves me alone whilst she enters the Temple and poses, once again, for the crowd.) You have seen the strength of her limbs, heard the power of her voice? And

111

you cannot have failed to notice her exquisite beauty. Ladies – my Angel was once mortal. When she came to me, she had a sickly, pale complexion, she was subject to fainting fits, her skeleton was weak and her voice a mere whisper. Now, with my remedies, you see her transformed. I call her my Goddess, for this Virgin Child is indeed Celestial. See her golden hair (she turns and runs her fingers through the lustrous strands, then raises her chin so her face can be admired). See her lips, fresh as rosebuds, and her eyes, clearer than a summer sky! See her pale skin, Ladies, and the fullness of her breasts. It is this perfection which you must aspire to. If, with my help, you can attain a mere ounce of her loveliness, you will be blessed indeed. Your husbands will come to you with fresh gusto, and you will conceive such children as you have never dreamed of.

2. *Advice to Young Men, Regarding Virility*

Gentlemen, do not think that it is women alone who must bear the burden of improving the species. You, also, have a responsibility, namely, to be Virile. And I tell you, I have spoken recently to a Bishop's lady, and even she has told me that she liked to have a GOOD THING in the house, or in the bed by her, whether she made use of it or not.

You should avoid early and frequent debauchery. For the discharge of seminal fluid dissipates strength, and if you indulge in secret, selfish practices, or spend your time with whores and trulls, you will surely lose your manly vigour. Not only this, but frequent venery (for a man of any age) occasions diseases which can injure the parts of generation in both sexes, and you will find that your member will shrink, shrivel, freeze and contract. Even in the natural connection between the sexes, with the loveliest of the sex, you risk disease if you emit too frequently. Yet the risk is worse in those horrid, solitary, joyless, early practices, the very ideas of which my soul has been reprobating and vomiting out! You may suffer infecundity, epilepsy, loss of memory, sight and hearing, distortions of the eyes, mouth and face, a tottering of the limbs. But if you are unlucky it will be worse – Idiotism, Horrors, Innumerable Complaints, Extreme Wretchedness or even Death. Thrice Happy are those who live to the age of twenty without ever having a seminal emission (whether awake or asleep, voluntary or involuntary). If a man can marry, in this state, then he is a hero indeed! – a Hercules! – an Angel! – a God! He will be the saviour of our Race.

3. On Fertility

In the Temple of Health, I have many treatments for improving fertility. But know, above all, it is your own behaviour which will affect your ability to conceive children. And there are two rules, which, if you follow them, will increase your fertility a hundred-fold.

The first, which I shall return to, is Cleanliness. You should ensure that you are clean at all times and under every circumstance.

The second is that man and wife should avoid the perils of sleeping in the same bed. To sleep, to snore, to steam together, to soak together three hundred and sixty-five times each year is no less, Gentlemen, than matrimonial whoredom. You cannot expect to conceive if you are too frequently drained of your precious fluids. Have two beds in the same room, if you must, but better still, have your beds in adjoining rooms. Your offspring, I assure you, will be the stronger for it.

And now, to the importance of Cleanliness. I cannot stress enough what effect this will have on your fertility. Not only should you frequently drink pure, soft water or rich, balmy milk, breathe day and night the cool air out of doors, and abstain from animal food (these steps being essential to maintaining cleanliness within) – but you should also bathe night and morning, if not your whole body, then at least your genitalia and fundament with cold water. I tell you – the Genitals are the true pulse and infallible barometer of the health and vigour of your body and mind.

But what if a person is lazy or timorous? Rather than not wash at all, I say let them wash and bathe in warm water; and if clean water cannot be procured, let them wash with the dirtiest ditch or kennel water that tumbles down Edinburgh streets, or that stagnates before a Dutchman's door. Anything, I assure you, is an improvement on our current habits of stewing within our own garments. And if you wish to avoid venereal infection then you would do well, after each amorous embrace, to spring up and wash, lave, and immerse the whole male apparatus and the female apartment of pleasure in very cold water. A couple who does this will remain favourites with one another, for if one of them were to stray to another bed, he would be abhorred by the lack of cleanliness there and would spring back to his partner. A man who washes daily in icy-cold water would be able to renew the tender combat two or three times, with less expense of strength and ten times more intense pleasure.

Remember this, Gentlemen. The male organs of generation are the rich pearl of Venus and the manly standard of love. As such, they should be treated with respect, and you will find, if you bathe immediately after the sweet, amorous engagement, that your member will be rallied, cooled, replenished and braced – crimped, and cabbaged up afresh! But think now of the man who does not obey this mandate. Think of him as an idiot who goes to drain off water, wine or liquor from a barrel. When he has done so, he leaves the cock half turned and the liquor continues running off and dribbling. Now, think – the male semen also dribbles and drains off for minutes and sometimes for hours after the voluptuous emission. But the instant application of the icy-cold vivifying water, or sparkling wine – effectively *locks the cock, and secures all for the next rencontre!*

How much better then, for you ladies, if the semen is not wasted. How much more likely that you will receive it and your embryos will be vivified. And if you, also, are clean, healthy and free of disease, then your offspring will certainly be strong and deserving of the name of Man.

More lives, it seems, are lost these days from the ravages of Venereal Disease than are lost in war. Yet does this excuse, I ask myself, that dreadful habit that many of our doctors have acquired, of prescribing mercury, which is itself a ferocious poison that can lead a man to an early grave?

I myself have often removed venereal maladies, even when complicated with rheumatism or gout. In addition, the most troublesome, painful and dangerous affectations of the urethra, prostate glands and neck of the bladder, which in general do prove so very obstinate – I can cure without the least pain or danger whatever. Perhaps, Gentlemen, you do not know the symptoms of this disease? Let me tell you some of them, for it will act as warning against excess. Think of inflammatory rawness and soreness and paralytic spasms and weakness of the neck and sphincter muscle of the bladder; scirrhous hardness and fullness, as well as ulceration and weakness of the prostate glands. Think of strictures of the urethra, occasioning a small, frequent, painful, interrupted and feeble expulsion of the urine, accompanied by shooting pains and spasms of the perineum and anus. And violent straining when you wish to void a stone. How easy it is for a doctor to look upon these symptoms and to offer mercury.

Indeed, I have heard of a new method, said to be recommended by some worthy and learned gentleman – of rubbing mercury on the inside of the lips, cheeks, and consequently on the tongue, teeth and palate. I know not what to say of this, yet think it is an idea spread by unprincipled and unemployed dentists and mouth menders, who have set this horrible practice afoot, in order that their healing dentifrices might sell, and the artificial teeth trade flourish.

But let me tell you now that my own cures are simple. I recommend drinking daily largely of pure gum arabic dissolved in chicken water or vegetable balsamics. To this I would add diuretics and strengtheners such as sarsaparilla, liquorice, marshmallow or parsley roots, linseed and elder flowers. This would be simply the beginning of my curative regime. For to this I would add those measures I have explained to you, namely bathing in ice-cold water, avoiding animal foods, sleeping with open windows (on a hair mattress if at all possible), and daily electrical treatments upon the Celestial Throne. In addition to this, I recommend my Electrical Aether, Nervous Aetherial Balsam and Imperial Pills.

Ladies, follow the example of my Hebe Vestina. She daily takes the cold air and bathes in ice water. She abstains from all polluting substances, and takes frequent doses of Aetherial Balsam. She will always be pure and disease cannot touch her. And a man who is lucky enough to possess a woman who has a tenth of her charms will never stray into the arms of another. Such a couple, who follow my regime, will be blessed indeed. They will never be fouled by the ravages of this unspeakable plague.

5. How to Heighten and Prolong the Joys of Venus

Enough, then, of the follies connected with the venereal act, for I wish to speak now of my greatest invention, my greatest stroke of genius.

I was, Gentlemen, some time in Philadelphia, where I studied electricity for two years, and became acquainted with the ideas of the great Benjamin Franklin. Indeed, I was five years in that boundless land, which then overflowed with abundance! – which glowed with liberality! and whose rising sun announced the great day of UNIVERSAL FREEDOM! and shone with intellectual light!

Whilst residing in that wise and all-tolerating city, I was, one day, suddenly struck with a thought: that the pleasure of the venereal act might be exalted or rendered more intense if performed under the glowing, accelerating and most genial influences of that heaven-born, all-animating element or principle of electrical fire! Indeed, so taken was I with this idea that I immediately set to work. I obtained a bed and insulated it, then filled it with copious streams of electrical fire, conveyed by metal rods in closed glass tubes. This was, I admit, a very primitive apparatus, yet I was convinced of the importance of my creation.

Eager that my bed should not be used for immoral purposes, I asked a venerable friend of mine if he and his wife would test the bed. This he did, and, Gentlemen, the next morning, I swear I saw a change in them. His wife, a young woman, but usually plain and rather jaded, appeared changed. Her pale complexion had acquired the full blooming sweetness and the freshness of the rose! the deliciousness of the nectarine! – and the blooming plumpness – the rich juiciness and the fine, glowing, juvenile down of the PEACH of beauty! – of the peach finely rounded by Venus's hand! But more than this – when I spoke to my friend, he revealed the effect the electrical bed had had upon them. He talked, not, as other men might have done, of the critical moment – no! – he talked comparatively, of the critical HOUR!!!

Yet I tell you now – this exaltation and prolongation of pleasure was, in a sense, the least important effect of the bed. For my next experiment had results that were even more astonishing. There was a Dutch woman who lived in Lancaster, a place fifty miles from Philadelphia. She had a paralytic complaint, she was barren, she had no speech, had lost the use of one side of her body and had a menstrual obstruction. The doctors she had frequented told her that her condition was incurable, and, having heard that my remedies were often gentler and more effective than those she had experienced so far, and that I often succeeded where more conventional doctors failed, she decided to ask my advice. First I inquired about her diet, and when she told me of it, I was horrified to hear that she drank strong coffee every morning, and that her usual evening supper consisted of old tea leaves dressed up by way of salad, with salt and vinegar. Immediately I set to work, prescribing a new diet and cold baths, but also, that she should sleep, every other night, alone or otherwise, in what I now named my Celestial Bed. I filled her room with aromatic green herbs, flowers and fruit. And I ground together, into a smooth paste, mint, sage, rosemary, lavender and juniper berries, and directed that this be rubbed into her skin by her husband after each bath.

The result, simply, was astounding. The lady from Lancaster was completely cured. After a short term following my remedies, she regained her speech and movement, her menses began to flow, and, soon afterwards, she became pregnant. Indeed, I am still in communication with this lady and she now has a large family consisting of six strong, healthy sons and two blooming daughters.

Encouraged then by this success, I shortly afterwards returned to England where I designed the new and wholly magnificent Celestial Bed, which you shall shortly see. And if any married couples amongst you wish to use the bed (which will cost you no more than fifty pounds per night), I guarantee a night of such pleasure and such exquisite sweetness that your whole body will seem, in the morning, renewed afresh. The joys of Venus will not only be prolonged and more intensely satisfying, but more fruitful also, for she who sleeps upon the Bed will be instantly cured of barrenness. My turtle-doves will coo and you will hear sweet music and smell odoriferous balsams, which will make the critical HOUR that I have promised you an hour of such furious delight that neither man nor woman will desire another so long as they both shall live.

17

EMILIA

I FIND IT difficult, this evening, to take up my pen, for a thing
has occurred which makes me feel yet weaker than before. I
know that death is near. I knew, from the moment that I first
began this work, that it might not be completed. Yet now it is
not the thought of death that drains my strength. No, it is a far
subtler enemy than that.

Helena warned me that this might happen; she told me that if
I allowed myself to delve again into the past, I would become a
slave, once more, to Vermilion.

'You have freed yourself from him,' she said, a few days ago.
'You think you are unravelling your story, but to do so is
impossible. You are simply binding yourself back to him.'

And to think that I upbraided her, when she said this, for
talking nonsense!

When the package arrived this morning, I knew the writing to
be his. If I had not begun these scribblings, if I had not recently
been thinking of that first night, at the Doctor's lecture, I would
not have opened it. I swear I would have sent it back to him.
Before I began writing this record of my life, I had more resolve.
I had no tenderness left for him. Indeed, I had thought that by
the very act of writing, my heart would have hardened still
further. When I began my tale, I had forgotten, almost, that once
I loved him. And love has a stronger power than ever we
imagine. Love can nestle under rocks, unseen, but it cannot ever
be fully dissolved. Love is the heart of the volcano, the fiery,
boiling liquid – invisible, but always ready to burst through the
rock. What is hidden is the strongest force. And so with my hard
heart. Against my will, my love for Vermilion resurfaced.

Yet still I continue, though for what he has done this evening I can never forgive him. I wish I could say that it has killed the love – perhaps it has. Perhaps love inevitably tends towards its own destruction. I would not call this hatred that I feel. I am simply vacant. When I am dead, let the doctors dissect me. They will find I have no heart remaining.

And so I will tell my story though I will not tell you yet of the gift sent by Vermilion. I fear it would shock you. You would be so full of loathing for him that you could not attend to my words of love. Though I have no feeling left, this does not signify that I have lost my memory. I remember Love. How can one ever forget?

Let us return, then, to the Temple. I have told you of the Doctor's words. Of their impression on me. All that he spoke seemed to me most noble and commendable. Even when, again, I was forced to come out of the shadows, to be turned and twirled by him. My lips like rosebuds – my eyes, clearer than a summer sky! I was no more than his marionette. But how proud I was! Celestial Virgin, pure as rainwater. Yet I was too coy, before, to tell you the truth of what happened next. So much easier to record the Doctor's words. With my love re-emerging, I did not feel able to write of Vermilion's actions without slandering him. But now what do I care if I spoil his name? When I am dead, he will spoil mine often enough.

We were in shadow then, and I felt Vermilion's hand press harder against my own. Next, I felt a movement against my neck, his hair, brushing against me, as he leaned down to kiss me there, at the nape. His lips, so light upon my flesh, they merely touched and hovered, yet still that flesh did seem to melt beneath the influence. I did not stir. I looked around me, afraid lest someone might be spying upon us, yet we were completely obscured here. The light did not touch us.

'. . . the discharge of seminal fluid dissipates strength, and if you indulge in secret, selfish practices, or spend your time with whores and trulls, you will surely lose your manly vigour.'

The Doctor's words seemed far away. Perhaps if I had heard them earlier, under different circumstances, I might have been shocked at his candour. But now, they were so distant. Slowly (it seemed like an age when his lips were no more than a presence) I felt something new. A moist flicker. His tongue. Could it be, I thought, that this was what the Doctor warned against? I considered it as I felt his teeth join in this delicate dance upon my skin. He pulled the flesh and bit upon it, sucked upon it. No, I thought. This could not be venery. The soft strains of the Doctor's small orchestra floated up to me. Before me, the Great Apollo Chamber glowed with the light of a thousand candles. Nymphs languished with Gods above my head. And at my side, this man that I barely knew was caressing my flesh. But I knew these were not mere mortal kisses. These sensations were quite different. They were Celestial. Elysian. I barely heard the Doctor's words any longer. For this Vermilion's fingers were tracing a line down my back. It was the reverence, I thought, that was due to a Goddess.

Even as I thought this, I believe I was shamed. Somewhere, deep inside me, I knew my thoughts were sinful. I was basking in a little paradise, and I could not sacrifice the sensation. No, not even when I felt him bend down and sit by my feet, his lips caressing my ankles, his hands stroking my calves – I could not stop him. It was too much pleasure. And the knowledge that the mortals below, with their painted faces, their fans, their eye-glasses and their walking-sticks, might turn at any moment and peer into the darkness, somehow served to increase the thrill I felt. I might have suffered anything, I thought, rather than lose this moment. For Vemilion now had buried his head beneath my shift and I felt his ruby coat against my skin, his dark tresses brushing against me, and his mouth upon my thighs. I should tell him to stop! For soon that tongue, that hot, sweet, wet tongue would be upon me, upon my delicate and private parts, where no man but a husband should roam. Stop! But my words were no more than a whisper. It was all that I could manage, for a fire was burning now inside me. I remembered my sensations when first I sat upon the Celestial Throne. Yes, my feelings now, though more intense, were made of the same stuff. And then it happened. I could not have believed it possible. With a single dart of the tongue, like the sting of a snake, he touched me in that vital place, that small, throbbing button of flesh between my legs, and I swear I would have shouted out, so intense was the pleasure, so mingled with pain. But I was stopped, right there, all of a sudden, as I felt a hand across my mouth and Vermilion emerged from beneath my skirts, looked up at my face, then, satisfied, smiled, turned and walked away.

I felt my legs tremble and give way, but the very hand that had stopped my mouth was now around my waist, preventing my fall. I barely knew where I was any longer, and I looked down to the only thing that gave me comfort – the hand which supported me. A woman's hand, adorned with a turquoise ring. My Peacock Lady. Her mouth was at my ear.

'Hold steady, Emilia,' she said. 'Do not let him see you suffer.' And I obeyed her, not knowing what else I could do. As the Doctor continued to speak, she said nothing more to me, but she kept her arm around my middle and the warmth of her presence soothed me. I found myself once again trying to concentrate on the Doctor's words.

'Ladies, follow the example of my Hebe Vestina. She daily takes the cold air and bathes in ice water. She abstains from all polluting substances, and takes frequent doses of Aetherial Balsam. She will always be pure and disease cannot touch her.'

The words were a knife that pierced my core. It was not possible that I could be all that the Doctor wished me to be. Yet I continued listening right until the end. From the shadows I could see the red rogue, across the room from me, seeming to hang on the Doctor's every word. I could not understand it. Could not make sense of it at all. Felt that I had sinned. Yet felt that I had not sinned. Felt that he loved me. And yet did not love me. That he was the sweetest creature that ever God did put upon this earth. And the most churlish villain. And I, myself – I was the chastest angel and the most defiled whore.

The rest of the evening passed as if it were a dream. I remember very little, except that the Peacock Lady was always by my side, smiling at me and encouraging me, yet I was constantly looking towards Vermilion, trying to catch his eye. He did not look at me. Even when, later, I was standing before the Celestial Bed, singing once again the Ode to Electricity, when the eyes of the two hundred guests were upon me, I glanced at him and saw that his eyes were fixed firmly on the Doctor. He had a defiant look, an uninterested air, and I felt my heart should break, for what had I done to deserve this treatment?

Even now I do not know how I continued to sing that evening. I do not know how I prevented my voice from trembling. Perhaps it was the thought of Smellie that did it, knowing that if I failed the Doctor, Smellie would be my prize. Or else my song was my only remaining purity, which I clung to, stubbornly. I wanted to melt Vermilion's hardness and this might be the only method I could use.

'*Haaaaaaaaaaaaaaaaaaaaaaaaaaaaaaaaail!*'

Afterwards I wept. The Peacock Lady accompanied me to my room. She was by my side as the tears flowed. Strange, to have so beautiful a creation so close to me. Like Vermilion, she was a stranger, and I did not learn much of her that evening. She was no more than a shimmering presence that seemed to offer comfort, yet in truth I did not know how much trust I could put in her. For her arrival by my side at the crucial moment, at the very moment that he shot out his poisonous tongue, delivering his venomous ardour into my body, seemed too great a coincidence. Did they intend, together, to bring about my downfall?

Eventually my sobs subsided, and I lay upon my bed, barely able to breathe. So tired, in fact, was I, that I do not know whether what happened next was real, or if I dreamed it. I remember her coming to my side. She seemed to float rather than walk. She whispered in my ear again.

'The Doctor has told me, Emilia, that he was pleased with your performance this evening. And Vermilion has told me that he loves you.'

Love! The word should have awakened a storm within me. He had no right to use such expressions! His actions had signalled not love but spite. Yet perhaps because I was tired, perhaps because I slept, I was lulled by the words. I hugged them close to me, and though my window was open and the chill January air blew into the room, I felt their warmth caressing me. If this was a dream, it was the dream I desired. This lie, I thought, would tide me over until morning.

And yet it did not. For though I know what followed was most certainly a reverie, I did not spend a calm night.

I was back in my father's house, my old bedroom, standing before a portrait of my mother. She was wearing her lemon-coloured dress and smiling down at me. For many years I had scarcely been able to bring myself to look at the portrait, but now I did look. And I saw a thing most disturbing, my mother in my own image. It was true her hair was curled and powdered, but the face was my own.

Never, not even then, at the height of my vanity, had I looked so closely at my own image. Never had I examined the features in this way. I saw that my beauty was different to that of other women. There was none of the pertness in my face that is seen in so many portraits. My face was not so simple as the Doctor made it out to be. For him, a Hebe Vestina was no more than a recipe – two blue eyes, clearer than a summer sky; two lips – rosebuds; two breasts, full and round. Yet here, in the portrait, there was so much more. A face of infinite complexity. A face that merited many hours of observation. And in the dream it seemed that I stood still, perhaps for a whole day, simply looking. I saw that the eyes were not large and long-lashed as one would imagine the eyes of a beauty must be. No, they were pale and a little deep-set and the lids were barely visible. The hair of my lashes and my brows was fair, so that the beauty came not from the strength of the eyes, but from their weakness. They were, I discovered, a picture of innocence. I was uneasy at the thought. For I was no longer certain of my purity.

I soon realized, in fact, that there was nothing in the face that I recognized as my own. It was mine, yet how did this nose, a little too broad and flat to be fashionable, reflect what I felt inside? And the lips. Rosebuds indeed! Nothing could be further from the truth. These lips were no buds, but full-blown, blooming roses! They were large lips, delicate and soft, swelling a little. No – I did not fit the picture the Doctor had made of me. If I was a beauty, it was not because I had the 'fine features' that he attributed to me. My face was not fine at all. It was a singular face. And it expressed nothing that I recognized to be me.

Suddenly I was awakened from this trance. Something had happened. The face of the girl had changed, become older. Now it was truly the face of my mother that I saw, not my own. Yet what frightened me was this – I was gazing *down* at her. She was standing, in my bedroom, staring up at me. And I was there, on the wall, trapped within the oils, contained within the picture-frame. I was not looking at the portrait any longer. I was looking from it and knew it was my fate to remain there. I could not move my hands to protest, for they were resting in my lap and though I longed to push against the canvas, I could not. I was inanimate. This was the price that I must pay for killing her. She was to live my life, instead of me, and as if to emphasize the point, the door of my room opened and a man entered. It was Vermilion, who, strangely, had a sword by his side. When he saw my mother, his face lit up, he wrapped his arms around her and kissed her with great passion. It is not me! I wanted to scream it, loud, but I had no voice. It is not me!

But I should have known that these words, even if they had reached his ears, would not affect him.

'Isabella!' he said. 'Isabella, how you fill my soul with joy!' He was in love with my mother and I was forced to watch as she, wearing her dress of yellow roses, plumped down upon the bed, with Vermilion clambering on behind to unbutton her. He kissed her neck, then seemed to tear the dress from her shoulders and pushed her backwards. Then he buried his head in her breasts, which were bursting out above her stays. She was laughing, heartily, at this, when he turned her over on to her stomach so that her hoop gaped in front of me, and he slapped her on the behind.

Her laughter haunts me still. And the rich voice she spoke with, so unlike my own.

'Oh Vermilion! Vermilion! Do not tease me so!'

And at this he helped her up and pulled the dress and petticoats over her head, so that she stood, quite indecent, in stays and skeleton skirt. But even this was not for long. This man was an expert in ladies' undergarments, and soon her hoop was discarded in a corner of the room.

Had my eyes been flesh, I would have closed them, but they were no more than tincture. I was oil and pigment and canvas. They could not see that I had a soul, also. How could they be expected to know? Behind those eyes that looked upon them was a depth of agony they could not imagine. No – the portrait made a simple statement. I smiled. I was surrounded by beautiful things. My needlework was upon my lap. All was serene and conveyed nothing but the deepest contentment. But there was so much more than this. I imagined the paints beginning to blur as I struggled to move within the frame. I was screaming, banging my arms against the canvas, spoiling the grace of the composition. Yet they did not see it. If they had looked, they would have seen only harmony and excellent proportion.

Vermilion, now, was unlacing my mother's stays, and her breasts were on the point of spilling out. Yet suddenly he stopped.

'I feel uneasy,' he said. 'As if someone is watching me.'

'Nonsense, my love,' replied my mother. 'We are all alone.'

'Perhaps. But still, I . . .'

He turned and looked right up at me.

'It is that portrait. Yes. It troubles me.'

'I cannot see how. That is a portrait of my daughter.'

'You have a daughter?'

'I had a daughter. She died.'

'My love. You never told me of this.'

'I did not wish to speak of grief at a time when I am so happy.'

'She has an enchanting face. So like your own.'

'They say there was a strong resemblance.'

'Indeed.'

'And now to bed.'

Again he turned to her. No! I longed to cry out. I am not dead! I am buried alive here! Please. You must liberate me.

He pulled her towards him, but I was relieved to see that his passion had somewhat abated. He made an effort to appear inflamed, but she sensed his loss of appetite.

'What is it, love? Have you fallen in love with the portrait?'

'No. Quite the contrary. I do not know why, but I cannot love you whilst your daughter is looking upon us.'

'Then we shall turn her to the wall.'

'No!'

He turned and paced the room. I saw his exasperation turn to anger.

'No! We must do more. I cannot have it in the room!'

And he launched towards me, drawing his sword, slashing and tearing my face, tearing my dress and my arms to ribbons.

'Stop!' my mother cried. 'Have pity, Vermilion.'

At these words, Vermilion vanished. His actions had liberated me from the canvas, but my body, my entire body, and my face were covered in deep scratches, and I was bleeding in my mother's arms, my bloody face resting on her naked breast.

'I am torn to pieces, mother,' I cried. 'There is nothing left of me.'

'Rest, Emilia,' she told me. 'Rest.'

'But mother – he has taken my beauty.'

'He has taken nothing of worth, Emilia. Nothing of worth.'

How I shudder to think upon this dream. I remember waking, crying, and seeing the Peacock Lady, still fully dressed, watching me from a chair at the other end of the room. I longed for her to be by my side, like my mother was in the dream, but she was detached. She merely watched over me, as I slowly took in this, my new room, her presence, the closed window and the thick air between us. A dream. Yes, only a dream.

Now, Vermilion's present lies before me, face to the ground. How cruel a gesture to send such a thing. No other gift could have wounded me so. Indeed, I dare not lift it again, for the gift that was delivered this morning was a mirror. A large and beautiful glass. A remnant from the Adelphi Temple. Gilded, elaborate – a most exquisite piece of work. A love gift, perhaps? A token of his affection? I remember this mirror – it hung above the fireplace near to the Celestial Bed. I have seen myself reflected in it many times. I have admired myself in it, turned and twirled before it. But this morning, when it was delivered to my room, when I opened it, believing it to be a portrait or a landscape, what I saw was very different. I tore the paper from the package, and stared in horror at the image before me. For a mirror is only as charming as that which is reflected within it. And I, Emilia, have changed. What I saw in that looking-glass was a sight that was most abhorrent to me.

18

VERMILION

THE BUSINESS OF the mirror was indeed unfortunate, but, I assure you, it is not what it seems. If Emilia had revealed the nature of the change in herself, then you would understand what a cruel gesture this must have seemed to her. Yet there was more to it than this. She does not tell you all. Indeed, she tells you very little, and though I, myself, might feel inclined to let the cat out of the bag, I shall respect her enough to let her tell her own tale. If you will be patient, all will be revealed in good time.

In the meantime, Gentlemen, I have a simple request. You have travelled thus far with me. You have placed your trust in my judgement. Do not then abandon me now. Not this evening, of all evenings, when I have suffered, more than you can imagine. Do not make judgements now, before you know the facts. Wait a while. All will come clear.

But enough of this. Whilst you have been luxuriating in my gentle seduction of Emilia, I, Vermilion, have experienced a thing which has left me weak and most distraught. You are aware, of course, that I have been entertaining a guest this evening. I had, at first, been inclined to extend a warm welcome to Lady Quinton. However, she has forced me, tonight, into an action which I never dreamed possible. She has made me confront a loss which I would rather have erased from my memory. Even now, I cannot stop my limbs from trembling. The image of what I have seen is etched in my mind.

Yet even if I were not so disturbed, I believe I would find it difficult, at this moment, to write of the Temple. For much to my irritation, the haughty Lady Quinton is sleeping in the adjacent bedchamber. I regret that I was so indulgent, after what she has done, as to allow her this liberty. Despite my earlier desire for company, I find I cannot think clearly whilst I sense the presence of another human creature. I am not accustomed to it. There is so much, I realize, about this woman that is abhorrent to me. For though, it is true, it was she who first led me to the discovery of Emilia's diaries, still there is one act for which I cannot forgive her. When Emilia died, she did not tell me of it instantly. She waited until the funeral was over and only then did she speak to me of my love's death. She made certain I was not present as they lowered my Emilia into the earth.

But now, whilst I am able, I must tell you, from the beginning, this evening's events, for I will get no sleep tonight.

I have said already that I am not superstitious. None the less, I did consider it strange when, an hour or two before her expected arrival, this rain, which has been most persistent for several days now, began to abate. I saw, for the first time in recent weeks, a break in the clouds; a small blue chink in their muffling thickness, so that the sun, though it was low in the sky, illumined the grounds with the deep yellow light of a summer evening. The trees threw out long shadows across the lawns, and even the folly, the tall white tower which has seemed so forbidding of late, seemed suddenly inviting.

It was preposterous. That she should receive such a welcome! When I myself had been forced indoors for so many days, that she should bring light and warmth.

Seven-thirty came, the appointed hour of her arrival, and soon afterwards I heard the sound of a carriage approaching. I had left the gates open, and watched as her driver, dressed in white and gold livery, drove his dappled mares towards the portal. She did not see me, I hoped, as I sat at the window (still streaked with rainwater), observing her as she was helped from the carriage. She was surely not so poverty-stricken as her letter had led me to believe, I thought, for she rode in style, and the dress she wore was as spectacular as any I had seen her wear at the Temple. It was of an emerald green colour with a bodice of an intense dark blue, so that she did indeed resemble that species of bird whose name Emilia gave her. And I saw, as she emerged, that her manner had not changed. She walked as if she were taking part in some elaborate dance.

I had ordered a servant to usher Lady Quinton into the house and ask her to wait in the library. However, once she was inside, I was surprised to see that the coachman did not immediately drive away. He began unloading luggage from the carriage – trunks, hat-boxes and the like, which he piled before the portal. I watched, astounded, whilst he chattered to John, who, I was glad to see, was arguing against these goods being brought into the house. It would have been amusing had I not been so angry, myself, at the implications of her arriving with all her chattels. Her letter had made no mention of a stay here. It was quite impossible. For the moment, however, it seemed we had no choice. My man was destined to lose this argument, for who, in his right mind, could send a lady's goods away, when that lady was already in the house and out of his sight?

When I entered the library, I was already on my guard. I was in a strange state of trepidation, desirous to see her, yet furious that she should impose upon me in this manner. The fury, I think, was uppermost, yet when I entered the room, throwing open the door, I was staggered by the sight that greeted me. I had forgotten that the library, like every other room, was hidden beneath sheets. I had deceived myself into thinking that it would be as it always was, when my parents were alive. The shelves would be redolent of polish, the deep leather chairs would beckon one to sit. I had imagined that the Lady Quinton would be waiting, like those guests my parents had when I was a child.

But when I saw her, earlier this evening, more fragile than I remember her, her dress a burst of colour against the white-sheeted chairs, I thought of the French Queen, the ill-starred Marie Antoinette. That poor lady, who languishes even now, imprisoned in the Conciergerie. I remembered the night that I saw her at the Opéra, only a year ago, at the Comédie Italienne, the last time that she appeared in public. She was in tears throughout the night and I could not bring myself to watch the stage, for the sight of the Queen was so much more moving, and my eyes, though they had no right to be, were wet as hers. Once she would have been in her element here, but now she seemed almost ghost-like.

All this flashed through my mind the moment I opened the door to the library. On seeing this lady, I felt as if I were seeing a phantom.

Such strange tricks the memory plays. For Helena had never been to Carmine Hall before, so how could she seem a ghost that lingered here? She seemed so isolated, alone, forlorn. Somewhat aged, yet still a remarkable beauty. She was staring at me as if issuing a challenge, yet all the same, I saw she suffered. She did not speak.

'I am sorry, Lady Quinton,' I said, 'for the poor reception that you have met. You will see that things have changed here since the death of my parents.'

'Indeed,' she replied, 'death disturbs us all.'

'Come,' I said, 'you must join me in my study. It is the only room, I am afraid, which is fit to receive guests in.'

'Very well. Though I admit, Vermilion, I had expected a better welcome than this.'

Her tone was not playful, but I returned her retort with a jest.

'What do you wish for?' I asked. 'A kiss?'

And I puckered up, as if to place one upon her cheek.

'I would wish, rather, for a comfortable place to sit, and perhaps a pot of tea.'

In my study she received what she had desired, but I felt that I should confront her about her luggage.

'I see that you are *en route* to a place of lodging, Helena,' I said. 'Are you moving away from London?'

At this she darted me a glance which disarmed me. It was a look I had seen so many times before, in so many different circumstances – I could barely believe that we were here together in my study; that we were talking such nonsense.

'To be frank with you, Vermilion, I have no place to go. Though I would wish for another solution to my current problems, I was hoping that I might stay here – only for a short while, you understand. Until I can find a position for myself.'

'A position?'

'Yes. I explained in my letter that my fortune has gone. Lord Quinton left Marcus's fortune in trust, not to me, but to his sister. I must make a living in any way I can.'

'Helena. A lady of your standing, and your age, should not be expected to work.'

'At thirty-nine years of age, I do not consider myself to be old, Vermilion. And my standing is of little importance now.'

'Some other way must be found,' I said. 'Have you not *friends* with whom you could reside? Must you throw yourself upon your old enemy like this?'

And again – that same look in her almond eyes. A proud look which yet somehow contained a plea. A look which shamed me.

'At times such as this,' she said, 'one becomes aware that an old foe has fewer faults than one imagined. An old foe is at least familiar.'

'So you have forgiven me my faults?'

'Your faults will haunt you, Vermilion, unto the grave.'

To this I had no answer.

She had changed. That much I realized immediately. For where once I had seen nothing but frivolity, I now saw a hint of pain, akin to my own. The woman before me, though she was physically the same (with the addition of a few lines on her face, some strands of grey in her hair), seemed to have a profundity that was not there before. Emilia and I would argue long on the subject of the lady's merit; while I would argue that the mysterious quality of her appearance was nothing but a sham, Emilia insisted that the Bird had suffered.

This evening I understood at once that Helena did not forgive me for all that had passed. And yet she was here. Her situation must indeed be desperate, I thought, and, wishing to know more, I asked about the circumstances of Lord Quinton's death, of his will, of the whereabouts of her bastard son.

'My bastard son, as you call him, is residing with his aunt – Lord Quinton's sister.'

'But no true aunt of his.'

'No indeed, sir, but I would hope that you are not so malevolent as to speak of this fact abroad.'

'Your secret is safe with Vermilion. But does the boy not miss his mother?'

'It appears that nature has played no part in the forming of my child's heart. He loved his unnatural parent more than he loves me. Though he is not a Quinton, he has grown like one. I see nothing of his true father in him.'

'Nothing at all?' I asked. 'Not even a glimmer?'

'Not a glimmer, Vermilion. Not a hint.'

'And has your experience of motherhood been all that you hoped for?'

'No, Vermilion. But let us speak no more of this. I wish to hear of France. Were you there, when his head rolled?'

I recognized her tactics, but I had no more desire to speak of the Revolution than she had to speak of her son.

'No, madam, I was not there,' I lied.

'But how could you miss such an event?'

'I loved the King too much to desire to watch his humiliation.'

'I see I cannot draw you on the subject.'

'Not this evening, Helena.'

I softened, for she smiled at me. Yet I did not know how I might continue the conversation. Was there no ground on which we could tread which would not be painful to one of us? Surely it was too soon to talk of the Temple, or of Emilia, so I could not yet tell her of my project. Perhaps I will not tell her at all. The silence divided us. It was too late to remedy things now.

'I was sorry to hear of the death of your parents,' she said suddenly. 'If I did not appear so earlier, I apologize. I am quite fatigued.'

'I thank you. It was indeed a grievous loss.'

'It does not seem as if we are favoured by the Gods, Vermilion.'

'I do not believe in fate, Helena. And you should not presume to know more about me than you do. I am happy.'

'Happy?' she said, mocking me. 'Loitering here on your own? No longer handsome? No wenches to play with. No Emilia to taunt. No coffee-house chatter to exercise your wit. No inns to get drunk in . . .'

I held up my right hand and could not help but notice the scars across the fingers.

'Enough. I am ugly, you say?'

'You cannot have failed to notice it. And ill, also, I hazard, though I would not wish to make your gout a laughing matter.'

'Tell me,' I said, not knowing why I was allowing myself to be drawn into this. 'Is there anything of the old Vermilion remaining?'

'Of his heart, I cannot say. But in person you are indeed much changed. I was quite shocked when first I saw you.'

'And yet you did not register that shock upon your face when I entered the library.'

'I saw a ghost at the window, Vermilion, when I arrived. A grisly, morose old man, bewigged and powdered, staring at me from the gloom, behind the glass.'

I was, you will understand, most dismayed at this, yet I continued.

'Surely you could not see me so well from there?'

'I saw enough to make my blood turn cold. My imagination filled in the rest. You have paid dearly for your years of indulgence it seems.'

'I ask you again, Helena – is there anything of the old Vermilion remaining?'

I was unable to hide my anxiety and the urgency of this question. She peered towards me, narrowing her eyes.

'I see traces – here and there. The structure of your face is ruined with the fat. Your eyes have grown bloodshot, Vermilion, and their colour has faded. Your lips are pale now, and your cheeks have grown bulbous. I would not like to guess what has happened to your hair which you have seen fit to hide beneath a wig. Is it your custom to wear it?'

'No. Not my custom.'

'So you are losing your hair. You have become portly. Indeed, you are losing all that made Vermilion, Vermilion.'

I had wished to avoid painful subjects, yet there could be, I realized, almost no subject more hurtful to me than this. I wished her gone. But I would not let her see that I was bitten.

'Surely,' I said, 'when we look into a person's eyes, it does not matter if those eyes have changed. We see beyond that. We see the soul.'

At this, she nodded and smiled in recognition of the truth.

'Would you could have said as much to Emilia, Vermilion,' she said.

Emilia. Vermilion. I had not thought, before, how the words echoed one another. This was not, of course, what Helena had desired me to think. Yet I would not give her the satisfaction of knowing the shame I felt. That is a private thing and I do not need her words to remind me.

I saw Helena watching me as she spoke. Her face glowed, golden, for the sun was setting. And I saw that she, too, was haunted. What matter – her son, the change in me, France? All we saw, each of us, was Emilia. Her beauty. The immeasurable loss.

Yet now, in my bedroom, I contemplate a different loss. There is no light left in the sky, no moon on this fateful night, but I write by candle-light and I find that the flicker of the flame and the act of scraping my pen across the page have somewhat lessened my agitation. The quaking has abated somewhat. In the corner of the room, the statute of Emma Lyon stares at me, and I am agitated by its presence. Emma Lyon? You do not recognize her name? Perhaps you will know her by another – Emma Hamilton. The new wife of Sir William Hamilton – a most scandalous match, it must be said. I cannot see her remaining faithful to one so old as he. I knew her when she was a

Goddess of the Doctor's, for she replaced Emilia. But though her beauty is much celebrated, and though she is renowned for her charm, she paled beside the Hebe Vestina that I loved. In truth, I only had this modelled to spite my Emilia.

My Emilia – how fond that sounds. Have I deceived you so much, gentlemen? For when you first joined me on this journey, was it my spite that you were attracted to? My bile? Did you truly think that this would be nothing more than a chronicle of my hatred? If so, I am at fault for misleading you. And you are at fault for being villains. I should have allowed the ladies on this journey. Methinks I would prefer their company at such a time as this.

And yet I have a lady, here with me this evening, and she is nothing but a vixen. I longed for company, yet when she came, I desired none. I wanted nothing more than to sit alone at my dining table, conversing with a roasted pig's head. But no – instead I was forced to sit opposite this Lady Quinton, who would not have such a thing set before her. I had wished to gnaw on the bones of the beast – to suck its trotters. Yet for her it must be all carved up and eaten with knife and fork. We sat opposite one another at one end of the long table in the dining-room. My only comfort was the wine in my glass and the three bottles before me, waiting to be drunk. Since my return I have sat alone here – one seat uncovered, the rest still draped in white. It is a stark room, with walls of white damask, a large, pale, marble fireplace where a fire burned this evening, and is decorated with much gilt – upon the chairs, the mirrors, the candlesticks and the ceiling. My marble busts, which I acquired before my departure to France, surround the room – Aristotle, Cicero, Milton, Shakespeare – but they too are covered. I have seen no reason to reveal them.

Not a word about the Temple was uttered this evening. I saw that Helena thought of nothing else, but she would not speak her thoughts. Instead, she asked again about my parents' death.

'What happened to them, Vermilion? It is a tragedy that they should both die – on the same day I have heard. Was it the smallpox?'

'You surely know, Helena, that my parents' death was no ordinary thing.'

'Yes – I know that the cause of their death was not made public. Why else do you think that I am curious?'

'Do you not think that family secrets should remain that way?'

'I had thought that you might reveal a secret to an old friend.'

'Ah – what a remarkable thing is this. I had thought that only an hour ago you were my foe.'

'Will you tell me, Vermilion, or no?'

'No – I will not.'

'Then I see this is some dark and unutterable thing, that will forever be concealed. A murder, perhaps,' she smiled, teasingly, 'or a love pact.'

'You are not so far from the truth, Helena,' I said, 'for I will tell you this – they did indeed die of love.'

'Oh, wonderful,' (the lady was sarcastic still). 'Did they expire upon a kiss?'

Yet her words, though she did not know it, were daggers. Did she have any idea of the nature of the secret that she wished to uncover?

'No, madam,' I replied, 'they expired upon a dance.'

'Upon a dance? What is the meaning of this?'

I chewed upon a piece of crackling whilst contemplating what my answer should be.

'Come,' I said, eventually. 'I will show you.'

And I stood up, wiping my fingers and mouth upon my napkin, and, not knowing what I was doing, beckoned her to follow me.

As we stood outside the ballroom doors, she appeared anxious. I think she realized then that she had taken her jest too far, for she saw the look upon John's face as he fumbled with the key. And I too, I believe, could not have failed to show my tremendous dread of what lay beyond these doors. I wished to turn back. Could barely believe that I was entering this room upon no more than a whim. To prove a point. To crack her smile. No – it would be too terrible. And yet I could not turn back now. I had no choice but to continue.

'Sir,' John said, when he had turned the key, 'I do not think that I should open this door. It should have been opened long ago, but now, though I know I speak out of place, I would advise you, sir, to let the room lie.'

'You do indeed speak out of place, John,' I said, though I nearly fainted at the thought of seeing this room again. 'I bid you open the door.'

'For the sake of their memory, sir – we should leave it be.'

'We cannot leave it forever,' I said. 'Now is as good a time as any.'

If I could change what has passed, if there were any way of remedying this, I would do so. But it is not possible. On my instructions, John swung the door open, and I saw, before me, a reminder of that tragic night. I forgot Helena and walked, dazed, into the ballroom.

In the dark gold light of dusk this seemed a faery-land in decay. For the gilded room, with marble floor and walls graced with Old Masters, with little chandeliers sparkling and windows draped with thick cream silk, was laced with cobwebs. Thick with dust, they hung like gossamer nets above our heads, illumined by the last rays of the sun. They trembled at our footsteps.

But it was the appearance of the floor that affected me most of all. At our feet were a million shards of glass, little tear-shaped drops which had shattered across the floor. Some were still intact, and these were like gems; diamonds beneath the dust.

Yet it was not these that Helena was drawn to. She was not attracted to the beauty of the scene, but rather to the evidence of the accident. In the centre of the ceiling, a large hole gaped in the plaster. The paint flaked around it, and moss and lichens had begun to grow, so that the faces of the Gods depicted there were mottled; half covered in green. The marble floor directly underneath was scarred and the room was thick with a damp, earthy scent. It spun before me, as I experienced, once again, the slow fall that killed them. The chandelier, too heavy for the ceiling to support, broke away, and its weight was the force that took their lives. They danced alone, on many evenings here, to celebrate their love. As a child, I would watch them, unobserved at the doorway, turning and turning and turning about, spinning a spell that would lead to their destruction. Without music they would dance, for they needed no other stimulus than that of touch. They seemed, in those moments, to exist only for one another. They could have been immortal. You could have starved them, refused them water, and still they would spin. They were nourished by glances, quenched by kisses. They had no need of me.

'Vermilion?'

Helena interrupted my reverie. I turned to her, and saw her brow tense, her face drained of colour.

'Yes.'

'What is the meaning of this?'

'Can you not deduce it?'

'A chandelier has fallen from the ceiling. This room has remained locked since . . .'

'Since their death. Yes.'

'Then they were crushed. You do not mock me.'

'No. Crushed by a chandelier.'

'But . . . how could this have remained private? Surely, if this is true, there must have been many witnesses.'

'They danced alone, Helena.'

And then, I believe, for the first time since her arrival, I truly looked at Helena. Her dark dress stood out against the pallid surroundings. Her thick black hair had more white laced through it than I had at first realized, and her large, slanting eyes had grown more heavy. The brightness of her skin, even, seemed to have faded.

She held herself with dignity, yet I saw that she was moved by my plight. And all at once, I remembered when we were friends, in the Temple. Accomplices even. We had thought ourselves so wise. So untouchable. But now, time has touched us both. Life has made fools of us.

*

Yet still I cannot forgive her for making me enter that room this evening. I had vowed that the room would remain closed, a pleasure-ground in which their immortal souls could roam, dancing again, each night renewing their love. Now I have broken my promise. The door is closed again and will remain so. It is too late, I fear, to make amends. When John brought me my nightcap, he ventured upon the subject of repairs.

'We could begin by a thorough dusting of the room, sir,' he said. 'I had my doubts at first, but now I believe you were not mistaken. Your parents would not be pleased to see Carmine Hall rot away. It would be best to restore the ballroom to its former glory.'

'Get out,' I mumbled.

'I beg your pardon, sir?'

I raised my head. My voice was gruff.

'I said, get out of this room!'

At which he turned, and left me.

I regretted it instantly, of course. I should never have spoken to John in that manner. Yet the idea of destroying those cobwebs, of wiping away the thick dust that was piled on every surface, of restoring the paintings and healing the floor, seemed sacrilegious to me. What need had I of a ballroom? How could I ever again hold parties and welcome guests into that place? No – even now, the image comes back to me. I was the first to see them. I was in the adjacent room and heard the crash and the high, unearthly shriek that was my mother's last breath. I ran towards the door and threw it open, and there, in the black of night, in a room lit by a thousand candles, they lay dead. I could not move, or speak. I was transfixed. That they should die, so soon after Emilia. As if to punish me. For my cruelty.

Yes, my faults haunt me indeed. A series of insults, culminating in that gift of a mirror. I had my reasons, and these shall become clear to you. But in truth there can be no justification. Emilia had suffered enough. Perhaps, if I had behaved differently, she might still be alive now. She would not have died alone; uncared for. If she were here now, I might learn to look beyond her face. But in my youth, I could not.

No – I could not love what she had become. For when Emilia looked in the mirror that I sent her, I knew what she would see. Horrible scars upon her face; the remains of pustules which had never quite healed. Perhaps the green-black scabs would remain there still (I am no doctor – I cannot be sure of these things). Indeed, though I did not know how far the disease had progressed, I knew it might be possible that her nose was beginning to rot. Her lips, even. Eventually, the bones might become exposed on her face. And she would watch that deterioration in the mirror I gave her.

And what of her body? Had this escaped unharmed? It is impossible. No doubt she would have seen it, scarred and spoiled as her face. She might have had pains in her joints, in the balls of her feet, the palms of her hands. If she had lived longer, the pain might have grown unbearable. It was better, perhaps, that she should die. But that she did not know of my love – this is what pains me most! That her diaries, written in those final weeks, show so clearly how she loved me. That she allowed her heart to wither, as her body had. This is what is unbearable.

I am alone, in my bed, an ugly man who cares for nothing. Who, though he will not sleep, does not wish to write more. Only Emilia's voice now can speak the truth. I am soiled, and feel I have no more to say. Only Emilia's voice can cleanse me. I must learn from her. I must be silent and allow her, once again, to speak.

19

EMILIA

THOUGH I HAD woken, in the night, to find the Peacock Lady by my side, the following morning I found myself alone. I was in a terrible sweat, yet I felt immediately relieved that my dream had been no more than a fantasy. My room in the Temple was dark and gloomy when I awoke, for the thick velvet curtains prevented any light from seeping through. Still, I was happy, knowing that once they were drawn, and the gauze cloths behind them, a winter light would flood in, and I could feast my eyes once again on the spectacle of the frozen river.

Suddenly, however, new thoughts crowded in upon me. I remembered Vermilion's actions the previous night. How could I have forgotten? Oh, the shame of it! I pushed my face into the pillow, half desiring to smother myself. How could I have excused this behaviour? Had the Doctor noticed my actions? If so, he would surely be rid of me before the day was through.

In the dimness of my chamber, I yet saw most clearly what a villain this Vermilion was. It was impossible that his actions stemmed from love. He had made me defy the Doctor, the man who had saved me from the Devil. And then it struck me – I thought of his ruby coat, his dark tresses, the glint in his eye. Then I thought of the Doctor, his fair face, his white silk coat and breeches. Surely there was no clearer sign than this. Vermilion was the Devil's agent upon this earth, who had wormed his way into the Doctor's affections. I had been beguiled by him. Cheated into believing that this was angelic love. But now that I recognized him, I felt sure I could avoid his wiles. I would stay here, in the Temple. But I would not go near him again.

There was a knock at my door then, and as my breakfast was

usually brought at this hour by one of the apothecaries, I bade the knocker enter. I was surprised, however, when I discerned a woman's shape, setting down the tray by my bedside. She moved to the curtains and threw them open, and the windows also, blinding me with the light, as she greeted me. When I was able to open my eyes again, I saw that she was a comely, friendly-looking woman of around thirty years of age. She had a generous figure, and chestnut hair, piled loosely upon her head. Her dress was not fine, yet neither was it the habit of a servant. Its looseness, and her bare legs, betrayed the fact that this woman was under the influence of the Doctor's teachings. Her face was plump and rosy, with bright green eyes, a fair and freckled complexion, and a sweet smiling mouth. I wondered that I had not seen her here before now.

'James has asked me to bring your breakfast this morning,' she said, setting down the tray before me. 'I took the liberty of bringing you some tea.'

'Oh no,' I said, 'I cannot drink tea. It will pollute me.'

'Nonsense,' she replied. 'One cup a day will do you no harm at all.'

'Pardon me, madam,' I said, 'but I have strict instructions from the Doctor to avoid such substances, and if, as I guess, you are some disciple of his, you would do well to abide by his maxims. I would add that, if it is the Doctor that you refer to by the name of James, you would do well not to repeat it.'

At this she laughed, a hearty, unashamed laugh, which angered me yet further.

'Child,' she said. 'I see you do not know who I am.'

'No, of course not. I have never set eyes on you before now.'

'Then I shall tell you, Emilia. I am the Doctor's wife.'

Nothing could have come as a greater shock to me than this news. The Doctor had not mentioned a wife. His manner and demeanour were not those of a married man. I had fancied him pure; untouched by female hands. But now this woman claimed she joined him in the matrimonial state! It seemed impossible, yet her gaze was so direct, I knew that she spoke the truth. It was not just the fact of his marriage, however, that shocked me. I was astounded that he should marry such a plain woman! For had I not, silently, believed that the Doctor adored only me? Had I not, in my weakest moments, imagined that one day the Doctor would take my hand in his, lean towards me, and kiss me full on the lips?

'You must pardon me, madam,' I said. 'I was not acquainted with the fact.'

'It does not surprise me,' she replied, amiably. 'I have been away for a month, visiting my sister in Pontefract. The children run wild up there. James is a little too strict with them.'

My mind reeled. The Doctor – a father? And yet, the more I thought about it, the more obvious it became. I knew, after all, that the Doctor advocated matrimony and that his greatest fear was that the race should degenerate. It would be vital, then, that he contribute to his own cause and help repopulate the nation.

'How many children do you have, Mrs Graham?' I asked.

'I have three children, and I am most proud of all of them.'

Only three! I was most disappointed. But I did not let her see it.

'I look forward to meeting them.'

But she shook her head. 'Oh no – I think not. The Doctor does not like the children to become involved with his working life. I imagine that is why he did not mention me to you. Whilst he is at work, he thinks only of work, and whilst with the family, only of us.'

'A pleasure I shall have to forgo then,' I said, somewhat insulted.

I wanted her to be jealous of me, I think, but she was clearly unaffected. Yet there was something on her mind. I saw her frown a little suddenly, and hesitate, as if she was somewhat afraid of what she should say next. I decided I would not help her. Perchance the Doctor had indeed spied me when Vermilion's head was beneath my skirt, his lips between my legs. This might be the end of my time here.

Yet when she did speak it was of a completely different matter.

'The Doctor is afraid,' she said, 'that you might be tempted to leave him.'

I laughed, with relief.

'Madam, I could never leave the Temple.'

'I am glad to hear you say it, Emilia. But surely you must feel you owe some allegiance to your family?'

'My family?'

And then I realized what was behind her words. It was on this day that my brother would be returning. With Smellie. The Doctor was afraid that I would go to them. I was about to dismiss the idea instantly, when suddenly the image of Daniel's face came to me. So open and trusting. He had been a little hard on me of late, but I knew that he believed he acted for my own good. He wanted to do as my father would have done for me. Yet how? With such a small dowry, I did not even understand how he had awakened this Smellie's interest in me.

Before I knew it, hot tears were scalding my cheek. It seemed to me, all of a sudden, that my time in the Temple had been nothing but a fantasy. The Doctor had offered to protect me, but I found that when I thought of my brother it was with a strange longing. He was my only remaining relative, the only person, beside the Doctor, in whom I could put absolute trust. And could I scorn him now? Could I reject the pleas of my own flesh and blood?

Yet I felt that I had no alternative. For I imagined this Smellie man. He would be a fat and ageing nobleman. He would have boils on his face and yellow, rotting teeth. His skin would be thick and coarse, his cheeks ruddy. I imagined the stench that must permeate him. He would never bathe more than once a month, I thought, and he would be a man who liked feasting. The smells of the food would emanate through his skin, and his clothes would stink of rotting cheese, old beer and pungent spices. Wherever he went, he would be accustomed to folk doffing their hats and bowing before him (for he was a rich man and there are few who will not show respect to such a one). But he would not know that there was a secondary reason for this behaviour. For to bow before him would be to avoid the odours

146

that sprang from his putrid mouth when he breathed or spoke. Men would bow lower before him than before any other gentleman, and whilst Smellie believed that this was proof of their enormous love of him, it was in truth a simple method for avoiding the worst – for if one bowed low enough, one could bury one's nostrils in the fabric of one's own breeches, and thus avoid the sickness that one would surely feel otherwise. But there was more than this. Dr Graham's wife sat, patiently, waiting for me to speak as these thoughts rushed through my head. The worst was this – if I were to become his wife, not only would I be forced to live my life in close proximity to him, but I would also be expected to share his bed. No doubt he would fart, constantly, throughout the night, sending forth a most unimaginable aroma. Then, when he awoke in the mornings, having recovered from his drunkenness of the previous night, he would remember that he had not, as a result of his intoxicated state, taken the pleasures that were his due. He would laugh heartily and roll his fat belly on top of me, so that I would be nearly crushed. His face would come so close to mine that I would feel I must die of the fetid air he breathed. But he would not have pity on me. He would place his mouth, his rotting mouth, upon my own sweet lips and force me to accept his kisses. If I dared open my eyes, I would see bulging, bloodshot, yellowing orbs, staring towards me, and no doubt a light drizzle running from his nose. He would tear my clothing from me and force his decaying member between my legs. I would be infected. I would surely die.

'You must tell the Doctor, madam, not to concern himself over this matter,' I said. 'My love for my brother is not so great that I would sacrifice my flesh for him. I will remain within the Temple.'

'I am glad to hear it,' she replied. 'The Doctor has told me, Emilia, that he was pleased with your performance last evening.'

I was struck, immediately, with the significance of these words. The very same words that I had heard the Peacock Lady utter. Words which I thought had come in a dream. Yet now I knew the Peacock Lady had spoken truly and I could be certain that the Doctor had not seen Vermilion's antics. I could remain here in safety. But there was more than this. My heart soared at the words and I was unable, at first, to think why.

And then it came to me. The Peacock Lady's words had not stopped where Mrs Graham's had. She had said something else. A thing of more significance.

'The Doctor has told me, Emilia, that he was pleased with your performance this evening. And Vermilion has told me that he loves you.'

A strange love, I thought, that will pretend he does not know me. That will not look me in the eye. It is the Devil's love, that much is certain. And yet I do not feel that I am evil. I know nothing. I understand nothing. I am filled with water and air and light.

These thoughts flash quickly through my mind. I was about to speak; to interrupt the brief silence between myself and Mrs Graham. Yet suddenly, from the open window, I hear a noise that startles me. A loud cracking sound, almost like a gunshot. We exchange glances, and together we move to the window. And immediately I see what has passed. The sky is white, yet the sun is burning through, throwing a pale yellow light across the Thames. The ice is breaking up.

And as we stand, watching, we hear it, over and again: the sound of the river as it begins to crack. Mrs Graham touches my shoulder and smiles before turning and leaving the room. But I could watch this for hours. The slow disintegration of the ice-sheet. Great chunks of frozen water beginning to move, one sliding against another, hurling themselves upwards as the river surges beneath. I watch as some of the boats, still trapped by the ice, are carried along; their sails, no longer stiff, but heavy with water. For me, it heralds another change. A new beginning.

It is love that has caused this change. I know it, as I half close my eyes and watch the surface of the river: slates of ice, slowly shifting, as far as the eye can see. Yet it cannot last. That is the worst of it. It cannot remain so.

And thinking this, I have a vision, suddenly, of a different London, some time in the future, after I am dead. I do not know from where it stems. I had not wished for it, for it is a black vision; a devil vision. The Adelphi is in ruins, a pile of rubble in a rain-drenched city. Grime covers the streets below and the river is thick with weeds. I want to stop this thought; to halt the progress of time. Yet I know this is impossible. Time will not stop its course. This ice-kingdom is ephemeral. Transient. And one day, London will be something other than what it is now.

20

EMILIA

WITH A LEADEN heart I watched the arrival of my brother. I saw he had not changed. Indeed, there was no alteration in his demeanour or in his carriage, and he leapt from the coach in his usual sprightly manner, a great, foolish, hopeful grin upon his lips. His eyes glanced up to my old bedroom window, but there was no one there to return his look. He was ruddy-faced and seemed invigorated by the ride and the weak sunlight. Daniel. My Daniel. Swathed in a new coat of green velvet, his corn-coloured hair glinting, his bright, protruding teeth shining, on the first day of the thaw.

It wounded me that I was betraying him thus. I longed to go out and hold him in my arms, kissing his cold cheeks, taking hold of his hand and leading him indoors. I barely remembered why I was avoiding him so, until I saw a strange gentleman, stepping down from the carriage and, laughing to myself, for I had never seen such a creature as this, I remembered Lord Smellie.

Yet this could not be he. For in every aspect of his looks and his behaviour, this man appeared the antithesis of that name. This must be a fancy manservant or dancing master, for no true gentleman could be such a fop as this, a King of Fops, a Macaroni Royal.

I watched in wonderment, fascinated by this thread of man-hood below. For though I knew him, somehow, to be a man, the very fabric of his being was feminine. He was of slight build, neither tall nor short, and though I saw him only briefly, I could make out the pure whiteness and tightness of the curls of his wig, and the thick layer of white paint upon his face. He had a dark patch upon his cheek and his lips were painted red as ripe cherries. But it was his dress that struck me most. For his suit was of canary yellow, embroidered with gold, and he carried a golden cane with a thick, tasselled knob which he clutched in his hand, a posture most ridiculous, for he held his arm as if it were the spout of a tea-pot, his wrist drooping downward. About his wrists, thick profusions of white lace billowed, and the same about his neck. His stockings also were white, and his shoes, both made brighter still by the dull hue of the melting ice beneath his feet. Was this the kind of company my brother wished upon me? The very type of man whom once he had so mocked. Though I loved my brother still, the sight of this dandy made me more certain than ever of my cause. I must remain within the Temple. The alternative, a life in the Essex countryside, surrounded by such fools as this one, was too horrible to contemplate.

And so it was that I obeyed the Doctor. In the week that followed, he advised me not to leave the Temple, and though he did not *forbid* me from venturing out, he made it quite clear that should I do so, he could not be responsible for my safety. He could not guarantee that my brother would not find me and force me to marry Smellie.

'But Doctor,' I said, 'if I do not run daily in the fresh air my beauty will fade'.

'Your beauty is too great to fade so easily, Emilia,' he said. 'Yet it would be hardly beneficial to confine you here for long. This is a temporary measure, remember that. I need some time to think about the matter. In the meantime, you must remember to sleep with your windows open, and to follow, with great seriousness, all other maxims I have suggested to you, that is, to spend time, daily, on the Celestial Throne, to take my Imperial pills, et cetera, et cetera . . .'

It was a lonely week that I spent. Both Vermilion and the Peacock Lady were absent from the Temple, and the musicians arrived only just before the nightly performances. The apothecaries, though they also lived within the Temple, were sullen fellows and I did not see them often. Yet though Dr Graham was a very busy man, tending the poor and the sick most afternoons, he was kind enough to spend time with me when he was able. But he rarely spoke of what was closest to my heart – my pain at not seeing my brother, and my deep regret at causing him such heartache. Every day, I saw Daniel and the Macaroni from my window, yet they never looked up to see me. The Macaroni – or should I say Jessamy? Tulip? Exquisite? (for such are the names that I am told are given to these fellows nowadays) – well, whatever his name, he was a source of constant amusement. If I could not bear to look upon Daniel, I would fasten my eyes on this creature, for his costumes were such as I had never before seen and I was much entertained by his appearance. Never before had I seen such a ridiculous man. All his clothes were of a brilliant hue – a glowing pink, a ghastly checked lilac, or green so bright one barely dared look at it, for fear one's eyesight would be irredeemably damaged. He never again wore the white shoes which he had worn upon his arrival, but now had a pair with high red heels and his walk was a totter, worse than any lady's. Sometimes he carried his golden cane, but I noticed he had another, even more ridiculous, for it was as long as a leaping pole, and very often he was wont to trip over it.

Watching, unseen, I also observed his hair more closely. It was longer than I had at first noticed, with white curls around his shoulders (borrowed curls, I do not doubt), and on the top of his hair he wore a miniature hat. Yet the most absurd aspect of his attire was this. The Macaroni carried a sword by his side, in a manner that seemed more graceful, I thought, than comfortable.

All of this was no more than a diversion for me. I tried to concentrate on the Jessamy in the hope that I would thus be able to avoid contemplating my dear Daniel. Yet often this was not possible. When I did look upon him, I thought that his face had lost the glow it had when he arrived; indeed, he appeared so wan that he nearly matched the painted pallor of that other fellow, and on one occasion I was so full of sorrow for my shameful act of leaving him, without knowledge even that I was safe, that I was about to open my window wide to cry out to him, and I am certain that I would have done had not the Doctor's wife entered my room at that very moment.

There was another subject, also, that I did not dare to broach with the Doctor. The name of Vermilion. For I feared that if I mentioned him, the Doctor might guess he was the subject of my love. In truth, remembering that time, I think he was afraid. He knew that the first flush of my joy at being here had faded. I had been solitary for much of my life, but I had always had my brother by my side. Now, with no friends, I was becoming quite desolate. And the Doctor sensed this.

Yet he did not show this fear. Instead, he talked to me of the world. He told me of Mr Franklin and the great influence that man had had upon him. He spoke not only of Franklin's electrical experiments but also of his involvement in America's Declaration of Independence. Dr Graham had great sympathy with this cause and spoke again of his regret at the bloodshed in that country. We should withdraw, he said, instead of spending our nation's wealth on such a war.

In spite of myself, I found that I grew a little interested in these affairs of the world. Never before had I been spoken to like this. The Doctor addressed me as if I were a man, and this, in itself, was enough to quell a little of my self-pity. Politics, after all, is a man's arena, and my father had never seen fit to tell me of these affairs. Did I not know, the Doctor asked, about the Catholic Relief Act? About Lord George Gordon and his fight against such an indulgence? He told me about the people's outrage against favours given to the Papists; how the Protestant Association was growing and how the direst actions were threatened if Lord North's Government did not give in to them.

'Is our peace really so fragile?' I asked.

'There is nothing more fragile than peace, Vestina,' he told me. 'Yet I do not wish to frighten you. I am certain some agreement will be reached.'

'How can you be so sure?'

'I have received, just this morning, a handbill petitioning against Catholic relief. I am certain that enough misguided idiots will sign it, and so the Government will relent.'

'Why do you call them idiots, Doctor?'

'Because, Emilia, as Defoe said, there are ten thousand stout fellows out there that would spend the last drop of their blood against Popery that do not know whether it be a man or a horse.'

'I have heard indeed that the Irish are a most vile nation.'

'And from whom have you received that opinion, Emilia?'

'Both my father and my brother have informed me of the degeneracy of the Irish. And you yourself, Doctor, are not a lover of degenerates.'

'But how do you know it is *true*, my Vestina? What evidence have you for your assertions? This is *received* opinion. It is not your own.'

And at this I could bear it no longer. Loneliness and frustration and a sense of the inadequacy of my female mind overcame me. I tried to prevent the tears, but they were already flowing. Immediately I saw he was affected.

'I am sorry, Vestina,' he said, in a soothing voice that reminded me of our first acquaintance. 'I move too quickly for you. Forgive me. My feelings run strong on this matter, but there is no reason why you should be burdened with men's business. Your realm is the Celestial.'

My mood, however, did not much improve for several days, and only the exhilaration of my evening performances made my life seem bearable. A week after my brother's return, however, the Doctor's wife, whose name was Mary, came into my room to wake me. I was most glad to see her, for I had hoped that she might spend some time with me in order to relieve my boredom. For though I had always been accustomed to solitude, I had never felt quite so alone as I did that week. With the Peacock Lady and Vermilion, I had glimpsed a possibility of friendship, but now I felt as if that had been taken from me. My own brother, it seemed, had turned against me (for how else could he wish to force me into a marriage against my will?) and the days seemed interminable, for though I was a Goddess by night, by day I knew I was no more than a mere mortal.

'Emilia,' she said, and she threw her arms around me, like a mother, smelling of tea and lavender. 'Sweet child' (kissing me on the forehead), 'I have told him that this is enough.'

'Pardon me, madam?'

'James has had his way for far too long. We cannot let a young colt like you remain in this place all day from morn to night.'

'The Doctor acts only for my own good, Mrs Graham.'

'Madam. Mrs Graham! When will you call me by my name? Cooped up like this! He'd have you fade away to nothing.'

'Oh no, I am not at all weak. And I eat plentifully.'

'Of fruit and vegetables – yes surely. Child, though I do not wish to speak against him, you are looking more and more like a skeleton each day.'

'That cannot be true. For I am following the Doctor's maxims with great care. It is true I have not taken my morning run of late, but I assure you, I have never been more healthy. If it were not so, how could the Doctor continue to display me as his Goddess?'

'I'll bring you some porridge this morning,' she said, as if she had not heard my reply, 'and a cup of hot chocolate. And there will be roast duck on the table at midday. I hope you will join us?'

I realized, at her words, how hungry I was. How I longed for the sweet taste of the breakfast stuffs and the succulent fat of the duck. Yet I was also full of shame at the thought. For if I had been feeling too full of mortal thoughts most recently, was this not because I had been eating too plentifully? Surely the food itself was contaminating me, for the food of angels does not grow upon trees or upon the bones of animals. And would this woman have me pour sugared chocolate down my throat? Polluting myself with cream and the fat of animals?

'I have no need of the nourishment that you speak of. I am nourished by more than mere food.'

'Child. If you do not eat, you truly cannot continue here at the Temple. James will not wish his Vestina to be a bag of bones. If you do not see that you feed upon nothing more than an illusion, you will surely suffer for it later.' A look of horror crossed her face; I saw her instantly regret her words.

'Do you call the Doctor a liar?' I said, my anger rising. 'His own wife! Then you are most treacherous.'

'Of course not,' she said, yet colouring, so that I knew this was exactly what she had intended. 'But you must approach James's teachings with care.'

'And you must learn to show respect for a man who deserves a better wife than you!'

Then I, too, coloured; felt the tears welling again within me. We stood, both silent for a moment, each of us staring at one another, with rage at first which soon dissolved into remorse. We were both shocked, I think, by the intensity of our outbursts. I had not wished to offend her thus, and, perhaps sensing this, she moved towards me a little.

'Emilia,' she said, in a more gentle voice that was yet suffused with hidden passion. 'Are you in love with my husband?'

'No!' I too spoke with great ardour. 'Of course not!'

'I no longer know what to think. I think that I trust you, and yet I see your beauty, child, and suddenly I fear you.'

'There is no need to fear,' I said, taking her hands in mine. 'For I am in love with another.'

I saw the look of relief on her face, yet no sooner did I see it than it was counteracted by a new panic.

'Who is it?' she said. 'Who is it that you love?'

'Not your husband, madam. I assure you of that.'

'I believe you, Emilia. But James will be furious if he hears you are in love. He would not wish to lose his Vestina thus. How is it possible? For he has told me that you did not seem to suffer from any such sickness when you came here. Was he mistaken?'

'I cannot say more. I beg you – do not speak to the Doctor of this. He that I love is unworthy of me. It is a love I must forget. I desire only to be the Doctor's Goddess.'

But even as I spoke, I knew it was a lie. I had thought, when I first came here, that there would be an end to sorrow, but it

seemed it was not so. It was a fault within me, surely, this
constant unhappiness that I experienced.

'Come,' Mrs Graham said, interrupting my self-pity. 'I did
not come here to probe into your secrets. I came, rather, to ask
you if you wish to venture out with me. It is a fine day. The ice
has nearly thawed now. It would be good for you to run again.'

'But my brother?'

'He has already gone out this morning, along with that
Exquisite friend of his. And you cannot remain a prisoner here.
Come. Let us breathe the January air together. Let us begin
again.'

'I do not like beginnings, Mrs Graham,' I said, 'but if we can
alter the course of our friendship, I should be glad.'

'Then that is what we shall do,' she said, smiling. 'Come. The
morning is ripe for it.'

EMILIA

TO BE FREE, once again, in St James's Park, filled me with the greatest elation. This was the first time that I had run here since the thaw, and I took off my shoes and my cloak (which Mrs Graham, against my will, had insisted that I wear) to thrill to the feel of damp grass beneath my feet. Whilst she watched from a small bench, I cavorted amongst the fallow deer, glorying in the air, in the fresh smell of earth and in the pale blue sky. I did not need to look at her to know what she thought of this. Our conversation, *en route* to the park, had made it clear that she thought I took the Doctor's maxims too seriously. She said he did not expect such strict adherence to his rules. Yet I could not believe her. I concluded that she was indeed jealous of me. She hid this beneath a façade of great friendship, yet in truth she wanted me to eat more, so that I would grow fat and unattractive; to cover my allure with a dull cloak, so that no men should look at me. Even now, as I danced, gazing down at the canal, enjoying the attention I invariably received from the passing crowd, I could imagine the set of her face. Perhaps she was thinking of this place at night, for though the park would be locked after nightfall, it was common knowledge that many thousands of people had obtained keys, and my brother had told me this was a notorious haunt for 'women of the town'. Was that what she was thinking? That I was no better than a whore? Our earlier conversation had shaken me. I did not like her criticisms, and would not believe that it was simple concern that made her act as she did.

I should, however, perhaps have been grateful to Mrs Graham. For, as you might guess, I do not recount any incident, any thought, or any feeling in this diary, without good reason. And though this day, as yet, might seem unremarkable, I write of it with a sense of anger, for there was one who watched me as I danced, and his interest was more than mere desire. I had noticed him, in fact, for though there were many who observed my movements, he had seemed to look more closely. Indeed, whilst most of my audience had their eyes upon my breasts and my limbs, he was the only one who watched my face. I caught his eye several times as I came out of a pose, but on each occasion he would immediately divert his attention to another part of my body so that he might seem more like the other men that gathered there. Yet he was not like them. I do not know why, but I felt, sometimes, as I danced, that I was casting some kind of spell; weaving a net around me of finest silk threads, which protected me from darkness and evil. I had found that it was not just the gentlewomen who avoided me, but the paupers also. Only gentlemen dared look. Only gentlemen were worthy.

But this man was not a gentleman. He was neatly dressed, in dark breeches and overcoat, buttoned full up, yet I sensed he was not a man of quality. It unnerved me, in fact, so much so that the attractions of the fresh air and the sweet smell of the thaw were not enough to keep me in the park.

We were on our way back to the Temple, passing through Charing Cross. I was silent, barely aware of what was around me. As I walked towards the Strand I did not look up to see the red-brick towers of Northumberland House or the Percy Lion that roared above its façade. What did I care that those towers had been there since the age of Shakespeare? I had more important things to think upon. My love for Vermilion; my desperation to see him again. I could not understand why, if he loved me, he had abandoned me.

It is not surprising, then, that Mrs Graham's words that January morning came as a shock to me, an intrusion into my private world, my separate sphere.

'Emilia – I do not wish to distress you, child, but I fear that we are being followed.'

'Surely not!' I replied, though in truth I was instantly afraid. 'You must be mistaken.'

'No. I swear that I am not. I have sensed it since we left the park, but I did not wish to alarm you unless I was certain that my feeling could be justified. Now I know it to be so. I have seen the man, and though at first he did not dart from sight, thinking perhaps that he might appear less suspicious thus, now he is aware that I am watching him and so has grown more furtive.'

'Could it not simply be that this man is walking in the same direction as we are?'

'I might have thought so, but he is hiding now, Emilia.'

'Hiding?'

'Yes, behind the base of that statue.'

'Are you certain?'

'Most certain. He is an ugly-looking man, dressed in a dark coat, but I saw a flash of red beneath.'

'You speak as if that has some significance.'

'It has indeed. It is the red waistcoat worn by the Bow Street thief-takers.'

'A thief-taker, Mrs Graham? But we are not thieves.'

'Look. There he is.'

I turned, fast, but saw nothing.

'Where?'

'You missed him again. He is behind the sedan now. A hunched little fellow. Wait now, it is about to move.'

I could not help but laugh as I watched the sedan being lifted, for though the carriers seemed strong enough, the passenger was an enormously fat alderman and the burden was clearly too great for them. They struggled, but did not seem able to lift it above a few inches and I anticipated that should they ever raise it higher, the man might keel from his seat, which indeed would be no more than he deserved.

'There!' Mrs Graham said. 'Do you see his feet?'

I could barely miss them: two black boots which turned as the chair was raised and began to walk away from us. Mrs Graham rushed to see where he had gone, and I followed her, but it was to no avail. The man had vanished.

'He will not have left us yet,' she said, as if she knew exactly what he was up to. 'But we must try to lose him.'

'How can we lose him,' I asked, 'when he is already lost?'

'Not lost,' she replied, 'simply waiting. He wants us to think that we have forgotten him. But I can guess his mind. He is still with us.'

At the time, I do not think that I fully believed Mrs Graham's suspicions. It was true that I had seen the boots, but it seemed, to me, so unlikely that one of these so-called 'thief-takers' should spend their time chasing women about the streets that I thought there must be a thousand other reasons why this man was behaving in such a way. Still, I did not argue when Mrs Graham suggested taking a different route back to the Adelphi. Indeed, I was much relieved that we arrived at Adam Street without further sightings of him, and more so when I was safe within my room at the Temple.

Refreshed and invigorated from the journey, my heart still beating a little quickly from the excitement of it all, I threw my cloak to the floor and went to the window, drawing aside the gauze curtain. I was about to step out on to the balcony, when, horrified, I recoiled. There, beneath, unashamed now, the thief-taker was standing. His coat was open and I saw the red waist-coat beneath, though his head was lowered so I could not see his face. He was a tiny man, with a slight hunch which was accentuated by his posture as he scribbled furiously in a small notebook. There was no doubt now that he was one of these detectives, though I could not see what interest Mrs Graham or myself might hold for him.

I saw a movement and, certain that he was about to gaze up at my window, I stepped back out of his sight, perhaps less afraid that he should see me than that I might see *his* terrifying face. I paused a moment, wondering if it would be best to remain here, yet curiosity got the better of me. I moved to the window again, but he was no longer looking up. Instead, I saw his dark figure vanish, his coat flapping out behind. It chilled my heart to see it. He had entered the house of my brother.

22

EMILIA

IT WOULD HAVE been a long and most distressing afternoon, for the Doctor had gone out of the house, with his wife and children, and I would have been left alone to contemplate the nature of this thief-taker, who, it seemed, was in the employment of my brother. I was lying on my bed, fretting, afraid of what the consequence of this might be, when there was a knock at my door. Immediately, fearing that the hunch-backed man stood on my threshold, I leapt up and hovered near the door, knowing that I had no choice but to open it, for there was no lock to prevent the visitor entering.

Trembling, I reached out my hand and held the handle for support. Then I pulled it towards me, and saw, standing before me, the person whose presence was all that I desired. I saw a red coat, and a white, silken shirt, billowing about a broad chest. I looked up, past the thick shoulders, to the strong neck, punctuated by the sharp rise and fall of an Adam's apple. I saw his face; his eyes – steadfast as a beam of light that would guide me, a lost ship in the night.

He did not smile at me then, but there was no menace in his look. I had thought that I could not forgive him for abandoning me thus, yet his regard was so frank and so sincere, so full of strength and so infinitely comforting, that I could not fault him for his actions. I had been told that he loved me, and if that were so, then I knew that I must trust the force of love, for I had no experience of it and must follow the lead of another. I knew, also, that I need despair no longer. I was a magnet for him, and though he might wish to deny the strength of my attraction, he would ever be pulled towards me. He must have the perfection of my face; the symmetry of my body. For they will reassure him that there is an order in this mad universe.

It was I that spoke the first.

'I have missed you of late, sir.'

'Has my absence caused you distress?'

'Of course not. Why should you think so?'

'I am sorry then, for I myself have been most tormented at not seeing you.'

'It were easy enough, sir, to relieve your torment by coming here sooner.'

'Ah – I see now the source of your anger. You have thought that I have purposely stayed away. But that is not so. I have been helping a friend at a time of great personal suffering. Indeed, I did not know how I should act. To betray a friend, to whom I have promised assistance – at a time when most she needed me. Or to cause you grief – you whom I hardly know, and yet desire only to make happy. Only to love.'

'That your friend is a woman,' I replied, burning with both rage at his desertion of me for another, and joy at his declaration of love, 'I do not doubt that had some influence upon your choice.'

'A *married* woman, Emilia. A woman to whom, if you saw the extent of her agony, you would not begrudge my presence.'

'And was her agony greater than *mine*!' I exclaimed, suddenly unable to contain myself. I knew I had no right to speak thus. And yet I continued. 'Did she suffer as much as I have – not knowing where you were? Was she alone, in a strange place, without friend or kin? Did she wake, in the night, feeling that she had been abandoned by every human soul? Tell me, Vermilion – had she experienced the shame that you have submitted me to – by making love to me with such ardour that I believed our union was blessed by the Gods, and then to walk away, and within five minutes to refuse to meet my eye. You speak of love, but I fear you must not know the meaning of the word.'

And at this he was silent for a moment. I saw a look of self-reproach flicker across his features. (A look, I now realize, that he had spent many hours, in front of the glass, perfecting.) I did not know what to do; thought how ridiculous it was that we should be speaking thus, upon the threshold of my room. And yet I did not wish him to feel that he was welcome here.

'Emilia,' he said, when finally he spoke again, his brow all knotted, his mouth pursed with the pain, 'I have a confession to make.'

At this I turned cold. Was it true that he had been unfaithful to me? That he loved another?

'Emilia,' (he looked uneasy that he should be speaking thus – I am certain that he wished to enter my room) '– I was afraid that my love for you was in vain.'

'This is your confession?'

'Yes, indeed.' (He spoke quietly, for fear he should be heard by one of the apothecaries.) 'How could I have known that my love would be returned? Had I dared to hope that you might reciprocate my feelings, even a little, I would have communicated my passion.'

And I, also, was drawn into the conspiratorial tone. Our voices were hushed, yet full of ardent emotion.

'You feared that I did not love you?'

I was incredulous. How could he not have known it?

'How could I have expected it? When you are made of such stuff as men fear to look upon.'

'What is the meaning of this?'

'Emilia – the Doctor, a man that is most revered by me, has chosen you as his Goddess. As his Angel. Do you not see that a man can be dazzled by the sight of you?'

'I had not thought of it.'

'How strange that you should not be aware of your own radiance. When I look at you, Emilia, I am awed by what I see. Beside you, I feel that I abhor my own flesh. It is too material. You are all air and lightness.'

It was most extraordinary that he should speak so. For, as you are aware, this is a thought that had often crossed my mind. Yet I was silent – unable to admit my vanity.

'Do you understand, Emilia – at least in part?'

'What should I understand, Vermilion? That you have treated me ill, because you did not know I love you? Surely *my* love is immaterial in these matters.'

'No – that is not so. When I walked away from you, after caressing you in the darkness, when I did not dare to look at you – it was because I feared the power you had over me. I feared that you would break my heart, Emilia.'

'And when you did not inform me that you would be absent for a week?'

'Why, I had thought you would not care for my apology. I had thought you would barely notice me gone.'

And I smiled then, at his humility. At human folly. How we make one another miserable, because we are afraid to communicate our emotions. He saw my smile and knew he was forgiven.

'Now will you come with me, Emilia? Will you let me show my love to you?'

'With all my heart, sir. Tell me – where will you take me?'

'There is but one place in this Temple where we may celebrate our love in a manner that is worthy of it.'

I knew his meaning instantly and was filled with pleasure at the prospect. And yet I feared it also. Knew that the Doctor would disapprove of the act we were about to commit. Still, I could not arrest it now. The force that bound Vermilion and me was great as the force of an electrical storm. And the Doctor himself would be the first to admit that such storms were unstoppable; that they would destroy anything in their wake. Such forces must exhaust themselves.

And so it was, with eyes bent modestly to the ground, that I ascended the stairs to the Grand Celestial Chamber. Vermilion trod before me, turning occasionally, whereupon I would raise my glance and he would look into my eyes and smile reassuringly. All, at that moment, seemed to fall into place. Love was the transforming power that would fill the void within me. There was nothing indecent about our love. Our union would be a coupling of souls. Yes – I remembered it now, as I moved, one foot and then another. My brother had told me about the words of Monsieur Descartes – that man and woman are but halves of a whole, and are only to be completed by a conjunction. We are incomplete and must spend our lives in search of our severed half. Some may find such happiness, whilst others may be destroyed by the seemingly fruitless quest. Yet I, Hebe Vestina, was to be most fortunate. In the meeting of our souls, Vermilion and I would discover the true meaning of consummation. I imagined, at the moment that he kissed me, full on the lips, we would evaporate. We would no longer be trapped by the flesh, but would become another element, a vapour that filled the air.

But now we had reached the top. Vermilion flung open the door, and there, before us, was the Celestial Bed, all charged with electricity, and swathed in the whitest silk sheets. So different it appeared to me now. For I had never thought I would participate in the joys of Venus. I had never thought that I would be initiated here into the rites of Love. I was more awed than ever by the beauty of the Bed. Though I sang before it each evening, never had it seemed so dazzling to me. The coloured glass pillars that supported it sparkled in the dim light, which filtered through the rose muslin curtains. I felt giddy with the clandestine nature of our presence here; with the fear that the Doctor might return early and discover us. Yet it was not a true fear, for with Vermilion present, I felt safe. I wondered anew at the electrical fire crackling from Hymen's torch, at the cooing of the turtle-doves above the Bed, at the piping music (which makes me understand, now, that Vermilion had accomplices in his villainy – his friends, the musicians, were all a part of his scheme to deflower me), and I closed my eyes to inhale the odoriferous balsams that quite overcame me.

Then, when I opened my eyes, I saw that Vermilion had closed the door behind him and had stripped off his red jacket. I was somewhat shocked at the speed of this, yet I did not show my unease. Soon we would be in the realm of angels, and we would barely notice our corporeal selves.

Shyly, uncertain of how to proceed, I sat down on the edge of the Bed. I believed I felt the power of the stallion-hair mattress course through me, as Vermilion also sat down beside me, and the scent of his skin became more potent than any of the spices that hung upon the air. He was so beautiful at that moment, so very manly, full of strength and yet with tender compassion in his eyes. How many times, I wonder now, had he practised each move of that seduction? How many girls had he deprived thus of their innocence? But no matter – however bitter I find myself now, at the unthinking cruelty of these rakes and libertines, I must not allow my emotions to intrude on my memory.

Vermilion moved towards me now, placing a strong arm around my shoulder, and pulling me, gently, nearer. The point where we touched seemed charged with energy, and when his lips met mine . . . I can barely describe the force that flowed through me. I gasped at the sensation and felt a deep heat engulfing me. My limbs became weak, and I was without breath or substance. Yes, for a moment I believed that I would indeed become aetherial, but then his tongue entered my mouth and I felt the warmth of it, probing my palate, my teeth. No – I knew at that moment that this experience would involve my body, perhaps equally to my soul. I could feel only the body, only the sweet tongue within my mouth. Then Vermilion withdrew for a moment, and when I tried, impatiently, to return my lips to his, he took hold of my shoulders and held me at such a distance that I could barely touch him, so that his breath no more than brushed against me. I could not believe the intensity of my desire to return my mouth once again to his own, for the air between us was charged, but he merely blew me little kisses, or flickered his tongue to briefly touch my lips.

And then, when I could bear it no longer, when I felt that I should die if I did not have his mouth upon my own, he released his grip and pulled me towards him with such might that I no longer knew where I was or what I did. Whether he was aided by the electricity of the Bed, I do not know. I felt myself being pushed backwards against the mattress and I felt his tongue stronger now, his mouth sucking my lips so hard I thought that they would bleed. I could think no longer; could only continue to respond to him, as his lips roamed across my face, my eyelids, his tongue upon my ear. Then, when I was robbed of power to move, when I was sunk deep amidst the white sheets, when I was crushed by the force of electrical fire, Vermilion ripped my loose gown so that my breasts were revealed to him. Then again he tore, so that I was naked before him, and though I recoiled from the violence of this, knew that this was not treatment fit for an angel, I did not object. I felt shame, deep inside me; anger – for I sensed it should not be like this. How could these actions take the name of love? Yet hatred was so mingled with desire that, as he fell upon my breasts, his hand between my legs, I could not deny him. Yes, as I watched him stand now, and look down upon me, I could not help but be awed by how handsome he was, by the new flush upon his cheeks, and, as he swiftly removed his shirt, by this sight that was entirely new to me. I had imagined it. Oh, how many times had I imagined what it must be like to see the naked chest of a man, bared before me; bared for my pleasure. But never, not in paintings of Apollo, nor of Mars, had I seen such magnificence. So dark was the flesh. Sprinkled lightly with black hair that covered his arms also. Though now I despise the very name of beauty, I cannot deny the power it has over us. I could have watched him for many hours, oblivious of my own nakedness. I knew I could not deny him the sight of me for if I took pleasure in his difference from myself, how much pleasure must he also take from my softness?

But Vermilion did not stop there. He slipped his shoes from his feet, removed his breeches and his silken stockings, to reveal a most terrifying sight. Indeed, when I remember how struck with fear I was at that moment, I doubt whether I should describe what I saw, for already I have stepped beyond the bounds of what is fit for a woman to write of. What if a young lady should read my work? When I describe what I then saw, though she may be shocked, she may also consider herself lucky that she has been told of this, for never had such a thing been spoken of to me. Never had I dreamed that this object, this strange machine before my eyes, had been so large as this. No – for I had seen it depicted all small and shrivelled, and though I had heard some suggestion, from the Doctor, that it must grow somewhat to perform the act of love, I had not imagined that it would swell to thirty times its natural size. What I saw before me, springing out from Vermilion's body, from its root in a coil of blackest hair, was a thing like an instrument of torture. A dark and throbbing instrument it was, so massive that I scarce believed it was a part of him. It stood erect upon his belly, its raw tip red as his name. It was such an ugly thing, like a piece of excess gristle upon his body, all covered in veins and spewing a little milky liquid on the top. I was filled with horror at the sight of it, for I knew the purpose of this tool and the thought made me nearly faint away. Yes, for though I knew that he must enter me, I was also certain that there was no space within me where such a gigantic member could sit. I might be split in two and die from the wounds I would receive.

Perhaps Vermilion sensed my fear, for at that moment he came beside me upon the bed, and, ignoring our nakedness, he began to kiss me over again, all gently this time, as if I were a child that must be comforted. He kissed my eyelids closed and stroked my hair, then I felt his naked body against my own, the roughness of his legs bristling lightly against mine. In that moment I pitied him suddenly that his body should be so deformed by this thing, and as I warmed again to him, I became aware of the music once more and the smells that surrounded me. Soon, he slipped his fingers between my legs and I felt the sting of pleasure as he brushed them lightly against me. He stroked softly, again and again, and I felt a ripple of magnetic power flowing down my legs, so that against my will I stretched them outwards and apart, and with each moment I became less of myself and more of the heavens, for now indeed the storm was raging and there was lightning in my legs, flashing furiously, until suddenly, unexpectedly, my whole body was overtaken with it; I was charged with electricity and the sky flared up in a sheet of white fire.

Then, hearing Vermilion chuckle beside me, I was relieved. It was over, and there had been no pain as I anticipated. I was not torn asunder, but instead had experienced a pleasure so exquisite that it seemed my whole life had been in anticipation of this moment. But then I opened my eyes and saw that I was wrong – it

169

was not over. It was just about to begin, for Vermilion was climbing on top of me, his great arrow poised at its target. He seemed not to see me then, for he, too, was looking down at himself, smiling at the sight of it. Now, with my eyes open, I saw the back of him in the mirrors of the dome, his naked buttocks, his strong back, his legs between my own. Somewhere, in the distance, I heard the cooing of the doves, and beyond that the sound of voices, lower down in the Temple, but then they were gone, as was my pleasure, for I felt, now, the hardness of his tool pressed between my thighs, pushing insistently against my skin as if he might find an entrance there, when I knew that there was none that would accommodate him. I could barely believe that he was doing this to me; to punish me thus, so soon after he had filled me with such pleasure.

'No, Vermilion. Please stop!' I cried. 'It is not possible!'

He looked again towards my face, and yet, I thought, he did not truly see me. Nor, I thought, did he hear the voices that echoed in my mind – my brother's voice, my father's voice.

'We cannot stop now, Emilia,' Vermilion said. 'This is the proof of our love.'

And at this I was silenced. I was afraid; and yet I did not dare deny him. I did not dare ruin our love by my cowardice. I steeled myself to be ripped apart by him; if this was the price of love, then I must pay it. I must suffer in order to be redeemed by it.

But the pain! The pain as he pushed, harder and harder against my tender parts, forcing them apart, yet making no real advances. Then, suddenly, he made a little progress, the very tip of it was inside me, no more than that. Yet even this was agony to me. All the pleasure of a few moments before had vanished and I was forced to bite into my own hand so that I might not scream with such intensity that the whole Temple would be roused.

'Now, Emilia!' Vermilion said, suddenly, his face contorted with pleasure. 'Now!'

He withdrew once again, preparing to make a final assault, and I steeled myself for the sacrifice. But then, without warning, the voices of my imagination, the sound of men, which had intensified with my pain to become loud shouts and exclamations, burst into the Celestial Chamber. Horrified, Vermilion heard the sound of the door being flung open, and he turned to face a large band of men, all fully clothed in hessian and sackcloth; intruders in the Temple. There were six of them in all, with swords by their sides and grimaces upon their faces. A pack of bearded hooligans, who, I feared, were here to murder Vermilion.

Ashamed at my nakedness and trembling with terror, I pulled the silken sheets around my body. That it should happen again! That I, Emilia, should be the cause of death. Yet Vermilion, to my surprise, merely laughed. He did not attempt to clothe himself, nor did he hide his weapon, but seemed proud that they should see its size.

'What can I do for you gentlemen?' was his request.

And at this, they stood aside, revealing, to my distress, three figures familiar to me – my brother, the Macaroni dressed in his vibrant yellow suit, and beyond them, in the shadows, the Thief-taker. My brother glanced at me, briefly, with such disdain and yet such sorrow that I felt my heart was breaking. For no apparent reason, an image came into my mind – that of the two of us, alone, eating biscuits on the day of my father's funeral. At the thought, tears welled in my eyes, and I could not look at him. Nor could he look at me, for his eyes, now, were focused upon Vermilion, who still lounged upon the Bed as if he were an artist's model, posing as a God. Daniel stepped forward. Then, surveying my love with a look of contempt, he spoke, with a harshness in his voice that I had never known before.

'You are a fool, sir, not to cower, for your life is in danger.'

'Oh, but sir,' Vermilion replied, 'if I am about to die, I should not like to die in a cowardly posture.'

'Clothe yourself, villain,' one of the ruffian band interrupted, 'before we cut your balls off.'

'Ah, you would make a eunuch of me?' Vermilion said. 'How charming – I have always been desirous of a beautiful voice.'

And at this the man launched forward, about to draw his

sword, but Daniel held up his hand to stop him. I was amazed at Vermilion's foolishness in tempting such a fate, yet impressed at his bravery and good humour in the face of such a threat.

'What makes you so confident, sir, that you will not be harmed by us?'

'It is a confidence born of experience, *sir* – I have never yet been punished for a crime before I have been accused of it. And besides – I trust you would not come here in search of me if you did not know my identity, and, knowing my identity, I am certain you would not dare to injure me.'

Seeing the uncertainty in Daniel's eyes, and in the eyes of our assailants, I was assured that they did not know Vermilion's name. Still, I feared for him.

'You are an accomplice of the Doctor, sir – that much I know. And your crime is most apparent. That of bewitching my sister' (at which word Vermilion turned to me in surprise) 'and of robbing her of her virginity, a prize that did not belong to you.'

'I should have thought it was a prize that did not belong to any man,' Vermilion replied. 'For a woman who is a virgin is possessed of that prize herself. And once it is gone, it belongs to no one, for indeed, it ceases to exist.'

And at this, I heard a little coughing sound, and the Macaroni stepped forward. In spite of my agitation at the circumstances in which we found ourselves, I could not help but stifle a laugh. Although the man (if I can call him that) was not as small as I imagined him, nor indeed as feeble in body, his whole attire being so preposterous (the little hat upon his head, the flowing curls, the white-painted face with little cupid lips upon it), it was not possible that I should take him seriously. Indeed, so pretty was this fellow, that if he had been of the female sex I might have admired his beauty, for his eyes were thin and slanted, his lashes dark and thick. Though his nose, being long with a little tilt at the tip, was not exactly suited to a woman's face, there was a simper about his lips that was almost sensuous. Behind the paint and powder, I thought, might lie an altogether different person. Yet he was obscured behind this mask, just as his natural smell was obscured by the odour that now wafted to my nostrils; a strong perfume, that was, I believe, the purest essence of lily-of-the-valley.

He coughed again, at which Vermilion also coughed (whether in mockery of him, or because the vile perfume caught in his throat, I do not know). And then, the Jessamy spoke.

'Sir,' he said, or rather 'Sa!' for that is how the word came out, so loaded with disdain it was, so cultivated that I thought he spoke another language to the one I had been taught, and if I will spell it out a little oddly, then I hope you will tolerate this, for I believe it is only thus that you will hear the full repulsiveness of his tone.

'Though indid you maay not be in possession of this gal's virginity, I would argyew that yew have most cartainly taaken it from her, for there is no other waay for it to go.'

His bottom lip thrust forward as he spoke, his head was held high as if it pained him to look upon us. There was no doubt, I thought, that this man was the victim of that thing called elocution, for unless he had a speech defect, there could be no other explanation for the strangeness of his voice. His vowels were so clipped as to be near non-existent, and the pitch of the sound was most certainly not akin to the masculine.

'Not so, sir,' came the velvet tones of my love, 'for I would argue that I have not taken this girl's virginity at all.'

'Yew are a liar, then,' the Macaroni replied, 'for wee have seeen the evidence with our own eyes. Yew have taaken that which is rytfully myne.'

At this I felt a chill as my blood ran cold. I could only half grasp the meaning of this; and I saw that Vermilion, also, was taken aback by the Beau's strange words.

'Yours!' he said. 'You say Emilia's virginity belongs to you?'

'Yas indid. At leest, it should have bin mine, for Emeelia is betrowthed to be my wife!'

'That cannot be, sir,' I exclaimed, suddenly, confident now that the ruffians were not about to attack, 'for I am betrothed to Lord Smellie.'

I barely knew why I spoke the words. For I would be betrothed to whatever man my brother chose for me.

'Indid, sweeet plum,' he said to me, 'and I am hee, come to claym you. Though I see now I am too layt.'

No! It simply was not possible. That this perfumed, high-pitched, dandyish man was Smellie. Smellie was covered in boils. He was corpulent, fleshy, stinking. This fop was the very antithesis of the man I had imagined. And yet he was equally repugnant to me.

'You are not Lord Smellie,' I said. I was trembling as I spoke. I was willing it not to be true. I felt my life was over.

'Mai the sun freckle me, if I am not,' he replied.

'You are not Lord Smellie,' I repeated, as if to say it again would make him accept it.

'Mai my clowthes mis-fit me, if I am not,' he said.

'And may my manhood wither if you will take Emilia's virginity!' Vermilion exclaimed suddenly (for still, indeed, his miraculous machine stood erect). 'For it belongs to her, and though no man can take it, she is free to bestow it upon whomever she chooses, and she has chosen me.'

At this point the Thief-taker stood forward, and I saw immediately that he was not the same man that had followed me that morning. He wore a similar dark suit and a red waistcoat, but now I saw that this fellow had a straight back and he was at least a foot taller than the man who followed us. It was another Thief-taker then, a tall and spindly man, with a narrow face and dark eyebrows that seemed to throw a shadow across his other features.

'You speak, sir,' he began, trying hard not to be affected by Vermilion's nakedness, yet clearly uncertain of where he should look, 'of Emilia's virginity as if it were still intact. And yet, it seems to me that you have recently withdrawn from the act of love.'

'If I had not been so rudely interrupted,' Vermilion said, 'I might have had the pleasure of withdrawing.'

'So you have not yet entered her, sir, which explains, perhaps, your . . .'

'Indeed it does.'

'And are you telling me that Emilia here is indeed a maiden still?'

'I am certain that she is, though I am equally certain that she shall not remain so for long.'

I shuddered to hear them speak so, as if I were absent from the room. I saw that Daniel and the Macaroni (I could not call him Smellie, for still that name was associated with the man I had imagined) also seemed uneasy, as did the other fellows. Indeed, all of us were somehow diminished by Vermilion's nakedness. He seemed to wield his phallus as a banner before us, and as he was not shamed by it, so we, also, were forced to honour its potency. Only the Thief-taker was not stunned, now, into silence.

'How should we believe you, sir, for Emilia here has been in this place for at least a week. Are you to tell me she has not yet been defiled? That we were lucky enough to arrive at the very moment when you were about to deflower her?'

'I will not answer your question if you do not call me by my name. I am tired of being "sir'ed" and would prefer to be called Lord Vermilion.'

At this I sensed the man's immediate discomfiture. Indeed, I watched as even the bearded fellows began to shuffle their feet somewhat and glance nervously at one another. The Macaroni Smellie, however, stepped forward. Waving his hand in an elaborate manner, he bowed before Vermilion and spoke once more.

'I see yew are a gentleman indid, sir,' he said, 'and as such I see I must treet yew as my equal. Yet tho I may no longer proceed with such crude meens as I had devysed to haysten your death, do not dowt that I *will* be revenged upon yew.'

I watched as Vermilion's eyes opened wide with laughter. When he spoke it was with tremendous irony and a mimicking of the Macaroni manners and voice.

'Oh Lord Smellay, I cower before you and beg that you will forgive me! For such a man as yew is graytly to be feared. Indid, I see that enaawmas sword which hangs so gallantly by your syde is impatient to be drawn, and if you should challenge me, then I do not doubt that I shall not long be for this earth.'

A sneer crossed Smellie's face as he listened, but I was surprised to find that he had courage enough to continue speaking, though his voice was as ridiculous as ever.

'If Emeelia here has indid been deflowered by that monstrous appendage of yaws, Lord Vermilion, then I have no desire to challenge yew, for she is now as a warthless daynty and my revenge has nought to do with honour. How can yew offend my honour thus, for if she gaave herself freeely, she is no maw than a slut' (at which I winced, and was so full of confusion that I wished I might sink so deep into the Celestial sheets that I might never more be seen) 'and if yew raped her, it is for her brother, here, to defend her. No, my revenge will be more subtle than yew suspect, my Lord.'

'If I have not offended your honour, sir, then I ask you – what is my crime that has so angered you? It seems to me your honour has indeed been offended, yet as you fear a duel, you would find other accusations.'

'That is not sew, Lord Vermilion. I assure yew.'

And yet his voice was full of uncertainty.

'No matter,' said Vermilion, 'for I do not wish to quibble over your cowardice. But, now that I am called by my name, I will answer the question posed by your friend here, in the pretty red waistcoat. Perhaps you have forgotten? He asked if you and your piffling mobsters might have "happened" to arrive at the very moment when I was about to deflower this maiden.'

'I remember the question well, Lord Vermilion, but we are alreaday apprysed of the answer.'

'Are we indeed?' Vermilion replied. 'I tell you, you are wrong. Here, before you' (and he flourishes his arm towards me) 'lies a virgin, sweet and pure. Emilia Beaumont is a maid. Her bud is not yet broken.'

At this there was wonder and amazement on all their faces. The men peered forward to look at me as if they might find the signs of my purity engraved upon my features, and, seeing my discomfiture, realizing suddenly that Vermilion might be speaking the truth, Daniel turned to the Thief-taker.

'I wish you to dismiss your men. I no longer require their services today. Please. Be hasty about it. We will conclude this business alone.'

Quickly, his will was achieved. Only myself, Vermilion, Daniel, Smellie and the Thief-taker remained in the room.

'I am sorry, Daniel,' Smellie said once they were gone. 'I cannot beleeve this story. My business here is ohver. If it is trew your sister has been kidnapped and mis-yewsed by this fellow, then I wish yew luck in avenging yawself. But it is no business of myne. I cannot marry a fallen woman.'

'Look at her!' Vermilion said, suddenly, and I was surprised to see him subscribing to this ridiculous idea that one could see innocence in a woman's eyes. 'She is unsullied. Can you not see it? She is the paragon of virtue. Or perhaps you would prefer for me to prove it to you?'

'Do you have proof?'

'Why no, Lord Smellie, I do not "have" proof, yet I can give it to you.'

'How can yew give that which yew do not have?'

'The proof of the pudding is in the eating.'

And at that I hated him, more than ever. All of them, these men who thought that they could discuss my virginity as if it were a thing to be divided up and shared out amongst them.

'What is your meaning, Lord Vermilion?' Daniel said.

'I mean that as you clearly do not believe me, as you are so certain that she is already defiled, then it would not be harmful to her for me to enter her now. Look! I am ready! I have been ready these last ten minutes. My tool of pleasure is aching for her.'

'You may do as you pleese with her,' Smellie said. 'As for myself – I am owrff. I have had enough of this business and I am tired of the sight of your useless tool.'

'Oh no, sir,' said Vermilion. 'Not useless. Stay! Watch the spectacle. Have you never seen a maiden deflowered? Perhaps

177

you are virginal yourself, Lord Smellie. With such a name as that, I would suppose it difficult to entice the ladies.'

'I will not staay to be insulted.'

'Nor will you be, sir. From this moment I promise I will behave most like the gentleman I am. If you will stay and watch me break her hymen. If you will stay and watch the blood flow and stain these virginal sheets, which will be proof enough, I think, even for yourself.'

At this, you can imagine, I was so distraught, I did not know what I should do. I despised them all; they made me feel like an animal, cringing before them. I could not believe that Vermilion would do this to me; yet his cruelty had already increased to such an extent that I realized I did not know him at all. I wanted to run from the room, yet I knew that they would stop me. I wanted to speak out. Yet I knew that they would not hear me.

'I still do not believe yew, Lord Vermilion. Yew are bluffing me.'

'No – I tell you – I am not! Stay, and watch. You will see the proof. It will not take longer than a few seconds. I need not achieve my satisfaction for you to see this. Now. I will prove you wrong.'

And he moved towards me, gently taking hold of my shoulders and pushing me down, again, upon the Bed.

'Sweet Emilia,' he said. 'I am sorry to have to do this, but you see – Lord Smellie doubts my word. Be brave, Emilia. Stop crying, my love. Stop your sobbing. It pains me to hear it. Remember – once I have broken your bud, you will be forever mine. Is that not your desire? To avoid the fate of becoming this man's wife?'

And then, finally, I found my tongue and broke free from Vermilion's grip.

'I wish for nothing, sir! I wish that I had never laid eyes on you – or you, or you, or you. Yes, Daniel, for you also are guilty of a terrible crime. I loved you, brother, but you have betrayed my love. And you also, Vermilion – you have betrayed me. I wish to be no man's wife. Nor no man's whore neither. I have a gift here – my virginity – which, it is true, can belong to none of you. So will I not give it, for what value has a gift without substance? I wish to keep it, for myself. I wish you all gone from here, and I wish to remain pure. Alone. Were it not for the kindness that the Doctor has shown me, I would say that I despise the masculine sex. Yet he *has* been kind to me, and I wish to remain here, in his Temple. As his Angel. His pure and virtuous Angel. Can you not leave me here? All of you? Will you not leave me?'

I do not know whence these words did spring. Like a hidden stream, they surfaced suddenly. And their power, I found, was greater than any action of Vermilion's. For a moment, all of them were silenced. Even Vermilion's manhood began to wither. Then Daniel spoke, softly now.

'Tell me truly, Emilia. Are you a maid still?'

'Brother, I am.'

'You would not lie to me?'

'What use would there be in lying? For I can tell, by the smile on your face, that you are still planning to marry me to this Smellie man. And I would like nothing better than to tell you I am deflowered and therefore worthless to him.'

At which Daniel turned to Smellie and said,

'Do not trouble yourself with her shrewishness. She will be easily tamed.' And Smellie replied, a grin spreading across his white face,

'Heavens be praysed! I beleeve it to be trew! I shall have my wyfe!'

And Vermilion, dressing himself now, pulling his breeches over his thighs, interjected.

'She shall be no wife of yours! Emilia is all mine, and you offend *my* honour to suggest otherwise. I challenge you, sir, to a duel.'

The very words, I saw, struck my would-be husband with shock. One needed only to look at him to know he would not survive one minute against Vermilion, yet, should he refuse, he would be labelled a coward.

'A duel?' he said. 'What is the meening of this?'

'The meaning is quite clear. Each of us claims the right to

179

Emilia's hymen. You interrupted my pleasure, sir. But I intend
to have her. And you will not stop me.'

'I am betrowthed to marry her.'

'And yet you will not. For I say that we will fight. And he
that survives will have her hymen.'

'Yew cannot do this, Lord Vermilion. Yew have no rite to it.'

'Nor you, for you have heard the lady speak. She will not
give it to either of us. Yet I have faith enough to believe that
she will change her mind. And so I think it a thing worth
fighting for.'

'I have not offended yaw honour, Sa.'

'No – you have offended the lady's. And I challenge you on
her behalf.'

Smellie seemed to consider this, before speaking again. They
stood, facing one another, Vermilion in loose shirt and breeches,
a boot in his hand, Smellie in daffodil suit, laced with gold.

'I am sorry, Sa. I cannot accept this challenge. Indid I wonder
whether yew are the gentleman yew say yew are, for yew do not
follow the "code duello".'

'To hell with that, man.'

'I say there will be no damning the code.'

'So you would I would write down my challenge and send it
by way of a second?'

'Ah – wanders! He is a gentleman indid!'

'And will you trust me, sir, until that time, not to change
my mind? With this sweet temptation laid out before me' (he
waved his hand across my body) 'do you not think I might
regret my decision to fight for her that can be mine without
it.'

Smellie seemed to consider this, weighing his desire for me
and his determination not to prove a coward against his fear for
his life. I saw a kind of flicker in his pretty eyes, a sinister smile
upon his cherry lips.

'The hymen is the pryze, you say?'

Perhaps he realized that he could have it no other way.

'Indeed,' Vermilion replied.

'And I am free to choose the weapon?'

Hesitation, quicker than the blink of an eyelid, flitted across Vermilion's face.

'Of course,' he said. 'Let the weapon be what you will. You know, as the offender, it is your choice.'

And Smellie beamed then, for the first time, revealing white-painted teeth. He was like a doll, I realized, a terrifying marionette.

'Then let it be pystols,' Smellie said.

'Excellent, and it is for you to choose the place also.'

'Yes. Yes, of course.'

'Only let it not be Covent Garden. I am tired of watching duels in that place.'

'And I am tired of Putney Common, which is indid a common spot.'

'Yes, indeed,' Vermilion said, 'on that point I am inclined to agree with you, Lord Smellie. And if you are to die, sir, I would not wish so unseemly a setting upon you.'

'Nor I, yew, sir. I should wish you to die in a pleasanter locaytion. I can think of no better plaice than Primrose Hill, for the prospect of the Marylebone farms is indid pleesing to behold. And let it be at dawn. Yes, death at sunryse would indid be pleesing.'

'At dawn then. I will be there,' said Vermilion. 'Tell me — who shall be your second?'

At this Smellie turned to Daniel, who turned quite pale, and nodded slowly.

'Myne will be Daniel, here. It is ownly fitting. And yaws?'

I did not listen for Vermilion's response, for the particulars of the battle meant nothing to me. Even my own fears suddenly seemed to fade as I saw the terror on Daniel's face. I saw the delicacy of his ruddy cheeks, the gentle, gentle flesh upon him. This was my brother. I realized now that no matter how he had betrayed me, Daniel was all that remained of my blood. The only remnant of the mother that I had killed.

And I knew he would not have the courage to stop it. No man did, it seemed. And I could say nothing. Not now. Though I knew that I must stop it, was certain that if I did not, something terrible would happen, again I could not speak. I had been numbed by their cruelty.

'You cannot have Daniel! Have you forgotten the "code"?' Vermilion's words pierced my reverie.

'To be sure – the man who is yaw second, must be yaw equal in rank.'

At which both Daniel and I breathed a sigh of relief.

'Yew have already flowted the code, Vermilion. So may not I also flout it? I can theenk of no person fitter than Daniel, for he, too, has a stayke in the hymen. What will he gayn if Emeelia were to continue her relaytions with yew, who do not offer your hand, ownly your tool! With me, Emeelia will gain a title. She will be my Lady Smellay, and her brother will be assured that his farther's will has been obeyed.'

Lady Smellie! The very words chilled me. Corruption and decay of my beauty!

'No, no!' Vermilion said. 'I will not have a man who is not a nobleman involved in this dispute. And certainly not if he is Emilia's brother. For our seconds should be neutral parties. I cannot see Daniel effecting a reconciliation between us. Choose another, Lord Smellie.'

I ceased to listen then, exhausted by their banter, barely able to believe that they continued to debate the matter thus. To them, I was a hollow vessel, containing nothing but a thin membrane which prevented them entering. They would die, not for the pleasure of discovering nothing, nor because they loved me. Simply, they were greedy for destruction. Each would be the one to break the membrane; to have the pleasure of causing pain. And I, being empty, could not speak against them. I, being empty, could only wait.

23

VERMILION

READER, THIS IS only the beginning of my cruelty. I must tell you this now, for there is more, and it will pain you (if you are not a villain also) to hear it. If, till this point, you have been a friend of mine, can I blame you if you do not wish to travel further with me? If you wish to be alone with Emilia's diaries, without interruption from the villain who is the cause of her distress?

I feel as if I have set a thing in motion. By opening these diaries once again – divesting them of their silken robes, which hang now, about my chamber, fragments of her presence – I feel that I have started something: a necessary process. For it is not just Emilia who speaks to me now, but Helena also. She has been here near a week, and I have been unable to tell her to leave. She lives quietly, after all. Her nose is buried in a book half the day, and she demands nothing of me. I sense that, like Emilia, she merely waits for events to unfold. When I see her, wandering in the gardens, or at the dining table, I sense a kind of serenity about her that was not a part of her when first she arrived here. She is calm, as if she believes that all will be well, and in my current state of agitation this is solace indeed.

Yet do not believe that Helena is silent. No – when she does speak, she forces thoughts upon me which I would rather have avoided. And when this happens I rail against her, detesting her for her intrusion. Yet afterwards, always, a strange thing happens. I am soothed by my memories.

Now, I feel, we are in the process of restoration. I am learning patience, and I have found that there is much virtue in faith. In this short space of seven days I have come to trust the lady who once had been my greatest foe. For when I watch her, carefully, I find that I experience sudden moments of illumination, when an event from my past (an event I have erased from memory) is laid bare before my eyes. And there I see it in its entirety. I see the horror of it.

I cannot say, you understand, what exactly is the value of all this. To face my own crimes is hardly a pleasurable experience. Yet I know, I feel, something strange is in the air. I feel charged with a sense of expectation; suffused with a sure knowledge that something is about to happen which will change everything. It is that smile I see upon the face of our Peacock: all-knowing; all-seeing. Yes, she sees more than I, and I cannot help but trust her vision.

What is it, then, you will ask, about this woman, that has set this Vermilion talking thus? Only a week ago he was railing against her and her over-bred manners. Was he mistaken?

I see now that I must tell the truth. Though it pains me to do so (it is not my nature, you understand – I am composed of dishonesty) I will speak justly of her. I will tell you what I know. Yes, I see that in my writing of this history I have, in a sense, played into Helena's hands. She is, you understand, a woman who loves to shroud herself in mystery. She does not wish to be known, or indeed to be understood. And yet I tell you, it is impossible to live under such pretences. Always one must reveal oneself to at least one other person. One must unburden one's woes; one's failings. Otherwise, one would most certainly go mad.

Yet though I have been, in the past, this 'other person' in Helena's life, her confidant whom she trusted above all others, I have chosen, until now, to portray her in the very way she would desire. It is true, I have at times attempted to explain her apparent impenetrable character by suggesting that there is nothing to her but the surface glitter. This I have done in spite, for if one so handsome as she does not dare to show her true thoughts and feelings, then either her sumptuous exterior is expressive of an inner depth or she has spent her life cultivating that haughty, elegant look, and the character has suffered as a consequence. I have encouraged you to think the latter, yet I believe that I have failed and it is possible that you do indeed think her full of mystery and glamour. But I will tell you all I know of her, and only then, perhaps, will you see her relevance to our tale. Only then will you appreciate the significance of her presence here.

Think of a child then, who, as soon as she began to walk, was put in stays: a tiny thing, no more than a year old, all laced up in a little whalebone corset. This was the young Helena Ashfield, a charming child, born into an idle, wealthy family. From the start, however, her father was jealous of the child, perhaps because her jet black hair and tawny skin suggested that she could be no offspring of his. There is no evidence, of course, to suggest that Helena was illegitimate, yet the fact remains – there had never, before this time, been a dark child born into the Ashfield family. Both the mother and the father came from families where fairness (both of hair and of skin) was a particular trait. Imagine the confusion when the tiny Helena emerged: a screaming little darkie, her head bruised from the forceps, her eyes like little fragments of coal.

It was Helena's father who insisted on the stays. If he had indeed produced such a moonchild as this, then he would do his best to ensure that she learn such manners and well-breeding as would befit an Ashfield. No matter how hard his little girl would scream as she was laced into the stays each day, he would not pity her, nor would he be moved by the pleas of his wife. There were many, he insisted, who followed this custom, and his daughter would later thank him for it, for what perfect deportment she would have; what a joy would her straightness be to look upon! And if, as her mother said, she appeared more of a cripple than a child (so that when she walked, it seemed as if her body were made of wood), then as an adult, she would walk with more grace than any other woman alive.

The effects of these restrictions on the child, however, soon became evident. As movement caused her such pain, she preferred to remain still. By the time she was four years old, she had learned that the most comfortable way of spending the day was to arrange herself on the nursery floor in such a way that the chafing of the stays was minimized, and to stay there throughout the day. Only at night did Helena find relief from her pain. Then, her mother would remove the whalebones and bathe her child. The little Helena luxuriated in a tub of warm milk. Her limbs were free, suffused with pleasure, and her nostrils breathed in the thick, sweet odour that reminded her of being at the breast; the time before she was encased in corsets.

As she grew older, Helena learned how to walk without causing pain to herself. By never moving a muscle in her back, her sides or her neck; moving the legs only but keeping the rest rigid, she was able to move. Seeing how handsome she was growing, her father began to love her rather more. He continued to instil perfect manners in his child, however, so that she would be well prepared for the time when she entered society. At the table, for example, he said that she must never eat too quickly nor too slowly, for the one would show she was too hungry and the other that she did not like the food. Before long she was apprised of such perfect manners that she never spoke a word out of place, nor did her physical presence ever offend, for she was always in the place where she ought to be, always dressed in a fitting manner, and always wearing the correct expression on her face. Each day she became less of a child and more of a miniature adult.

Yet throughout all, the young Helena had one pleasure which kept her strong: her relationship with her mother, which was renewed, each night, when her mother bathed her. She was able to wallow in warm liquid and be soothed by stories of other lives. Never had Helena felt so close to another human being as she felt to her mother. Never had she felt so totally accepted for what she was.

Yet is anything ever what we desire it to be? Is ever our trust deserved? I, Vermilion, say it cannot be. For when Helena Ashfield was only nine years old, she discovered the truth behind this nightly ritual and after that she refused to be bathed and she never loved her mother more.

What happened was this. One night, when Helena emerged

from the soothing milk, little white drips flowing down her body, she caught her mother turning to wipe away a tear.

'What is it, Mama?' she asked.

And when her mother failed to reply, Helena urged her once again.

'Please, Mama. What is the matter?'

And unable to contain her private grief, the mother eventually gave in to her child. Not thinking how her words might affect the girl, she spoke something like this:

'It is the milk, Helena. It has not worked.'

'I love the milk, Mama. What do you mean?'

'Not like she said. Then I am indeed to blame.'

'What is it, Mammy? What is the matter?'

'I have not told you about the wise woman.'

'The wise woman?'

'Yes. She said that I should bathe you in milk, each evening.'

The child nodded, pleased to hear this story.

'She said I must be patient. There would be no effect for many years. But by the time that you were eight years old, the milk would make you fair. If I were an innocent woman, the milk would turn you fair.'

And at these words, the black hairs on Helena's neck began to bristle. The jet stones that were her eyes began to spark. Unlike her mother, she was no fool and she saw, instantly, the meaning of this. All those nights when she had thought the baths were a healing balsam that was meant to comfort her! Yet the ritual had been nothing more than a little attempted white magic. Her mother had wanted to blanch her.

After that, Helena Ashfield leaned towards neither mother nor father for support. Though her father dictated the shape of her life, her education, her pastimes, and Helena was outwardly obedient to these restrictions, she began to lead a life quite separate from her own. By this, I mean that though she was trained to be all that a woman should be (namely a most splendid and attractive servant to the man she might marry), she led an inner life of great richness. Or at least, this is what she told me, though still I cannot believe it entirely to be true. For it is evident that, in such circumstances, one must surely wish to escape the confines of one's life, and if it is not possible to run away (for a young girl, alone, must surely perish or else turn to a life of sin) then one must retreat to a place of safety, and such a refuge is the mind.

I speak in riddles? Yes, I see you are confused by my rambling. Is there, or is there not, you ask, more to her than meets the eye? And the answer is, 'of course'. For if the Peacock Lady, when she was young, was not the complex and fascinating character that she desired to be, there is no doubt that she was shaped by her experiences, both then, and since. Indeed, of late I find she has become quite the intellectual, reading works by the likes of the wanton Wollstonecraft, as well as the admirable Burke and (there is no accounting for taste) the revolution-monger Paine. She is, it seems, fascinated by the revolution in France, yet she senses my reluctance to speak on the subject, and, I am glad, no longer pesters me with questions. Perhaps, wrongly, she believes that I will tell all, if only she waits long enough.

But I rush ahead, and should return to my tale. At the time that I met Helena, she was twenty-seven years of age. She had been married for several years to the haughty Lord Quinton, a shell of a man, old enough to be her father. Indeed, this hapless marriage, in which she had no choice, was in a sense the very occasion of our meeting, for had she married a virile, younger man, full of the luminous principle of life, she might have found happiness. She might have dropped her curious façade and become such a dull and satiated creature that she would have no place in our story. Instead, however, the new Lady Quinton suffered herself to be mounted by this man half in the grave. This is not a scene that I care to imagine. It is not my memory after all. Just my imagination. Inflamed because I have ploughed the same furrow as he.

Had you not guessed? Gentlemen, you disappoint me! I had thought it was quite clear that a rake of my quality would not have let this gem pass me by. Why, she was a most obvious target for my arrow (how sweetly Emilia phrases these matters –

I cannot help but imitate her). 'What was she like?' I hear you ask. 'Did she writhe and scream?' 'Or was she still and straight, like a twig beneath you? Were you afraid that she should snap?'

Friends – I will tell you nothing. What purpose would it serve to tell you this, except to further excite your swelling members? Do I need to remind you of the purpose of my tale? Emilia's tale, I should say. I have no wish for needless diversions which will do nothing more than animate your lust. Suffice to say that she went to it like a veritable goat. Once I fell upon her breast, she was somehow released from imaginary stays, becoming again the child in the milk-bath. Her limbs were freed, and with them her tongue. I tell you, she had a touching line in obscenities which she would whisper in my ear. Think of it. Darkness all around. Her husband is away, but she has house guests and they sleep in adjacent rooms. You go to it silently, knowing that at any movement they might wake and discover your pleasure. The window of the room is open, blowing a soft breeze across the bed. But you scarcely notice it. You are burning beneath the sheets. You had not dared hope she would give in to you again, but there she is, naked beneath you. Your tongues are serpents, entwined. At such a time, she will do anything for you Gentlemen. I tell you, anything. Because your breath can scald her. Because your tongue can set her soul on fire. Because in those moments, when she is beneath you, when she is so full of you she thinks she will die when you withdraw from her, being left so empty and so hollow that her whole life will seem a void – in those moments she is possessed by you. Not just your prick, but your very essence has penetrated her. She is suffused with your odour. Your image is so engraved upon her mind, that she cannot think of spending another night without you. And yet you know that this will be the last. Even as you withdraw from her, sensing suddenly the moon, piercing the darkness, and seeing her face, briefly illumined, so pale and knowing, you might think she was possessed – even then, you know that you will never have her again. This is the end of it.

Yes, that is how I remember it; the last time I shared Helena's bed. It was just before I returned to the Temple, ready to seduce

Emilia. And though I admit I was quite taken with the Bird, how could I give her what she desired when I knew that her only wish was to desert her husband and to spend her life with me? How could any woman expect this of me? I am, by nature, a rambler. I will roam wherever I please, and if the Bird will always love me, then that is her fault and not my own. Did I say that I would give her my heart? No! I promised only pleasure. And that she had in great abundance. More variety of love has no woman ever had. We first touched in a garden, beneath the stars; we made love in the room by the rotunda; we fucked upon a staircase, and we dined together when she was sad. Could she have asked for more? And if we are so formal now together, is it my fault? Can she not accept it?

Enough. I said I would tell you nothing of this and once again I find my old self will resurface and brag of his conquests. You see, of course, the implications of my words. The reason for our initial coolness when first we met again. Perhaps you also wonder whether I have some connection with Lady Quinton's bastard son? Is it not most evident? The Lady Quinton is not a promiscuous woman. Having spent some time testing the Doctor's fertility treatments (Aetherial Balsam and the like, cold water and a diet devoid of meat), is it surprising that she should listen to the Doctor's most ardent pupil, one Vermilion?

I promised her that it was her husband who was faulty. If she had not conceived, there was no doubt it was because he was shrivelled and dried. There were no vital liquids left in him to animate her ovaria. And even if he should, one day, by chance impregnate her, he would plant a seed so unworthy of her soil that if it should grow it would surely wither before it came to full maturity.

Yet there was another option. If she would produce an heir that her husband would think worthy of the Quinton name, she could do much worse than to copulate with a man such as myself. One such as I, a nobleman, in the bloom of youth, might make a fine father for a child, and I knew of one, a friend of mine, who would most certainly fit the bill and would doubtless plant an astonishing seed. It did not take her long to suggest that as she had not seen my friend, and was in every sense a stranger to him, would it not be better (if I had no objections) that I should do the job myself?

All this, my friends, passed shortly after the opening of the Doctor's Temple, when Emilia was no more than a shadow at an Adelphi window. Yes, whilst she, with her mirrors turned to the walls, gazed down upon the spectacle of the Doctor's guests, I was already entangled in the life of Lady Quinton. It was not an easy affair, I grant you that. We could not chance too many meetings, for Lord Quinton was a jealous man and did not like to have her long out of his sight. Many of our conversations took place in the shadows on the platform where first I seduced Emilia, whispering, so that neither the Doctor nor his guests might hear us arranging our next rendezvous. And so that we might not be discovered, Helena continued to consult the Doctor on the matter of her barrenness.

The time came, however, when I had had enough of her. I had discovered more about this lady in the space of a few months than ever had been revealed to me by one of her sex before. Indeed, it could be said that I had come to know her too well. I had been a lover of her mystery; the secrets that she seemed to hold. But now I had devoured them all. I knew of the stays, the blanching baths, the humping husband, and the desperate desire for a child (for without one, what kind of a woman, what kind of a wife, was she?). Now they were revealed, she no longer held any fascination for me. I knew her vanity, her moods, her miraculous manners. I knew her wit (which grew with our acquaintance) and I knew that, unlike other women, she had an ability to sting me. A woman who has suffered, as she has, cannot help but acquire a caustic tongue. And I was certain that very soon I would be its object. For I was on the point of abandoning her. I had met a new creature who had recently entered the Doctor's establishment. One Emilia Anne Beaumont. Hebe Vestina. A Goddess. And, moreover, a virgin.

What, then, was I to do? It is easy to jilt a woman when one has only fucked her once or twice, but having *known* that woman, promised her a child, even, what *can* be done? And yet I found there were no real difficulties. For Helena knew me well. That very evening when first she met Emilia, she did not doubt what the consequence of her presence here would be. She knew Vermilion for the rake he was, and anticipated her own demise. Yet my Peacock is a charming bird. She would not accept simple rejection. She would pretend that jealousy was not in her nature. In order to keep her Vermilion, she would love Emilia.

And that is how it happened that the Lady Quinton taunted me into seducing Emilia, there, in the Temple, before her very eyes. In her opinion it was inevitable that I should deflower our Vestina, and so her one desire was that she should not appear an obstacle to it, for, if she did, she knew that I would leave her. No, she would be my accomplice in this (she thought) and in everything.

'Come, Vermilion,' she whispered, before I even introduced them. 'I'll vow you cannot get your head beneath her skirt.'

Then, the moment before Emilia arrived, once I had accepted her challenge:

'And I'll vow you will not be heartless enough to scorn her afterwards!'

'I'll scorn her for a week,' I replied, 'but still I will have her.'

And so, you see, it is not I, alone, that was to blame for Emilia's harsh introduction to the world of men. It was your beloved Peacock (yes, I know you did not suspect it of her). She is not such a friend to Emilia as you might have anticipated. She had suffered so much herself, she wanted to watch the symptoms in another. But how to do so without encouraging suspicion? Would not Emilia guess Vermilion's game? No – the friendship would be the very thing that would disguise our passion. And how to build the friendship? Why – to play the martyr! To talk of her suffering in such terms that Emilia would be overcome with pity. To speak of her barrenness with such a degree of regret and dismay that Emilia would feel an instant duty to soothe her, calm her, bind herself forever to this woman, who is, in fact, her darkest enemy.

Yet by the time that Helena reached the point of confessing

her barrenness to Emilia, it was already too late for her. I loved her no longer. Still, she had her week of gloating. Whilst her husband was away, and she was left to entertain a party of guests, I was invited to her house. Why should I not be there, after all? To divert the young ladies of the company and to charm their fathers with my quicksilver tongue. I was most welcome, especially at night, when the servants had retired to their chambers, and I crept across the passageway, bathed in a pale blue light. And I knew, each night I knew, that soon it would be the last. I knew there was another fruit, waiting for me in the Temple. Ripening in my absence.

Yes, and though I did not know it, I had, at this time, already completed my office. Emilia told me, of course, with the greatest pity, of the Bird's longing for a child, of the years she had suffered, being sterile; empty. And it could be true that when she said these things to Emilia she was not aware of the lie. Yet it *was* an untruth. There, within her, as she befriended my new lover, was the grain of a child. *My* child. A little embryo, growing within her, curled like a fern within her womb.

But I did not know it. In fact, the idea of seeing Helena's stomach swell and distend was quite abominable. There could be nothing worse than seeing a son of mine born to a woman I did not love. Nothing worse than seeing that son become the son of Lord Quinton, who apart from his decrepitude was also, I had recently discovered, a Catholic. *My* son, I thought, would grow up a Papist. No – it was too horrible.

And now, you ask – what is my opinion of my son? No matter. Suffice to say I do not love him, nor he me. There are times, of course, when I contemplate the matter: melancholy times, when I imagine how it would be to have a son, now that I am alone. Would it have changed me? Made me less bitter? What kind of father would I have been to him? No father at all, I think is the reply, for I cannot imagine forsaking my time in France for a mere child. No, from what I have heard, the twelve-year-old Marcus Quinton is a spiteful brat, who adored his decaying would-be father and now heartily mourns his loss.

It seems then, in these matters, that blood is of no consequence. For if it were; if it suffused our bodies in such a way that we were constantly reminded of our origins, then he would shed no tears for a man who is nothing but a surrogate. He would wonder what it was that prevented his grief, and, in examining his heart, he would find his father to be false. He would be drawn towards me.

Yet this is fantasy all. And I will not waste more time with talk of him. No, my thoughts have wandered on too far already. So far that I have not yet told you of my latest conversations with the Peacock. Of how this history unfolds, each day, revealing truths that I have hidden from myself. Yes, the very fact that I have mentioned the name Marcus, and called him my child – that is a proof of how things are changing.

But enough of this. There will be time to tell you of our talk. But I know you must be impatient. It is not talk that you desire, I can tell. It is action. For compared to the past, the days in the Temple, the present is a dull place to be. Indeed, we barely live in it. Our existence here is nothing but a shadow world. We have no weight. We are merely images from the past, I think. Lost souls who long to find their way back to their origins. We live in a kind of dream world where little exists beyond our minds, which hanker back to that place where our thoughts, our longings, could be corporeal. Yes, perhaps Helena's presence here is simply a part of my dream. She is the agent who will guide me through the labyrinths of my memories, uncovering all that we pass by.

So now, if I may choose the direction of my dream, I will be guided to Primrose Hill. Come Helena, strange spirit – show me the way! Never a day passes when the images of that morning do not flit through my mind. The first day of February, in the year of 1780. Yet the images are vague. It was so long ago. I was so young then. A different Vermilion to the gouty creature that I have become. I wish to remember myself as I was. For my wiser self not to intrude. Only then will I remember the horror of it. Only then might I see clearly. Come – let us travel together! Let the duel begin!

24

VERMILION

ON THE TOP of Primrose Hill, I await my rival. It is still quite dark, and the sky swirls above me. Huge, aery clouds, tinged pale by the crescent moon. A few yards away from me, my second, Lord Herbert, is checking the pistols. He is a man of experience; one whose friendship I do not doubt. I would trust him with my life.

Yet he knows I do not want him near me now. Now is a quiet time. I had desired to get here early, simply to savour the break of day. It is that still, blue time of morning and the world sleeps below. Yes, as I sit here, upon a jutting stone, I breathe the sweetness of the air, and am overcome by it. And by the chill in my throat, the scent of the dew upon the grass. By the sound of birds, just beginning to sing.

I tell you – never have I, Vermilion, known such a sentiment as this. To sit, completely still, watching the hues of the heavens begin to change. I feel a strange up-beating of my heart, as if a butterfly flutters in my chest. Yes, I am near sick with it, short of breath and giddy; I cannot possibly describe it to you. Soft! Listen. Do you hear that soft sound? I swear it is a nightingale singing. Yet there is none here to hear it. Only my friend, Benjamin Herbert, who seems barely aware of it and hums a little ditty to himself as he polishes the guns. Can he not feel it too? My throat constricts with love for the world; for all the day-breaks I have missed. For all I may not see again.

I dismiss the thought instantly. Surely it is not fear that makes me feel thus? How can I be afraid of one such as Lord Smellie? A Tulip like him? How could he ever harm me? It is not possible. And if I do not know my pistols as well as I ought, I feel certain that I know them better than he knows his. I try not to think too much on this point, for it is a well-known fact that duelling pistols do not shoot straight. At twelve yards they will lose at least a half an inch in accuracy, at fourteen, at least an inch. A clever fellow will test his guns beforehand; will take a target, and with his gun in a vice, determine the level of inaccuracy. Indeed, some men have made an art of pistolry – it is said that the admirable Lord Darkman and his near neighbour Viscount Swaby have schooled themselves so well in this that none dare challenge them. They have hair-triggered pistols for speed of shot, and various other fancy refinements such as hydraulic barrel testers and the like, the purposes of which are a mystery to me.

It seems preposterous to think upon such things now, as London begins to unfold beneath me. And yet I cannot help myself, for I am full of regret that I have never taken time to know my pistols better. Indeed, if truth be told, I do not know my pistols at all, and it is only a sense of my own superiority that convinces me that I will win this duel. I have a steady hand, at least, whereas I imagine Smellie will be shaking so much that he will shoot far wide, missing my body completely. Or he will misfire, or overload his pistol. It is not possible that he will kill me.

And, it is true, I have no wish to kill him either, for he is a harmless piece of frippery. I only desire to teach him a lesson. To show him that a fop cannot hope to marry a woman such as Emilia. To revenge myself on him, for interrupting my pleasure.

Why is it then that carnal pleasure seems, in this instant, to have no meaning? What seems important to me now is solitude; is the feeling I have now, within my breast, of love for the morning; wonder at the way the sky above has paled, and the sun which has not yet emerged illumines the horizon with shades of lilac and lightest yellow.

Soon the first rays will reach out across the metropolis, lighting spires and domes, bridges and fields. Is it simply the presence of death that makes these things remarkable? Things that I have never viewed with particular wonder. Or is it just the morning? And Primrose Hill, which I have always thought of as a magical place. Some spell is upon me; that is how it seems. Though logic tells me I am in no danger, I am suddenly convinced that I will die today. This beauty is a revelation to me. Tomorrow, the sun will rise again, but I will not see it. Another man, awaiting another duel, may sit here, and he will breathe the air of a morning that is suffused with my absence. He will hear the humming of his friend, toying with pistol-balls and powder, and he will know, like no other, what I have felt today. There is music in the city: horns blowing in the streets, bells in the churches, percussion in the homes and flutes in the hills. Each note is never to be repeated.

But my time for contemplation is over. Benjamin has jumped up and is pointing down to the foot of the hill.

'Hey, Vermilion! Your Fribble's here.'

I leap up and fill my lungs with grass-scented air. What a sight to behold! There, beneath us, struggles Smellie in all his finery. His little hat comes first, balancing precariously on his superabundance of curls. His face is down, watching his unsteady feet, which I suppose are supported, even now, by silly red heels. But what a suit is this he wears? It is difficult in the dim light to make it out exactly, but as he approaches I see it is of a deep sea-green colour, laced at the front with so many white frills that I swear he is decked out rather for a wedding than his own funeral. He has lace handkerchiefs protruding from his pockets, and large rings upon his fingers which catch the first rays of the sun so that he seems a little magnet for the light.

Only look at him! His shoes slide in the mud so that his white silk stockings are spattered brown. He can barely get a purchase. He is helped, however, by his second, a handsome man to be sure, who takes his hand and leads him slowly upwards, whilst Smellie, short of breath and unaccustomed to such exertion, concentrates on keeping hold of his gold cane.

I turn away. I will not watch him ridicule himself thus. Yes, I have time, instead, for one more glimpse at the morning, the bare hint of blue above, scattered with billowing white clouds. Looking back again, towards Hampstead, I see a thing which startles me. On a distant hill, a white tower seems to catch the first rays of the sun. The folly at Carmine Hall. How small it seems from here. Yet how significant.

I am reminded, suddenly, of a thing I once read about this place.

'Benjamin – there was a prophecy, was there not, about Primrose Hill?'

'Indeed, Vermilion. It was Mother Shipton that said it. Around two hundred years ago.'

'And what did she say?'

'I am not certain that I remember her exact words, but I believe it was this. That when London surrounded Primrose Hill, the streets of the metropolis would run with blood.'

I pause, stilled by his words. What is it that made me think of this? Seeing London all around me? Yet London does not yet surround this hill. It is true that whichever direction I turn in I might see some suburb of the capital. But that is not the same thing surely? No, there are fields about me, not dwellings and churches and dirty streets. There are no great shopkeepers here, no chop-houses. Surely that was her meaning. We are safe here. The prophecy has no relevance today.

And now Smellie has emerged, panting, above the brow of the hill. There can be no turning back, I see that now. Smellie, also, seems reluctant to look at me. He is fiddling with his pocket watch, wishing, perhaps, that time might halt. I cannot imagine what spirit possessed him, that he should come decked out in all his finery. He looks so ill-at-ease here, in his tight breeches and golden trimmings. A man that should never be seen out of doors.

Yet though Smellie and I do not greet one another, our seconds are engaged in conversation. Who *is* that man who plays Lord Smellie's second? I swear I have not seen him before, and yet he looks somewhat familiar. I received a message last evening, giving the name of Viscount Gainsford, but that name means nothing to me. One of his country acquaintances no doubt. I am surprised to see such an apparently level-headed fellow. He has a kind of simper, and is not entirely manly, yet he seems a man of sense. I had almost expected Smellie to bring a second Macaroni.

Any moment now, I expect that Benjamin will bring an apology from my rival, but I shall find some grounds on which to refuse it. I must fight. My reputation depends on it.

Yes, here he comes.

'Vermilion, I have tried all ways to effect a peace. It seems the foolish fellow is determined to fight. Perhaps after the first shot. I feel he needs one attempt, for the sake of his pride. After that, I'll swear he will not take it further. It will not go to two.'

I raise an eyebrow, pretending I feel nothing other than surprise.

'So – is he prepared to die?'

'His second says he has no fears.'

'I cannot promise he will survive the first shot.'

'Of course not.'

'Very good. Are the terms fixed?'

'They are. You will fire from a distance of fourteen yards, and I will signal the moment when you should fire.'

I am not ready. I know I am not ready.

'I am ready. Let us begin.'

Fourteen yards is better than I might have hoped for. At this distance, it is unlikely that a flimsy Beau like Smellie will make a hit. And though I may be less accurate than I had hoped to be, still I should wound him (that is, if my guns are to be trusted). Yet as I watch our seconds loading the guns, how full of regret I am. The sun has risen further now, and though it is partly obscured by cloud, it is too bright to look upon. We are standing in such a way that neither of us will be disadvantaged more than the other by its brightness. If a ball should, by accident, enter my skull, would the image of that sun be imprinted upon my memory? If they dissected me, would they find it there?

'Your pistol, Vermilion.'

'Thank you.'

I imagine myself, how I must appear to the others. Larger,

more muscular, more handsome; my scarlet jacket complementing my visage. How I must fill Smellie with fear. A wind has started up, and my hair blows loose around my face. Emilia! Yes. It is almost too late. I should have thought of her before now! If I lose, she will be smothered by this mockery of a man. And if I win ... No, I cannot think now of conquering her. These thoughts of death have wrought a change in me. I try to remember why I am here – to win her hymen. To break into her flesh. To tear her maidenhead. But those desires have vanished. So many thoughts, so much to contemplate, yet there is no time. My second has his hand in the air and we are ready to fire. The pistol is at my side and once his arm is down, there will be no time to aim. Only to raise the pistol and fire. Otherwise, I may be hit before I myself am able to fire. Go for the frills upon his breast and let the pistol do the rest. Take a breath. No time. Lungs full for the last time? Bright sun. Keep it there. Remember it. NOW!

The sun seems to reel about me. I hear the echo of the shot in my ear and I am on the ground. Sensing the smell of something burning, I put my hand to my head. At my right temple, the hair is singed. Nothing more than that. For a moment my mind was empty, but now I feel again the graze of the pistol-ball against my head. Yes, there is a spot of blood upon my hand, that is all. I have been brushed by the ball. And now I look up, to see, fourteen yards away, a sly smile upon the face of Smellie. Not his usual smile at all, for it is his custom to grin like an ape. No, he seems quite different.

Benjamin is approaching me.

'Are you well, Vermilion?'

This is the worst possible outcome. To fall to the floor when the ball has barely touched me. The duel must continue and he must be hurt.

'No,' I say, as I stand again. 'Not well at all.'

'This should be the end of it. I shall speak to Viscount Gainsford.'

'This will *not* be the end of it, Benjamin. We will shoot again.'

And with this, he walks away, to consult with the Macaroni's second. I am furious. It seems my ball did not even touch him. Yet it was surely chance that he came so close to killing me. The thought chills me. A lucky shot. Yes.

I have never yet seen a fop who knew how to shoot. He is seated now, reclining upon a large cushion which his second carried here for him. What kind of a man is this who needs the comforts of the drawing-room, when he is upon the battlefield? I'll show him the meaning of manhood.

Benjamin has returned.

'I'll swear he had a hair-trigger, Vermilion. It is impossible that he could be so well schooled otherwise. The speed of it was quite astounding. And yet you say he seemed to fear the duel?'

'He quaked in his ribboned shoes, Benjamin! I cannot make sense of it.'

'I have told Viscount Gainsford that you are fit to continue.'

'And what does he say to that?'

'You truly wish to know?'

'I do, indeed.'

'His exact words were, "Then he is a silly ass who deserves to die. The hymen is not worth the price."'

You can imagine how this inflamed me. If I had been possessed of the second pistol, I am certain I would have turned it upon the villain. To offend both Emilia and myself! Instead, I vowed that Smellie would suffer for his second's words.

'How does this Jessamy get such an impudent fellow for his second?'

'Vermilion – he is not worth your scorn.'

'You are right. His words are worth nothing. Come. I am ready for the second shot. Are the pistols loaded?'

Once again I take my place. The pistols are not yet loaded, but I know that simply by striking a pose, I may intimidate my rival. I see him reclining still. The cushion is gold, and fringed, and when I strain my eyes further I see that Lord Smellie is taking no notice of my actions whatsoever. The audacious man is looking into a pocket-glass. Yes – he is preening his curls! He is re-painting his eyebrows! I take a deep breath, swelling my chest in the hope that my presence might strike fear into his heart. I twist my mouth into a sneer. I tauten the muscles in my arms. But he sees nothing.

I remember now those moments before the first shots. My thoughts were of Emilia, and would I leave contemplation of my love till last again?

My love? Did I say those words? It was surely a mistake! For though, to inflame Helena's jealousy, I may have once said such a thing, it is not possible I could truly feel this frivolous sentiment. Yet if it were true? To discover it now, whilst Viscount Gainsford loads the pistol that might blow out my brains! I have no time to think upon the matter. And yet I must.

How can I know? There is no time for this. Now the seconds are through with their work. They are satisfied it is well done. The turquoise-suited one is leaving his cushion, and Benjamin approaches me, pistol in hand. Think only of Emilia, Vermilion. Emilia, Vermilion. Our names are intertwined, and if you do not wound this man, we will be torn asunder. Benjamin reaches me, before Lord Gainsford is with Smellie. I take the pistol, without speaking, and watch Smellie's face, for signs of weakness. Yet he has a handkerchief across it. He is blowing his nose! Viscount Gainsford is with him now – he lifts the gun and . . .

'AAAAAAAAAAAAAAAAAAAAAAAAAAAAAAAAAGH!'

It cannot be! No – I'll not believe it. Chaos has come. Lord Smellie is on the ground, his body shuddering violently, his legs kicking against the ground. Even from this distance I see a red stain, oozing across his turquoise jacket, spreading from the heart. His second is panicking, seems barely to know himself. He has shot his friend!

I rush towards my dying rival, but by the time I am half-way there, Gainsford is upon me. He does not seem in control of his emotions and tries to stop me. He pushes my breast and will not let me approach.

'No! Do not go near him! Do not go near him!'

And in a daze, barely knowing what I do, I allow myself to be commanded by this villain. I stand, stock-still, staring at Lord Smellie as he raises his frost-white face and moves his painted mouth as if to speak. Instead, I see a small trickle of blood, the colour of his lips, spew out from that opening, and his head falls back against the earth.

Benjamin is at his side, staring gravely down and shaking his head. He closes the eyes. There is no need to take a pulse. I can see, even from this distance, that he is dead. I am so full of confusion that all I can do is watch, as the crimson blot spreads out across his chest, like an early blossoming flower, petal upon petal unfolding beneath the February sun.

'An accident!' Lord Gainsford cries, and though his voice is not a Macaroni's voice, still I swear it is akin to such a sound. 'Dear God, it was that trigger-spring! That damned gunsmith. I'll have him imprisoned!'

And Benjamin moves towards him now, taking his shoulders and speaking firmly to him.

'Take it like a man, sir. Take it like a man.'

Yet he cannot.

'My fault. No. It is my fault.'

'There is none to blame in this, sir.'

'I have killed Lord Smellie.'

'He came here to be killed, sir. Does it matter, amongst gentlemen, who pulled the trigger?'

'He would have won the duel, I swear it. Oh, my friend. My friend.'

'Now he has lost the duel. The Gods are just, Gainsford. If you wish, we can make matters simple and say our friend Vermilion shot him.'

'Oh heavens – that would make a liar of me!'

I do not move much closer, yet even here I can see how death transforms us. I never knew this man. I only met him once before today, yet to me, in life, he was nothing more than a jester. How much more dignified does he seem now. His face, more like a man's. It is painted still, but as it is no longer held in fixed expressions, the truth of it shows through. Suddenly I imagine a man of reason behind that face, a different spirit animating it.

And there I might have lain. Inert like him, scarlet on green. How fresh the air is today. How verdant the fields.

'Go, Vermilion.'

It is Benjamin who speaks to me.

'You are in no fit state to remain. Call us a coroner here, and I will do the rest.'

'What shall I say?'

'Why, say that you shot him in a duel.'

'Of course. I will see to it straight.'

And then, realizing that I grasp my pistol still, I point the barrel into the air, and squeeze the trigger hard. As the explosion rings in our ears, I think of Emilia. The hymen is mine now. Mine to break or cherish.

25

VERMILION

GENTLEMEN (AND RECALCITRANT Ladies who have not heeded my warnings), I have received, this morning, a letter, which, I must confess, has quite unnerved me. The past, it seems, is chasing at my heels. Thus, although the letter has no direct bearing on the events of thirteen years ago, I will transcribe it here, for I cannot but think it has some significance. I feel myself, once again, charmed by its author. And yet I should pity him. The madness of his words demands nothing more.

Edinburgh, July 23, 1793

My friend, Vermilion,

Having heard, abroad, that you are once again residing in Carmine Hall, I write with news of the utmost importance to you. I will waste no time on preliminaries for there is little enough time, and my business is the salvation of your soul. Believe me, friend, we live in the days when the measure of British and European iniquity is nearly full. You have seen the atrocities in France, and it will not be long before the people of Albion follow suit. There can be no doubt about it. The Avenging Angel is standing ready to unsheathe his tremendous and irresistible sword. You must be ready for it.

I tell you, Vermilion, I have misled you. Whilst you have been away in France, I have discovered the errors of my ways. I have continued to study medicine and I am convinced that the most wholesome cure for all our ills lies not in the heavens but in the earth, the all-bountiful earth. As for the solar or celestial fire, I mean the electrical, sulphureous, aetherial, fermented-vinous and ardent spiritual fires, which flash from and snatch down to hell, I have made many too bold, sinful and nearly fatal experiments. For electricity is not an element that should be handled by man. It is a

*power, Vermilion, that should only be handled by the most High
God! The eternal Creator, Preserver and supreme and absolute
Ruler of all systems and worlds and beings and things in the
universe. And as you, also, have handled that which belongs to God,
alone, you also must recant. You must reform your life.*

*Vermilion — know that every act of fornication or of amorous
commerce between unmarried persons is expressly forbidden by God
and is a stroke from the hammer of death and condemnation, to
every thing that virtuous and wise human beings ought to cherish
and hold sacred. The frequent use of these pleasures, my friend,
makes the hair fall off, obscures the lustre of the eyes, changes the
florid, lively colour of the face and lips and brings on deafness,
tremors and palsies by weakening the nerves and extinguishing the
heat and dissipating those spirits which animated and cherished those
parts.*

*Know this, also, Vermilion. In your absence, I have been abused.
I have been imprisoned both in the Edinburgh Tolbooth and in my
own home. They have called me lunatic. Though hundreds of people
over these last eleven years have flocked to see me and my Goddesses
bathing in earth, still they have called me mad.*

*I tell you, Vermilion, and I know you will believe me, the source
of our salvation lies in the earth. I have recently written a pamphlet
which further explains my thoughts on this subject and which I urge
you to read. It goes under the following title:*

*A New and Curious Treatise on the Nature and Effects of
Simple Earth, Water, and Air when applied to the Human
Body; How to Lie for many weeks, months, or years without
Eating anything whatever*

*For your convenience, however, let me lay down the most basic
concepts of my new methods, that you may begin using them
quickly, for there is not much time. I wish, simply, to show the
perfect congeniality of the simple earth to our corporeal frame and
to prove to mankind that nature may be supported, and better
health maintained, by eating and drinking things less cooked and less
compounded, and in far less quantities. The earth has indeed most
wondrous properties and will cure want of appetite, indigestion,*

bilious or nervous disorders, pains, inflammations, swellings, gouty, rheumatic or scirrhous tumours, itching, scurf, scabs, blotches, tetters, rawness, recent wounds, sores, or scrophulous, callous and offensive ulcers, fistulae, bleeding and also the bites of mad dogs or other mad animals.

Having been buried, myself, my friend, naked in the earth, in sand and in mud, in almost every soil and clime and season, more than three hundred times in the course of the last eight years, generally up to my lips and sometimes over my head so as that I could breathe, which is very safe and easy, the earth being porous, I can tell you the true benefits of this method of curing one's ills. I have been buried naked up to my mouth in the fine earth at Pontefract in Yorkshire for six hours daily for eight successive days and on the ninth day for twelve hours successively, without any sensation of hunger or thirst. Yet once I emerged from the earth, my appetite returned and I was ravenous with hunger. Why is this? Think, Vermilion, of the humble vegetable. So long as a carrot, parsnip, turnip, potato, cabbage, tree or any vegetable is in the earth, and acted upon by the air, rain, light and sun, they are plump, nourished, alive and, as it were, happy in their element; but take them out of the earth and expose them to the air and sun alone, they presently begin to droop, wither, languish and die for want of necessary nourishment from the earth and water.

I urge you to discover for yourself the benefits of earth-bathing. If you find that to do so is inconvenient, then may I suggest a most valid alternative. That is, to strap raw turfs to your naked body by means of a strong girth belt with leather straps. The best type of turfs should be from high grounds (the turf from your native Hampstead would be most ideal). These you should wear for as many hours of the day as you are able, yet I do not advise you to sleep wearing the turfs as I have found this to be extremely uncomfortable. Instead, you could apply, at night, a large fresh-cut raw steak, externally to your stomach and bowels. This I have found to be most beneficial to health, and is a sure factor in my increasing vigour, for I swear that I will live to be a hundred and fifty years of age. Indeed, there is more than this. I swear, Vermilion, that from the last day of December, 1792, to the 15th

*day of January, 1793, I neither ate, drank, nor took anything but
cold water, sustaining life by wearing cut-up turfs against my
naked body.*

*And yet, Vermilion, I would not wish for you to think that the
earth can redeem you of your sins. You must repent of them before
God and you must recant your use of electricity. You cannot find
salvation if you do not do this and I am powerless to save you.*

*Do not, therefore, my old friend, fancy that this is the genial
spring or summer of life, or that you, yourself, are evergreen. Alas,
the hoary winter of life is fast coming on – sensual love is for ever
fled. Do not, like the Phoenix, wilfully burn and consume your
body, vainly expecting to spring anew from the ashes of human
nature.*

I am, your most humble servant,
Dr James Graham M.D.
Servant of the Lord O.W.L.

Oh Wonderful Love! And what has it done for him, this new-
found religion? He is indeed insane. And I find, on transcribing
this, I am moved by his plight. His wife is dead now, I hear, and
so the worst of this is that he is alone in his madness. And yet
this interest in earth-bathing started innocently enough. When
his second Temple in Pall Mall was seized for debt, he moved to
an establishment in Panton Street. Having very little money and
having sold most of his electrical equipment, he was forced to
find more simple cures in order to continue working. And so
he established the earth-baths. This was shortly before I left
London for my travels in Europe, yet I no longer associated
myself much with the Doctor. Nevertheless I was curious, and
on several occasions I went along to Panton Street, lurking at
the back of the room, so that he might not notice me. I tell you,
his performance in that place was, for me, a supreme example of
the genius of his quackery. Together with a whole new team of
Goddesses, he demonstrated the joys and benefits of bathing in
the earth. Yet what was this, Gentlemen, other than an exhibition
of the ladies? They would strip naked in that place. The room
was full of young men with swelling cocks, enjoying the spec-

tacle of these young nudes before them, being buried to the neck in a pile of earth.

With such a money-making exercise as this, Gentlemen, I am somewhat astounded that the Doctor did not recover his fortunes! But he was always too serious a man. He truly *believed* in his miracle cures. And when he discovered God, he truly believed that he was his agent.

Yet why do I divert you thus? The Doctor, in my opinion, no longer has any place in our story. That he is a madman, living in Edinburgh, is quite irrelevant. It is his ghost, his shadow, that concern us. The man he used to be. So why should my emotions intrude upon our story? What does it matter that I weep to see what he has become? What I have become. We have changed, all of us, yet we live on. Only Emilia has vanished.

In truth, we witness our own decay. That is what disturbs me most. Only yesterday, I was in the library, reading with Helena. It was an extremely hot day, and the doors were open on to the garden. Yet even outside the air was still and no breeze filtered through to us. I felt myself stifled beneath layers of cotton and silk; my breeches were nearly wet through. Indeed, I would say that I was veritably stinking. It was near impossible, in fact, to concentrate on my book, yet I felt that I must attempt it, as before me were a whole stack of small volumes, which Helena had recommended to me. Mere trifles, in fact, little books of verse composed by women, yet I had vowed to her that I would survey these lines – she would have been intolerable company had I refused.

In any case – there was I, my scalp itching beneath my wig, little beads of sweat running down my face, when I heard Helena cough. Looking up, the sight that greeted me was most disturbing. Helena's right eyebrow seemed to be sliding down towards her eye. Clearly she had not noticed it herself, but my eyes did not deceive me. Yes – the whole black brow was moving, as if it were alive. And where it should have been there was nothing – a blank space upon her forehead.

'Helena!' I said. 'Helena – what has happened? Your brow. Your eyebrow!'

And hearing this, a look of pure dismay crossed her hitherto composed features. She reached her hand to the little slither of moving hair, and seemed to push it back into place. Yet it would not stick, and in her shame she made to move from the room, brow in hand.

'Stay, in God's name, woman,' I said. 'What is a fake brow, between friends? Here' (I held out my hand) 'let me look at it.'

But, after a slight hesitation, she would not have it, and left the room.

Helena returned, shortly afterwards, with her eyebrow freshly glued into place.

'Tell me, Helena?' I said, 'what are those brows made of?'

'Of mouse-hair, Vermilion,' she replied, without a touch of humour.

'And what has happened to your own?'

'My own were grey, and so I plucked them out.'

And though I saw, inside, she was quite mortified, she would not let me see her horror at being found out; her shame at her deterioration.

Yet we are all the same. All of us. My gout makes me so ugly that I truly cannot bear to look at myself. My hands are so swollen they are barely recognizable as such. They are deformed, like the paws of some mythical beast. And the shoes upon my feet are four sizes bigger than those I wore as a young man. I do not stride, as I was wont to. Rather I hobble, taking care with each step not to cause myself too much pain. When I remove my stockings, at night, I am sick to see the stunted shapes beneath. Stumps of feet, gnarled by the disease.

Yes. Dear Reader, I tell you, do not be fooled. Though your Vermilion may laugh and jest and speak as if he is still the handsome rake, surely you have not forgotten that he is none of that? Your Vermilion is not only half crippled, but he experiences such pain as he can barely describe; or sobs, alone in his study, his whole being consumed by self-pity. I told you once, did I not, I would not leave Carmine Hall, considering the world outside a place no longer my domain. But there is more to it, my friends, than this. I am confined here by my condition. My pain makes the very thought of a journey into Hampstead quite unbearable. And my pride, also, forbids it. The truth is, I do not desire to be seen.

There is nothing, Gentlemen, will stop my decline. No. Rather, we must bear our fates. We must distract ourselves from pain. And I cannot help but think that, as our own decay is unstoppable, so, it seems, is the Doctor's madness. I do not think there will be an end to it. Not until the day he takes his last and long earth-bath. When he returns to the element from which we spring.

I will not follow his advice then. I will not bury myself alive. I am stifled enough within the confines of Carmine Hall. And though I feel I should reply to his letter, what would I say? That I wish he were the man he was. That, whatever his own opinions, I loved the man that was. The younger man that first I met in Bristol; the great Dr James Graham, oculist and aurist, who could not cure Emilia's father.

I remember it so well. Dr Graham turned her father away because he did not like to take money from incurables. Yet, being desperate, John Henry Beaumont returned to the Doctor's house each day, offering more and more money, for he had heard that the Doctor had had great success in curing the blind. Indeed, money was no object for Emilia's father in those days, for not only was he a successful merchant in the immoral slavery trade, but he was also a gambling man. In Bristol, no doubt, he was most successful at this sport. But London is a different country. In Brooks's Club, I have no doubt, as many villages are lost each evening as in the earthquake that overwhelmed Herculaneum and Pompeii! And I do not think that Walpole was exaggerating when he said that a thousand meadows and corn-fields are staked at every throw. This is how the father of my love lost his fortune. It was no accident; no cruel stroke of fate. Sheer stupidity left my Emilia poor.

But I forget myself. Let us return to the Doctor, who told

John Henry Beaumont, each time he visited, that a cure was not possible. He had tried, before, to cure similar conditions, but with no success. He repeated – he would not take his money.

Yet the insistence of Emilia's father became too great.

'I do not expect you to cure me, but I would pay you simply to try, Dr Graham. Already my eyesight is fading and I have a pretty young daughter whom I long to see grow up. I wish you to attempt it, Doctor.'

And so the Doctor tried, knowing that it would be in vain.

The Doctor was admired by all in those days. All except John Henry Beaumont, that is, for the chief reason I remember that man is his strange behaviour on the final day that I saw him. An outburst the like of which it is impossible to forget. A strange confession which has its place later in our story, and for this reason, I will not describe it here. Suffice to say, the Doctor did not deserve such treatment from his patients. It is true, he had not succeeded in this case, yet he had, on many occasions, been known to cure the blind. The *Bristol Gazette*, on the day he left for London, lamented his going, and wished that he would stay.

How I admired him then. Though he was not a handsome man, he had a knack of attracting the ladies which I could not help but respect. I used to stare at his face, wondering what it was they were attracted to. Some elements that made it were simply ugly. The heaviness of his chin spoilt the otherwise perfect oval of his face. His eyes, it cannot be doubted, were magnetic, yet their impact was lessened by the bags beneath them. And the lips, though full and sensual, were often set in a rather mean-looking and hard expression. Still, the sound that those lips emitted always seemed, to me, a kind of song. A deep, compelling tone that none but the Scots may possess. He was broad-shouldered and strong, that I will not deny. And I looked to him with awe.

But how is he now? Older than I, yet if his body is less infirm than mine, his mind is surely gone. They used to call him the Genius of Nonsense, yet now he would receive no such honours.

I do not like to think what his fate might be. Perhaps it would be fitting for him to receive the latest treatment for the insane – a current of electricity through his head! Or might a bleeding be preferable? Leeches on his head and on his back. They could give him a potion to make him vomit (for some say the evil spirits that occasion madness reside in the stomach), or might they simply confine him again, alone in his house? This would surely be the cheapest solution. Keep him out of our sight! It will not do to have him wandering the streets.

But that is enough of our Doctor. I tire of him and I tire of myself. What if I should invite him here? How strange it would be to have the three of us gathered at Carmine Hall. One gouty, one mad, and one without eyebrows. We could invite Emilia's ghost along, also, and dance in the new ballroom. Ah – did I not tell you? The Peacock has made the arrangements – the workmen are arriving shortly to begin restoring it to its former glory. She says I have had enough of death and must begin to think of living again.

But without my Emilia, how is that possible? I would indeed dance with her ghost, if I could, for even if she were made of air and I could not touch her, I would like to see her face before me. I would like to see her smile at me. Yes, to spin to the song of violins, seeing her little hand within my own ghastly paw, yet feeling nothing. It would be enough. I would see, not Emilia's face, but her essence. Her soul, bare before me. So brilliant it would be that I would be fair dazzled by the sight. I think of gold-dust, floating on a garden air, illumined by a summer sun. Wherever I walk within the garden, the air is suffused with it. It is so fine, like a honeyed dew that settles upon the skin. A mist of yellow light. Yet that is not it. For, being mortal, I can think only of objects; things composed of matter. And the spirit world where she lives is made of some other stuff.

Most of all, however, in this place, I would that Emilia could see a portion of Vermilion's soul. And though it might be clouded with a thick grey dust, if she will trust me enough to blow it off, she might find a little ruby core. For I feel, though you may doubt it, some good within me. The dust that has settled over my soul is already lifting. If you do not abandon me, you might see a different Vermilion. If you will wait for it, Gentlemen. If you will wait.

26

EMILIA

I AM GROWING thin. Yes, as I lingered in the Temple, befriended now by my Peacock Lady, this was the thought that cheered me the most. I am growing thin.

For there was little enough comfort for me. Since the day of the duel, I had refused to admit Vermilion into my chamber. I could not help but see him, each night as I sang and posed before the Doctor's crowd, but I did all in my power to avoid catching his eye, and when he spoke to me I acted as if I did not hear him. Though, in secret, I longed for his touch, dreamed of those moments on the Celestial Bed before we were interrupted by my brother's rogues, I could not forgive Vermilion for his consequent behaviour. He had wounded me so deeply, I half doubted whether I would survive. I had thought myself an Angel – the Doctor still told me, daily, that indeed I was – yet Vermilion had made me flesh and blood. Vermilion had made me meat.

I was determined to prove him wrong. He was, after all, nothing but a coarse murderer. Oh, all the Gentlemen of the town would describe it some other way. They would say that to die in a duel was honourable conduct, but what kind of honour is it that allows men to kill one another for trifles? For though I would not call my hymen a trifle, I would say it was foolish of them to fight over a thing that they might never 'win' in this manner.

How sickened I am at the world of men. I found, at that time, the more I knew of the sex, the less sense I could make of their actions. With the exception of the Doctor, they were all bravado; all flourish and clever words. I began to doubt their capacity to *feel*. They knew so much more than us. Their educations gave them access to philosophy and Latin, yet what use did they make of these privileges? None. They behaved like spoilt children who cared for nothing beside themselves. They toyed with women; they toyed with pistols; they toyed with their own lives. Indeed, though I had despised Lord Smellie, when I heard that Vermilion had killed him it made me hate Vermilion even more.

My only friends then, apart from the Doctor, would be women. And though I had never been accustomed to the company of a woman who was not at least twenty years older than myself, I welcomed the new friendliness of the Lady Quinton, who was a mere ten years my senior. For no reason that I could ascertain she began visiting me each day, bringing me dainties and sweets and garlands of flowers.

'You are so gaunt, Emilia,' she said to me, early on. 'You must eat more.'

'That is what Mrs Graham has said,' I replied, 'but to speak frankly, I can see no reason to eat more than I already do. I do not like to eat. It seems somehow – unwomanly.'

'Unwomanly?'

'Yes. Ungainly. It would make a mortal of me.'

'But you *are* mortal, Emilia. Surely you are not taken in by the Doctor's talk of Angels?'

'The Doctor is a wise man, who knows many things.'

'If you do not eat, you will die.'

'Perhaps.'

'There is no perhaps in this matter, child. If you do not eat, you will die.'

'Child! Child! Child! Why am I *always* called a child?'

'Perhaps because you are one, Emilia. You are only sixteen years old. You have so much to learn.'

And that was how it all began – with a squabble. It was the third time that she had visited me since the duel. Till then, we had exchanged mere pleasantries; frivolous greetings and light compliments. But now, for the first time, I knew there was more. A thing as yet unspoken, but hovering none the less, there, in the air between us. We were seated in my chamber, with the window open wide so that we could hear the noises from the street below. A chill air blew in, and the Peacock Lady leaned forward to the fire which had been lit by Mrs Graham. Her body was like a scissor blade, so straight it remained as she inclined towards the heat. Yet in spite of her grace, I watched her disdainfully. Though I had not been warm for many days, I despised the fire. I knew that its forked flames were little tongues, that longed to consume my beauty.

I remember well the way she looked on that occasion. She wore a dark dress, the colour of the sea in winter, and her jet hair was pulled harshly from her face and piled a foot high on her head. It was a strange mixture of the wild and the regal, which I never saw in another person. When she spoke, the tone was so low-pitched I thought she must surely have some gypsy blood in her, yet when she smiled, she seemed all-knowing, all-seeing. And those eyes! Black diamonds and alabaster. I looked for some light there, but found only a starless night.

I discovered that morning that we had much in common, and that, behind the peacock mask (which still she wore on visits to the Temple), behind the enigmatic face, lay a woman of great complexity. I learned about her childhood – how she was forced to wear stays by her father, how her mother betrayed her trust, secretly despising her dusky skin, and how she doubted often whether her father was indeed her father. She liked to think her true father was some wanderer, she told me, some great, exotic man, who wrote poetry and fought in distant wars. She thought it funny, indeed, that one who looked as she did was brought up as a Catholic. But she did not feel the truth of the religion in her bones, she said. It was all form for her; form without substance. She did not dare speak her thoughts abroad; indeed she had never uttered such a thing before this moment. Surely I would tell nobody?

I assured her that I would not, and continued to tease her story from her, whilst being very open also in the telling of my own. And I found that the more Helena uttered, the more she wished to say.

One thing, in particular, I discovered about her that day, which truly struck my imagination. She told me she was childless. That the Lord Quinton, her husband, greatly desired an heir, yet she could not seem to give it to him. It was for this reason that she visited the Temple.

'To seek the Doctor's help?'

'Yes. Indeed,' she said.

'And yet, Lady Quinton, you do not heed him.'

'What is your meaning, Emilia?'

'Look how you lean to the fire. I would never do such a thing. It will cause impurities to rise within you. It will pollute your blood.'

'Nonsense!'

'How can you say nonsense? It is the Doctor's teaching.'

'Oh Emilia – I have seen so many doctors. Their opinions conflict so, I often wonder exactly what the right course of action must be. It seems to me, whatever advice we follow, nothing changes the fact that we are inadequate.'

'Inadequate? Surely you cannot say this of yourself?'

'Why might I not? It is the truth.'

'Is being childless such a terrible fate?'

'Of course it is. You are still young, Emilia. You have not yet felt the urge to suckle an infant. But it will come to you. I promise it will come.'

'Oh no. I will never wish to suckle a child, because I never wish to be contaminated by a man.'

'Contaminated?'

'Yes. Early or too frequent venery will sap one's vital juices, and I have no wish to be sapped.'

'That is not your meaning, Emilia. That is simply the Doctor's jargon. Tell me – what do you truly mean?'

'How can I say? I barely know myself.'

'You said you would be contaminated by a man. Why do you say that?'

'Because I have discovered men to be unkind and false. Vermilion . . . Oh, what is the use?'

'What did he do to you?'

'He made me think he loved me, but then he humiliated me, in front of my brother, and Smellie . . .'

'How did he humiliate you?'

'I cannot say.'

'Then is it Smellie's death that angers you?'

'No! No! I love Vermilion still!'

'Emilia – how is that possible? I know not exactly what has passed between you, yet I know enough of him to know that he is not worthy of you. You should continue to avoid him. That much is certain.'

'How can I avoid him, when I love him?'

'Why do you love him? Do you have reason to love?'

'I do not know why. I cannot help myself from thinking of him.'

'If you do not respect him, then this is nothing but infatuation. You are lonely, Emilia. You place your love with him because you have no other guardian for it.'

'And yet I am certain that there is another Vermilion, beneath his brutish behaviour. At moments I have seen it.'

'I tell you; no other Vermilion exists. I am certain of it.'

'But he is so handsome. I have never seen a man so handsome! And when he touches me . . .'

'And are you fooled by trifles such as this?'

'What do you mean?'

'That his soul is ugly, Emilia. Do not be fooled by his swagger. He is a brute.'

'And yet he is your friend.'

'As a friend, perhaps, he is less of a brute. But I have seen him with the ladies. He is a rake, my friend. He has deflowered more virgins than one would believe possible. He wishes only to break your maidenhead, and then he will be done with you.'

How could I have known her self-interest in this matter? Though, it is true, Vermilion had shown himself to be the very man that she described, I desired him to be more than this. I longed for her to tell me to give him another chance; to allow him to speak, at least. And when she told me I must not, I felt obliged to follow her. I knew that I must indeed, as I had resolved, seek happiness in the company only of women.

And so our relationship continued, over the space of several weeks. As each day passed I learned to trust her more. With the dawning of each new sun, I came to feel more calm, glad that I had the strength to resist Vermilion. And yet, in truth, my strength came only from her. He whispered in my ear each evening. Or he passed me little notes, which I could not refrain from taking.

My dear Emilia,

I cannot tell you how I suffer, to know that I have injured you. When I see you in the Temple, my whole being is suffused with your beauty: your inner beauty which sheds light upon the world.

I am not the man I was, Emilia. I do penance for my sins. I cannot sleep at night. I cannot eat. I am wasting away, my sweet, and can be nourished only by your love.

I tell you, my Angel – love has transformed me.

I am your own,

Vermilion

When I read these words, I could not help but think of a novel I had once read about poor Werther, and the way he killed himself for love. The images of that novel began to pervade my mind, and without Helena's knowledge, I began to read the book again, at night. When I reached the end, tears were running down my cheeks.

'Charlotte! I do not shudder now that I hold in my hand the fatal instrument of my death. You present it to me, and I do not draw back. All, all is now finished; this is the accomplishment of all my hopes; thus all my vows are fulfilled.'

I imagined my Vermilion, dying thus for me. I began to fear what should pass if I did not speak to him.

When, however, I finally confessed my fears (and my reading matter) to Helena, she upbraided me. She made me tell every-thing that had passed that day in the Celestial Chamber, and as I spoke I saw her flinch with the pain of it. I thought, at the time, that it was pity for me, but now I know it was more than that. He had made love to her on the very morning of the day that he attempted to take my hymen. Since then, he had barely spoken to her.

'If you speak to him again, Emilia,' she told me, 'he will surely break your heart.'

'It is breaking already,' I told her. 'Look, I am certain that he regrets his actions.'

And I thrust one of his love-notes beneath her nose. She held it gingerly, with disdain, as if she might catch some horrible disease from the paper. Only now do I realize the hurt she was subjected to. I thought she was cold and a little hateful in her reactions to the note. Yet behind her manner must have been a wealth of emotion.

'Do not believe this can be love, Emilia,' she said. 'I know love when I see it. This is not it.'

'But how do you know, Helena? How can you tell the true from the false?'

'True love will never be expressed in such sentimental phrases. He cannot eat, or sleep? Have you ever heard such nonsense? He has borrowed the notion from a novel, child. Do you not see – he wants you to think he is a Werther. But if anything, I would say he has grown fatter and more ruddy recently, whilst you are growing so pale and skeletal that before long you will fade away. You are growing consumptive with your passion. If you do not eat soon, the Doctor will surely notice.'

'I am happiest without food, Helena. I have no need for it.'

'There is no person alive who can live without nourishment.'

'Without the nourishment of love, perhaps.'

'No! Emilia, trust me.'

I thought I had every reason to trust her.

'Trust me. I am twenty-six years old. I have lived ten years longer than you and I have known what it is to pine for a man. Yet I tell you: without love you may be sad, but without food, your flesh will waste upon your bones; you will soon be in the earth.'

'Unless I am not mortal.'

This made her furious. In a gesture more sudden and extravagant than was her wont, she grabbed me by the shoulders, and turned me to my mirror. She pulled my shift above my head, so I was naked. And I had not the strength to resist it.

'Look at yourself, Emilia. You are still beautiful. But not for long, girl. You see your ribs there? Do you see them?'

I nodded, aghast at the sight. Beside the Peacock Lady, who was growing, I thought, a little fat, I was indeed so thin I wondered how my frame supported me. I was still beautiful; my eyes seemed to shine with unnatural brilliance and my skin clung to the contours of my skull, so that the perfection of its structure was plain to see. Yet my body, I saw it instantly, was sapped. My breasts had shrunk; my little rounded belly had become inverted.

'But if I should speak to him,' I said, 'surely . . .'

'Vermilion is not the cause of this, Emilia,' Helena said. 'It is you yourself that causes it. You must eat meat and cheese and butter. You must eat bread. I am told by the Doctor's wife that you touch nothing but fruit and vegetables, and even then, not enough to sustain life.'

'What sort of life will I *have*, Helena!' I said, turning away from the glass and donning my shift once again. 'I have no family. Few friends. No occupation besides posing and singing before strangers, charging myself with electricity and dancing in the park.'

'How *do* you spend your days, Emilia?'

'When I am alone I read, I do a little paper-cutting or japanning, as I was taught to do when I was young. I am *tired* of the Temple. It holds no wonder for me now. Each night when I sing before the Celestial Bed, I can think only of my own shame. Yet if only I would allow Vermilion to apologize to me, perhaps I might be happy again. Without him, this place is barren.'

'Oh no, Emilia,' she said, her eyes flashing. 'You do not know the meaning of the word.'

And instantly I was sorry. Full of pity for her, as well as for myself. I saw how my only hope for happiness might lie with this woman, whose pain was equal to my own. Both of us had been disappointed by the masculine sex. Her womb was hollow as my heart. Empty as my stomach. I wondered, if she stayed with me, if we would grow full again. We might feast together on pomegranates and partridges, on breast of duck, and oyster loaves. Might I be nourished by these foods? What might pass, I wondered, if I sat at a table that was piled high with delicacies? A platter of sea turtle, a dish of anchovies, a salmagundi, a bowl of green pea soup. Yes, I saw them all before my eyes: the curried meat, the strawberry fritters, the truffles and the cold neats' tongues. Salted haddock, Scotch salmon, Stilton cheese and piccalilli. Guinea fowl and quail, plum pottage and potted venison. I would eat them all in the company of this Peacock.

I turned and saw her, moving towards the window, herself in a reverie.

'You see how the water flows again, Emilia,' she said, though it seemed more to herself than to me. 'Don't you feel it signals something? A change? Perhaps all will be well.'

I followed her footsteps, and, suddenly tender, placed my arms around her waist, my head against her shoulder.

'I notice nothing any longer,' I said, my words muffled by the thick emerald silk of her dress. 'I have not thought of the river for several weeks.'

I wondered why I had not thought of it till this moment. Had Vermilion's absence so affected me that I should lose my sense of all that was outside of myself? Or was it this hunger, that I could feel now, gnawing my innards, that made me forgetful?

They say that in Hell there is a river, Lethe, which is the river of forgetfulness. There, the souls of the dead must sip their fill, so that they will forget all they said and did in their lifetime. I wonder, if Vermilion goes to Hell, will he forget what he said to me? What he did to me?

Have I forgotten? I thought. Already? Is this murky river some relation of the one beneath the earth? Has it been contaminated by some lurking spirit who would not stay below the ground?

Whatever its force, I know that I must fight it. I have been stilled this last month, since the ice began to melt. Yet I am free now; there is no need to dwell in this oblivion. Without my father, without my brother, without Smellie, without Vermilion,

I am at liberty to do as I please. They say the moon controls the tides, yet I will not be a slave to the moon. I will be the moon itself. I will be the moon-goddess, Isis. I see myself, shedding silver light upon the world. I am all-seeing, like the Peacock Lady, all-knowing. I have no need of men to show me the way.

27

EMILIA

VERMILION CAME TO the Temple every evening. I had thought
he would soon grow tired of playing love-sick and find some
other woman to fawn upon. And yet it was not so. I discussed
this, often, with Helena.

'If he does not love me,' I said, 'if all he desires is my
maidenhead, why does he not give up the fight? Sure, there are a
million maidenheads no different to mine.'

'It is the fight he loves, Emilia,' she said. 'But once you do
give in to him, then he will no longer desire you.'

Yet though I considered her words carefully, there were times
when I was not sure she knew enough to judge Vermilion's
behaviour. For I remember him at that time. And I know what
passed afterwards. Even now, though I may try to believe that
he has always been a most despicable man, I cannot pretend that
there was not a time when he seemed to love me. I say 'seemed',
yet in a sense I have faith he did love. It is only what happened
afterwards that makes me doubt him. In that spring of 1780, I
do believe I saw the best of my Vermilion. I do believe I saw
the man I love.

You will think me weak, of course, for admitting love for
such a villain. Yet what is a villain, but a man who has been
confused? What is a villain, but a man who soaks up all the
hatred that surrounds him, and does not have the strength to
wring himself free of it? Yet Vermilion was surrounded by love,
you might say. Think of his parents – people so loving, kind
and generous that a child of theirs who turns out demon must
surely be at fault. Yet can we blame the parents for all? We
women, being the weaker sex, have learned to be despised. And
men have learned to despise us. The whole world turns upon

225

this truth. Why may we not study, as men do? Why did Helena weep for lack of children? Why was I considered a fallen woman, whilst Vermilion remained respected and admired by one and all? Why is marriage the only place where *we* may be respected? Why can a rich man rape a poor girl and still be considered 'a good sort' whilst she will be ever defiled? When the word in the coffee-houses was that girls were for the taking, just as books were for the reading and duels were for the fighting – could Vermilion truly have learned a different kind of manners?

You will say he could. He could have followed the example of his father, who treated his mother with nothing but respect and love. Ah! But there's the rub. A mother is different altogether. A woman who has given birth within matrimony. She will not wish to usurp your power. She will only desire that her child is kept warm and well fed. She will sew a sampler for the wall, and put a chicken in the pot. One day, perhaps, Vermilion is sure to find such a one, and then, though he may not love her, he will sit at the fire with her in the evenings, and take her to his orange-tree garden at Carmine Hall, where, he has told me, white swans swim upon a lake, and the scent of the fruit perfumes the air.

Think of him as you will. I have told you of his cruelty. Is it not fair that I tell you of his love, also? A love that seemed, if only for two short months, to be a flower so rare it should be locked in a glass case and preserved for all time. More fragile than a midnight orchid, more potent than a blood red rose. I tell you, it is true. Though afterwards the most callous and unfeeling side of his nature re-emerged (the poison in the stamens, the thorns upon the stem), I will not have the bloom itself defiled.

Helena, of course, could not see it. She continued to teach me to despise him, yet as the days passed she became less successful in her quest. Though I found, in her, a better companion than any I had known before, there were times when her rants against Vermilion grew tiresome. I desired her to speak on some other subject. And then she would talk about her barrenness. In that deep, smooth voice I now love so well, she would tell me, again, of her despair. Lord Quinton had grown to hate her, she said, for failing to furnish an heir, yet still he punished her with constant efforts to produce a child. Yet it was God's punishment, also, she said. Helena's mother had surely sinned, by giving her husband a child that was not his own. Helena herself must be the product of her mother's wicked liaison with a gypsy. Being the fruit of sin, she told me, God had ensured she would not be fruitful herself. She would not be able to perpetuate the crimes of her mother.

The more I knew of Helena, the more I saw how similar we were. She was the darkie daughter, a child born of vice; I was the Devil Child, an infant who murdered the one who bore her. I did not tell Helena about this of course – I was not ready to speak of my crime. And yet, inside, I began to think that I had found my Platonic double. Suddenly I doubted the words of the philosophers, for who could say that man and woman are halves of one whole, when I saw nothing in a man that corresponded to myself? No – here, in this tall, straight woman, lived a wilder spirit than my own, which none the less seemed to move in harmony with it. I thought that if spirits were visible . . . No! More than that – if they were material – ours might fit together as if we were figures carved from a single piece of wood. Each, alone, would seem a touch misshapen; beautiful and yet imperfect. Yet when they were placed side by side, we would seem almost a perfect oval. Yes – we would be egg-shaped. We would fertilize ourselves.

'Vestina! Vestina! Have you heard the news?'

It was the Doctor that spoke, on an early March evening, as I descended the staircase to visit the apothecary. He seemed agitated – his hair was only half powdered, his neckerchief not properly tied.

'What is it, Doctor?' I said, terrified suddenly, lest his alarm was due to some incident regarding myself. Since the day of the duel, my brother had not been seen in the Adelphi. Perhaps he had returned with another husband for me?

'It is that Gordon man. He has made threats against the King.'

'The King?'

'Yes. He claims he has one hundred and sixty thousand men at his command in Scotland. They say, if he does not have his way, he is determined to cut off the head of the King!'

'I do not believe it!' I cried. 'It is not possible!'

'Yes, Vestina. It is possible. I have a friend in the House and he has told me this. I am afraid it is most true.'

I reached out and took his hand.

'Doctor, what shall we do?'

He helped me, then, to seat myself upon the marble stairs. And he sat down, beside me, overcome with the news. His face was pale as his white silk jacket and he was silent a while, seeming to compose himself. When he spoke again, his voice was calmer.

'We must hope he does not carry out his threat, child.'

'What sort of a man is it, Doctor – that would make such a threat?'

'A dull man, if my friend Vermilion is to be believed, so dull that he has been known to empty the House of Commons. Yet, though I despise Lord George's morals, Vestina, there is some sense in what he says.'

'What does he say?'

'Like myself, he despises this pointless war across the Atlantic.'

I looked quizzically at him.

'In America, my Angel. In America.'

And feeling foolish, I allowed him to continue, in awe at the extent of his knowledge.

'I tell you, Vestina' (he said my name, and yet he spoke almost to himself) 'there is only one reason why our Government passed the relief act for Catholics. Only one reason.'

'And what is that, Doctor?'

He did not look at me when he replied. His eyes were fixed on the crutches at the foot of the stairway.

'With France and Spain about to enter the war against us – what could they do? They needed more man-power. They needed the Catholics to enlist. And so they had to give in to them.'

'And Lord George – he would not have the war go on?'

Dr Graham turned to me when I spoke, suddenly aware again of my presence.

'Why – you are learning quickly, child. Very quickly. That is right. Lord George Gordon – who according to *some* is not dull at all, but rather gay and elegant, with high spirits and a liking for good wine – where was I?'

'Lord George Gordon would not have the war go on?'

'No – he would not. And I am of accord with him on that subject at least. It is a mad, accursed war. Butchery! Lord George is against setting *our* Catholics against America's Protestants. He would have us hate all Papists!'

I thought about this for a moment, whilst the Doctor quietly fretted by my side. I thought of Helena.

'Doctor. If a person is a Catholic, does that mean they are in sympathy with our enemies, the French?'

'No, child – no, of course not.'

'I am glad of it,' I said. 'For then I should have lost a friend.'

And he smiled, no longer listening to my words.

To me, it did not seem Vermilion had a ruddy look at all. Each evening, when he came to the Temple to hear me sing, to watch me pose, I thought that he, like me, had paled somewhat, was looking thinner and more haggard. Though at first, after the duel, I had felt an aversion to his presence, now there was something different about him. I could not place it exactly, but I was unnerved by it. I wished he would not watch me. I wished he would not hand me these notes, on which he scribbled fine words and little sketches of roses. He would give them to me as I stepped down from the Celestial Throne each night, at the very moment when I was most charged with desire. I would hold my hand out for them, but would not look him in the eye. Only when I was safe within my chamber would I unwrap them, hastily tearing the seal. Yet even then, once they were open, I was sceptical. Helena had taught me to be so.

There was one night, however, when I felt worn down by his protestations of love. I knew that this was a most dangerous time. I knew that I must not give in to him. And yet I had seen with my own eyes that this was not the same Vermilion I had known. Who would do such a thing – deny themselves food, forget to comb their hair, affect a look of great distress, and, more than these, visit the same lecture four times each week for more than a month? Surely, I thought, to let him talk could not harm me? And when I saw his note that evening, I became convinced what I must do.

O Emilia,
    If you do not let me speak to you, I fear that I must leave the metropolis. Your forgiveness is all that I desire.
    Your own,
    Vermilion

I knew I could not let him leave London. Perhaps it was no more than a threat, designed to make me relent. And yet – if he went away, if I never saw Vermilion again, I knew I would not be able to forgive myself. Though in many ways I hated him still, the thought of life here without him seemed intolerable. And even Helena's warnings could not prevent my desire to see him.

With a thumping in my breast, I sat down at my table to write to Vermilion. Then, realizing that the single candle was too dim, I stood up again and moved about the room, lighting several more. The flickering orange light was a companion to me, and I felt the strength of it, as I lifted my pen. I was determined that never again would Vermilion offend me as he had that day on the Celestial Bed. If he truly loved me, then I might return to him – but only if he could prove his love and his regret for his deeds.

Yet I struggled with my words. Remember, if you read this and think me foolish, I was only sixteen years of age. How was I to know how to address such a man as Vermilion? Even now, as I write, I am no more than nineteen. Yet I am so much wiser than I was then. I have experienced so much and I have had time to reflect upon it. Yes, these two years past, I have spent more time with my books, and I have emerged a somewhat different person. With Helena to encourage me in my learning, with little else to occupy my time, I feel that I am ready for what I must now confront. Death will be a friend to me. Though my mind, and my will, are stronger than they have ever been; though I am no longer the shrinking, quivering creature that once I felt myself to be, still my life has grown intolerable.

But to return to my chamber, where my mind was in turmoil. I could not write the letter. It seemed to me that words were spinning in the air: a million pale leaves, caught in a whirlwind. Some toyed with the flames from the candles, catching alight before my eyes and flaring up, more words, lost to me. They were meaningless now, little black fragments upon the air; charcoal and ash, settling at my feet. But surely there were more! They had not all been burned. Yes, but now they spiralled out of the window, or were sucked by the wind outside, into our fireplace and beyond. They must be spouting from the red chimneys of the Adelphi; a veritable dictionary, spewing from our rooftop. The following morning, perhaps, an early boatman would push his skiff from the shore, and find, as he dipped his oars into the water, that the Thames was scattered with words.

I was relieved to hear a knocking at the door. I bade the knocker enter, and turned to see Helena, standing in the doorway.

'My, what a little scholar do we have here!' she said, a smile upon her face. And, as she walked towards me, I sensed an aura of gaiety about her that I had not known before.

'Tut tut!'

She rapped my wrist.

'The Doctor will not like to see you wearing out your pretty little hand by holding a pen!'

I determined, almost immediately, that as she seemed so well disposed this evening, I would tell her of my new resolve. But not straight away. First I would speak of other things so that she might be caught more unawares by my admission.

'What are you doing here at this hour, Helena?' I asked. 'Surely Lord Quinton will be angry that you are so often out without him? Does he not wish to visit the Temple also?'

'Why no. For as the Doctor has told us, Emilia – infertility is almost always the fault of the woman.'

'And he thinks you come here for treatment!'

'As I do, Emilia. As I do!'

'So far as I can see,' I replied, 'you never heed the Doctor's advice. I cannot think why you are so often a visitor!'

'You know, as well as I, that I come only to be with you.'

'So?' I was truly curious now. Why *was* she here?

'I have news for you, Emilia.'

'Ah – do not say it – Lord George Gordon has threatened his men will chop off the head of King George!'

'No, no, though I have heard this news also, and I am indeed terrified of the prospect. But I have something of a more personal nature to convey to you.'

'Come then – what is it?'

I had never seen a smile like that upon her face. Always she had seemed so full of sorrow. But now I watched as the little upturned lips began to broaden, spreading wide to reveal the teeth that I had barely ever seen. Suddenly, I knew what had happened.

Without saying a word, I moved towards her and embraced her. We held one another for a few moments, my head against her breast. Then I moved away and put my hand out to touch her belly.

'A child – yes?'

'I am near certain of it.'

'Oh, Helena – I cannot say how happy I am for you. And have you told Lord Quinton the news?'

'Oh yes – already he swears that it will be a son.' She swelled her chest, tossed her head backwards, pulled her mouth down at the corners and looked down with disdain, feigning the posture of her husband. The voice she spoke with was much higher pitched than her own, and each vowel was perfectly pronounced. 'An heir for the Quinton estate! I have produced – a son!'

I laughed, for though I had never met Lord Quinton, I had imagined him exactly as she portrayed him.

She looked at me then, and in the orange candle-light I thought I saw the black of her eyes seem to soften, almost to shine, a look of such trust and intimacy that I felt it was the time to speak. Now she would accept my decision. Surely she would understand.

'What is it, Emilia?' she said, sensing my hesitation. 'Is there something you wish to say to me?'

'Oh! A thing of little importance, compared to your glad tidings. And yet . . .'

'Come – speak.'

I took a breath before I gave air to the words.

'I have decided to meet Vermilion. I am convinced now of his love for me.'

How many shades of emotion, I wonder, is it possible for a face to register in the space of a single second? I thought I heard thunder bellow in her throat and saw lightning flash from her eyes. I thought I saw tears begin to gather, and yet the set of her mouth became so hard, one would imagine her almost incapable of emotion. Perhaps it was the flickering of the muscles in her cheeks that convinced me of her hatred, yet the sudden pallor of those cheeks seemed to betray nothing other than shock and fear. And somewhere, in that brief instant, I saw another feeling begin to well. I saw it in the trembling of her hands. I *sensed* it, in the air between us. She loved me still.

'Emilia – you *cannot* do that. You cannot go to him.'

'Why not?' I asked. 'Am I not free to make my own decisions?'

'Of course you are, and yet I know Vermilion will injure you.'

'Why is it, Helena, that you hate him so? Surely – I have more reason than you.'

I was resentful now of her intrusion. Tired of her scolding.

'I tell you, Emilia, he is poisonous and vile. And once his venom is in your blood, you will never be free of it.'

'Helena – his poison has been in my blood from the very day that I met him. Do you think that I can rid myself of that now? No – the name of the poison is love, and I am struck with it. There is no doctor that can cure me. I must go to the source of the infection. Only there might I find the antidote.'

'No!' she cried. 'No – I tell you – seek it in vain. There is no antidote, Emilia! I know it. I know it.'

And with a sudden gasp she swung to the window, and took hold of the open door to steady herself. She seemed to cling almost desperately to it, laying her head against it for support. And then, her body was racked with convulsions. Her sobs came intermittently. I had never seen her like this before. So calm she had always appeared. So free from the demons that had visited my own soul. Yet here she was, sobbing at my window, as a cold breeze filtered past her, disturbing the little candle-flames. The light of the moon, behind her, made her no more than a black, weeping shape, throwing a long shadow across the floor. I wanted to move towards her, to make her real to me again, but I felt that if I moved, the whole room might blaze up in an inferno.

So I stood still, afraid for her and for her child within her womb. And when she was quiet again, I took a candlestick and moved towards her as she looked up, and met my eyes. Her face glowed in the darkness.

'What is it, Helena?' I said, quietly. 'Have you known love, as I know it? Before you knew Lord Quinton, was there another man who caused this pain?'

'I have known love, Emilia. I *know* love. This is a love-child, this little seed within me.'

'You love Lord Quinton? Surely not?'

But even as I spoke, I knew this was not her meaning.

'No, Emilia. Some other love has done this to me.'

234

'Some *other* love? But that is vile!'

'No. Not vile. You must not believe the Doctor when he says that infertility is always the fault of the woman.'

'Must not believe the Doctor? What has this to do with . . .'

'Everything. Emilia – Lord Quinton is infertile. I needed a child. I found another man who gave me what I desired.'

'Another man?'

'What else?'

'A lover, then?'

'Yes, Emilia! Yes – a lover! Is that so terrible?'

'It goes against all nature. It is a sin.'

'No, not a sin. Love cannot be called a sin. And yet we are harmed by it. We cannot escape unscathed.'

I did not wish to argue with her. Yet I was horrified that she was carrying a child that did not belong to her husband.

I understood now why she railed against men. I saw it was not Vermilion that she hated, but the whole of the sex. I placed my candle upon the table, and she followed me to the soft chair by the fireside. Together we sat in silence for a moment. I felt I could not speak without offending her.

'Emilia,' she said, after a moment. Her voice was hushed. She seemed herself again. 'Vermilion is the blackest villain. He will tear your soul out.'

'You can speak thus, against one whom you profess to be a friend?' I said, 'Why? I *know* his faults. Yet he has changed. I am certain he has changed. *Why* would you turn me against him?'

'How can I convince you of his perniciousness?'

'You cannot.'

'Unless I speak the truth.'

I could not remain sitting and rose from my chair to pace the room.

'What truth is this?'

Helena turned her head to face me.

'I do not wish to hurt you, Emilia.'

'Then if you have proof of his "perniciousness" as you call it – give it to me now.'

'And yet you will not love me after.'

Her voice was calm, which only served to aggravate my anger.

'I will not stop loving you, if you can prove he is a villain.'

'I fear you will, Emilia. But I will tell you. This child inside me,' she said. 'My little baby . . .'

She was quiet a moment.

'His father is called Vermilion.'

I felt the world sway. Little points of orange light went spinning round me, as the room began to turn. My own reflection taunted me; a whirlwind of faces. And then I saw the nymphs that adorned my ceiling, and the god, Hymen, in the shadows. They seemed to have turned malevolent now. Spinning about me in a void. Yes, the heavens themselves revolved around the one still point that bore my name. Emilia. Voices beckoned; called to me from distant stars. Came closer now: shooting stars. Chaos all about me. Yet still I shone, a pure, silver luminary upon the revolving world. Isis again. Moon-goddess. Heaven knows how the ships below were suffering in this wind. Even I, with all my power, could hardly control them. Tiny things, bobbing about on the dark waters. I should give them my gift. The gift of light.

When I recovered, I found that Helena, again, was by my side. She had seated me on the chair beside the fireplace and had lit a small blaze. She held a compress against my head.

'Aetherial Balsam!' I cried. 'Please – bring me my Balsam!'

And she did as I asked, placing my own hand against the compress. I railed at her as she fetched the liquid.

'Why have you lit the fire? You know I cannot stand the heat. And the window! You have closed the window!'

She did not reply, merely returned to me, took the compress from my head and gave me the small bottle. She sat down beside me, and watched as I poured the balsam on to my palm, and inhaled deeply. I rubbed the rest of it upon my neck.

'So,' I said, barely able to contain my spite. 'It is you who are his love, not I.'

'Calm yourself, Emilia. You are weak. You must calm yourself.'

I knew the truth of her words, but could not temper my anger. Merely, I spoke more softly. Little whispered arrows.

'You told me that he loved me! Yet he was *your* lover. Why? I do not understand why you lied.'

'I did not lie, Emilia.'

'Ah – I see. He loves us both!'

'No.'

I saw her meaning before she spoke it.

'He loves only you.'

And yet I could not accept it.

'I was a mere toy for the two of you! That is all.'

Inside her, a little Vermilion seed was growing. More than anything, I realized that I longed for that little part of him, within me.

'No toy,' she said. 'His passion for you is true, Emilia. I have never known him to suffer thus!'

'I can believe nothing that you say, Helena. I wish you would go to him. Leave me, now. I am tired of this.'

'At first I thought that if I let him have you, he would love me still. I thought that you would be no more than a trophy for him, whilst I would be more than that. Yet that day, upon the Celestial Bed, he truly came to adore you, Emilia. I promise you. He told me this, soon afterwards. And now, he will not have me near him!'

I could not believe this. I knew it was not love that he had shown me upon the Bed.

'Does he not know about your child?'

'Of course. It means nothing to him. He says it is Quinton's now.'

'And you fear that if I go to him, I will receive a treatment equal to your own?'

'How can I know, Emilia? I think he will love you. Truly, there is more love in his heart for you than I had ever believed could be contained within him. But I do not know how long it can survive. I fear for you.'

'And yet I might think, if what you say is true, that you are driven by jealousy.'

'Of course I am jealous. At first, just to look at you was torture! And even now the very thought of you within his arms is enough to drive me to the brink of madness. Remember, Emilia – it is you who stole *my* love. Before you entered the Temple, Vermilion was mine.'

I realized, as she spoke, the truth of her words. I recognized my own guilt. For had she not been a friend to me in spite of all?

'And yet, against my will, I have grown to love you, Emilia. I would not wish you to suffer, as I have. Why should we be bound to such a villain as he? Together, perhaps, we might find strength. We might find a way of forgetting our unworthy love.'

'What do you mean?'

'Do you wish to be a slave to men?'

'No. Nor will I be.'

'And yet you would be a slave to Vermilion?'

'No. I will not be his slave. I am decided. If he will be mine, he must change.'

'You would scrub the spots from the leopard?'

'I do not believe him a true leopard,' I replied. 'I think him rather . . .' I paused '. . . a large cat who has merely disguised himself in a more dangerous form. The spots will be easily erased.'

And at this, Helena sighed, realizing now that nothing could be altered. She had played her final card, but even that had not distracted me from my purpose. I pitied her, yet my passion for Vermilion was too strong. I was ready to plunge from the moon into the sea. Perhaps, if she had not betrayed my trust, I might have been content with sisterhood, but now she was not the Helena that I had loved. Vermilion had come, like a piece of steel, rending apart our perfect oval. And now that it was broken, I did not believe it could be repaired.

Turning to her, slowly, I saw her take her hand away from her belly. I pretended that I had not seen.

'I wish to be alone now, Helena,' I said. 'Please, will you open the window before you leave?'

Silently, not looking at me, she raised herself. She walked to the door, ignoring my command.

'If you would freeze, Emilia,' she said, 'I would not be responsible for it.'

'And if I should burn, Helena,' I replied, 'I will not blame you neither.'

When she was gone, I placed my hand beneath my shift, upon my abdomen. It was hollow as a sea-shell, washed up upon the beach. I stroked it, gently, feeling the lustre of my skin. I might scour the shore for a million shells and all would be empty, as I was. This brilliant lustre was not enough. And I knew now that I searched in vain. I would not find the pearl here, within me. The pearl lay elsewhere. For though it was a thing of great beauty and value, my brother had told me that it was formed from a piece of sand. A piece of grit within the shell. And there was no such substance within me. I was pure as Aether. Thin as air. And, for the first time, I wished it otherwise.

28

VERMILION

IT WAS DURING dinner that Helena brought up the subject of
my sojourn in Paris. Being aware that I will not say one word
on the subject of the Revolution, she took a more gentle
approach this time, and in return, I told her a little of my life
there. Strange, I thought, as we spoke in this civil manner, that
this is the very woman of whom Emilia wrote. The woman who
cried for me at the window of Emilia's chamber; who was
convulsed with sobs. This is the woman who called me the
blackest villain. Who told Emilia that I would tear her soul out.
And yet there is nothing in her manner, now, to suggest that she
has ever loved me. Perhaps it is my altered appearance that has
changed her attitude towards me. But whilst I write this, I do
not believe it to be true. I think that she has found a thing of
more value than a yearning after a man who has never truly
loved her. She has found a stability within herself and has no
need for such frivolity.

'Tell me, Vermilion,' she said. 'How much were you wont to
drink in Paris? Your gout is far advanced for one so young.'

'Ah — you are much mistaken, Helena. I have never been a
heavy drinker. Whilst in Paris . . . Let me think. It is certain that
I never drank more than three bottles of port in one sitting.'

'I cannot believe it. That is surely enough to kill you.'

I laughed at her naïveté.

'Do not be so foolish, Helena. I had many friends in Paris
who drank three or four each evening.'

'Most likely they are dead now.'

'Yes, surely. But it was not the port that killed them, but the
guillotine.'

She nodded at this, seeming to sympathize with me, but I was glad she did not take the subject further. Rather, she inquired what it was that led me to drink in such great quantities.

'I tell you,' I said, 'I do not consider a bottle or two of port each evening to be excessive. Any less, and I would not be considered man enough to sit at the table.'

'And are you more a man, now, Vermilion, hobbling about this place like some octogenary?'

'I did not make the rules of the coffee-houses, Helena. I am not to blame for this.'

'I had not known there was a rule-book. Pray, tell me what is written therein.'

'You know very well that these rules are not written down. And yet, if one does not abide by them, one is certain to become a laughing stock. They would have called me a Dandy.'

'Oh – most horrible fate!'

I laughed at her manner. She is better company now than she used to be. Whilst I am speaking to her, my pain seems lessened somewhat.

'You know I could not have risked ruining my reputation thus.'

'Then tell me how you upheld your reputation.' She, also, was laughing.

'Ah – it was simple,' I told her. 'After dinner, it was of course customary to drink the health of a lady.'

'Of course.'

'But once we had all drunk to the first lady, then another would be proposed, and the port would be passed once again.'

'I see.'

'And so it continued, until all the ladies that we knew had been toasted, and we were all blind drunk.'

'And that would be the end to it?'

'Oh no – by the time that we were drunk, and could not remember the names of any more ladies, we had no objections to drinking to whores that we had known, for in that state we really could not see the distinction between them.'

'Indeed,' Helena remarked. 'There is no distinction, Vermilion, for the whores are ladies who are not lucky enough to be of high birth.'

'Helena – I do not see that you yourself have suffered.'

'There you are wrong, Vermilion,' she said. 'For once you made a whore of me, and I will not forget that.'

I looked at her then, fearing, for a moment, that I was about to lose her because of my carelessness. I have grown used to her presence here and would no longer wish to be alone. I remember those days of rain, before her arrival. When I had no one to carp at but myself and John. When my only connection between myself and my past lay inside my head, and in the pages of Emilia's diaries. I am afraid of what might happen if she should leave.

'Yet I hope that you will forgive me for it, Helena,' I said, 'for I am truly sorry that I was unkind to you. I am full of regret for my actions.'

'I know it,' she said, 'and it is clear that you are not the man you were. But I cannot forgive you, Vermilion. Instead, I will put my hurt upon a scale, and I will balance it against your recent kindness. If you had not allowed me to stay here, I do not know what I might have done.'

'And how well do you find this scale is balanced?' I asked her.

'Right now, the hurt weighs too heavy on the left-hand side,' she replied. 'Yet for the future, I cannot say.'

'I might be forgiven then?'

'Only if you will tell me more of Paris!' And she smiled again, and I knew I must continue.

I do not know how long I spoke after that. I spoke of the Paris I knew before the Revolution. It was impossible for a person of good breeding to live there, I told her, if they were not in possession of a coach, for not only were the streets filthy, but they were dangerous too, filled with one-horse cabriolets, driven at great speed by men of fashion and their imitators. Indeed, once I saw a child mown down by some such rascally, would-be gentleman, and he did not even look backwards to see what he had done.

No, it was no place for a lady, I said, for walking on those streets one would most certainly be spattered by mud. It was a toil and a fatigue for a man, and an impossibility for a well-dressed woman. And do not think that a sedan chair would be an alternative to a coach, for it would most certainly be knocked down in the streets! Indeed, people of fortune at that time were, for the most part, forced to dress in black, for the mud would otherwise soon be all too evident on their fine clothes.

In all of these matters, as well of talk of the Comédie Française, the Trianon and the Champs Elysées, Helena seemed most interested. She laughed when I told her of the rouged ladies who used to play lotto from dawn to dusk, and great was her mirth when I told her about the fellow who attempted to cross the Seine in elastic shoes.

Yes, it is quite remarkable, in fact, how at times like this we are able to put the past out of our minds. Yet she does not know how recently I have been remembering her; how indeed she must have suffered, to have felt my seed growing within her, whilst I had eyes for none but Emilia.

I am alone now, once again, within my study. I feel I cannot begin to explain to you how tired I am of this place. Yes, however I look at it, always the walls appear the same. I might pull the false ones back, of course, if I so wished, to see my Hogarths or my naked Bouchers, and yet I do not desire it. No, as each day passes I realise that it is *life* that I desire. I wish I were able to walk in the garden without pain in my legs and sorrow in my heart. I wish I might walk around Hampstead village or visit the market at Covent Garden. And indeed, it is possible. If I so desired it, I might hire a coach or a chaise. I might join the world again.

And yet I fear it. Yes. I fear what I most wish for. For I would be reminded of my former self. The Vermilion whom the ladies stared at. Yes, there was no public place where I could walk without feeling a thousand long-lashed eyes upon me. My legs were long and perfectly formed. My hands were strong with elegant, straight fingers. Now I will not look down for fear of catching sight of them.

But if I do not go outside, what then? What is the worst fate, I wonder – to ride through the streets in a carriage, peering out at society from behind the window drapes, terrified lest they should see my altered state? Or to remain here, feeling a kind of madness beginning to well inside me – feeling myself dragged backwards through time, sucked into the past, knowing nothing but the one emotion that dwelled within my breast when Emilia was alive. My walls breathe around me. They exhale the odours which they have gathered over many years: tobacco smoke, coffee fumes, the perfume of books and the essence of learning. Yes – a manly smell it is; so untouched by female presence that I am suffocated by it. My walls seem malicious creatures. They would enclose me entirely if they could. The walls have absorbed a part of me also. I feel I cannot go outside.

It terrifies me, you must understand – the idea of being seen. So long as I remain here, people will remember me as I was. I will be a kind of legend: forever young, in their eyes. They will think of a man whose eyes were so powerful that he could dazzle a woman and make her fall to the floor, though she were standing ten feet away. They will think of a man whose dark locks were desired by every wig-maker in town. Yet if they saw me now: bewigged myself, and bepowdered. If they saw me, peering from behind a curtain, afraid to leave my coach, lest the crowd should laugh at my crumbling façade – what would become of me? I do not think that I could continue to live, having endured such ridicule.

No – better by far to stay here in Carmine Hall, in a room without mirrors. Better to be locked in a dungeon without light or air! Better to breathe dust than see the smirks upon their faces, when they say:

'There goes that Lord Vermilion! Once he claimed that he could walk a mile with a girl impaled upon his prick! Now they say he cannot even support himself. He cannot walk ten yards without a stick!'

The very thought of it is intolerable.

*

Here, with my memories, I am safe. There is not much for me to do, besides thinking on Emilia, but at least, when I take that journey, I am seldom disturbed. Often, I cannot bear to travel to the past. I will do anything rather than go there. I will speak to John about the state of the wine-cellars, or idle my time away in the library, reading nonsense that Helena has passed on to me. For why *should* I go there? Why should I go to the one place where I will find only sorrow?

And yet I do go, over and again. Emilia and I had but one month together, yet in that time we found a bower, where brier roses grew, and in that place a miracle occurred. You will not believe it of me. But at the beginning of March, in that year of 1780, I, Vermilion, learned to love.

Indeed, you may believe what you will – but had it not been for a single unfortunate incident, I tell you it is possible that the course of my life might have changed entirely.

Angered by Helena's deceit, Emilia came to me at the beginning of March. Yet by the time the snowdrops that grew outside my lodgings in St James's had withered, that is within the first few days of April – she was lost to me.

But I will not think of that now. I will think only of beginnings. We had no need, in those days, of anything, but that which was contained in one another. When I kissed her, I tell you it was like sipping nectar from the honeysuckle. My thirst was quenched by her and my hunger sated. There were times when my lips were upon hers, and I shut my eyes. I felt her petals closing in on me. Translucent, gossamer shields surrounded me. I breathed the air, thick with pollen, and was intoxicated by it.

Yet do not take Vermilion's word for this. I know now that Emilia is winning at her little game. Her diaries have a greater force, I fear, than any words that I can conjure. How everything has changed these last weeks! I began this work hopefully, certain that I could prove the rectitude of my actions; my innocence in this unpleasant business. I told you I would be rational. Yet I begin to find her words have more sense than mine. I am drawn in by her presence. I no longer stand apart from her, disentangling the strands that she throws out, but rather am enmeshed within them. This story is out of my control. I feel I am merely an element of it, and only Emilia has power to dissolve these threads. Sometimes, late at night, I swear I feel her, close to me, in my bedchamber. The window is always open of course. Though I fear her spirit, I would not shut it out. Indeed, I believe that she can sense my anxiety, for when it is at its height, that is when she comes to me. So often now, when I read her diaries, I feel I am no more than a pawn in her elaborate game. She comes from beyond the grave, yet still she seems able to exert great influence upon my life. There is one passage in her diaries which I return to, again and again. I will give it to you here, in the hope that you might understand my sentiment. In the hope that you will not think me mad.

EMILIA

THIS ROOM, IN which I write, is bare, and devoid of ornament. It is so different from my room at the Temple, where I was surrounded by painted mythologies, and little objects shining with gilt. There, everything was procured for my convenience, or for the enjoyment of my eye. Here, I am offered no comfort, nor no diversions. And yet I feel I want for nothing.

It is a dark room, at the back of a house. I very rarely see bright sunlight, for I am too ashamed to go out and face the world. Instead, I remain indoors, and receive no visitors, except for Helena and one other, whom I shall not yet name. I make the most of the little light I do receive, by placing my desk before the window, and reading there in the mornings. In the afternoons, I am forced to light a candle, and that is when I write in this journal.

Yes, such plain, dingy walls these are, that I have decided to mount Vermilion's mirror above the fireplace. I do not like to look at myself. Indeed, to do so is to inflict a kind of self-punishment. And yet if I am to die, I must not, like my father, go blindly. I will look at myself, each day. I will see what I am. I will see the face that has ruined me. For it is true – I blame my downfall on this. This face that is not what it should be.

When Helena comes each day, bringing food, and books, she often asks me why I have hung that mirror there, in such a prominent position. I try to explain it to her, but always I falter, knowing that she will laugh at me. She is not so superstitious as I, and much that I have experienced, she would not believe. She would say I make up stories, or that I dream. But there is more to it than this. I will tell you. You must believe me.

There is another reason why I hang that mirror there. For at night, when I am alone, I often see a movement in it. Something outside the window – a branch disturbed by the wind, or the flutter of a bird's wing – causes the moon-shadows to shift. I have adjusted the mirror so it is at the right angle from my armchair. Because it is this that sparks my thoughts; makes my mind begin to whir. There is something magical about the nights here. When the sun has gone from the sky, I cannot see the dampness of the walls, nor the reflection of my face. I see only the moving shapes of the trees, cast across my room. Often, I blow out the yellow flame of the candle, and I sit in silence, in my chair, feeling the shadows leap over my face. The stories of my life seem somehow to focus then. I am able to order the past; give each incident its just place and significance. I see the *form* of things. And during these times, I feel almost possessed. I am myself, and yet I am more than I. How could I write these words, if I were no more than a simple girl of nineteen years? It is not possible. Rather, when the night comes, I believe I am entered by a much older spirit. One who has roamed the earth since ancient times; a female spirit whose knowledge is un-bounded. And when she is inside me, I find I am transformed. I am sibylline. Prophetess. I say nothing. I do nothing. And yet I feel as if I am acting within another sphere. I am sitting in my trailing, dark robes, and my life, and that of Vermilion, are a tangled mass of threads beneath me. Effortlessly, I unravel them, and I find I have a kind of net, which I cast out, across the future. Helena says I bind myself to him thereby, but it is not true. I merely wish that, when I am dead, he will not forget me. He will feel my influence, pulling him, shaping him, even then. At first he will try to escape the net, but soon he will see it is impossible. The net is a part of him. It is made from his flesh and mine; his thoughts and mine. He will see, if he looks hard enough, that he does not need to work to understand the past. I have done the work for him. Here, in my words, are the strands of that net. And in his words are the cross-threads. When we both were alive, those words were always struggling; fighting against each other. But now I have disentangled them. I have made everything plain. All he must do is learn that what we see has no meaning. It is the shape of things beneath that is important. The pattern. The form. The given. The unchangeable. No effort is required by him, either to weave or to unravel. Eventually he will learn to understand this. That the prophetess has done it all. The shape is plain.

After my death, Vermilion will do anything to escape me. I know that, and it does not concern me. For the net will do its work. Slowly he will be drawn back to the place where he began. He will return to Carmine Hall, and there he will understand that there is no fighting what is pre-ordained. There is no escaping love. Once he accepts that, he will find the net begins to dissolve. And when he closes his eyes, he will find me in his heart.

VERMILION

NOW DO YOU understand me? How can a man struggle against powers such as these? What she has predicted has come to pass. Though I fought so hard to escape this place, in the end I had no choice but to return to it. To face the truth. And the truth is simple. One morning, upon Primrose Hill, I contemplated death. The startling beauty of the morning made me aware, as never before, of the value of life, yet I had no choice but to watch a bullet speed through the heart of another man. And when I saw this, I believe there was a metamorphosis. All my bravado, my manly actions, my cavalier wit, seemed but nought. I was soiled by the occasion. By its sheer futility. And I wished, in an instant, to be pure again. Pure as the scent of morning. Pure as Emilia. I vowed to myself I would be cleansed.

Yes, as my carriage rattled up Haverstock Hill, to fetch the nearest coroner, I could think upon nothing but her, and how I had wronged her. My shame coursed through me, as I remembered my antics in the Celestial Chamber. I saw the fear upon her face; fear which I had occasioned. And I wished for nothing but that I might counterbalance my villainy, by offering her a thing that I had never offered to any woman. My hand in marriage.

29

VERMILION

OF ALL THE nights that I remember, there is one, above all, which remains with me. I do not know why it sticks thus in my mind, for there were others, later in that month of March, when we experienced a union much stronger than was possible on our first evening (I call it our first, for it was the first time that we had ventured outside the Temple with one another, and it was the first that I spent with her when my intentions were nought but honourable). Images from that evening resurface, often, in hopeful dreams, and occasionally distort themselves and form the basis of my nightmares. For what could be a worse reminder to me of my failings, than to fall asleep and watch that strange yet marvellous evening turn vile before my eyes. To watch her, laughing and smiling, but then to witness a hole appearing where her nose should be, a hole which spouts serpents that devour her eyes and wind themselves around her neck, squeezing the last drops of life from her body.

But I grow morbid. I had not intended to burden you with my visions. I should tell you, instead, of the events of that evening. As the Doctor was not giving a lecture, Emilia agreed that she would steal out to meet me. The twin porters would not be attending the door, and with the use of my key, Emilia would be able to return without alerting any person to her absence.

I felt as if our outing would be a kind of beginning for us, and I resolved that I would take her to a place that reflected her beauty. I would show her a side of the metropolis which she had never seen. Thinking how to impress her, I considered what setting might be most appropriate for a declaration of my love.

Only one was perfect in all respects. I would take her to Ranelagh.

Yes – and though I long to tell you of the event, I fear, more and more, that you are doubting my honesty. Like me, you are beguiled by Emilia and you have heard so much about my malice that only her own words will convince you. Prepare yourselves, then, to be taken to a place which is the quintessence of loveliness: the jewel of the metropolis. Prepare to enter the Rotunda.

EMILIA

IN THE GLOOM of the garden, I wondered where Vermilion had brought me. It seemed mean-looking and ill-lit, and there were very few people around. He glanced at me, and I thought I should look pleased that he had brought me here. This was, after all, the much-boasted Ranelagh. I had heard tales of its wonder, and had accepted Vermilion's invitation with as much pleasure as trepidation. Yet the little Chinese Pavilion and the canal that I had heard of were not visible in the dimness. And I wondered if this were some obscure joke that he was playing on me. If he wished to make me a laughing stock, I would not take it lightly. I would tell him of my disgust at his behaviour. I would threaten to inform the Doctor of his antics upon the Celestial Bed. And to tell Lord Quinton the name of the true father of Helena's child. If Vermilion would punish me, I would punish him also.

But then, cautiously, he took my hand, and said,

'Come, Emilia. Let us go inside.'

And at that, I had to force myself to reply. I vowed that I would be strong, yet there could be no denying the force concentrated within him. Most truly, it was stronger than the fire of the Celestial Throne; a veritable store of electricity! It flowed between us, and all at once I remembered why I was here. Because this power was greater than I. Because he and I were magnets, compelled to meet. I knew, suddenly, that he was powerless as I. Yet I also knew that I must find at least a show of strength. He must not see how he affected me.

'Inside?' I said. 'I had thought we came to see the gardens.'

'Ah no, Emilia,' he replied, 'the focus of this place is not the garden itself, but the Rotunda. Come. I will show you.'

And I followed him to a place where I saw a number of people entering a door, and, close behind them, we entered.

Never, not since my earliest experience of the Doctor's Temple, have I experienced such a sense of wonder as when first I saw the Rotunda. I was overcome by the sight of this pleasure-dome. By the thousand glittering lamps high above my head, bright as the midday sun, and by the very magnificence of this round building, higher than a cathedral, more splendid than anything I had ever seen. It seemed, to me, as if the whole of the beau-monde of London revolved about the four central pillars, and Vermilion busied himself instantly with pointing out a Prince of Some Place here and a Duke of Some Other Place there. Yet it was not the people that interested me most. My eyes were flitting at a tremendous speed, wishing to absorb all that they could see. Above, there was a gallery, divided into boxes, and in one part of it an organ with a beautiful choir, from which such sounds poured forth as would make even the Doctor jealous. Below the gallery, and all around the room, were little painted boxes, also illuminated, where people were taking refreshments, and it was to one of these that Vermilion beckoned me.

'So, Emilia!' he said, once we were sitting. 'What do you think of Ranelagh?'

'It is surely the most beautiful place in all the world,' I replied, noticing how pretty were the little vases of narcissi that adorned the tables. 'I have found, of late, that even the Temple can seem too small a place, and I am often confined within my chamber. To be inside a building of such a magnificent size is like being in the open air again. I am glad to be here.'

He smiled at me then, and all at once I felt myself to be extremely confused. Here was Vermilion, a man who had subjected me to such trials as would shame a harlot, and here was I, simpering before him, as if I had no grudge to bear. I knew that he wished me to be overwhelmed. Too overwhelmed, perhaps, to think of expressing my anger at him. I had to find a way to move beyond this politeness that I had been taught always to observe. Yet at first, it was impossible.

'Shall I order you some coffee, Emilia? Or some punch?'

'Oh, no,' I said. 'I will drink only water.'

'The Doctor is not here to watch you.'

'No. But I respect his teachings. And I wish only for a glass of plain and simple water, that will doubtless revivify me.'

'I cannot think that one so vital as you would need revivifying.'

'My beauty would soon fade if I drank the vile brews that others are foolish enough to swallow.'

Not wishing, perhaps, to anger me in any way, Vermilion smiled, and indulged my wish by ordering not one glass of water, but two. I tried to avoid looking at him when he smiled thus, for I did not wish to be beguiled by him. Rather, I focused my eyes again on the marvels that I saw about me. I looked towards the high, black, central pillars of the Rotunda, where little fires burned in fireplaces, and was glad that I was not near them. I regarded the women, who paraded the room quite shamelessly, and was shocked to see how many of them endangered themselves by adopting hairstyles more elaborate, even, than that which I myself once had worn. I swear I saw, upon their heads, an acre and a half of shrubbery, besides slopes, grass plots, tulip-beds, clumps of peonies, kitchen gardens and greenhouses! The thought of what lurked within those pretty flowerbeds was enough to make me feel quite ill.

Added to this, I could not but remember how the Doctor had spoken of the foul and putrid exhalations of other people, the stench of their dirty bodies and garments and the corrupted substances that might leak from hidden sores. I was glad to be seated in one of these painted boxes which were a little isolated from the main walkway, where people circled around and around, making me dizzy to watch them.

A serving man came towards us shortly, bearing two glasses of water on a silver tray. I imagined, suddenly, that the water would, as it was placed before us, turn into a boiling mass of blood, proving, once and for all, that I was a Devil Woman, and I must have shuddered, for Vermilion detected my unease.

'What is it, Emilia?' he said. 'Are you cold?'

'Oh no, not at all,' I said. 'I was thinking on a foolish thing. No matter.'

'Come – tell me of this foolish thing.'

'I cannot,' I replied, forcing a little laugh. 'My mind is full of too many imaginings. They are best left unspoken.'

'I find that difficult to believe,' he said.

He spoke so civilly that I could not understand the change in him.

'If they are your thoughts,' he continued, 'they must surely merit expression. I tell you, Emilia, though you will not believe me, there is not a thought in your head that I do not wish to know about. I wish to know all there is to know about you.'

'Why so, sir?' I said, surprised at the vehemence of my expression. 'For before now, you have cared only for my body. I cannot truly believe that you have an interest in my mind.'

'Indeed – my behaviour has merited this treatment, and yet . . .'

'And yet, what, sir? Do you think that, all of a sudden, I will love you again? I am here, Vermilion, but do not think that means I have forgotten what has passed. You have used me ill.'

His face, as I spoke, bore a most strange expression. It took a few moments before I realized the meaning of this. The expression was strange, simply because I had never seen him in such a mood as this. His brow was furrowed, his mouth drooped, his eyes were without focus. In short, he seemed to suffer.

'And is there no way,' he said, 'that I can convince you that I have changed?'

'Sir,' I said, then paused to take a sip of my water, relishing the refreshment, 'only time will convince me of that.'

'I wish you would not call me 'sir', Emilia. Why are you so formal with me?'

'Because I do not know you well, sir. Because you are, as yet, no friend of mine.'

'And how long will it take, Emilia, before you will call me friend?'

'I cannot say,' I replied, thinking 'Never, never can I be a friend to you,' then was immediately saddened at my thought. 'I cannot say.'

'How is it you are so hard on me?'

'I?' I said, with true astonishment in my voice. 'I? Hard? Who are you to speak, Vermilion? You tried to make love to me, Vermilion, when you were hot from the Lady Quinton's bed. How can you call *me* hard, when you continue to court *me*, whilst the Lady Quinton has your child growing within her?'

He looked aghast. This was not at all the Vermilion I had known before. That man was so in control of his senses that he might hear news of an impending earthquake and respond only by raising an eyebrow. He might, whilst dining out, hear that his lodgings had burned down, but he would do nought but wipe his mouth upon a napkin and inquire coolly whether this news merited an interruption of his dinner. But what was this display of emotion before me? It was so unlike him, that I could not believe it was merely a performance. No, he seemed to stutter almost, 'I do not ... I cannot ... How can you . . .?'

And he half stood up from the table, then sat down again, then took a sip of water, before he finally blurted out, 'Emilia, hear me . . .'

'I am listening.'

And then he paused a moment. His look was an entreaty that I should believe his words.

'If you do not think that I care for the child within her, you are mistaken. I am not so cold as you think me, Emilia. But think. Do you believe that she will own the child is mine? Do you think that ever, for a moment, she would even dream of harming her reputation thus?'

I hesitated.

'No. I do not believe she would. And yet . . .'

'Emilia — Helena wanted a child, more than anything. And Lord Quinton was incapable of giving it to her.'

'And so you obliged her?'

I was astonished that I should speak like this to him.

'It does not look good, I warrant it.'

'How can I forgive you for this, Vermilion?' I asked, despairing suddenly. 'How can I?'

'Remember, Emilia. If I could love the child, I would do so. And yet, to protect my own heart, I must distance myself. I will never be acknowledged as the father.'

'I do not care!' I said. 'I do not care about this! I do not know why I am here. I do not know where your affection lies.'

'With you, Emilia,' he said, with such earnestness that I almost believed him. 'Only with you.'

'But you are expert in deceiving. You could make any woman believe that you love.'

'Yet I would not offer my hand in marriage ... to any woman.'

His words trailed off as he spoke them, not in regret, I think, but rather in embarrassment.

You can imagine, of course, my reaction to his words. Young and capricious as I was, I was so moved by them that I barely knew where to look. Though I should not have let him win my heart with such an easy stroke as this, though he had done nothing to deserve my love, I could not but be exhilarated at the promise of his words. I could feel the force of his gaze upon me, that was no arrogant look, but rather one of tenderest regard, and anxiety. How can I explain, to you, who read this document of my life, how I seemed to give in to him so easily? Perhaps I can only remind you of my surroundings. For while we spoke, even when I was angry, I could not help but be aware of the beauty of this place. I was so pleased to be outside the Temple, and to be, once more, a part of the world's throng. Just for once to be attired in a full, brocaded dress (without stays, you understand), and to feel as much a part of society as every other person here, was marvellous indeed. Slowly, almost imperceptibly, I had grown to feel somewhat belittled by my role at the Temple. Perhaps I had for too long thought of myself as superior, yet now I saw that there I was nothing more than a freak. The looks I received in this place were so different from those I received at the Temple. There, men drooled, rubbing their eyeglasses the better to observe my breasts, leering at me as if I were a common trull. Though they were rich and dressed in fine silks, their eyes bulged from their sockets, just as another part of their anatomy bulged beneath their breeches. They dared to pick their noses whilst they ogled me (for what did they care of my opinion – I was only there for their eyes to devour), and they whispered in one another's ears, before bursting out with obscene laughter, which I knew I had occasioned.

Only think, dear Reader, of Ranelagh! However I might now wish that we mortals were not led by such fragile things as outer beauty (desiring only that my spirit might soar; hoping that the mind might discover regions more delightful than any known in this material world), yet I am as susceptible as any to sensual delights. Yes, all that was before my eyes pleasured me. Nor were my ears, my nose, my mouth or my hands disappointed. For the sound of the orchestra, the scent of the narcissi, the taste of . . .

His lips upon mine! The touch of . . .

His rough chin which I cradled as I kissed!

For how else might I reply to such a statement as this? Yes, I will admit it – when I was seemingly most safe from Vermilion, when he trembled like a young boy before me, in truth I was most in danger. I leaned towards him, and took what was mine. His breath. His essence. His very soul.

You will not believe it? You think him undeserving, and me a fool? And yet I tell you, if you think this, you have not understood me; you have not understood that at that time, for me, he was necessary as water.

And then, I pulled away. I disentangled my arms from his; looked at him. I was speechless.

'I take it that you accept my offer?' he said.

'You are truly serious, Vermilion?' I asked. 'You do not mock me?'

'I had rather mock the sun for shining. I would rather throw derision on the moon for being crescent, Emilia.'

But though I was moved by his words, a sudden fear enveloped me.

'I think my brother has reserved some dowry for me, and yet I cannot think that he would give it to you, Vermilion. I have reason to suspect he would rather starve than connect our family's name with yours.'

'I have no need of a dowry, Emilia. Material things, to me, are worthless as shadows. It is only love that has substance.'

I do have faith that, at that moment, he truly believed in the words he spoke. Though now I am certain his world would have crumbled, had his chattels been stripped from him, this does not signify a lack of honesty in his intention. There was much, between us, that was still necessary to discuss, before I could be certain that I should accept his proposal, and yet I could not help rejoicing at the prospect. For a change *had* come over him. He was suffused by a different spirit and I was convinced of his integrity.

'And Helena?' I said. 'Did you love her?'

'You know I was mistaken. I have much to regret. You must marry me, Emilia. Say you will have me.'

'I can say nothing,' I said, 'until . . .'

And then I broke off my sentence, for I had seen something that truly startled me. I must have been gaping, wide-eyed and open-mouthed, for Vermilion waved his hand before my eyes, and even then, I could scarcely find breath to speak.

'Look!' I said. 'Vermilion, look!'

And he followed my eyes, yet clearly did not see what I had seen.

'What is it, Emilia?' he said. 'I see nothing.'

'Over there, near the orchestra!'

'Tell me what you see, my love. I do not know what you are looking at.'

'If I had not known that he was dead . . .'

'That *who* was dead?'

'Vermilion – I swear . . . Oh, he has turned again. Would I could see his face.'

'Whose face? Emilia. What is this?'

And then I told him what had so alarmed me.

'Lord Smellie! That man. I know it is not possible, and yet – I could almost swear it is him.'

Vermilion began to laugh. He turned and saw now what I was looking at. The Rotunda was a little emptier than when we had first arrived, and there was a clear passage through to the orchestra. Occasionally people would pass in front of the object of our attention, yet he was standing there, plain as day. How, after all, could one miss a Macaroni?

He had his back to us, yet one did not need to see the painted face to know what breed of man was this. A mass of borrowed curls cascaded down the back of a tight jacket of violent pink, and on top of those curls a tiny matching hat was balanced. As we looked towards him, we saw the man gesture with his tasselled cane. I had often watched Lord Smellie from my window and this movement was most surely a part of his dainty repertoire.

Vermilion raised an eyebrow at the sight of the Beau – his laughter had indeed been stopped by this striking resemblance.

'They are invading the capital!' he said. 'I am certain their number is increasing.'

'I could have sworn it was him, Vermilion,' I said. 'And yet I am foolish. You killed him in the duel, did you not?'

'I did indeed.'

'And are you certain that he died? Perhaps he was merely wounded.'

'I tell you. I saw his dying breath. I saw the wound through his heart.'

'Of course. I am sorry, Vermilion. I am much prone to imagining. Yet . . .'

And at this, the Macaroni turned, and once again I saw the

astonishing resemblance. Vermilion must have seen it too, because he became a little pale at the sight. We watched the Macaroni bow before his companion, flourishing his free hand before him, then turn and move towards the door.

'Come!' he said, cheerful now. 'I warrant you, he is indeed most like him. Let us follow him, so that we may satisfy our curiosity.'

Vermilion took my hand and helped me traverse the Rotunda. We wove through the crowd, bright threads pulled across a tapestry. The music continued all the while, and I worried lest I should trip and find myself beneath the feet of those couples who were beginning to dance. Always, the bright pink spot in the crowd remained at the edge of our vision. Then, as we reached the central pillars, he slipped quickly through the doorway to the garden.

'Come on, Emilia!' Vermilion said. 'We'll catch him yet!'

I realized then that this was sport for him. He had been shocked at first, but good sense prevailed. He knew this was not Lord Smellie, but he thought it might be amusing to chase this fellow. I laughed too, to see the pleasure etched on his face.

My laughter continued as I moved across the Rotunda, towards the garden door. I felt a rush of blood to my cheeks, and my heart was beating fast. Vermilion's hand was hot to the touch, and he stopped, before the doorway, to kiss me again, full on the lips.

'So!' he said, as he pulled away. 'Let us find this rascally deceiver.'

And, reeling from the impact of his embrace, I followed him from the sparkling light of the Rotunda into the cool caress of the garden.

Before, I had not liked the garden but now, after the brilliance of the interior of the Rotunda, after the noise of laughter against the melodies of violins, and after the heat of so many bodies in one place, I could think of nothing more desirable than the slightly dank air that I now breathed. What a contrast it was — the blue moonlight was soft upon our faces, such a relief after the lamps inside. And how welcome this new silence was to my ears!

But where was the Macaroni? In those first few pleasurable seconds, I did not think upon him, but I saw that already Vermilion was rushing ahead, peering down the dark avenues before us.

When Vermilion came back to me, shaking his head, a shiver ran through me. The look on his face seemed to echo my thoughts. Could it be that this Macaroni had vanished into the night air? All was so still here in the garden, as if the ground had not been disturbed, before our arrival, by human footsteps. The air was unruffled. The trees seemed to hold secrets. The rustle of the branches whispered that ghosts were all around us.

But Vermilion, if he did harbour similar suspicions, would not speak of them.

'We were too slow,' he said. 'A shame. I would like to have seen his face.'

'Do you not think it strange, Vermilion, that he vanished so quickly?'

'Ah,' he said, putting his arms around my waist, and pulling me towards him. 'These fops are wily creatures, did you not know it? They are always quick to deceive.'

And with this he placed a kiss upon my lips and already I had forgotten the Macaroni. Lord Smellie, the perfumed, powdered, primped and piffling suitor, was dead. He could not harm me now. Now, all I knew was the warmth of a thick cloak that surrounded me. In the chill of the garden, a sheet of red velvet was wrapped about me. It flapped in the wind a moment, but soon held me close and tight, so that I never wished to escape from its embrace. I was safe here. Safer than I had ever been. Though a vile pink ghost had dissolved into the air, it was impossible that he could harm me. With my eyes closed I had entered into a different realm, which spectres cannot enter. A realm where only pleasure has a place.

Slowly, only slowly, did I emerge. I saw Vermilion's face first of all, blanched beneath the moon. His eyes shone in that light, reflecting the stars perhaps. But though I was drawn by that face, I could not help but sense, at the edge of my vision, another thing, a movement, that demanded attention. I turned a little within Vermilion's arms, and saw a thing which most astounded me. A flash of pink, which, had it not been for the bright moonlight, I might not have seen. The man who would be Lord Smellie moved so quickly, I was certain that he desired not to be seen. And I was certain this was no good omen for our love.

30

EMILIA

WHENEVER THE DOCTOR was not at home, Vermilion and I would linger upon the Celestial Bed. At first, it is true, too many unpleasant memories lingered in the Celestial Chamber. I could not help but think of what had passed before. It was a scene imprinted upon my memory. And yet, in spite of this, the Bed continued to have a strange fascination for me. I remembered, you see, the feel of Vermilion's naked flesh against my own. I remembered how his touch had electrified me, and I longed to feel this again.

Yet this time it was not long before I realized that I truly had nothing to fear from Vermilion. Above our heads, as we cavorted on the Bed, the sculpted figure of Hymen seemed to be watching us. Hymen, you know already, is the God of Marriage, and Vermilion, being changed, would not offend such a God by disregarding the rules of matrimony. No, for the sake of our love, Vermilion said, my own hymen should remain unbroken until the night of our marriage.

To me, this was the proof of his love. If he had desired that I let go of my virginity, would not I have said yes? Vermilion had acquired a new sweetness, and I fed upon his words, his look, his touch. His former wickedness seemed submerged now. A different Vermilion had emerged, and I felt certain that together we might renew ourselves.

Yet from where did it stem, this trust? You think I was beguiled by the lights of Ranelagh? Or by the perfumed odours of the Celestial Bed – the lavender flowers, the rose leaves, the oriental spices? By the gilded mirrors, perhaps, was I ensnared, or by the magnetism that continually flowed through the Bed? How, after all, could I have thus forgotten my poor friend

Helena, who had more right to the company of Vermilion than I?

I tell you – I had not seen Helena since the day she revealed that she was with his child. I scanned the crowd for her, each time I sang before the Doctor's audience. When I stood at the head of the Temple stairs, beneath the dome, and I watched the ladies arrive, all incognito, I always looked for that Peacock mask, but there was none so elaborate, no woman so tall, so straight, so perfect as Helena. I felt most sorry to have lost such a friend. I wished she would return. And yet I knew that she was a married woman. Now that she was with child, she had no excuse to frequent the Temple. I was not certain that I would see her again, and the thought filled. me with regret. I did not think she would forgive me, for what worse injury could I do her than marry her love – the father of her child?

All I could do was embrace my new-found happiness. For happiness it was, to be with Vermilion. My desire for him increased with each new day, occasioned not only by his physical charms, but by other things. Gone was the man who paraded naked and erect about the room. In the place of that arrogance, I found a new reluctance. A sense that he desired only to please me. I tell you, though you may laugh to hear the words, Vermilion had become kind. He was vain enough still, and his high opinion of himself had not waned. He remained a witty man, who would not tolerate fools gladly. But, simply, though still he pleased me with his kisses, which could not exactly be called chaste (kisses upon my breasts, upon my thighs, his fingers lingering in such places as could not but give me pleasure) he became what I would, without hesitation, call a Friend.

You doubt, even now? Perhaps, when I have told my story, you will gain some little sympathy for him. You will think he is not entirely evil. This is not the purpose of these journals, you understand, for ultimately the old Vermilion returned, came up for air and gained strength to conquer the new Vermilion I had come to love. But believe this: that once he was good to me. Believe that without him, I would be about to die in ignorance.

In ignorance of what?

I have told you that I am a murderess. When I was a little child, I murdered my mother. Let me tell you the story I told Vermilion. Picture us, if you will. It is early afternoon. Rose-coloured curtains are drawn across the windows of the Celestial Chamber. The Celestial Bed emits no sound (for the orchestra in the adjacent room is not playing), yet still we are lulled by the magical moving landscape, situated at the foot of the bed. Vermilion is winding this little toy for my amusement, and together we watch a nuptial scene: a bride's procession enters the Temple of Hymen. And as we watch, we are invigorated – by the stallion hairs beneath the rose sheets; by the air, thick with rich balsams. Vermilion and I are easy together. We have spent an hour or two in this place, caressing one another; giving and receiving pleasure in a multitude of ways. And now we are sated. We are quiet. The March sun beyond the curtains gives the room a warm, pinkish hue. I have been lulled by this soft light, yet suddenly, for no apparent reason, I am disturbed by it. This light is womb-like.

And instantly I am afraid. I think of my mother who kept me thus, within her, guarding me safely as the room guards me now. I showed no gratitude for her care. No, rather, I punished her for nurturing me thus. I killed her.

The very words chill me. My secret marriage to Vermilion is set for the beginning of June. Yet what if, on that night, he should discover my crime? What if, on the night my hymen breaks, more blood should pour from that place than is usual? Guilt-blood. Like the bloody water that gushed from the Hot-well. I feared that the Doctor was wrong. That my cleansing in the Temple was only superficial. When my new husband thrust into me, breaking my hymen, how would he react if a stream should flow? Blood not just from a broken membrane, but from a broken heart. My mother's heart. If all the blood in my mother's body should pour from between my legs?

'Vermilion,' I said, and I felt his hand instinctively stroke my thigh.

'What is it, Melia?' (This was the name he had coined for me, since he had come to love me.)

'There is a thing I have not told you. A thing of which I am much ashamed.'

'I cannot believe my love has more to be ashamed of than I myself. Surely it is a trifling thing?'

He kissed me tenderly upon the forehead.

'No,' I said. 'Not trifling at all, my love. I have committed a crime greater than any that even you have been guilty of.'

He laughed at this.

'It is not possible!'

I pulled away.

'It is most possible. Vermilion, I murdered my mother.'

I saw his shock but, after that, I remember very little. The instant that I spoke the words I regretted them. I felt unable to breathe, suffocated by the intense rosiness of the room that seemed to swell around me. I closed my eyes, unwilling to face the consequences of my words, and found that the red light flooded through even here. I put my head upon the pillow and it was soft and spongy as a mother's belly. I felt myself revolving within this space, my head against a silent, fleshy wall. Somewhere, beyond, a voice was summoning me. It echoed in my ear, far away as the sea.

'Come, Emilia. You speak nonsense, my love.'

'Go away!' cried the silent voice within my head. 'Go away. You cannot love me now.'

'My love – speak to me.'

It was Vermilion's voice. But so distant.

'I know how your mother died, Emilia. I tell you, love – you did not kill her.'

An impossible dream. A voice that I had conjured up to take away my guilt. Not Vermilion's voice at all. But all the same, I open my eyes and meet those of my lover. I wish to speak to him, but fear my voice will be too weak.

'I killed her,' I said, not lifting my head from the pillow. 'When I was only a child.'

'And how do you suppose that you killed her?'

'A knife, perhaps. I am certain it was a bloody death.'

'And what makes you so certain that you committed this crime?'

'Why do you question me, Vermilion? I speak the truth. I only desire to know if you will love me still.'

'I question you because you are wrongly informed. Tell me – what makes you think that you are guilty?'

'My father said certain . . . things. If I had not been born, my mother would still be alive. He said that once. "The cause of my agony" – that is what he called me, when I was no more than five years old.'

'And what if she died as a result of giving birth, Emilia – would you think yourself guilty then?'

His words struck a strange chord upon my heart. I wished to believe him and yet I could not. Slowly, I found the strength to push myself up from the pillow.

'How can you know about the circumstances of my birth?'

'Your father visited the Doctor, Emilia – do you not remember that? In Bristol.'

'Yes but . . .'

'There was a time – I could not forget it – he wept before us. When the Doctor told him that he was incurable.'

'My father wept?'

'Yes. I vow it.'

And then Vermilion told his story. He told it slowly, his arm around my shoulder, soothing me; reassuring me. And he painted such a picture of my poor father that, had my sorrow not been balanced by my relief, I would surely have wept copious tears. Instead, I merely listened, quietly.

When my father learned from the Doctor that there was no cure for his disease, he began to rail. These were the very eyes that watched his poor wife die, he said. These were the eyes that looked upon her in her last moments, when she lay with her new child in her arms. According to Vermilion, so delirious with grief was my father on that day, that he gave a most gruesome, unasked-for account of my mother's death. And that, above all, was why Vermilion and the Doctor could not forget the meeting. Vermilion did not wish to alarm me, yet I insisted that I know the full story. What was it that was so unpleasant he would remember the words of a stranger, spoken to him over six years ago?

This is what I learned. When my mother was in labour, she was attended by a male midwife. I know nothing of this man, so I cannot say how far the fault was his. All I know is that my mother was in pain. I, being a babe too large for her liking, was pressing within her; pressing, pressing, pressing; yet I was reluctant to emerge into the world. So it was that, in order to help relieve her misery, the midwife got out his forceps. In my dreams I see them now as large metal instruments of torture, descending towards my head. I repeat – this may have been a good man who clutched my head thus in his vice. No doubt he behaved according to the strictest laws governing his profession. Yet the fact remains. As I was thus pulled from my mother's womb, the force of the movement rent her vagina horribly. My mother was torn asunder.

No doubt, also, the doctors did their best for her. My father would have paid the highest prices for their services. Yet the fissure did not heal. It became infected and began to ooze a kind of yellow pus. Soon after, a fever was upon her. Within two weeks, the doctors diagnosed a poison in the blood. Death came quickly.

Perhaps you will not think my Vermilion kind for being the bearer of such news as this. And yet he relieved me, finally, of my guilt. Though it was indeed true that I was the agent of my mother's death, I was innocent of murder. And the peace that this knowledge brought me was tremendous indeed. I felt, on hearing Vermilion's words, that the robes of the Goddess were no longer necessary for me. For what was Emilia the Goddess, but a negation of the Devil Child. And if the Devil Child did not exist, then what remained was a mortal. A woman. And for this, more than any other gift, I thank my Vermilion.

EMILIA

DURING THIS MONTH of March, a change came over me. Already, by using the Celestial Bed without his permission, I had betrayed the Doctor. Now, slowly, I found his doctrines were becoming less important to me. Even, I would say, I avoided him when I could, for fear that he would remark this alteration in my being. It was not difficult. The Doctor's wife had once again left the Temple and taken her children to Pontefract, perhaps because she sensed the Doctor's desire for solitude. It seemed that all and sundry were deserting the Adelphi Terrace, for my brother was still absent, the Peacock Lady had not been seen, and even the Doctor's audiences were beginning to dwindle somewhat. He was not in the best of tempers, knowing that he needed to ensure the Temple's continued success. He would write a pamphlet, he said, which would be entitled thus:

A Sketch or Short Description of Dr Graham's Medical Apparatus, erected about the end of the year 1779, in his house on the Royal Terrace, Adelphi.

This pamphlet, he said, would be distributed to many important personages by his twin porters, and would serve to illustrate to all who had not yet visited the Temple what wonders he had in store for them.

For Vermilion and me, the Doctor's withdrawal to his room could not have come at a better time. It seemed that the apothecaries and the porters and the members of the orchestra all knew of our alliance, yet none were so malicious as to tell Dr Graham this news. I knew that once we were married, I would leave the Temple, yet for the moment, I desired to stay here.

Still, more and more, I felt distant from Dr Graham. For several weeks I had not run in St James's Park, I did not always take my Aetherial Balsam, and often I closed the window at night, because I was cold. Vermilion had begun to convince me that some of the Doctor's 'remedies' might be as injurious to my health as my former bad habit of wearing stays. In principle, he said, the Doctor's methods were sound, but they should not be taken to extremes.

I remember, in particular, one afternoon when we entered the Celestial Chamber, furtive as usual, and not a little terrified that we might be discovered there. Vermilion carried with him a box, which he placed on a cabinet beside the Bed, refusing to tell me what it contained. Then, delicately, and with extreme tenderness, he undressed me (as was our custom – do not think that, though I remained a virgin, we were entirely chaste). Yet rather than placing his lips to my breast, he shook his head, and there was a pained expression on his face. He traced his finger across my ribs, which had no flesh upon them. His fingertips were lost in the hollows between the bones.

'Melia,' he said. 'My love, you will surely vanish if you do not begin to eat properly.'

I looked down at myself then, and saw, for the first time, what others had seen before. Not the body of an Angel. Not some unearthly, aetherial substance, but a body, wasting away. A starving girl of sixteen years. A pale and skeletal frame.

'I thought,' I said, suddenly afraid of the sight of myself, 'that Angels did not need to be nourished. I thought I might live on air.'

'On air?' he said, horrified.

Vermilion traced the features of my face, with such care that I nearly wept. Then he reached over to his box, and opened the lid. Within, to my surprise, was no necklace, no jewellery box, but a small cake, no bigger than the palm of my hand. He took it, on a saucer, from the box, and said:

'Emilia – I would like you to eat.'

And though I felt the protestations growing in the back of

my throat, though my stomach turned over at the thought of eating a thing so rich, I knew that he was right. In my attempt to embody my own ideal of Goddess, I had suffered enough. If I were truly to become mortal again, I must eat the stuff that mortals eat.

'I do not know if I am able to, Vermilion,' I said. 'The cake is too large.'

'Then you must eat a smaller portion,' he said, breaking it in his hand, and offering me the morsel.

I hesitated before taking it, but take it I did. I had expected to be revolted by the taste, for it had been so long since I had eaten such a thing. Yet I was overjoyed by the sensation. The sweetness of the cake astonished me. It seemed to swell in my mouth, filling each crevice with a buttery warmth. I tasted cinnamon in the mixture, and caraway seed. And as I sucked the spongy substance against my palate, I watched my Vermilion smiling at me. Smiling upon his Angel turned corporeal. Smiling upon his Melia.

I had begun to eat again. And, truly, it seemed that I had come to my senses at exactly the right time, for I discovered, with some alarm, that they had begun to lampoon the Temple upon the stage. Yes, one George Colman had written a play entitled *The Genius of Nonsense*, which was now playing at the Haymarket Theatre!

The Doctor, during one of our now rare conversations, told me about it. He had been present, in a stage-box, on the opening night. There, besides seeing his Temple ridiculed, he had had the mortification of being refused the opportunity of purchasing one of the bills sold by men imitating his own twin porters. Strangely, however, the Doctor did not seem entirely displeased, perhaps because it provided, in a sense, some additional publicity for the Temple. Yet I was less than happy. When one of the apothecaries read me the newspaper report later that day, I was agitated by the description. On the stage, so it said, the Doctor was shown exhibiting a 'satin sofa on glass legs' and the actor who played him was said to have perfectly captured the Doctor's 'grotesque mode of sliding round the room, and the bobbing bows he shot off to the company'. Most of all, however, I was alarmed by these words. 'His Goddess of Health can be seen dying of a sore-throat, got by squalling songs at the top of his cold staircase.'

The lack of reverence appalled me. Squalling indeed! Finally I realized that there was no grandeur remaining in this role I played. I had thought myself above the world, but in fact I was no more than a laughing stock. What hurt me most of all was that the world at large perceived that my health was in danger. The apothecary also let slip another rumour, this one suggesting that I was dying of a cold, caught from sleeping on the damp sheets of the Celestial Bed. Yet none knew the truth. I had been starving myself. I had wanted to efface myself.

Still, I had much consolation. An invitation from Vermilion sat upon my mantelpiece. It was most unexpected, for I had seen Vermilion the previous evening and he had told me that he would be visiting his parents at Carmine Hall, to speak to them of our marriage, and to prepare the way for our meeting. It might be a difficult task, he had said, for although he would not mention my role at the Temple, still he would have to present me as the orphan of a merchant; hardly a fitting match for a nobleman.

I had been disappointed at Vermilion's intended absence, for I was not performing that night and thus would have to spend it alone. Yet he had clearly completed his business early, for here was the most delightful message.

My dearest Emilia,

In celebration of our forthcoming nuptials, I have obtained tickets (one here enclosed) for a grand masked ball, to be held this evening in the New Spring Gardens at Vauxhall. As I shall be travelling direct from Carmine Hall, I will arrange for a carriage and a chaperon to collect you from the Temple, this evening at seven o'clock. Be sure to wear the mask which I enclose. The chaperon

will accompany you to the Turkish dining-tent where I will meet
you.
Yours, ever,
Vermilion

Already, by the end of the day, the invitation was becoming a little ragged at the edges. I lost count of the number of times I held the card to my lips, kissing the gold embossed corners, and the curve of his signature. I tried the mask on, over and again, admiring the image that I reflected. For the mask, also, was golden, and studded with rubies at its winged edges. It covered my eyes only, yet when I coiled my hair on top of my head, and wore the vermilion-coloured dress which my love had recently bought for me, I was as different from the Goddess of Health as I could ever hope to be.

When the hour of seven struck, I left the Temple, once again without the knowledge of the Doctor. My carriage awaited me, and I found my chaperon to be a most polite gentleman. Through my eye-holes, I saw he wore a suit of rusty velvet, a bronze-coloured mask and a heavily powdered wig, which seemed to leave a little puff of smoke in the air each time the carriage crossed a bump in the road. I was beginning to think I might suffocate in a cloud of powder, when we stopped by the York Water Tower, and the chaperon told me that we would be travelling from here by water.

Vermilion had procured a barque, for my comfort, upholstered with red velvet, and covered by a canopy. There were two oarsmen to take me to Vauxhall, and I delighted in my good fortune. It was early April now, and the river was stinking somewhat, but this mattered little to me, for I had not ridden in a boat since I was a child and was elated at the prospect. The chaperon took my hand, and helped me aboard.

How can I ever forget that journey? The barque seemed to glide like a slow lament across the Thames. The splash of oars in the dark blue-green water was cool upon my ears. But more than these, it was the light that astonished me. Great, billowing storm-grey clouds gathered in the sky beyond the towers of

Westminster Abbey, giving the impression that the building was spewing smoke. Yet through these clouds, the sun, low in the sky, shot rays of pale yellow brilliance, which yet had power enough to illuminate the evening. All this was set against a backdrop of the most delicate blue, and the whole combined to make me aware that another change was in the air. I felt the rise and swell of the waves beneath me. I inhaled the smells of damp wood and musty cloth and early blossom, odours which cut across the stench of the river. For the first time (and only now do I know how wrong I was to trust in this), I believed that we might experience a kind of rebirth. And thinking this, as we now emerged from the arches of Westminster Bridge, I opened my mouth to sing. Not for the Doctor; not for his crowd; but a song for the sun and a song for the spring, a song for the plashing water beneath me and the air that surrounded me. But most of all, it was a song for myself. A song for the woman I found myself to be. A song for Emilia Anne Beaumont whose voice was a mortal voice, and a loud voice. Whose voice was entirely her own.

32

EMILIA

READER, HAVE YOU ever been to the Spring Gardens at Vauxhall? Who are you, I wonder, who read my words? Like the folk
who promenaded that evening, that April 6th, at the masquerade,
you will not reveal yourself to me. Perhaps you are the only
reader of this document. Perhaps I speak to my friend, Helena –
you who have heard this history a thousand times. And if it is
you, my dear Lady, believe that my spirit watches over you.
Believe that love can exist beyond the grave.

Or is it Vermilion who reads this? Vermilion, who cannot
keep from fingering these pages. Yes – do you weep, Vermilion,
to think upon me? And if you weep – do not think it is enough.
Do not think I will forgive you so easily.

If I am fortunate my words will travel beyond the hands of
those who knew me. My words will be equal to men's words.
Perhaps a time will come when we women cease to be invisible.
When they look beyond our faces to what lies within. When
they listen to our voices. I wonder, if men, one day in the
future, should read these words, what will they think? Will they
criticize me, saying I lack reason and hard fact? Will they say,
because I am a woman, my words are not good enough? Or
will they find some reason to reject my meaning? It will not be
fashionable, say, to probe into the past. They will say – she is
dead! Why should we listen to the voices of the dead?

Did you not know, sir, what the dead can teach you? Do you
not wish to know the hidden stories? The stories told by women
such as myself, whose only desire is that one day we shall be
heard, even if it takes a thousand years. We do not dream, as
you do, Gentlemen, of immortality. No, we have no such vain
ambitions. We only ask, I say it again, that you listen. And how

many reasons, I wonder, will you find, to refuse that simple request?

Only the modern! (perhaps that will be your cry). The past is gone, you will say, and has nothing to teach us. Be new! Speak to us in our modern tongue – the tongue of men! But sir (I say), I do not know your tongue. Your man's tongue speaks facts; abounds with knowledge. I can speak only in the tongue I know. And this man's world, which dictates to us what language we may speak, and bids us hold our tongue if we understand it not, is an unjust world. His story, I have said it before, must not be the only story. His story is a lie. I will found a realm whose name is the heart, and there I will abide. My symbol will be the open ear. The ear that is open to hear women's stories. To hear ancient voices. They will imprint themselves upon the memories of those who will listen. They will bear fruit.

And now, for those who listen, let me take you to the Spring Gardens. Long straight groves of elm and lime, formal walkways, criss-crossing themselves endlessly. If you are at the centre of things, you will see over a thousand lights, illuminating the avenues. You will see the Chinese kiosques where folk take refreshment, a Gothic orchestra, where over fifty musicians play. Along those avenues that are illuminated, you may see triumphal arches, or you may come across a cascade or an imitation of some ancient ruin. All, you understand, is designed for your enjoyment. This is a pleasure-garden. It lies before you. Will you take what you desire?

Or are you of a more cautious nature? Will you wait before you taste the offerings? I will tell you more. Yes, think of the gardens that evening in April. The trees were all beginning to bud, the yellow flowers of the limes were open. All around me was the sound of laughter and music. The sights were marvellous indeed, and if I was a little anxious that Vermilion had not yet arrived, and the chaperon had left me alone, I was distracted enough by my observations from the Turkish dining-tent to remain calm.

For what a masquerade was this! There was an air of absolute gaiety. I heard groups of men guffawing, and the chatter of the ladies seemed almost frantic, their voices spiralling upwards in an ever-ascending pitch. The very movements of the visitors suggested a kind of desperation to be seen; to be heard. Men's hands flourished elaborately, women's fans flickered like the wings of tethered swans.

Yes, though I was awed by what I saw, though I marvelled at the jewelled masks, like birds of paradise, perhaps even then I detected the underlying tension in the air. I could not give it a name, and I did not feel a part of it. Yet I believe, if the colourful masks worn by the visitors to Vauxhall that evening had been removed, I might have seen a most disturbing sight. I might have seen faces marred by fear: a fear they could not justify; a fear that ran thick in their blood.

Unable, however, to see what lay beneath the masks, I told myself I was a fool for beginning to feel thus uneasy. Vermilion would surely be here soon enough. And how fine it was to be in such a place. How thoughtful of my love to meet me here, in this blue-domed pavilion, where I might sit, almost unobserved, peering from behind the pillars at those cavorting all around. I sensed that this was a naughtier place than Ranelagh, for here was none of the soberness that had marked that other place. No, I had some inkling that not every person invited to this ball was of high rank. I noticed, too, that there was some bottom-pinching afoot, and recoiled from such gross behaviour. How glad I was that my face was hidden, as if my mask, sent by my Vermilion, was a kind of talisman which would protect me.

Anxiously, I looked about me. How unlike my love, I thought, to leave me stranded here. For the light had gone out of the sky, and only the lamps illuminated the arbour. Sure he was safe. Sure he had not been harmed by some footpad on the road! Yes! Why else should he alarm me thus? He had met some danger then. He might be lying dead upon a muddy Hampstead pathway, his bloody head against the earth.

As the thought struck me, however, I spied a figure in a coat of red velvet, with dark curls about his collar. My Vermilion! He wore a mask, of course, similar to my own, excepting that

277

his covered his whole face and had a large curved nose like Pantalone's. I knew that it was he, although I did not at all understand why he did not approach me. Still, I stood up and, holding up my skirts, I wove between the tables to meet my love. As I did so, however, Vermilion teased me by walking backwards towards the main lighted avenue. I laughed at this, sure that my love had some surprise in store for me. Yes, it was not like him to take me to a masquerade, without providing some little intrigue for me. This was his game, and I would play it.

I followed Vermilion into the avenue. There were moments when I lost sight of him altogether, he was obscured by the crowd, and then, suddenly, he would appear again, his scarlet mask peeping from behind the shoulder of some unsuspecting person. Perhaps I should have wondered whether this was decent behaviour for a man about to marry. I was certainly amazed by his antics, yet I was captivated, also. I was convinced that Vermilion was leading me to some most beautiful spot, a lighted lake, perhaps, or a grotto. And, indeed, in that atmosphere of jubilation, there was nothing unusual about his behaviour.

Still he continued to weave his way along the avenue. Sometimes it was difficult to see him, for only the stars and the lamps lit our way. Concerned lest my skirts should be spattered with dirt, I gathered more of the thick red velvet between my hands, as I jostled against the other visitors who moved towards the pavilions, not away from them as we did.

The avenue stretched ahead of us, with four pale, high, classical arches spanning the pathway at regular intervals. I was beneath the first, and Vermilion was approaching the second. Already, I began to wish some friend was with me, for I was a little uneasy as the music began to fade behind me, and Vermilion would not let me get closer to him. When I moved faster so did he, so I slowed again, knowing that he would always be able to out-run me.

Suddenly, without warning, Vermilion turned from the path ahead, and I was glad, believing we had arrived, finally, at our destination. Yet when I reached the cross-ways, there was no sign of him. The path, ahead of me, was not illuminated, and I could see very little. Immediately, I was afraid again. What was this game of his, that would have me wandering here, alone, with no one to accompany me? Was I mistaken? Yet no! There! From behind one of the trees, quite near, Vermilion beckoned once again. But what was it that he wanted? Why did my love lead me here, where he must know I might be anxious for my safety. I only longed to reach him now. To remove his mask from his face, and to be held in his arms, whilst he pressed his lips to mine. But he continued to walk forward, and I, having no other protector, continued to follow. Sensing this, perhaps, Vermilion held out his white-gloved hand to me and though he did not quite touch mine, if I stretched out also, our fingers were barely a foot apart.

Thus we travelled, along this first dark avenue and around a corner, along another. As my eyes grew accustomed to the faint light, I began to see faces forming in the shades of the trees, strange forms, like tree-gods, lingering there. Slowly, as we moved, however, I realized that these were not supernatural figures that I saw, but the forms of lone women, whose attractiveness, in this light, I could not judge. Sure, they were loose women, plying for trade. And I was instantly saddened at the thought. That they should be reduced to this. That each of them should be alone here, beneath the stars.

We turned again into the third of the dark walks. This must be some short cut, I thought. Some unpleasant prelude to a sight that will astound me. Still Vermilion held out his hand, yet now, at once, I was afraid to follow further. For as my night-sight was improving, I saw, at my feet, a most horrible sight. At the base of a tree, I had at first detected what appeared to be a woman kneeling. But almost immediately I realized my mistake. This woman was kneeling over a man. His breeches were about his ankles. And she, her breasts loosened from her dress, was riding him, as if he were a horse. She cantered in gay abandon, oblivious of our presence.

Had not Vermilion, at that moment, taken hold of my hand

and pulled me away from the sight, I am certain I would have turned on my heels and run from that place. Even with my hand in his, I no longer desired to be with him. For with his red mask, in this dimness, he appeared more a devil than a man. Surely he had betrayed me once again. All his wooing was no more than a joke. And now he wished to show me, once and for all, how much he despised me.

Still, he continued along the dark walks of the garden. I saw other couples, their clothes awry, limbs entangled upon the ground. And, knowing then that the game was over, I pulled my mask from my face, and spoke.

'Enough!' I said. 'Vermilion – I am tired. I cannot go on.'

He clasped my little hand tighter in his then, and pulled me, somewhat roughly, a little further along the path, to a place where a single lamp was glowing. There, he clutched me to his breast, and though I was angry at him, I allowed him to hold me close for a moment, whilst I prepared myself to be strong, to demand an explanation. Yet even then, I sensed that something was terribly wrong. I experienced a chill that turned my bones to ice. Everything about this embrace was wrong. And at the very moment that I understood what was happening, I looked up towards the scarlet jewelled face above me, and saw the mask being removed. A white gloved hand unloosed the ties that held it, and as the mask was pulled from the face, I saw a sight that will haunt me to this day. Beneath the red, gilded mask was a second mask. A painted mask. The white-painted visage of Lord Smellie.

33

EMILIA

WITH THE DEVIL-MASK, came the hair also. The locks that I had thought to be Vermilion's were peeled away, leaving a shock of short, dark curls beneath. I could not understand it; and yet, in the lamplight, there was no mistaking that face. How thick the paint was upon it. How the dark eyes glittered, echoing the sky. He held me close to him, so that our faces were no more than a foot apart, and I watched his red lips curl into a contemptuous smile. Then I saw a sight most strange. Around the edges of his white-painted teeth was a thin blue line. Even in my terror, I could not help but notice it. A blue line across the gums. A most unnatural thing.

'My Lord . . .' I said, and then could find no other words.

'You thought me dead, did you?' he said, in a voice I did not recognize. 'Or rather, "Yew thort me daid did yew?"'

I was thrown into confusion. What was this man who had two voices? For the first was the voice of a man, and the second, the voice of a Macaroni. The second was Lord Smellie's voice, but the first that of an impostor. He was dead. Vermilion said that they had buried him. And yet the face was the Macaroni's face, Smellie's face.

Yet how unlike a Macaroni in every other way. His grip was cruel, and his movements lacked the affectation I had once witnessed. One thing was certain. This was no ghost.

'I had been told that you were shot dead by Vermilion.'

And then he laughed, so hard that the lips pulled back against the gums, and again I observed the strange markings in his mouth. I could not escape his grip, and I could do nothing but watch him. And watching, I became convinced of the truth.

This was indeed the dandy Smellie I had known. Yet though he had retained his face, he had discarded every other foppish affectation. But how odd it was to see him without his finery; without his powdered curls and miniature hat. How like a man he was now, despite that painted visage. Despite the heart-shaped patch upon his cheek, despite the long lashes and the slanted eyes. I feared him. Especially now, as he pulled me closer to him, pushed himself against me, so that I could feel, even through the thickness of my dress, the throbbing presence beneath his breeches.

'Does this feel dead to you, "my sweet"?' he said, pronouncing those last two words alone in the Macaroni voice. 'Does this feel like a dead man's machine?'

I understood now that the Macaroni voice was entirely affected. This other voice, instead, was his own. And though it was not entirely masculine, yet it was much deeper than the voice that I had known. It had a menace that penetrated me, and I feared it, perhaps more than I feared his 'machine'.

Still, I had no time to articulate my fear. I struggled against his hold, pushing my hands against his chest; kicking his shins. In vain. He used my movements to help manoeuvre us away from the light, but never once did he release his hands from around my back. Just a few steps it took, a few moments when I could see very little. And then, not far from the path, yet hidden entirely from it, we came to a small clearing. Even in the dim starlight, I could make it out, for it glowed in the darkness. The earth here was covered in some kind of white cloth. And the trees, also, that surrounded it, had the same cloth draped between them, all around.

'What is this?' I said. 'I do not understand.'

'Do you not, Emilia?' he said. 'And yet I had thought you would be so grateful!'

'Are you Lord Smellie? What is this place?'

And in speaking I suddenly feared myself to be in some underworld. I feared that I had died, without knowing it. But immediately I banished the thought. If I was to escape this place, I must remain strong. Though he held me cruelly by the wrist, so that I felt he would crush my fragile bones, I knew I must resist him.

'I am indid Lord Smellay,' he said (Macaroni again). 'And this plaice, Emeelia, has been creaited for your playsha.'

'It gives me no pleasure . . .' I began, but he interrupted me, in a voice that was now his own.

'Welcome, Emilia, to your Bridal Chamber.'

How could I have begun to understand what passed here? My bridal chamber? Was Vermilion a part of all this? Had he simply pretended to kill Smellie? For I was certain that this was he, and yet I could not grasp the meaning of his double-self. His double-voice. And would Vermilion appear now? Would he appear now, to banish my fears? To embrace me, and tell me all was well? For this was indeed a pretty place. A place where, in other circumstances, dreams might be fulfilled.

'What is your meaning, sir?' I said. 'I understand nothing.'

'Then I shall make you understand,' he said, releasing his grip from me, 'but first you will seat yourself upon the Bridal Bed.'

'I see no bed, sir. What do you want from me?'

'This,' and he flourished his hand to indicate the cloth-covered earth, 'is our bed.' His voice contained a threat.

And though I feared the consequences, I silently vowed, once again, that I would not bow to the will of men.

'I will not do your bidding,' I told him. 'I would know why I am here.' These words, however, only served to inflame his anger, and he threw me to the ground. I felt pain in the small of my back, and found myself shaking. The cloth beneath me was soft, like layered muslin, yet not soft enough to cushion my fall. I felt rise within me a feeling I could not have anticipated. It was a rage. Immense rage at finding myself once again the victim of these men. A rage at my own weakness. A rage at my beauty.

'You are here,' he said, looking down upon me, 'because I wish to claim what is mine.'

'And what might that be, sir?' I asked. 'What do you claim?'

'You could have been my bride, Emilia!'

And at this, he began unbuttoning his breeches. I knew what

was next, yet if I could continue to talk, if, in spite of the pain in my back, I could reason with him, I might prevent my fate.

'What double-faced creature are you,' I asked, 'who has two voices? Who dies and yet lives? Who has been a fop and now is a man?'

'What double-faced creature are *you*, Emilia, who would marry the man who once abused you? Oh yes, I have heard about your forthcoming nuptials to that Vermilion fellow. Did you think that he could keep it to himself? But remember, Emilia, that day' (he knelt down, and stroked my bare shoulder) 'upon the Hill – he did not win your hymen. He did not kill me. There was no victor in that battle, and thus the hymen should have been mine, not his. I am the man to whom you were truly betrothed. This marriage, *our* marriage, is just. I will take nothing that is not mine.'

I pushed his hand away, but he responded by grabbing me harshly at the base of my skull, twisting a little hair between his fingers, and pulling my head backwards so that I was forced to look at his face.

'What do you mean, *our* marriage?' (I near spat at him) 'I will not marry you.'

'Nor would I take Vermilion's whore as my wife.'

'Then I do not understand your meaning, sir.'

'My meaning, Emilia,' he said, releasing, suddenly, his grip with a tug, so that my head fell backwards again, to the earth, 'my meaning will soon be clear.'

And with this, he pulled each finger, slowly, from the white gloves, and threw them on the ground. He discarded his red jacket and I, knowing full well his meaning, began to push myself up from the ground, determined to run. Yet as I moved, he knelt over me, pinning my thighs and holding down my shoulders.

I had never been so afraid. Had my Vermilion lied about Lord Smellie's death? Did he know that I was here? No – I would not believe him capable of such mischief. I would not believe that he had deceived me. Nor would I cry. Still, nothing could temper my fear. If Lord Smellie took my virginity, I could not be sure that Vermilion would love me after.

Uppermost in my mind, however, was my revulsion. When he was the Macaroni, he had been nothing more than an object of ridicule, but now I saw a thing far more sinister, a blacker villain than ever Vermilion might have been.

'Tell me, Emilia,' he said. 'Are you still pure?'

'I do not know your meaning, sir.'

'You know my meaning well enough. I say, are you a virgin?'

'I will not tell you that, sir.'

'Not if it would save you?'

'Might you release me, if I tell you the answer?'

'If you were still a virgin, I might pity you. Yes, then I might indeed release you – if I believed you spoke the truth.'

'Then I tell you, with all my heart, sir – I am pure still. I ask you please to pity me, for I would not be defiled before my marriage.'

He leapt up then, and began to remove his other clothes. I sat up again, watching in horror as his pale limbs (lit now by a moon which emerged from thick cloud above) were revealed. His body was smooth and sleek and hairless; like a girl's body, for I noticed a slight swelling about his nipples. Yet this was most certainly a man. For his tool stood erect, like a monument beneath the moon. So different from Vermilion's. Vermilion's was large and thick and full of blood. Yet this was thin and long and pale; an alabaster ornament. I imagined it would be cool to the touch, insensitive as stone. And as these thoughts struck me, I was myself again. And I feared him. I felt a nausea stirring in my stomach. I made to stand; I knew that I must get away.

But it was too late. Again, he held me down. He ripped my clothes from me with a terrible ferocity, but I was mute. I knew no way of stopping him, and he continued until I was naked. Then he pushed his vile, smooth body against mine. He seemed to slide across me like an eel.

'No.'

I mouthed the word but no sound emerged. I felt the foul softness of his girl-breasts against my own.

'No.'

Then his head was next to my ear, and I smelt the sickly odour of his painted face; the smell of powder and metal. The white paste from his cheek brushed against my own. And he whispered, again in a double-voice, each word charged with malice.

'I will hef yore haimen, Emeelia,' he said. 'Do not doubt it. I will have your hymen.'

And when I did not respond, he continued.

'That is, if you speak truthfully. These bridal sheets will be the proof of it.'

Still I was silent. And he responded to my silence by gathering a layer of the muslin and wrapping it about my hair.

'And what a wonderful bride you would have made, Emilia,' he said. 'How sweet you would have looked upon my arm. How proud your brother would have been.'

He wrapped the cloth about my neck and I prayed to God that I might be absolved of my sins. He pulled the cloth tighter so that I could barely breathe.

'What beauty!' he said, and I felt he was in a kind of trance that none could break. 'What perfect beauty is this! Oh my bride! My beautiful bride!'

I did not cough. I did not stir. Death, when it came, I thought, would be quiet. My soul would fly up to find a place amongst the stars. This little arbour then, draped in white, would seem but nothing. The cloths would fold around me, and men would take my body away and bury it how they pleased. The trees, alone, would know that my soul had flown.

But then I felt the cloth, released from around my neck. And I knew that death would not release me. Almost instantly, I felt what most I feared. A hard and cold insistence, pressing between my legs on my softest parts. This was not his for the taking, and yet he would have it. He would force me open. I knew the wound would never heal. I knew his foulness would permeate me.

And then I felt the pain. It came in an instant, like nothing I have ever felt. And with it, as my soft membranes were ripped, my voice was released. My scream pierced the chill air. But he kept at it. Pushing, pushing, pushing. Like a murderer who will not pierce the heart once, but will keep stabbing it through in a frenzy of hatred. His thin rod sent waves of pain out from my loins, into my abdomen, down through my legs. He pressed his red-stained lips against my own, and I was forced to taste his metallic breath. Then thankfully he moved from my mouth, across my neck, across my breasts, and there left the marks of his paint, and the marks of his teeth as he bit into my flesh. I felt the slither of his skin against mine. I saw the ecstasy upon his face.

And then, finally, it was over. In a little puff of pleasure, he finished and collapsed against me, silent. I did not dare move, for fear that it would commence again, but as he lay there the pain still throbbed between my legs. And I felt a little trickle there, and wished only to be alone, so that I could clean myself.

After a moment, however, Smellie lifted himself up from me. He was holding his stomach, and moved slowly, as if it were *he* that had been hurt. He stopped still a moment, and he winced, as if he felt some agony. But then it was gone, and instantly he pushed me aside, so that he might examine the sheets. Even in that light, I could see that he had gained what he desired. The muslin, a pale, glowing lilac beneath the moon, had a number of dark patches that seemed to spread across the fabric. A virgin's blood. The proof of his victory.

34

EMILIA

I REMEMBER A coach, full to the brim with Macaronis. The whole journey, in my memory, recurs in sudden images which I thought I had forgotten. It was too cruel, that scene. That I, dressed in a torn red dress, feeling a harsh pain between my legs, and the irritation of dried blood increasing that discomfort, should be subjected to this.

So helpless was I, so stunned by what had happened, that I had no choice but to accept a passage home in Lord Smellie's carriage. I did not speak to him of course, yet I followed him to his coach, where his friends, gilded Jessamies all, awaited him. There, they helped him don a checked jacket of his own, and handed him his wig, his hat and his red-heeled shoes. Almost instantly, he donned the Macaroni manner once again and was entirely the Lord Smellie I had known before. There, in the dark walks of Vauxhall, I had seen the true Lord Smellie. But were his friends aware of his other self? Were their manners equally false?

I did not have time to ponder this mystery, for immediately I entered the coach, the Macaronis followed, speaking in loud and ostentatious voices, making thought impossible.

At first, they taunted me.

'What did you theenk of your Bower of Bliss, Emeelia?'

And, to Lord Smellie:

'We trust yaw Bridal Chamber was to yaw liking, Thomas?'

To which he replied that it was indeed a most elegant work, and should he ever again wish to deflower a notable virgin, he would employ their decorative skills once more.

I was too tired, however, too drained, to respond to such jibes. The whole scene was so nightmarish that I could barely believe myself a part of it and I remained silent and dazed. For here was I, who should have been an object of their pity, a young girl, destroyed, yet soon, once the coach had begun to move, they paid no attention to me at all.

Indeed, when I think of that journey now, I find that I must somehow have absented myself from their company that evening. For in truth, I remember very little. My mind had fled the scene perhaps, with the result that I cannot remember whole conversations, only fragments.

'What is there to make so much of in the Thames?' I remember one of them saying. 'I am quite tired of it – there it goes, flow, flow, flow – always the same.'

So many meaningless phrases, amusing phrases, which fill me with anger when I think of them, for what right had they to speak such trivial words, whilst I suffered so?

'. . . and then the parson stopped his shayving cut, by applying a hapless moth, that happened to be flying too close . . .'

'I vow that it is better to have all one's teeth pulled out and artificial ones inserted, than to use that disgusting Pearl Lowtion, which is, in any case, not a permanent solution.'

'. . . But have yew visited the urine-gazer? He swears he sees the future in a bucket of piss!'

They chattered endlessly about nought but frivolities, and only Lord Smellie remained silent. He sat as far away from me as was possible, and would not look at me. Indeed, I would say he was even somewhat sullen until we had crossed the bridge, and reached the Houses of Parliament. There the coach stopped, and I noticed that several parts of the House were still lit, and people milled about the place as if something of importance were happening. Lord Smellie alighted from the coach without a word, whilst the other Macaronis began to speculate upon the progress of events. But I could barely listen to their words now. No doubt they babbled on about the stubbornness of the King, the indifference of the people, the ineptitude of Lord North and suchlike. It meant nothing. Nothing could change my plight. I felt, in those moments, as I closed my eyes against the gaudiness of the coach, against the sight of their repugnant faces, that I desired to die. Even the thought of being with my Vermilion once again could not comfort me. I was changed now. I was polluted. And even if I did not tell him what had passed, surely he would see the alteration in me. My purity was to have been his prize.

After a few minutes, Lord Smellie entered the coach once again. There was nothing in his manner to betray the existence of the man I had encountered among the trees. Though the paint upon his face was somewhat smudged from our encounter, he seemed entirely the ridiculous fop. I could barely believe that this was the man who had so recently defiled me. For before me was a weak and fragrant creature, one who might burst into tears if he should so much as step upon a ladybird. And so excited did he appear that it seemed impossible he could, only an hour ago, have stolen my honour and my self-respect.

'The Bill has paarsed!' he said. 'Dunning's Bill has paarsed!'

'Oh maaarvelous,' replied another. 'But what does it meen for us?'

'It meeens, dear Friend, that that silly German Keeng of ours has been finally put in his plaice.'

'Will he be deposed?' asked a third.

'Oh no,' Smellie replied. 'But his power has beeen diminished, and that can ownlay bode well for us!'

I did not fully understand, of course, the meaning of these comments, but I thought that they appeared full of treason. Yet I was afraid, also, for my ignorance was a further expression of my powerlessness. Perhaps the King might be overthrown, and the whole country would fall into chaos. For me, at least, chaos had already come.

The carriage stopped outside the Adelphi Temple. The door was opened for me, but I stumbled, and fell on to the pavement. Lord Smellie did not look at me then. But as the carriage drove off, I thought I saw a movement at the window. I imagined his face, turning to look upon me, cool and impassive. He would smile to himself and his heart would be warmed by his wickedness. Whilst I lay alone, in the darkness. Whilst I lay alone, and listened to the river's song.

35

VERMILION

IMMERSED IN STORIES, I, like you, have lost track of time. Nothing changes in the past. Yet here, in Carmine Hall, the flow of the seasons will not stop for us. I might wish we could be sealed off here, from history. I might wish that it were winter and the frost of 1780 had come once again, so that the leaves of the evergreens might freeze, and I, unable to see the movement of the wind, could believe, if only for a short while, that time stood still.

But look! Outside my window, the trees are adorned with red. Red, the colour of my coat; the colour of my blood. How they blaze against the lawn. They seem to taunt me with their brilliance. They are wounds upon the landscape. Yes, Emilia is alive among the trees. She laughs at my sorrow.

July then, has turned to August, and still I am no closer to my object. What is my object? In truth I have lost sight of it. I only have some obscure notion that I must finish this work. When I began, I believe I wanted to prove to you the severity of Emilia's judgement of me. I wanted to improve upon her story. To enrich it as only a man is able; to imbue it with Reason. Indeed, I wished to prove myself a clever fellow and point out the inaccuracies of her words. But how senseless do these things now seem to me. For who can say where truth lies, except that it belongs to no man (nor no woman, neither). Truth lies not in the words that we utter, but in between them, beneath them, above them. We weave our cloth, Emilia and I, but neither my threads, nor hers, alone are adequate. Yet those points where we meet! Yes, in the interaction of our threads is some grain of honesty. If you hold the fabric to your face, you might sniff it. Truth.

Alone, however, I have no words. Already I find the will to write is leaving me. Let it go, I tell myself. Let it go. Be like Helena who accepts her fate with dignity. Whose quiet smile suggests she is confident that the future will not be bleak. Who does not wish that time would halt.

But I cannot let it rest. This, perhaps, is why I have barely spoken to Helena these last few weeks. Her presence is a comfort to me, yet I find I do not wish to speak. I am afraid, I think, that her words will somehow influence me. I am afraid that if we speak too often we will not be able to prevent ourselves speaking of Emilia. And that I could not abide. There is a private space, inside me, where I converse with my Melia. And I cannot let her go until the cloth is made. Until the tale is told.

Let us return, then, to that fateful night in April. When the talk of the town was Dunning's Bill. That the power of the Crown has increased, is increasing, and ought to be diminished! Well might the fine ladies and gentlemen at Vauxhall hide behind their masks on such a night. Emilia did not know how right she was to detect the fear that hovered in the air. For the King is ours by divine providence, so what right have men to challenge him? It is the road to Revolution. The French road, which must be avoided at all costs.

All this, however, is nought, compared to the events of that evening. I have no means of expressing my detestation of Lord Smellie. He it is that has brought me to this sorry state. He that killed my Melia. But what use to chronicle my hatred? A lifetime spent penning poisonous portraits of him would not do justice to the depth of my loathing. Nor would imagining tortures for him be of service to me. My wound will not be healed so easily.

No, Gentlemen. What use would these measures be? The sharpness of my pain will be clear soon enough. And I have not forgotten (in my self-pity) that I have a duty to my Readers. For no doubt you are in some confusion.

'Was this Lord Smellie not shot dead upon Primrose Hill?' you ask. 'Did you not see the blood, spreading across his chest, unfolding petals beneath the sun? Were you lying to us, Vermilion? Or did he somehow survive this deadly wound?'

I will tell you this. That evening, when Emilia was lured by Smellie's false invitation to the Ball at Vauxhall, I was indeed at Carmine Hall. Having dined with my dear parents, I was left alone with my father after dinner, and, having drunk two bottles of port between us, and about to embark upon the third, I was plucking up the courage to ask him about a marriage to Emilia. I felt sure that, if I could find the right words, he would agree to a love match.

Just at that moment, however, there came a knocking at the door. I started, because it was unusual that John should disturb us thus, but my father bade him enter.

'Sir,' John said (for his reverence towards my father was great, compared to his reverence, now, to me), 'sir, Lord Herbert has arrived unexpectedly. He is waiting in the library and says that he has urgent news to convey to your son.'

My father raised an eyebrow, both amused at John's refusal to call me by my name, and surprised at our visitor's presence. Yet he did not question my need to see my friend Benjamin, and before long I was seated before him in the library, anxious to know what could have brought him here at this hour, for I knew that no man in his right mind would make the journey after dark, for fear of the footpads known to lurk in the ditches hereabouts. Indeed, Benjamin did have a most agitated air that evening, and even the thick dust and tobacco smell of the library did not seem to calm him.

'I shall come straight to the point,' Benjamin said, his brow knotted in concern. 'We have been deceived, Vermilion.'

'Deceived?' I replied. 'What are you speaking of?'

'Have you not heard, in recent weeks, the rumour that Lord Darkman has not been seen?'

'Indeed I have,' I said. 'But what is this to us? The sharp-shooter was never a friend of mine.'

'No, indeed. But he was a friend of your enemy, Lord Smellie.'

'I am surprised to hear that such a Dandelion as he had

294

friends of such quality. Yet I'll believe it. Come, come. What is this?'

I could tell that the news he had to impart was of some great consequence, and finally he spat it out.

'Vermilion – Smellie is alive!'

My blood ran cold. I remembered the pink-suited Macaroni at Ranelagh. And yet I would not believe it.

'Nonsense, Benjamin! I saw the bullet wound in his heart. No man could survive that.'

'No indeed.' His expression was deadly serious. 'And yet the man that was shot was not Lord Smellie.'

I heard Benjamin's words, yet at first I could not comprehend them. Of *course* it was Smellie that was shot. I *saw* it was Smellie. I could not mistake that mincing manner. Yet Benjamin recognized my confusion, and rather than waiting for a reply, he continued to speak.

'Do you truly think that Lord Smellie would have had the courage to fight a duel with you, Vermilion? Can you not remember how strange his impudence was that day? How he insisted on a second shot?'

'I remember it well. Yet still I do not understand.'

'Vermilion – Lord Smellie was not your opponent. Smellie was the second. Your opponent was Lord Darkman!'

And finally I saw his meaning. I shook my head in disbelief. The implications were devastating.

'He hired Lord Darkman to imitate himself?'

'Indeed.'

'How do you know this?'

'I had thought, mistakenly it seems, that Lord Darkman was a friend of mine. I hired a thief-taker to investigate his disappearance.'

'And yet you did not tell me this?'

'Vermilion – I have not seen you since the day of the duel. And I had no idea that Smellie was a part of this.'

Still I was dazed. Unable to fully believe it.

'But I *saw* Lord Smellie.'

'You saw what you expected to see. A Macaroni. Can you truly say that you can tell one Macaroni from another? You did not get near to the man at all, Vermilion.'

'But his manners . . .'

'Easy enough for a talented man to imitate.'

'And you say Lord Smellie was the second? The clumsy oaf who shot the . . .'

And only then did I see the true implications of this. I was going to say 'sharpshooter'. And I saw, instantly, how I had been favoured by the gods that day. For if it were not for Lord Smellie's clumsiness, I would have had my brains blown out by Darkman's notorious hand.

'And the villain is alive . . .'

So much was changed by this news. I recalled the impudence of the second, after the first shot had been fired. *He* was a man, indeed. And if this were truly Smellie, then he was more cunning, more dangerous than I had thought him. And what of Emilia? If Smellie was alive, surely he would not yield his claim.

'I shall go to him now,' I resolved. 'Do you know where he lives? Is there room in your carriage?'

'Yes. To both questions. But do not be hasty, Vermilion. You will achieve nothing at this hour.'

'I'll kill him!'

'My friend — it would not be wise. First sleep on it.'

'No. I cannot sleep. And if I will not kill him tonight, do not doubt I'll most certainly teach him a lesson for thus deceiving me. And I must ensure that he never goes near my Melia again.'

As he could not dissuade me from this course, finally Benjamin relented, and allowed me to ride back into town with him. My mother and father were far from happy at my going at this hour, and insisted that I take a pistol with me. But I had no fears, for rage made me blind to any other emotion. And yet I did not know what I should do when I stood face to face with Lord Smellie. I knew I would not challenge him to another duel. I knew I did not wish to die. Yet I knew, also, that I must not lose my head. I must not murder him in cold blood. How else, though, to defend my honour? When he had deceived me so, how could I face the world with pride?

I was quiet in the carriage. I had a bottle of port with me, and in spite of Benjamin's disapproving glances, I continued to drink as we rattled along. It was gone ten, and the night was pitch. My thoughts were blurred by drunkenness, and I was feeling sentimental. I imagined the coach, lit by little oil-lamps, driving through this blackness, a toy of the gods. How fragile we mortals are, I thought. We create these little spaces in which we feel safe, yet in truth they do nothing but fend off the darkness; fend off our fear of the endless night.

Before long, however, Benjamin, sensing the blackness of my mood, began to speak, and my thoughts were diverted to matters of more urgency. And in spite of my drunkenness, I found that I was able to listen to him. He told me that (according to his thief-taker), on accidentally shooting Darkman, Smellie had begun to panic. Not wishing that his deed be known, nor that he should have to assume a new identity, he waited till Benjamin had left Primrose Hill to speak freely with the coroner. He told the coroner the truth, omitting, however, to mention that this man who had assumed his own identity was the famed Lord Darkman. He said the man was an orphaned servant, whose disappearance none would question, and paid the coroner well to keep his secret. The coroner was to ensure that the man was buried quietly in an unmarked grave, whilst he, Smellie, would leave town for a month or two to stay with his family in Essex, allowing the rumours of his death to spread. On his reappearance he would tell his friends that I had been mistaken. That he had been wounded, not killed, and was now well again. Perhaps, Benjamin suggested, Lord Smellie did not think that I would attack him again.

Throughout this explanation, however, only one thought filled my mind. That this man who plotted my end, this man, whom I had thought once lay dead before me, was living. He lived and breathed and moved about the metropolis, his very being an insult to my pride. It was like some strange dream, for once one believes a man to be dead, it is near impossible to believe him alive again. And the fact of his life gave a strange poignancy to Lord Darkman's death, also. That the quick-shot should be killed by an imbecile who did not know how to handle the hair-trigger. That the man I watched, seated upon a gold cushion and painting his eyebrows, was none other than that most manly of men, Darkman. I watched the blood trickle from his mouth. A man as strong as I. A man they called invincible.

'What do you intend doing, Vermilion?' Benjamin asked, and I started from my reverie.

'Doing?'

'To Smellie.'

'In truth, Benjamin,' I replied, 'I do not know.'

'Then are you wise to knock upon his doors, if you cannot be responsible for your actions?'

'In love,' I told him, 'there is no wisdom. Nor in hatred, neither.'

'But you will not shoot at him?'

'I wish only to see him,' I assured him.

36

VERMILION

WE WERE SHOWN into the house by a manservant, who wore a livery of brilliant blue and a black diamond patch upon his cheek.

'Lord Smellie is unlikely to receive you at this hour,' he told us. 'He has just returned from a ball at Vauxhall, and is mighty tired.'

'Tell him it is Lord Vermilion, and his friend, Lord Herbert,' I said. 'He will see us soon enough.'

We were shown into a small sitting-room, lit by a large number of candles, where he asked us to wait, a room as vulgar as the first entrance hall. Imagine it, Reader – whilst the walls were covered in red damask, the pillars of the doorway were of yellow-streaked Sienna marble! The chairs on which we sat were elegantly designed, in what appeared to be gilded oak, yet they, also, had been upholstered in yellow. Indeed, it seemed to me that here, in this house, Smellie's rotten nature was displayed. Here there was no order, nor no Reason. Had he learned nothing from the master-craftsmen of our age? Did he know nothing of harmony? It seemed not, for even in this room I saw the Rococo mixed with the Oriental, the Gothic combined with the Classical. And as I sat, awaiting the return of his servant, the many gaudy colours of the room seemed to force themselves upon me. Objects seemed to flicker in the brilliant candle-light. Gold and silver, dazzling blue, yellow and red. I felt a queasiness building in my stomach. I felt I could not remain here a moment longer.

But then the manservant returned.

'Lord Smellie wishes to see Lord Vermilion – alone.'

Benjamin glanced at me uneasily, but did not protest when I agreed to these terms. He knew better than to counter my will.

Thus it was that on the night this villain raped my Emilia I trod upon his staircase, a visitor in his house, ignorant of his crime. And in my ignorance, I had time to observe, in more detail, the revolting decorations in this house. Here, once again, the yellow-streaked marble clashed with red carpets; a gilded chandelier hung above our heads, illuminating paintings so nauseating that I had to suppress my laughter. For on these walls were all the hackneyed themes that I had seen a thousand times before, yet never so badly painted. Here Apollo flayed Marsyas and the Olympian Gods feasted; here Christ dined for the last time, and Saint Sebastian received his arrow wounds. Yet what matter whether feasting or flaying? So sickly was this style, so idealized the figures and so weak the colours, I swear the artist must have painted them in soap. What an inadequate fellow it was, I thought, that I was about to meet, who would choose such images as this for his walls.

I had not reached the top of the staircase, however, when my attention was distracted from such musings. For though I had not realized the cause of it before, a sudden sickness swept over me, and I knew, all at once, it was the port I had drunk that affected me thus. I was most giddy in fact, and somehow distant from myself. Upstairs, as we continued walking, one vulgar candle-lit room opened up before me, and then another, like flowers, bursting into sudden, violent bloom. And I prepared myself for what was to come. The final, extravagant and tawdry flourish which would be his private apartment. I wished to be gone from this house.

Eventually, however, we came to his door, and I remember holding the pillar at its side, as the mouldings seemed to swirl before my eyes. The servant knocked and a thousand doubts passed through my mind. Yet, though I had no idea what I was about to say to this detestable fellow, though I felt extremely ill, I knew I must face him.

'The door is open.'

Lord Smellie must have said some such thing, for the servant acted on what seemed to me no more than an inarticulate grunt, and he pushed the door ajar.

*

300

Nothing could have prepared me for what I saw. I blinked, thinking at first this was purely an imaginary scene. A room so plain and bare, that the eyes had difficulty accepting the sudden change. A puritan room. Nothing adorned the creamy-pale walls. The candelabra overhead had no frills nor fanciness. And the furniture consisted of little more than a simple, oak bed, a wardrobe that ran across a single alcove, two stools and an enormous, plain dressing-table on which stood a mirror, a second candelabra, his wig and various closed boxes. But it was not these things that my eye was drawn to. For facing me, sitting on the stool beside the dressing-table, was a man whose face was at once familiar and alien. Sitting opposite me was the man who had been Lord Smellie's second in the duel. Only this was the true Lord Smellie.

He smiled at me, the slow, smooth smile of a man who has no fear; a man who is not afraid to demonstrate his contempt. And I admit, it startled me. I felt instantly at a loss; inferior even. And all this, in spite of his strange appearance. Yes, that is what is most incredible. Had Benjamin been beside me, we might have turned to each other and laughed. Yet alone and drunk, I was too taken aback to mock him. Still, I moved towards him, though he seemed, to me, almost monstrous. And that impression was confirmed by proximity. He wore a dark blue, elegant powdering gown, and his feet were bare. His dark hair sat closely upon his head, although I noticed he was growing bald at the front. Yet it was his face that was most disturbing. He had begun to remove the paint from it, but as he had not completed the task, his visage was part white, part fleshy, and part yellow. Yes – I swear it is true. Beneath the white paint, some of his face seemed to be turning yellow.

I should not have been shocked by this strange deformity, for the paint these dandies wear upon their faces is called ceruse, a mixture of white lead and vinegar. Spirits of Saturn they called it. A most toxic substance. And yes, I have heard it said that it turns the face yellow and then black. It makes the hair drop from the head.

'Vermilion!' Lord Smellie said then. 'Will you not take a seat beside me?'

And I was shocked by his voice. The voice I had heard on the day of the duel, belonging to the man I thought was Smellie's second. A voice most unlike a Macaroni, for though it was a little high-pitched, it was none the less full of menace. I knew, immediately, I must find strength within me.

I did as he bid, and he spoke once again.

'What brings you here, my friend?'

'No friend of yours,' I replied. 'Explain yourself, Smellie.'

'Call me Thomas, Vermilion. For my name is indeed most unfortunate.'

And it was then that I noticed his gums. I had known that there was something peculiar about his mouth, but I had not been close enough to see it. Yet now it was clear. My eyes had not deceived me. Smellie's gums were turning blue!

'What *are* you?' I asked, for indeed my purpose in being here seemed almost forgot, so shocked was I. Perhaps it was because he seemed to come from the dead that he frightened me so. Half-man, half-Macaroni or half-fool, half-devil.

'You have come to ask me that?' he said, as he picked up his long wig and began, almost absent-mindedly, to roll the curls.

'No – I have come to accuse you of treachery, but first I would have an explanation for your double-self.'

'Why should I explain myself to you, Vermilion? You come to my house when I am preparing to sleep. I give you an audience. Must I also dissect myself before you?'

'You did not play fairly in the duel, sir. I could have you imprisoned for thus flouting the code.'

Perhaps he realized then that I knew nothing of his crime against my beloved. Perhaps, inside himself, he heaved a great sigh of relief, knowing that dishonesty were a lesser charge than rape. Yet if this were so, he showed no sign of this relief. He continued with his wig, as if he were aware that I was fascinated by the spectacle he made. He seemed nonchalant.

'Oh, draw your sword and be done with it, Vermilion,' he said. 'I am tired of your accusations.'

At this, finally, I was enraged. I leapt up and grabbed him by the neck, pushing him against his wardrobe. The wig fell to the floor as his head banged against the wood. Close up, I saw how thick the remaining paint was on his face. A poison that seemed to eat his skin. I realized, also, that he was stronger than I imagined. If he fought me, I could not keep him here for long. Yet he did not fight. He remained passive. Half choking beneath my grip, but not struggling at all.

'Tell me!' I said. 'What are you?'

'A man!' he whispered, with much difficulty. 'A man!'

'No,' I said. 'You are too womanish.'

I released my hold, suddenly, then, and to my surprise he collapsed to the floor, coughing. And as I watched him there, a strange and unexpected emotion came upon me. The sleeves of his gown had ridden up, and I saw his bare arms, which clutched his stomach as if he had some kind of pain there. His arms were thick and rather muscular, yet they had no hair upon them. Then I saw his legs had the same look about them. And I felt pity for this creature, who seemed barely, himself, to know what he was. He began to push himself up from the ground, yet seemed to find it more difficult than the size of his frame suggested he should. Surely I had not injured him so much?

Yet he was slow in getting to his feet. His movements were almost clumsy. Gone was the obnoxious Macaroni, with slick, affected manners. This truly was a *man*, in some distress. But I reminded myself of my hatred for him; I vowed I would not offer help.

Once Smellie was in his chair again, however, I saw that he remained almost doubled-over in pain. He clutched his stomach, and his piebald face seemed quite contorted with some agony, whose cause I did not understand. For sure, such pain could not be connected to my attack. I felt, almost, as if I had pounced upon an invalid, and I could not summon back my rage. Indeed, I felt almost ashamed of myself, and as my eyes roamed the room, that shame increased. For what was this Smellie but a painted sham? Here, half crippled before me, was the man beneath the façade. This room, I thought, devoid of ornament, was where he hid from the world. And here, only here, could he discard the trappings of his everyday self. I did not know why he chose to be a Macaroni. Yet I saw these trappings, scattered about, and felt quite moved at the sight. In the corner was a pair of false calves, all the rage then for slim gentlemen of means. A little pile of clothes sat upon the white marble floor: a black and white checked jacket, a pair of red-heeled shoes, a miniature hat. My curiosity was roused, and I moved to his dressing-table, opening the little boxes thereon. They were full of jewels. Rings and pocket watches, an eyeglass and a selection of snuff-boxes. In frustration (for I could not find it in me to attack him), I pulled open his drawers and discovered more. Pots full of ground white lead, a hundred pocket handkerchiefs, a dozen pairs of gloves.

'Stop!' he managed to whisper, though he had no strength to prevent my actions.

And I continued, pulling open the wardrobe now, discovering, behind the thick, oak doors, a collection of tiny hats and red-heeled shoes enough to dress a whole army of his dandy friends. I saw rail upon rail of brightly coloured suits, glistening in the candle-light, the ribbons of the knee-breeches dangling low. A shelf full of pomades and powders, little luminous tins, and curling tongs. Lace collars I saw there in profusion, and waistcoats, pantomime masks spilling from a box (two red ones, balanced precariously upon the top) and a stand full of swords, all sheathed and harmless. Yet none of this was enough for me. It fed my curiosity rather than satisfying it, and I continued, pulling open a door here and a drawer there, as if I thought, amongst all these possessions, amongst these vanities, I might discover some little thing that might reveal the truth to me: a pile of stays, such as I have heard that Jessamies wear; a rack of tasselled canes; a drawer of silk stockings.

Finally, I turned. Thwarted. Beguiled. And I saw that Smellie had recovered. He was looking into his glass and wiping the remainder of the lead-potion from his face.

'Did you find me?' he asked, his voice having returned, full of scorn.

304

'I beg your pardon?'

'I asked, sir, whether you found me, there amongst my vêtements?'

'I do not grasp your meaning,' I replied.

'Those glittering baubles are not me,' he said. 'Oh no. Look at me now. As I am. You are privileged, Vermilion.'

'I see nothing when I look at you, sir,' I said, most honestly. 'You have very little substance.'

'Substance enough,' he could not resist saying, though I did not, at the time, understand his meaning, 'to take what is mine.'

'You speak in riddles, sir. And I have no patience for such jests.'

'You will understand me soon enough,' he said, and he smiled, a miraculous smile, for though the muscles around his mouth were put into motion, revealing the tincture of his gums, above the nose all was still: frozen, as if painted in oils. 'I have offended your honour, Vermilion. Best kill me now, while you may.'

'I did not come to kill you, Smellie,' I replied. 'I came to find you out.'

'And that you have not done.'

'On the contrary,' I lied. 'I find there is little to discover.'

'Thin as air, eh?'

'I would say you are too preoccupied with fashion, sir,' I said. 'And it is a frivolous occupation.'

'One had as well be out of the world, as out of fashion, Vermilion,' he replied.

Yet again, as he spoke, I saw him cringe and clutch his stomach. He tried to disguise the pain, but it was near impossible, and as he saw me move towards him, he halted me by holding up his hand.

'Just a little consti-pation,' he said, relishing the last syllables of that word. 'Nothing more. Too much rich food.'

There was nothing more then that I could do in his house. I had not known why I came to Cavendish Square, except that I had been drunk, and I was now sobered by this experience. How ridiculous, suddenly, the idea of murdering him seemed. I did not know, of course, what he had done to my Melia that evening. And I was too confused by what I had seen, to act. For the man who sat before me, who seemed, suddenly, full of lethargy, was not what I had expected. There was malignity in his voice and in his visage, yet his body seemed weak and incapable of action. I could not help but feel he was being somehow destroyed by his Macaroni act. As if the pretence had become too much for him. As if he was attempting, now, to reassert his manliness, but was prevented from it by the feminine side of himself, which was inherent in his blood. I thought that he was maddened by it. That if I stayed much longer in the room with him, I might be infected by his lunacy.

Wishing I might find some threat which I could carry out, but failing to find adequate words, I spoke.

'I wish you well with your constipation,' I said.

Then I turned, and stumbled, dazed, through the gaudy chambers of his house. By the time I reached the door, where Benjamin was waiting, I felt a stirring in my stomach. A recurrence of the nausea I had experienced earlier. Outside, on the pavement, I felt a light drizzle, falling on my face. I turned to the side of the road and vomited in the gutter.

37

EMILIA

I ENTERED THE Temple quietly, terrified lest I should be seen in this condition. Inside, all was still. The apothecary had not yet come to extinguish the candles, but they were near burned out, down to their stubs. Even so, I could not help, as I walked through the entrance hall, but catch a glimpse of myself in the mirror. The sight was shocking enough to make me stop for a moment, and move closer to the glass to examine what I saw.

There, in the dim orange light, flickering with the flame, was a face of such beauty that I could barely believe it. It was small and frail, but the eyes had little tears forming at their edges and this made them shine like the eyes of a radiant spirit. I felt as if I were looking at the image of an aetherial being who had transcended earthly beauty.

Do not think, however, that I relished this sight. I did not want to think of myself as more than mortal. I did not want to be light as air. The face before me in the mirror, the faint and helpless face, whose very fragility was the essence of her loveliness, that face was my burden. That face it was that made men wish to possess me. That beauty was the thing that they desired to conquer. As if, in taking me, they might punish me for some obscure crime committed by our sex. As if, in seeming innocent, I was an insult to them. As if, in sullying me, they might say, 'There – she will not bother me more. Now I know I am superior.'

And thinking this, I turned from the mirror and ascended the stairs. I was still very sore between my legs, and my back hurt from being hurled to the ground.

The Temple, that night, seemed a different place. Such a gloom there was across the upper landing, and such terror in every mirror. Once or twice, when I had not intended it, I caught sight of my reflection echoing endlessly, as the several mirrors stole images from one another. I could not help, when I had reached the top of the stairs, looking down at the platform where I stood to sing for the Doctor's guests. I remembered the first moment that I saw the Doctor appear there, like an angel come to earth. Swathed in light he was, and dressed in white; a kind of saviour for poor Emilia.

Yet what good had he done me? He dressed me too in white, and held me up as the essence of purity. But he could not protect me from the world of men. Now I wore torn red velvet, a costume fit for a harlot, and my body was torn, and my heart was bleeding red. This glittering Temple, which I had thought would protect me, did not glitter now. One by one the candles were burning themselves out and another corner was bathed in darkness. The spell was broken, it seemed.

The Virtues of Simple Water! How many times had the Doctor preached the importance of bathing after the carnal act? The Genitals are the true pulse and infallible barometer of the health and vigour of your body and mind! After the act of love, in order to avoid disease, a woman must spring up to lave and immerse her apartment of pleasure in cold water! Yet what if there were no love in the act? What if a woman's barometer was smashed and broken? What should her actions be then?

When I returned to my room, nothing was further from my head than the Doctor's doctrines. I will not say I did not think about Aetherial Balsam, but I no longer had faith in it. Nothing could heal these wounds. Nothing could quell the throbbing, there, in my softest parts. Nor would any balsam, ever, any ointment, any potion, cure the ache inside of me. I desired to be plain. I desired that my beauty would fade away, would rot, even, so that I might move about the world invisible, unremarked by any man.

Still, it was water that I turned to. I did not use it icy cold, but lit a small fire and warmed the basin before it. Whilst the water was warming, I removed my torn dress and my petticoats and threw them upon the fire. Immediately it was extinguished by their weight, but I would not be defeated by this. I lit another taper and this time I set the dress itself aflame. The scent of burning velvet was thick upon the air.

Naked, I watched the flames, licking the white lace of my underskirts, consuming the delicate threads. And when the water was warm, I used my hand to clean myself. My little hand, rubbing at the dried blood, making it wet again. My little hand, dipping into the water, turning it pale pink. To my wound again, then to the water, until the water, also, was scarlet.

That night I slept very little. In half-dream, I thought I saw white-faced phantoms, lurking in the embers. I thought I saw a man come to my bedside and place a vase of lily-of-the-valley there. Their fragrance, I found, was overpowering. But I did not dare touch them or move them away from me. I watched them, as their stamens began to bleed.

When I was more awake, I thought about Vermilion. Would I tell him what had passed? Could I marry him still? I remembered stories I had been told by the Doctor, of women who, fearing that their would-be husbands might discover they were no longer virgins, came to him asking for help. He always refused such women, telling them that not every woman bled when her hymen broke. Equally, it may be broken by sneezing or by coughing. Yet the Doctor's words were no comfort. My mind turned to the quack remedies that he had spoken of. He warned against such actions, yet if I were to marry Vermilion I could think of no other solution. A little phial of pig's blood, concealed within the vagina. Surely it would not be difficult.

How long the night was, with thoughts such as these my only companions. For Smellie's act had done more than defile me. It had divided me, once and forever, from my love. During the month of March, Vermilion had been a friend to me: our bond had been one of honesty and trust. Yet I knew Vermilion well. If I told him of this incident, our love would never be the same. He would think it sullied. He would not blame me for what had passed, but he would not love me more. Yet if I did not tell him, what purgatory that would be. To have a locked chamber in my heart, which none but myself might enter. What he saw upon our bridal sheets would be no more than the blood of a slaughtered animal. It would be a false beginning.

Only once, for a brief moment, was I comforted that night. Exhausted from tossing and turning in my bed, when I thought that morning might never come, I felt the presence of my mother standing by my bedside. I saw nothing. Knowing that darkness was all around, I did not even open my eyes. No, I simply felt her there, watching over me. I thought, perhaps, that I was near death, and that she came to take me away. The thought was sweet, and comforting. And when she left me, alone again, and I knew that I had not died, still I knew her visit had given me courage. Her perfume carried me through until the morning.

38

VERMILION

THE FOLLOWING MORNING, the bundle arrived. Yes, I must continue the story here, even though I ache to tell you my emotions, now, as I read her words. But what does it matter what I feel? You are tired of my regrets. Of my gout. In the present, at Carmine Hall, nothing of interest comes to pass. All that drives me now is the need to finish this tale.

I was shaken, that much you will know, by my visit to Lord Smellie. When I arose the following morning, however, my mood was not so grim as I might have expected. It was a bright day with high, white clouds, which defied me to be glum, and I determined, immediately I awoke, that I must speed my marriage to Emilia. With this villain on the loose, I knew I must not delay. And, I admit, it was not simply fear that made me wish to hasten the day. Love and lust both played their part. And I did love her. I woke, longing to see her. No, not simply to *see* her, but to *feel* her presence. To be sure, I longed to feel her fair hair fall upon my chest; to stare into those ghost-pale eyes of hers. Yet it was not this, most of all, that fired my thoughts. I longed to hear her voice, but that was not it. I longed to smell her perfume, but that was not it. What was it then? Her soul? Is it that which defines our being? I cannot imagine a soul. And yet I know (and this is all I need to know) that Emilia is more than hair and lips and voice and scent. Emilia (I know it now) is more than cunt and hymen. She is all these things and yet these things, together, do not make her. Emilia. Vermilion. Emilion. Vermilia. No. That is not it. I will not find her complete within myself.

How then (you will ask), if my love was so great, can I justify my actions on this day and during the months that followed?

My answer is, I cannot. When I began to write this account of the past, perhaps I believed that it was possible. But now I know this was nothing but self-deceit. I was blind. And the knowledge of my behaviour during the months leading to her death is the burden I shall carry unto the grave.

What was it then that sparked this change in me? Let me enlighten you. A parcel, a large parcel, arrived at my lodgings that morning. My landlady presented it to me at breakfast, yet though she eyed me curiously whilst I sipped my coffee, I (through some presentiment) did not open it there. After I had finished eating I returned, with the package, to my room. Though bulky, it was extremely light, and I ripped the wrapping from it almost without pause for thought. Yet almost instantly I knew this was no pleasant gift. I saw the blood and shivered lest I had been sent a piece of severed flesh, by some unknown enemy. Yet as I fumbled with the cloth, the white muslin, stained with large droplets of red, I realized that it contained nothing. The cloth, itself, was the gift. There was no grisly object, nestled within. I was disturbed, yet it made no sense to me. After a second or two, however, my alarm increased. For whose blood was this? A friend's? A parent's? Or worse? With a sense of the world collapsing about me, I let the cloth fall to the floor and opened the small envelope which was contained within the loose folds. These were the words I saw written there.

My friend, Vermilion,

How I enjoyed your visit of yesternight. Your civility, under the circumstances, was most impressive. And yet I always knew you were a gentleman. Who else, but such a one, would accept defeat so gracefully?

I enclose, for your perusal, a small token which may help compensate for your loss. For who would have guessed it? That Emilia should have been a virgin, indeed? What a fool you were not to take her when you were able. Now, as you will know, there is nothing to take.

Or am I wrong? Perhaps, Vermilion, you know nothing of what

*has passed? Perhaps you have not recently seen your dear Emilia?
Indeed, I cannot wonder that she hides from you. For what
woman would not hide thus from a man that she has so deceived?
Do you understand me now, sir? Yes, Emilia and I had our
nuptial night, after all, Vermilion. And how sweet it was. Oh,
she was ripe for it, Vermilion. A little tight, perhaps, but that
is natural in one so pure. And when I entered her, not a cry did
she utter. No, she bore the first pain like the angel she was.
Indeed, only the blood convinced me of her innocence, for once the
hymen was broken, such pleasure she seemed to take in the act I
might have sworn she was the Whore of Babylon. Indeed, I ought
to thank you, sir, for surely you must have prepared her well for
this.*

*I send these nuptial sheets as a token of my respect, Vermilion,
and I hope you will accept them thus. Though it was I who took the
hymen, you may keep the proof, and I hope they will serve as a
reminder of the fate that you so luckily avoided. She was never a
suitable match for the likes of us, my friend. Now I have
taken the only attraction she ever held for us. Her innocence. For what is beauty without that?*

Be glad, Vermilion, that I have released you.

I am, your most humble servant,
Smellie

I did not, at first, read every word. I closed my eyes and let the
pages drop to the ground. No! It began as a low cry. No! I kept
repeating it. I remember howling, like a dog. After that there is
a blank spot in my memory. All I know is that when rational
thought returned, I was on the floor, my right hand and wrist
covered in gashes. I felt no pain, but saw the lacerations and the
glass scattered about the floor around me. On the bloody cloth,
also, little piercing shards had fallen. I looked up, and saw the
broken panes. The wind rushed in, but I felt barely able to
move. I could not remember doing this.

Now, trembling, I picked up the letter once again. I sat there,
upon the floor, and read it through, the tears streaming down
my face. I barely knew what to think nor to believe. Each word

313

was a wound that penetrated far deeper than the glass had. For though I doubted Smellie's description of Emilia's behaviour, still I could not but think this blood was hers. More potent than Othello's handkerchief were these sheets, where now my blood mingled with her own. And when I had finished reading, so full of disgust was I, so broken, that I could do nothing but hide my head in those sheets so that salt water, also, was spilled upon them.

Yet for whom did I cry? Because I did not know how willing Emilia had been in the act, I could not yet cry for her. I sobbed, now, for myself and for my own loss. Yes, as she had predicted, something had changed between us. I have heard that an earthquake may change the direction of a river, and this, it seemed, is what had passed. My love no longer flowed out, towards her, but was forced back inside me. A love condemned to move nowhere. A love trapped yet volatile still.

I do not know how long I sat there. The tears subsided after a while and I was silent, yet still I did not move. Eventually, however, I was roused by a sound in the house, below. My landlady, having heard, no doubt, the sound of breaking glass, was on the stairs, on her way to my room. As I awaited her approach, the real world began to filter in again. I felt the wind against my face, and I looked down and saw how badly injured my hand was (though still I felt no pain there).

Her reaction, when she arrived, was predictable. Uncertain whether to fuss over the damage I had caused or the cuts that covered my hand, she was rushing about the room, shrieking like a harridan. She demanded to know what the contents of my parcel were that had so angered me. She demanded that I pay immediately for the repairs to the windows and to clean the bloodstains from the floor. She demanded that I let her wash and bind my hand and that I go, post-haste, to visit 'a doctor, but please, Vermilion, not that quack friend of yours'.

I let her scream at me a while, I let her wash me and put me in a bandage. And then, emptying my purse of coins and promising she would have the remainder by the end of the day,

I put on my dark greatcoat and left, quietly folding Smellie's letter into my pocket and promising that I would visit a doctor.

Paper was hurled about the streets. The wind was high indeed that morning and brought the stink of the Thames and the smell of dung to my nostrils. The sky was bright and streets were full of carriages, carts, child-beggars, fruit-sellers, and all manner of people rich and poor, as they always were. I saw a fine lady all a-fluster when her hat went flying off towards the Mall, and all around people were clutching their head-gear, fearing a similar fate.

I walked speedily. The wind blasted my face and my greatcoat billowed out behind me, but I was not impeded by this. Rather, walking against the gusts seemed most fitting to my mood.

By the time I arrived at the Temple, I was exhausted; puffing and panting, my cheeks pricking, my eyes sore. The twin porters were standing at the door, as the Doctor was holding his afternoon sittings, where the poor might visit him at no cost. Before, I had always avoided the Temple at this time, and even now, when my mind was elsewhere, I was shocked at what I saw here. I barged past the porters and marched towards the staircase. But though I tried to avoid looking at them, these people, sitting on the benches at the foot of the stairs, were a disturbing sight. I saw a face that appeared to be rotting away, a young man with only a single leg, and a woman, her belly so large I feared she might give birth whilst I looked on. I saw spotted faces, sneezing faces, yellowing faces; I saw vile, fat bodies, a hunchback, and then – I was out of their sight.

These images echoing in my mind, I ascended the stairs to Emilia's room. I threw open the door, was ready to spill my emotions, but was halted by the sudden sight of her. She was sitting at her window, staring out towards the river. Though she was shivering, she wore nothing but her white silken shift. In spite of my noisy entrance she did not start, but merely looked round, calmly, as if expecting me, then turned her face back to the window.

I stopped there, suddenly tamed by this vision. Her fair hair tumbled loosely about her shoulders. Her eyes were lost. Even when she turned to see me, I felt she looked right through me. And I knew then, before I asked her, there was some truth in Smellie's words.

'Tell me, Emilia,' I said (feeling the tears smarting once again), 'what has happened to you?'

She turned and looked at me then, as if she were afraid of me. And still she did not speak.

'Tell me, Emilia – are you still pure?'

I thought for a moment she would deny it. But then she said, in a voice so quiet I could barely hear her, 'No, Vermilion. I have been abused.'

She did not cry. That is what angered me most. I did not understand it. If she had been raped, surely she would sob and cry and throw herself into my arms, begging that I would believe her. But no. Emilia seemed serene. Surely she should have screamed and raved and railed against her fate.

'You are no longer a virgin?'

She shook her head, slowly.

'And whose doing was this?' I asked.

'The man you said was dead,' she replied. The words were near inaudible. 'The Macaroni-jester. Lord Smellie.'

'And you assented, Emilia? You betrayed my trust?'

'No, Vermilion,' she said. 'I was much deceived. I am . . .'

And there she lost her voice. She looked down towards her small, white hands and did not speak.

At this, I turned. I would, with all my heart, I had not turned, and yet I did. I cannot – do you understand that? – I cannot take it back. I cannot change it.

My life pivots on this moment. It is the central point of my life's sphere. Past, present and future, all revolve about it. Yet at the time, it had no gravity. The moment passed, like any other, and I was unaware of its significance. I should have truly looked at her, so that I might remember her, exactly as she was that day. One final look. One last encompassing of all she was. At the very least I could have talked to her. Let her talk.

For Gentlemen, Ladies (yes, I hope you did not heed my warnings — I hope you are here with me, now), after that moment, I never saw Emilia more. After that, she was lost to me. Without a leave-taking. She was in such pain that she could barely speak and yet, hot-headed, selfish, proud, I walked out on my Melia and did not say farewell. No final kiss. No final glance. Nought in my mind but revenge, my sword, smarting at my side, and my desire to ram it through the throat of Lord Smellie.

Yet even there I was thwarted. I took a carriage to Cavendish Square, but when I arrived, there was no dandy servant, and no Lord Smellie. A short gentleman in a dark frock greeted me at the door, and told me Smellie had gone.

'To Italy, I believe, where, they say, the climate may benefit his condition.'

The gentleman would not tell me the nature of Smellie's condition, and insisted he was only the auctioneer's assistant. I would not believe him, of course, and pushed past him to enter the house, where instantly I saw the truth of it. In addition to the auctioneer, accountants, lawyers and other such folk busied themselves arranging Lord Smellie's affairs. The auctioneer, as overgrown as his assistant was stunted, was scribbling in his notebook, whilst the poor assistant, who now returned to his duty, appeared to have been assigned the task of noting descriptions of each ornament. Each man, indeed, seemed so dedicated to his work that none seemed to notice me, or ask me what my business here might be.

I knew now that this was no trick or ruse to fool me. How else would Smellie have dared to taunt me so? He knew that he was leaving England, and the bridal sheets were his parting gift. Yet I *could* not have anticipated it. That were impossible, for only the night before I had spoken to him here, and seen no sign of his quitting the house. Unless I fancied gallivanting over to Italy, I had missed my only opportunity of revenge.

How could it have happened thus? That is what you will wish to know. Why did I not, once I discovered his flight, return to Emilia at the Temple, and tend to her needs?

317

How many times, do you think, have I asked myself that question? And how many times have I failed to find an answer? Surely my failure here, you will say, is proof indeed that I did not love her?

My only defence is that I had never, until that day, known the meaning of suffering. Because love was new to me, I had never before been injured by it. And in my pain, I desired solitude. Like an animal, I wanted to be alone, to lick my wounds.

It is not enough. Of that I am certain. And there may be other explanations. (I did not know that time was so short. I was not capable of imagining the extent of her suffering. I was too blind to see our love should be unchanged by this event.) But what good comes of searching to justify my actions thus? It is done. I am guilty. Even when I was in Paris, I continued to convince myself otherwise. My pain was buried deep inside me. A fault, at the heart of my diamond self. A small, black flaw, that spoils the jewel. Yet I barely noticed its presence. A diamond is the hardest stone. They say it is near impenetrable.

What is it then, that has cut me thus, after so many years? A jeweller's knife? A hammer blow? Not possible. No. Vermilion's glittering surface is quite gone now. A woman named Emilia took a pen once, and wrote the story of her life. The words she wrote, upon that parchment paper, were so finely crafted that they, alone, have cut the gem. Those words have more power than the hammer or the knife. They have cut away the surplus, to seek out the wound. And now it is exposed, yet cannot be healed.

My life now is nought but regret. Even the pain in my legs, which plagues me now, as I write, and soon will force me to lay down my pen, cannot rival the hurt inside me. The worst, I know you have guessed it, is still to come. Emilia's story is not yet finished. Many pages, there are, that chronicle her pain; her suffering after I had deserted her. But these, my friends, I will keep from you. These pages are for my eyes only. They tell you nothing that you cannot guess at, and I would not inflict such raw distress upon you, when there is no purpose in it. Rather, let us join her two months later, at the end of May. You will

318

learn, easily enough, how she had been hurt in the preceding months. But here, also, you will learn the worst of it. You will see how Smellie's actions, how my actions, destroyed Emilia. In these pages, which I will place before your eyes, Emilia suffers for our sins. Her life is changed. London is changed. And nothing will ever be the same.

You must forgive me then, if, with these last drops of ink upon my nib, I indulge myself with reverie. This is a last luxury, before I face the truth once more. I wish to remember her, you understand. I wish to re-enter that room where last I saw her shivering and afraid and I wish to place my arms around her. Enfold her, like a blanket. She would be comforted by my touch. She would know there would be no more pain. And there, in that room, our story might be changed. Truly, she would learn the meaning of beginning.

39

EMILIA

WHEN, AT THE very end of May, I became ill, the Doctor, you will not be surprised, was most concerned. In those last days of the month, I developed a headache and a fever. The muscles of my body began to ache, and I felt I did not wish to rise from my bed.

Daily he came to me. Though I felt sure these were none other than the symptoms of my sorrow, I could not tell the Doctor this, and thus I listened whilst he pontificated on the likely causes of my sickness. He had noticed I had begun to neglect my early morning run. The servants told him that I lingered in my bed in the mornings, and had been known to warm my water before a fire, and keep the windows closed. Even, he said, he had not seen me of late upon the Celestial Throne.

'My dear Vestina,' he said, his voice so sweet I nearly sobbed for love of him, 'Vestina, I have tried to neglect these aberrations in your behaviour. I have noticed that your voice has become less sweet, that your skin seems less radiant and no longer shines with such translucence. And yet I have said nothing. I had hoped that this change in you was merely temporary, and that soon you would remember that the road to true beauty and eternal health was in my remedies. My Angel – now I see that you are fallen indeed. Your health is fading. Your beauty is in grave danger. But do not concern yourself. I will bring you fruit and Electrical Aether. I will bring you such scents as will rouse your spirits from their present torpor. And more than that, I will bring you sea-water, my Goddess, the most perfect cure for languor and debility! You will be Venus, rising from the sea! You will be rejuvenated! Come, let us open your windows wide! Let the balmy wind invigorate you!'

When he was gone, I felt a great anger, welling inside me. I got out of bed and closed the windows once again. I put more wood upon the embers of the fire. And I realized, all at once, that I had lost my faith in him. I was left with nothing. For once, the Doctor's words, the Doctor's wisdom, had been a refuge for me. No matter how I had been punished, no matter how I was hurt by the looks and stares of his obnoxious guests, I had thought that I could be safe, here in the Temple. I had thought the Doctor's way to be the true way. A path, which if I followed it, would lead to some salvation.

Now I saw it was not so. I knew that happiness, if it existed, must come from love, but there was none who loved me. What good were the vibrations from the Celestial Throne, when one had thrilled to the touch of Vermilion's hand? What good was everlasting beauty, when one was alone with no company but a looking-glass?

The days, then, continued to be long, and lonely. Whilst I was ill, I did not perform in the Temple, so I had little distraction from my fever and my sorrow. I was becoming weaker, full of lethargy, and I also began to suffer from little ulcers which swelled inside my mouth, and made eating painful. Only the Doctor's morning visits prevented me from total despair. For though (I afterwards learned) he had already employed a new Goddess, one Emma Lyon, who performed in my place each night, he did not speak of this to me. Indeed, as May turned to June, he stopped speaking of my illness. He talked instead of other matters, and though I was disturbed by some of the news he conveyed, still I was glad to think upon something that was not me.

Once again, the Doctor spoke of politics, and once again, in spite of my malaise, I found myself interested in what he said; comforted by a sense of a world beyond my chamber. The Lord George Gordon furore was continuing still, he said. In protest at the new liberties being given to Catholics (such as allowing them to exercise their religion freely in licensed chapels and to erect schools for the education of their young), Lord George had gone so far as to call the King and the ministry Popish. On this very day (which was the second day in June), he said, Lord George had called upon at least forty thousand people to gather in St George's field, to prepare to deliver his petition against relief to the Houses of Parliament. They would be wearing blue cockades in their hats, he said, to distinguish them from the Papists. Dr Graham doubted if so many people would join the rally, but still he was concerned at the prospect of a gathering so large.

'The nation is corrupted, Emilia,' he said. (He had begun to call me Emilia once again. I knew it did not bode well.) 'We have bred a race of fools, a nation bred in foul and steamy beds, not purified by love or by compassion. You must learn from these mistakes, my child! You must find strength again.'

But I took no notice of his words. I had heard them all too many times now. And I was no longer certain whether I desired to get better. I could see no prospect of any future for me, either here, in the Temple, or elsewhere. When I looked in the mirror I saw, in spite of my illness, a face that continued to be stubbornly beautiful. It was a lie, that face. A lie that concealed a tormented soul. For now that Vermilion had deserted me, I knew that my value was nought. Now I knew that I had not purposefully murdered my mother, that I was not a Devil Child, I had to look elsewhere for blame. And if I was not guilty, then I could only think that God was cruel, and I wished, most earnestly, to die.

So far, however, release had not come, and I was exhausted through lack of sleep. Even when, on that second day of June, I did eventually succumb to slumber, I was not comforted. I do not know how long I slept. But I woke sweating and uneasy, my shift soaked right through. I closed the muslin curtains of my chamber and ensured the door was locked. Feeling my legs weak beneath me, I moved slowly, but I found the strength to kindle a fire, so that I might warm a little water. Then I sat on the edge of my bed, and I pulled my shift up, over my head. I was naked beneath.

Immediately, I saw that I had changed. Across my belly, my

breasts, the tops of my arms and my thighs, a rash of pale pink spots had appeared. I ran my hand across them and felt the roughness beneath my palm. And despite myself, I was afraid. For though I desired death, I wanted it to be quick and painless. I wanted my soul to be stolen whilst I sat in contemplation. Instead, my skin would become scarred. I would lie for days in a high fever. For sure, this was smallpox or the measles. Diseases of bodily suffering. Earthly diseases.

Fearing suddenly lest my face, also, be scarred, I turned to the glass above the dresser. But no. The face remained unblemished. I could keep my illness a secret from the Doctor.

In a daze, my limbs weak, my head so hot I was certain I would faint, I dipped my cloth into the water before the fire. I bathed my head first of all, and then my body. As drips of water ran down the inside of my legs, I was reminded of the blood that had poured from that place. Blood shed too soon. For tomorrow was to have been my wedding day. I would have carried roses the colour of an open oyster-shell. I would have carried cornflowers, blue as I imagined foreign skies. Roses, for love. Cornflowers, for hope. All woven about my head, to ward off the spirits of evil.

I lay upon my bed, still damp and shivering, unable to find the strength to dress myself again. I pulled a sheet across my speckled body, propped a pillow behind my head, and closed my eyes once again. I saw myself, in an ivory-coloured dress embroidered by a mother who loved me. All made of silk, it was, the bodice covered in lace. Such happiness! You cannot imagine such happiness! My brother was there, dear Daniel, as he used to be, and my old nurse, Mrs Holland, and Miss Bright, the music teacher. My father played the harpsichord and my Vermilion, my new husband, kissed me, there, before all the guests at the wedding feast. And the sky! How blue it is on my wedding day! And the grass beyond the open windows is so green! So fresh! Summer is upon us! The world begins anew!

There was a knocking at my door. I opened my eyes and saw the door handle being turned, but, as it was locked, it turned in vain.

'Emilia! It is I! Open the door, Emilia!'

It was the Doctor's voice, that seemed to call from a far-away place. I closed my eyes again.

'Emilia! They are burning the chapels! Chaos has come!'

Even those words barely roused me. Yet I heard him rattling the door, and finally I found strength to stand, and to pull a fresh shift over my head, and to place a shawl around my shoulders to hide the rash.

'They are attacking the Palace of Westminster!'

And then I opened the door to him, and he walked past me, a vision in white, leaving a puff of powder trailing behind him, and bringing a scent of jasmine into the room. Exhausted, I clambered back upon the bed and pulled the sheets around me, whilst he drew the muslin curtain aside before perching on the edge of my bed, innocent as a father.

'Vestina!' (And I warmed to him, hearing that name, once again, that I thought he had forgotten.) 'You will not believe what has happened!'

I shook my head, feigning interest, yet wishing I could return to that wedding scene. That summer's day, in a place that was not London.

'Over fifty thousand people, they say, marched upon the House! Did you not hear them, Vestina?'

'No, Doctor,' I replied, still unable to lift my head from the pillow, 'I have been sleeping for most of the afternoon.'

'Astonishing!' he continued, 'I heard them from my study. How could you not have woken? The streets were packed with them! Vermilion has brought me the news.'

'Vermilion!'

'Yes, he has returned now to his parents' house at Carmine Hall, but he said he was much in danger, as were many of the other peers who voted for relief.'

'In danger?'

'Yes. Many of them were attacked on their way to the House. Lord Bathurst lost his wig and had his legs kicked. The Bishop of Lincoln was seized by the throat and had the wheels removed from his carriage! And Lord Mansfield narrowly escaped with his life!'

'But Vermilion is safe?'

'Yes, yes. But think of Lord Stormont! His coach was broken to pieces and he was half an hour in the hands of the mob, who pelted him near continuously with mud!'

'And all this because the crowd hates the Catholics?'

'Sweet Emilia! This will not be all. There will be more than this, I promise you. In spite of the violence, Lord George insisted that the House of Commons vote upon his motion, and when it was defeated, the crowd dispersed, some to Lincoln's Inn Fields, some to Golden Square, to plunder the chapels there. They say the Sardinian ambassador's chapel is burning now! Oh, Vestina! Chaos is come! We will all be punished for it!'

And I saw then, as he spoke, that tears were welling in his eyes. I could not understand it. Yet I pitied him. And not knowing whether I did right, I put my arm around his shoulder, and pulled him to me, so that he half lay across me. There, his head upon my breast, he cried in silence. Not for the Lords, I thought, who had been taunted by the mob, nor even for the Catholics. He cried, I thought, for some other reason that I knew I could not quite comprehend. Only now can I begin to make sense of his tears, and even now, I may be wrong. But I think the Doctor cried for the loss of innocence. I think he knew the meaning of all this, more, perhaps, than any man. I think, in that moment, he saw the future. He saw what would come to pass.

But then, I did not think of this. I thought only of my dear Doctor, who might have saved me from my fate. I thought of his sweetness. His sweet, soft, Scottish voice. That even he should cry! All was crumbling around me. Melting. There was nothing solid remaining. No. Not even my own flesh. Even the light, the last orange rays of the day, searing trails across the floor, seemed malevolent. A fire that would burn the Temple, also, to the ground. A fire that would eventually burn us all.

And then, I remembered them. The spots beneath my shift. Little burning spots, that might burn through the silk, burn through my skin and through my flesh. We would all be punished, the Doctor said. Was this my punishment? Surely, we were caught in a strange whirlwind. We were blown about, like little leaves, not knowing what our fate might be. We were nothing to God. All was arbitrary. Nothing we did, whether good, or evil, could affect our future.

'My Goddess!' the Doctor whispered, as he continued quietly to sob. 'My Hebe Vestina!'

I held him close, knowing that his need was great as mine.

'My Angel!' he said. 'The world does not deserve you.'

After that, he did not cry much longer. He was exhausted from emotion. Overcome. His head rested upon my collar-bone, and he closed his eyes and began to breathe more evenly. The weight of him was a little uncomfortable, but I did not wish to disturb him, so I waited until I was certain he was sleeping, and then shifted myself a little beneath him, so that my breast became a pillow for his head. Though I knew it was not right that the two of us should lie together thus (what his ever-absent wife would make of it, I would not like to think), but at that moment, I did not think of what was right, or decent. I did not dwell on the thought that he might, by resting so upon me, catch the measles or the smallpox. No – all I could do was be glad that he was near. How strange it was, to see his face so closely as this. I saw the little lines, etched across it – around his full mouth where he was wont to smile – and I saw the bags beneath his eyes. But more than that. Even his forehead – which, though he was asleep, was furrowed in a frown – was marked with hair-thin trails, the lines that make us mortal. I realized, looking at it, that my face, if I should grow old, would become like that.

The light was fading. The searing, orange fire-sun had departed from the room and, at least for this night, we were safe. Calmed, desiring to forget all that had passed, I, also, closed my eyes. The last I thing I remembered, before I fell into oblivion, was the movement of his breath against my chest. I felt the rise and fall of it, regular as the waves upon the shore.

40

EMILIA

NEXT MORNING, I awoke to find the Doctor gone. I could not, of course, have expected him to stay, and yet so soundly had I slept, with him by my side, that the knowledge of his absence now struck me instantly with pain. I felt it as a constriction in my chest; from the very core of me, I ached with the loss.

Determined, however, not to suffer more, I rose, vowing that I would find strength to walk in the park that day, for I was so tired of the Temple. I pulled the curtain aside, and, as was customary, moved to the mirror. Perhaps I had guessed it, even before the sight greeted my eyes: a patina of disease upon my face. Finally, almost as I had desired it, my loveliness was marred. Across the whiteness of my skin, small pink bumps arose. Against this background, how odd my features suddenly looked. My pale eyes seemed almost insignificant now. My large, reddish lips seemed to glare, the greatest imperfection of all. I knew I could work for the Doctor no longer. Nor, of course, could I leave this room, and allow others in the Temple to see me. I believed my only course was to await my death.

To chronicle that time, where, once again, I stayed within my room, with nought to do but think (for I did not wish to sew now, nor were there any books I had not read), would serve very little purpose. For three whole days, I would not even allow the Doctor to enter, nor, at first, would I open the door to receive my meals. I will ask you, however, to imagine the movements of my mind during that period. Often I cried, remembering that night when the double-faced Smellie had forced himself upon me. I cried, when thinking how Vermilion had abandoned me. Yet there comes a time when crying is no longer possible. When the body, parched from lack of water, can produce no more brine. I sat, in silence, watching the changes that took place in me. What a marvellous thing is the human instrument! We may sit, perfectly still, doing nothing, and yet it continues to function. I was still, yet something within me was moving. For on the first day, the Saturday, I saw the rash seem to intensify. To spread to the palms of my hands and the soles of my feet. Indeed, my whole body (and my head – yes, once again, my scalp was not spared) was covered in these tiny spots, which by Sunday were beginning to swell larger, and to harden, like pustules. When I peered into my mouth I saw my ulcers, grey lumps against the flesh. And though my face, as yet, remained merely speckled, I feared that it could not remain so lightly touched by this disease.

During those three days, the Doctor, do not doubt it, showed the greatest concern for me. He banged upon my door, and demanded to be allowed to enter. He threatened to knock it down himself if I did not open it, or at least reassure him that I was well. Cunning, in spite of my fever, I found a voice to talk to him.

'Doctor, I am well,' I said (on the second day), 'I tell you – I am completely recovered from my illness. But I desire to be alone for several days. Please – if you leave my food outside my door, I will eat it.'

Perhaps he thought I had taken offence at his sleeping on my breast. Perhaps, because he had a new Goddess, he did not need to force me to come out. Whatever his thoughts, he remained quiet for the rest of that day and on the third, he merely spoke to me once or twice through the keyhole, telling me if I would open up, he would speak to me of the mob, which was continuing to destroy the Catholic chapels.

But in spite of my promise, I did not open the door, nor could I think much on the chapel burning. Instead, I began talking to myself. In the absence of others, I became, for myself, both mother and father, brother and lover. I wrapped my arms around my shoulders and rocked myself. I told myself stories. I reminded myself that as it was my beauty that had caused my pain, it was good that now that beauty was being destroyed. I looked in the mirror and saw that – yes – pustules were swelling on my face. Yellowing lumps upon my skin. I told myself I was glad to see my body do my bidding. It killed the thing that had made me suffer. Though the sight pained me, I vowed I would not pity myself for my ugliness. Still, I saw ghosts in the room. Ghosts of myself, in many different guises. I have told you of them before. The Babe, the Murderer, the Devil Child, the Goddess. I spoke to them like friends.

On the fourth morning, however, I was woken by the sound of a heavy banging at my door. Within seconds of me realizing where I was, the door collapsed inwards, into my room, and briefly I saw the apothecary, who, it seemed, had achieved this destruction. He vanished immediately, however, and there, at the door, was the Doctor, pale and dishevelled. I saw a look of sorrow on his face, but the instant he saw me, that changed into an expression of such shock that I near wept for him. He rushed towards me (and I was glad to see that he was not suffering from this strange disease), and took hold of my hand, where the pustules now were hardening and becoming almost scaly.

'Emilia!' he said. (Not Angel now.) 'What is this?'

I shook my head. Still there were no tears. The Doctor cried for water to be brought, and Aetherial Balsam.

'Emilia! What has happened?'

'I do not know, Doctor,' I protested. 'Can you not tell what is the matter with me?'

'If I did not know better . . .' he began.

'What is it, Doctor?'

'Let me see your hands . . .'

I held my palms out to him, knowing what he would find there. He took them in his own and I realized how hot they were. He looked at them then, and seemed most shocked by what he saw. He examined my feet, also, and then he put his hand to my forehead. Finally, he asked if he might see the rest of my body. When I had removed my shift, he examined a pustule or two, asked if he might see my back, and then, having run his hand over the surface of the spots there, said he had seen enough and I could dress myself again.

329

For the first time, I was forced to contemplate the fact of my illness; of my impending death.

'Is it the smallpox, Doctor?' I said, bracing myself to receive the news.

'Oh no, Emilia. Not smallpox.'

'Are you certain?'

'Your fever is not high enough,' he said, dismissively. 'The spots are all wrong.'

'Then what? Is it measles?'

He seemed almost confused; as if he were still trying to figure it out.

'No. Not measles neither.'

'Then *what*, Doctor? What is wrong with me?'

'It seems . . .'

And then he sat down, on the edge of my bed, shaking his head from side to side, still silent, as if he would speak, but did not know what to say. He began, once or twice, but could not seem to find the words, then took a deep breath, as if he wished to calm himself.

'Emilia – I do not know how to ask this, child. I do not wish to offend your sensibility. I am sure I must be wrong.'

'Please. I must know what has caused this.'

'Forgive me,' he said, swallowing hard. 'Emilia – are you virgin still?'

The question shocked me. I had not expected it. Though my instinct was to avoid the truth, I found my tongue would not lie.

'No, Doctor,' I said, my face crumbling. 'No. I am not.'

Which caused him to give in to grief once more. I watched his face contract in pain; his mouth distort, his eyes close tightly. Then, when he opened his eyes and saw me once again, his grief seemed to mingle with anger. I had never seen the Doctor thus.

'Who? Who has done this to you?'

I did not understand. Did he speak of my virginity or my illness? I said nothing.

'Is it Vermilion? Has he deflowered you? I'll kill him.'

'No!' I cried. 'No! Not Vermilion.'

'Then who?'

Spittle foamed at the Doctor's mouth. He gesticulated, wildly.

'Lord Smellie,' I said. 'Lord Smellie.'

'What?'

'I have told you.'

'You copulated with that Tulip!'

'No!' I cried. 'Or at least – not willingly, Doctor. He took me by force.'

And suddenly the Doctor was quiet. The creases on his brow unfurled. His mouth hung open. His arms dropped to his sides. And in silence he shook his head. I waited to see if he would speak, but he did not.

'Doctor,' I said then, imploringly. 'What is wrong with me?'

'When did this happen, Emilia?'

'Perhaps two months ago,' I replied.

'Then there is no doubt of it,' he said, gravely. 'It is the Neapolitan sickness, Emilia.'

The tone of his voice frightened me, but I had never heard of this disease.

'What is that, Doctor?' I said. 'Will I die?'

'Possibly,' he said. 'Emilia – I cannot tell.'

'But Doctor – what is this disease? I do not understand.'

He paused a moment before he spoke.

'Syphilis, child. The pox.'

I could not speak nor move. My eyes fixed not on the Doctor, but on a point far distant, whilst my mind fixed on a memory. Of a man with little budding breasts, metallic breath and a face thick with paint. Of his hairless body, sliding across my own. Of the pain that he inflicted.

That moment now was more significant than ever. I knew it, and I could think of no other thing. For as Vermilion had planted his seed within Helena, a seed that would grow and form a perfect little child, so Lord Smellie had planted a seed within me. A seed of death, that would eat my flesh away.

'I know your meaning, Doctor,' I said, recovering my senses, appearing, no doubt, more calm than I truly felt. 'What is the worst that will happen to me?'

'Ask what is the best prognosis, child,' he said. 'Not the worst.'

'I know about the pox, Doctor. I have seen your patients, waiting to be treated. I have seen how their faces rot. I have seen their noses, half eaten away. Their black teeth. Or their toothlessness. Their lifeless eyes. I have heard that the pox can stay with a person twenty years, Doctor, and then it will turn them mad. And I have heard you speak of paralytic spasms and shooting pains. I know the worst. Indeed, I know the worst. But dear Doctor, I tell you – I wish to die. I cannot tell you enough how I have wished for death. Yet not this death. Not decay followed by madness. I do not wish for that path to the grave.'

He took my hand then, and held it tightly, and if he felt repulsion on looking at me, at that moment he hid it well.

'Emilia, my fallen Angel. You must not forget that many sufferers make a full recovery from this accursed disease.'

Then he turned away and seemed to speak to himself, yet I heard him clearly.

'Oh, that he should rape her. My perfect virgin. That he should rape her!'

But I interrupted his mumbling.

'Doctor, I do not wish to recover. Nor do I wish for a slow death. Is there no potion you could give me that might . . .'

'Do not think on it, Emilia!' he said, clearly shocked by my words. 'You must not think on such a sin. I have remedies, you know it, that may cure you.'

'Oh Doctor. I do not mean to doubt your cures, yet – I must speak my mind – your cures have failed me. You held me up as an example to all women. You said that by following your maxims, I would be safe. You said, each time you gave your lecture, that I would always be pure, and disease could not touch me. I have done all that you asked me to do, yet still I am here and I am diseased.'

He shook his head and looked at me as if I had betrayed him.

I knew that we were divided now. That there was no returning to the purity of our old bond.

'I said you would always be pure, Emilia,' he said, great sorrow in his voice, 'and that disease would never touch you. But your purity was the very reason that I predicted no disease. Had you remained a virgin, I guarantee you would be in good health now.'

'But now that I am not in good health, you would have me continue to bathe daily and to take your Aetherial Balsam! Now that I am diseased, you will cure me, no doubt, with your gum arabic dissolved in chicken water!'

He ignored the fury in my voice, and continued to speak calmly.

'Yes,' he said. 'With sarsaparilla, liquorice, marshmallow or parsley roots. It is your only chance, Emilia, or else . . .'

'Or else, the slow death,' I interrupted. 'The rotting face, the pain in my bones.'

'Or *else* you take the quack's advice,' he said. 'And fill yourself with mercury, which in my opinion should be confined to barometers! It is, itself, the cause of loss of teeth, and not the pox. If you do not wish to salivate four pints of spittle a day, Emilia, I would advise you to avoid the mercury cure.'

'Doctor – I would take no cure at all. For I do not believe there are any actions I might take, nor any potions I might swallow, that would prevent this worm from multiplying within me. I have desired that my beauty might fade, and now my wish has been granted. I must only hope for a quiet death. A quick death.'

'There is no quick death from syphilis, Emilia. Either you will recover or you will die, slowly. You must allow me to help you.'

'No, Doctor. I will find a way, myself. Please . . .'

But my words were interrupted by shattering glass. A brick came flying through the window, and landed at the foot of my bed. I screamed, as the Doctor rushed to the broken window to see who had committed this act.

'For shame!' I heard him cry to some person in the street below. 'What do you hope to achieve by this violence?'

In my desire to understand the cause of this, I pushed myself from the bed and, in spite of my aching limbs, donned my shoes to avoid the broken glass and moved nearer to the Doctor.

'They say,' came a gruff voice, 'that you are a Catholic sympathizer, Doctor, and I have come to discover if this is the case.'

'Why?' the Doctor asked, leaning so far from my window that I feared he would fall out of it. 'Pray – what will you do if I say I am? Will you destroy my Temple as you have destroyed the chapels in Smithfield and Moorfields? Will you treat my house as you have treated Sir George Savile's house?'

All of this was new to me, and I was afraid to hear that, outside the Temple, the destruction continued.

'Sir,' came the voice. 'We will not touch your Temple today. Yet if you do not wish it stripped bare and your furniture, including that famous Bed of yours, burned in the streets, you would do well to declare your allegiance to the Protestant faith, and hang blue ribbons from your door.'

'No doubt you would have me close my shutters and chalk "No Popery" upon my door also.'

'You may do as you please, Doctor,' the man shouted. 'But if we find you continue to treat Catholic patients, you'll soon not have a place to treat anyone!'

At which the Doctor, perhaps not daring to reply, did indeed pull the shutters closed, so that they slammed together, and we were enclosed in darkness.

'What is happening, Doctor?' I said.

'I fear for humanity, Emilia,' he replied. 'The mob have stripped Catholic houses of furniture, chapels of ornaments. They have torn up altars and pulpits, pews and benches, and have made huge fires of them. When I was out walking yesterday, almost every man who dared to walk the streets wore a blue cockade, for fear, no doubt, that he would be attacked if he did not.'

'Will this continue?' I asked. 'What will be the end of it?'

334

'There is no knowing,' the Doctor replied. 'Yet I am sure we have not seen the worst of it. Certainly I shall not continue my work until it is over.'

'You will not be lecturing this evening?'

'No. Nor will I until the peace resumes.'

And then it struck me.

'Helena! What will happen to Helena?'

'I cannot say, child. I truly cannot say.'

After that, there was a silence between us. Once again, there, in the semi-darkness, he took my hand, covered in pustules. He held it lightly for fear that he would hurt it. I think we did not speak for near a full half-hour. We merely sat, neither of us knowing what should come after this, each of us caught up in our own despair, yet somehow linked to the other, in spite of all. Eventually, it was I that spoke.

'I cannot be your Goddess, now, Doctor,' I said. 'That much I know. You must find some other Hebe Vestina.'

'Yes,' he said, simply, not mentioning Emma Lyon. 'Yes.'

'Go now,' I said. 'Leave me alone here. I know what I must do.'

Though I do not know if he understood my meaning, he must have sensed the seriousness of that moment. He took my other hand and kissed them both, which act made me wish to cry for love of him. Then he leaned forward and kissed me on my forehead and held my hands tighter still.

'My poor Angel,' he said. 'You have been much misused.'

At which I tried to smile at him, and he at me.

'Go,' I said. 'Please go.'

And he turned, without looking back, and left me, alone in my chamber.

41

EMILIA

KNOWING THAT THE Doctor would not be lecturing that
evening, I took the liberty of ascending, one last time, to the
Great Apollo Chamber. I could be alone there, for the Doctor
would be in his study and the musicians would be absent. I only
feared lest I be seen by one of the apothecaries, for I could not
bear it if they saw my face, which was beginning to harden with
scabs. I walked, wearing a long-sleeved gown of dark satin,
through to the Chamber.

There, in the fading daylight, I saw the room that had been so
dear to me. I saw the Temple of Health, raised above me. The
glass pillars. The Chinese railing. The metallic globes and the
massive dragon. And though they were not illumined that
evening by electrical fire, still I could imagine myself sitting
within it, watching the sparks play above my head, experiencing
the thrill of the fire running through me. In the empty room, I
hear the Doctor's words, echoing.

The day is closing now, but the sun, low in the sky, still
throws light against the stained-glass windows. A solemn and
celestial gloom, the Doctor would call it. A mild lustre! But his
words mean nothing now. I stand beside the crimson and gold
curtains, and look up to see, for one last time, the figure of
Victory crowning Apollo. None of this has significance. It is
beautiful, but empty. These symbols do not touch me. No – my
strength comes, not from the room itself, nor the objects within
it, but from a new sense of myself. I had thought, when I sailed
towards Vauxhall, that I knew myself. I thought that I had
found myself, through love. But now I see this was not so. I am
cynical now, perhaps. A fallen woman. But now, at least, I see

what is true. I close my eyes, and I imagine the Temple, crumbling around me. The glass melts in the windows, the paint dissolves upon the wall. I see the curtains fade to dust and the iron-work turn soft and molten. As my body is but mortal, so the Temple is but matter. Nothing is permanent. I understand that now. I had thought that love might live eternal, but now I know I was mistaken.

When I open my eyes, nothing has changed, but I decide to step out on to the balcony to take the air there, one last time. I unlock the window and step outside. I am astounded by what I hear and see.

The sound, of course, had been there all along, but, in a trance, I had barely noticed it. Yet now I heard the voices of the mob, a thick and fearless roar, which seemed to come from the direction of the Strand. I saw how almost all the houses in the area of the Adelphi had blue ribbons flying from their windows. But more than this, I saw a most fearful sight. From beyond Holborn, I saw flames that licked the heavens. The sky itself was obliterated, it seemed, in this huge, red blaze, and the distant air was thick with smoke. Worse still, this was not the only fire. Over towards Leicester Fields there seemed to be another burning, and just beyond the Strand, a third. The voices seemed louder now. I could make out the cries of 'No Popery!' amongst the general shouting.

And suddenly, I could think only of Helena. Knowing that the blazes would most probably be Catholic houses (though what that distant blaze must be, I was not entirely sure, for it was too large to be a single burning house), I feared for her. I realized how selfish I had been not to seek her out sooner. I did not know if she would forgive me. Turning then, into the Chamber, closing the doors of the balcony behind me, I moved towards the door. But as I reached it, I was startled to see a young woman. She had been about to enter the room and no doubt was herself startled by my ugly appearance. I stopped and looked at her. And I understood, instantly. For this girl was dressed in a white silken robe. Her hair was a lustrous brown, and her face! I could hear the Doctor speak already – lips, fresh

337

as rosebuds, eyes, clearer than a summer sky! See her pale skin, Ladies, and the fullness of her breasts!

'You are the Doctor's new Goddess,' I said. 'His Hebe Vestina.'

'My name is Emma,' she replied. 'But yes, I am the Doctor's Goddess. I am afraid that he has not spoken to me of you.'

Her tone was questioning, as if she would know more of me.

'No,' I said. 'I am not a frequent visitor here. It is unlikely you will see me again.'

'I am sorry for that,' she said. 'I should have liked some female company here. I think it will be quite lonely.'

And as she spoke, I longed to take her in my arms. I longed to hold her close to me and warn her to stay away from masculine company. I longed to tell her to leave this place, where she should be friendless, or else betrayed by those she loved. Perhaps I might have spoken out, had I not known, full well, that it was likely the girl had no place else to go. How strange it was, to see her thus: an echo of myself. I was no older than she, and yet I *felt* so much older. In the space of a few months, I had aged more than I had ever dreamed possible.

I took her hands then, in mine, and as she flinched a little, I assured her that my illness was not contagious. I wanted to speak but found I could not. How could I tell her what her fate might be? I knew how hollow and bitter my words would sound to one so innocent as she.

Instead, then, I broke away from Emma Lyon and, not looking back, hurried down the stairs to my chamber.

Even now, I feel the weight of my failure that evening. The girl ought to have been warned. She *deserved* to have been warned. Why was it I could not speak to her? Was it jealousy? Did I hate to see what seemed a near mirror image of myself, as once I had been? Did I despise her because she was beautiful?

I think not. Rather, I believe, simply I was too full of pain that evening. The present and the past seemed all rolled into one. The wheel had come full circle, and I knew I could not stop it. Time, insisting always on continuing, had dealt me the cruellest blow. I was given a glimpse of the hope I had felt when first I entered the Temple. Now the metropolis was burning. And my body was rotting away.

In my room, I quietly packed my remaining belongings into my trunk. I folded each silken shift, carefully as if it were made of spider threads, and wrapped them in fine paper, knowing their value. And though I scarcely had need now for any fine dresses, still I packed these also, for each dress held a memory. Next, I tied a bonnet on my head, and wrapped it about with blue ribbons, for whilst I was against the actions of the mob, I was not courageous enough to be seen to oppose them. Though still I desired to die, I did not wish to die at the hands of an unruly mob; to be raped again, perhaps, or to be beaten.

I left the trunk all packed and locked, within my chamber. I would send for it, in a day or two, once I had reached Helena's house. I did not know if she would forgive me, or whether she would allow me to live in her home. I did not know if her home were still standing. Yet to seek her out was my only option. I vowed I would not return to my father's house. Though I still had the key about me, I could not bear to live so close to the Doctor. And I did not wish to be in a place where Daniel might find me, and seek to sell me once again, to the highest bidder.

As I walked down the stairs towards the entrance hall, I became aware that I was shaking. There was no light flooding through the dome that evening. It was too late for that eerie effect, and too early to see the Temple illumined and glittering in the lamplight. How unsteady I was on my feet, I realized. I held on to the banister to ease my descent. No music played to accompany my step. No crowd to stare up at me from the foot of the staircase! How hard I tried to banish my own ghost who lingered on this stairway. I saw her, the Goddess Emilia, ascending on that very first day, bathed in light, clinging tightly to the Doctor's hand. I remember the chill she felt, half-way up the stairs. The sudden feeling that she was being watched. Could it be that she, also, felt my presence? She senses me. I swear she senses me. Would she but heed her fears, she might *see* me. A slow and huddled figure, hiding her face. If you will look, Vestina, you will see my young face, deformed by scabrous lumps. You will see a sight that will make you turn and run from this place. And as I reach the foot of the stairs, and glance around at the crutches, discarded there, suggestive of miracles, I hear a sound. A distant sound, but none the less, I hear it clearly.

'Haaaaaaaaaaaaaaaaaaaaaaaaaaaaaaail!'

No! It could not be. I will not believe it. But I turn and there, at the head of the stairs, beneath the dome, is a figure in a white shift. Though the entrance hall, where now I stand, is still in shadow, the evening sun has emerged from behind a cloud and now filters through the dome, to illuminate this Goddess.

'Hail! Vital Air – Ætherial! – Magnetic Magic – Hail!

Thine Iron Arm – thy bracing sinewy Arm! – is everlasting Strength!'

I strain my eyes to see her, but her face is near obscured by the light. Only her body is clear, for her dress has become transparent. I see her breasts, her belly, her thighs. Is this flesh, I see, or mere illusion? Emma? Or Emilia's ghost? Is it no more than this? An imprint upon the air?

Her voice fills my ears. Such a full voice it is, as if a whole choir sang. Yes, a sound that builds to such beauty, such intensity, that I am humbled by it. I close my eyes, and feel the tears swell in my throat.

'*And thou, celestial Fire! – Thou, FIRE ELECTRIC – GREAT
    RENOVATOR –
    THE LIFE OF ALL THINGS! Hail!'*

But I no longer wish to hear it. It is a false God that I have worshipped here. And so I turn, not daring, first, to open my eyes to see if I have been deceived. The voice continues, but I will not look back towards its source. Nor will I look in these gilded mirrors that adorn the walls. No. The door is before me. What is remaining of my life lies beyond it. I reach out, and turn the handle. Outside, a hundred blue ribbons flutter in the breeze.

42

EMILIA

AS I WALK along the Terrace, towards Adam Street, I can find no carriage to take me to my destination. Usually the front of the Terrace here is brimming with life; one can hear the chatter of tradesmen beneath and the clop of hooves on the road. Yet today it seems that every living soul is locked within doors. None dare venture out. For though a silence pervades the Adelphi, broken only by the plashing of the river, there is a distant rumble on the air. Distant, yet strangely loud.

Disturbed by this strange atmosphere, still I continue to walk. The sun is gone behind the Terrace now, yet I feel my forehead burning. As I turn into Adam Street, I am surprised to find that here, also, the street seems to be sleeping; it is as if some dreadful plague had come to London, and whilst half the population were dead, the other half cowered and did not dare come outside. I am relieved, however, to see a small carriage, bedecked in blue ribbons, moving away from me towards the Strand, the only movement in this graveyard thoroughfare.

'Sir!' I shout, though I know my voice is too weak to reach him. 'Sir, stop!' Yet he does not stop, and I despair, for I do not know how much further my legs will carry me, nor how far I will be able to travel on foot, without encountering some danger, for already, the sound of voices is becoming louder. Shouts, screams and huzzahs fill the air. I sense the voices are jubilant, but somehow menacing also.

I hurry my pace, though I am aware my chase will be fruitless, for I know the driver will not hear me. Yet suddenly, when he reaches the corner, he stops. At first I think he has, by some miracle, heard my cries, but then I realize the reason for his delay. The mob is upon us. There, at the top of Adam Street,

I see a sight that makes me stop, reeling in my shoes. The Strand, ahead, had appeared quite empty, but now, all of a sudden, that street is full of men. They fill my vision, and their voices fill my ears. I am afraid to continue, and yet I know my only hope for reaching Helena is to mount that coach, so I find strength, somehow, to walk on.

Eventually, the din hurting my ears, I reach it, for the mob has made the coach's progress impossible. As I come closer, I see how even this coach has a slogan chalked upon its doors. 'This coach is driven by a True Protestant,' it says, 'and none but those of that faith are transported within it.' The driver, quite terrified by what he sees, does not observe me at first, but I tug at his ankle, and when he looks down at me, he seems immensely startled.

'Miss!' he shouts, so that he might be heard. 'What are you doing out at such a time as this?'

'I need to get to Bloomsbury, sir,' I reply as loud as I am able.

'Now's no time to travel, miss,' he said. 'This mob's just burned the Newgate Prison down. I've been told the whole place is ablaze and the prisoners have been set free. They'll stop at nothing, I tell you. You must get yourself back inside the house from whence you came.'

I started at the news, yet determined to get myself a place within this coach, I used every last reserve of energy within me to shout up at him one final time.

'Let me inside, sir,' I said. 'I have no place else to go. Would you have me walk through this crowd?'

'You may get in, if you please, for I'm heading through Bloomsbury myself. But I'll not vouch for your safety.'

Thus it was that on one of the worst days of what have since been called the Gordon Riots, I came to be seated in a carriage, watching part of the mob return from burning down the prison at Newgate. We could not move into the Strand, so my driver waited there, on the corner of Adam Street, for them to pass, whilst I watched incredulously. For I must have seen, that day, near a thousand men, armed with axes, iron bars and fire-brands, knives, saws, clubs and ladders, parade past me, in the direction of Charing Cross. Some rode on horseback, but most of them were on foot, blue cockades upon their heads, and massive banners held between them. 'The Devil take the Pope!' they declared. 'No Popery!' Yet what startled me, more, even, than *their* appearance, was that of the men who moved ahead of them. Filthy men, bound together by chains, yet cheering, and joining in the general racket. The prisoners at Newgate, let loose. Criminals. Men who had been waiting only for death. Now these hollow-eyed creatures frolicked and japed and danced along the road, their dirt-smeared faces lit up by their yellow smiles. They seemed like ghouls that had emerged from the earth. And on seeing them, I shrank further back into the fraying seats of the carriage. The very thought of what this rabble had done was enough to make me fear for humanity.

As the voices of the mob died down a little, the carriage jolted to life again. I was startled to see one of the men from the crowd grab hold of the carriage window and hang on to it, peering in at me. He said nothing, staring at me with pale eyes in a muddy, bruised visage. He wore a blue cockade upon his head, and he smiled at me, almost in a friendly manner.

I cowered in the corner, for he had an iron bar in his hand. I said nothing, for fear I would provoke him, and he also remained silent, staring at me with a gaze so intense that, in spite of his fixed smile, I thought he might be about to climb in and murder me. Suddenly, however, he opened his mouth to speak.

'You've got the pox!' he said.

And then the iron bar fell from his hand, and he tumbled forward so that the top half of his body fell into the carriage, and I saw he had a gaping wound in his back, as if an axe had entered there.

When I think upon these moments now, of my reaction to this man's collapse, I often experience great shame. I could have stopped the coach. I could have checked whether he was dead or no, but instead, so horrified was I by what had happened, that I peeled his warm fingers from the carriage door (how stubbornly they clung, like little hooks), lifted his head, and pushed him, backwards, into the street. It was not until I saw him fall that I regretted my actions. And then I realized that my hands were wet, and I looked down to see that I had his blood upon them. I could not help but look now, from the carriage window. I saw him, twitching on the roadside.

My witnessing of this man's death was but the beginning of that day's horror. London was in the grip of a kind of madness. A group of soldiers lingered on one street corner, armed with muskets, but I could not imagine that they could resist the mob should they come this way. Many of the shops on the Strand had their windows boarded over, for fear of looting, and barely a soul was to be seen out of doors who did not wear the cockade.

I suddenly became aware of the dangers of my actions that day. I was *en route* to Helena's house. Helena – a Catholic. If I was allowed to stay there I might wake to find my bed burning around me. I might find my hair on fire; my flesh melting. All around me, now, I saw distant fires. Indeed, I realized, as we came closer to Bloomsbury Square, that I might be too late, for flames were leaping in the air before me, and black smoke was choking the air.

Soon after I spied this, I heard the voices once again. The sound of the mob. But worse than this, I heard a noise louder than anything I had ever heard before. A sound that seemed to pierce my skull, so that for a moment I thought I had been shot. And then again. A most unnatural sound, that seemed to repeat itself over and again in a single instant. I knew this must be the sound of muskets firing. Finally the soldiers were acting against the crowd.

To my surprise, the driver of my coach seemed determined now to reach his destination. I was glad, for I had no place else to go but Helena's house. As we turned into the square, however, I felt the blood drain from me. For there, before me, was a vision of such devastation, such violence as I have never before, nor will ever again witness. The armed soldiers were leaving the scene on horseback, moving in our direction, and I saw that the mob, in panic, were all attempting to run from the place. But though these men in blue cockades were all around me, and women too, many with blood smeared on their faces and hands, I could not help but be most awed, most terrified of the house-fire that blazed before my eyes.

Flames flickered from the windows, lapped the stonework, blackened the façade. In front of the house an enormous bonfire also burned, and as the frightened mob allowed our coach to pass ('Make way!' I heard the driver shout, 'Here's a notable Protestant lady on board!'), I saw a great pile of once-beautiful furniture burning there, wooden cabinets, upholstered chairs, and a great number of portraits, faces half burned away. Helena! I feared at once that this might be her home, yet no sooner had the thought struck me than I witnessed the worst horror of all.

I had not seen the bodies at first, for they were lying there, on the ground, before the bonfire. But now that the soldiers had gone, the mob seemed to gain courage. An unspoken change came over the rioters, and, though they had been fleeing, now, though I saw no order being given, they turned about, and surged towards the fire. Our coach, happening, at that moment, to be passing right in front of the burning house (which crumbled now before our eyes), was caught right in the middle of this tumult, yet they did not heed us. The noise that surrounded me, the terror I felt on seeing their metal bars and axes so close, and feeling the heat of the flames begin to scald my face – these were nothing compared to my emotions on seeing the dead bodies. There were around six or seven of them, with most horrible wounds, and the crowd hauled them up on to a small cart that had been abandoned at the roadside. But worst of all, they did not lay them in the cart, but rather sat them up, and fixed weapons in their hands to make them look as if alive. I was astonished by the barbarity of the act, particularly when I saw them haul up the final body, which had belonged to a woman. They leaned her against the other seated dead men, so she was a kind of masthead for their strange vessel, and at first I could not see how she had been wounded. Suddenly, however, as a group of men began fixing a large knife within her still pliant hand, I

345

saw blood that dripped from a lock of hair on to her face. Like a teardrop it ran down her cheek. And then the men's movements made her head slump forward, and I saw the gaping wound in the back of her head. Half her skull had been torn away.

Caring not, they pushed her upright again, and, having re-arranged the weapons in the hands of the dead men, seemed to contemplate their work a moment, before beginning to push the cart before them. One man picked up what looked like a dinner bell from the pile of plundered goods and began to ring it with all his might, while those with the cart followed him, right past my carriage, towards the north of the square. As they went, I saw the dead men, so close I might have leaned from my carriage and touched their faces, contorted in agony. They had died, each of them, in a state of terror. And now their pain was displayed in this deathly freak show.

Yet where was my Vermilion at this time? As I felt the grief well within me, this was the thought that passed through my head. Though I hated him, I could not help but remember the touch of his hand upon my shoulder. But I was alone, in an unmoving carriage, and, as the mob peered in at my window and waved as if they thought I would support them in their deeds, I thanked God that I had worn blue ribbons that day. I did not dare imagine my fate, had they thought me to be Catholic.

The coach was still now, and I stepped from it, expecting to see the coach driver, stunned as I. But not only had he disappeared, his horse had gone also. The harness had been cut right through, and I was alone, watching the departing mob. I could not move at first, for I was weak still, and the intense heat of the flames, so close to me, seemed to increase my fever. I held on to the side of the empty carriage for support, coughing, for there was a mass of black soot and smoke in the air, and my eyes were stinging. I was able to see little besides the flames, the smoke, and the shadows of burning objects, disintegrating between them. I felt a kind of relief, in spite of all, for though I could not see them any longer, the cries of the crowd were diminishing. And now, the only sounds that filled the air were the crackling and the hissing of the fire. The sun was low in the sky, but it seemed that these flames would light the square till morning.

So awed was I by what I saw and had seen, that even the thought of Helena could not rouse me. Suddenly, however, I saw a movement, a black shape moving at the base of the bonfire. It did not take me long to be certain that this was a human shape that seemed to be scrabbling about, dangerously close to the fire. Over and again, I saw his arm reach almost into the blaze and remove an object, which he would hurl away as far as he could from the flames. Large flakes of ash, so light that they floated upon the air, rained down upon me, and as I brushed them from my cloak, my bloodstained fingers became covered in black dust. Then, before I had a chance to think what these flakes might once have been, a heavy object landed at my feet, flung by the man whom I watched. It was a little gnarled, but still intact, and I bent down to pick it up. What I held in my hand was made of leather and paper and ink. I had never thought a book could be so dear.

'That's about all the good I can do.'

I saw it was the fire-fellow talking. He was moving towards me, gathering the books that he had saved. And I felt I could not help the tears from falling, finally, from my smarting eyes.

'These are Lord Mansfield's books,' he informed me, seeming glad as I for the company. 'They chucked them out the winda', in t'the fire. And then they set the rest of his library ablaze.'

'Who is this Lord Mansfield?' I asked. 'A Catholic?'

'I can tell you're no Londoner,' he said, as if he were quite shocked by my ignorance. 'He's the Lord Chief Justice 'imself – that's who he is. They've burned 'is life's work, lady. This,' he continued, nodding at the pile of books in his arms, 'is all that's left of it.'

Though I was overjoyed that this was not Lord Quinton's house, still I was horrified at such destruction.

'The rarest collection of manuscripts in the world is burning up there. And there's no one, not even I, that can save 'em.'

*

We were alone, in the midst of the flames, yet I did not fear the man, nor did I hurry away from that place. Though I assumed he was some servant of Lord Mansfield, in truth I did not ask his name, or his identity, nor did he question me why I was there. And when he made to leave (having first pointed me towards Lord Quinton's house), I did not question that he took the books with him, nor ask what he would do with them. Indeed, it seemed to me that, having saved the books from their fate, this man had more right to them than any person. For whilst he talked, he once shuffled the books so that he held them in the crooks of his elbows and not in his hands, which could take the strain no longer. Then I saw, in the light of the flames, a quite unbelievable thing. Much of the skin had been burned from his fingers, and where it remained, it was blistered and very damaged. On the backs of his hands, also, the flesh was clearly charred, yet he made no mention of this fact. Nor did his face betray any sign that he was in pain. When he left me, I wondered if I had imagined him. For I could think of no human creature that could sustain such injuries and not cry for help, nor no servant who would deform himself thus for the sake of his master's words. I think, even now, this man was some unearthly creature that I had conjured from the blaze.

When first I saw the house I was convinced that there had been some mistake. For though it was extremely grand, there were blue ribbons flying from every window, a sure sign that these were not Catholics that lived within. Still, I knocked upon the door, and when there was no reply, I summoned the last of my strength to beat upon it. I was certain that I saw some movement behind the curtains, close to me, but still no person came to the door. Completely exhausted, I collapsed on the doorstep but continued to knock, my head resting against the door, only my arm moving, above my head.

My persistence, eventually, was rewarded, and a maidservant came to the door. I looked up and, before she could slam it again, I spoke.

'I wish to see my friend, the Lady Quinton. You must tell her it is Emilia, come to see her.'

She hesitated, then closed the door once more. I waited for at least five minutes, fearing lest I was in the wrong place, or that Helena would not see me, and was about to begin knocking once again when the door did open, and I was lifted up by two liveried men, and carried inside. Then, knowing that for a short time, at least, I would be safe, I finally allowed myself to sink into oblivion. Now I had only to wait, and hope that all would be well.

43

VERMILION

THE FINAL HUMILIATION is upon me. Ladies, Gentlemen, I must beg your forgiveness for interrupting, once again, this narrative. But, I am obliged to tell you, your friend Vermilion (if he may still presume such an intimacy with you) may soon be incapable of writing. We are in danger of a tale without an end, for so swollen are my hands become, that I can barely hold a pen. Yes, though I am loath to admit it, I am become what is commonly termed an invalid.

I blame Helena for this. She came to my room yesterday evening, when I was quite happy to be alone. I was enjoying a bottle of port wine from my cellar and, this being my second bottle, the pain was dissolving. Indeed, though when John brought the bottles I was quite unable to walk, by the time that she knocked on my door, I had overcome my agony, and, with the aid of my stick, managed to cross the room.

'Vermilion, you are drunk again!' she said, the instant I opened the door.

'Is that a line you have prepared, Helena?' I asked. 'For I swear you said it before you even looked at me.'

'Not true, sir,' she replied. 'I had time to look before I spoke, but it did not take me long to come to the conclusion. Oh Vermilion, if you could only see yourself.'

'What would I find?'

'A man old before his time,' she replied, most candidly. 'A man bound for an early grave.'

'I thank you most kindly for that remark. Though I would suggest, if you wish to continue relying on his charity, you would not offend your host.'

'You forget who I am, Vermilion. I am the mother of your child.'

'But I am not a father to my child, Helena. Remember that! I am deprived of fatherhood.'

Even so, in spite of my carping, in spite of my drunkenness, her words touched me. I had been thinking that very night of my child who was a stranger to me. Young Marcus Quinton. Indeed, I believe that Helena saw the change in my demeanour when our son was spoken of. She took my arm, and said, 'Come, Vermilion, let me help you downstairs. I have a thing to show you.'

I had not been down my staircase for at least a month, for my gout had kept me to my room. Yet as the pain was temporarily lessened, I allowed her to lead me, and, with her help, I was able to descend. When we reached the foot of the stairs, however, I was exhausted with the effort, and I asked if I might sit a while there, to recover. This she helped me to do, and said she would fetch the object that she wanted me to see. I looked up at her as she spoke, and was struck, all at once, with her beauty. We were of near equal age, yet whilst I was ravaged by disease, age had not really harmed her. Lines were etched around her almond eyes, but the greying of her jet-black hair gave distinction to her face and her back was straight and long as it had always been. For an instant I remembered a moment when she had arched that back beneath me. When those dark-lashed eyes had closed in ecstasy. But then the thought was gone, for there was no such link between us now. I knew we were not equal. Helena still held herself within her. Though I might nearly reach her, I knew that a part of her would always remain untouchable. Whereas I – I have a heart that spills out within me. He who has been most heartless finds that that organ wreaks revenge.

When Helena returned, looking cold and stern, it was clear that she planned to make a invalid of me. She was pushing an object that made my blood run cold. A gout chair. A seat on wheels. A cripple-wagon.

I flew into a rage. What did she mean by this? Did she think I would be pushed about by her? What were my legs for if not to walk? If I sat in that thing it would not be long before they seized up completely – was that what she desired?

Strangely, as I screamed and shouted at her, there was a part of me that watched my drunken, raving self in horror. Indeed, that part of me knew that not one word I said would disturb the calmness of Helena's countenance. She simply waited for me to exhaust myself, and then she spoke.

'Vermilion,' she said, 'the last thing I desire is that you should remain long in this chair. I wish for you to see a physician so that he may speak to you of how you might recover. But until you agree to that measure, would you remain locked up in your study? I know that you mourn, still, for your Emilia. Do not think I am ignorant of that. But you are wrong to think you betray her by learning to live again. Vermilion – I wish you to live, not to rot in that room. I am lonely here. I wish for your company.'

'I'll not sit in that thing and be pushed about,' I said.

'No indeed, nor is there need for that. For look – here is a little handle that you may turn. It makes the wheels revolve. If you keep to the paths, it is possible you may see the garden yourself.'

'I'll not be a cripple, Helena!' I said. 'I'll not do it. Look, I am quite capable of walking.'

And with that, clumsily, I pushed myself up from the staircase and, with the aid of my stick, began to walk. I regretted this instantly, however, for I felt a spasm sear across my knees. I landed hard upon my wrist, which twisted beneath me as I fell, causing further agony. But worse than this was the shame, as Helena helped me up and I allowed myself to be placed in the gout chair. For no reason that I was aware of, an image of Emilia came to me, looking at herself in the glass that I had sent her. Surveying the scars upon her face. Watching it begin to rot away, as the pox took hold of her. I think I knew then there was no forgiving myself for that. The truth was that Emilia had suffered, more, no doubt, than I did now. However many times I tell myself another story, it comes back to this. For I can say – I did not know that she was raped; I believed she had consented to it. I can say – I thought she had betrayed me on purpose, so shortly before our marriage. I can say – I thought she had taken a sword and plunged it through my heart. But what good are these excuses? If I had simply talked to her, she would have convinced me. If, on that day when I found Lord Smellie had left the metropolis, I had returned to the Temple to speak to my Melia, how soon might my hatred and self-pity have been dissipated. How soon would I have learned that love cares not for disease, nor for the decay it spreads, but only for its object, the soul of the beloved?

So it was that in my realization of this fact I said to Helena, 'I will stay in this wretched thing on condition that you bring me a mirror in which I may survey my appearance.'

'I would not advise it, Vermilion,' she replied. 'You are still drunk, and are by no means at your best.'

'I would see myself at my worst,' I said. 'I would see a true picture of myself.'

But still she would not have it. She said I was clearly in no position to argue, and she was determined that I should come outside with her and take some air. She was tired of my antisocial behaviour, and this evening she would have some company.

Thus it was that I learned to use my cripple-wagon, in which I remain seated, even as I write. It is a great, bulky, oak thing, most strange to look on, with a sickle-shaped handle attached to the right arm, which I can turn about in order to make the wheels move. Such a peculiar object have I never before seen, for it is like the plainest chair you can imagine, yet it sits upon a little platform which is supported by three wheels, two large, at the front, and a small one behind. It does not move smoothly, but rather seems to jolt across the marble floors of Carmine Hall. And how like a child I feel within it! One who has not yet the strength to use his own legs.

In truth, I had no choice, last evening, but to do as Helena requested. For once I was within the chair, I found that, due to my portliness, I was wedged in. Still rather drunk, I did not turn the handle but allowed Helena to push me through the dining-room, from which I noticed she had removed the sheets, and through the tall doors that lead directly into the gardens. And I admit that I was glad to be outside. I had forgotten, I think, what it is to feel this freshness.

Outside, the moon hung like a cradle in the sky. The triangular trees along the paths threw long shadows across the lawns. All was still save for the cooing of a wood pigeon, the trickle of a fountain, and the crunch of turning wheels beneath me. How beautiful it was. The chill air, the scent of dew, the knowledge that Helena trod behind me. We moved without speaking. Along the avenues we passed, close by the statue of Hercules, and the fountain where Neptune rode. Does not the stone rebuke me, I thought, for being more stone than it? Yes, these figures seemed to mock me with their silence. I closed my eyes, not desiring to see their manly forms.

Eventually, we reached the orange-tree garden, and I admit I was delighted to see this sight, which I had not visited since I first returned to Carmine Hall. Helena stopped by a little bench, and there she sat down beside me. Still she did not speak, respecting, I think, my need for contemplation. I would never say how thankful I was that she had brought me here, but I looked at her then, and smiled, and I think she knew my meaning.

The garden was spread out beneath me. We were seated half-way down a little valley, at the base of which lies my ornamental lake. The trees of the garden form a semi-circle around the lake, and opposite where I sat, my Pantheon could be seen, glowing white beneath the moon. How strong the scent of oranges was upon the air! I heard scufflings in the undergrowth, saw shadows flickering across the grass. My Melia should have been here now. The thought came to me all at once. Without her, all this was meaningless.

'Tell me again about Emilia's funeral, Helena,' I said, suddenly.

'What!' she replied. 'Why do you ask me this?'

She was defensive, I think, because she knew she should have invited me. But I pretended not to notice this.

'Sometimes,' I said, 'I find myself thinking that she is still alive. I can barely explain it, except to say I *feel* her. I feel she is with me.'

'If that is so, if you wish to believe her alive, why should I speak to you of her funeral?'

'Because often I wish I had been there. I hear her spirit, screaming from the grave because I was not there. Other times, I think she haunts me because I did not witness her decay and death. I often cannot believe her dead, because I did not see her buried. Nor did I allow myself time to mourn her.'

'From what I have seen, Vermilion, you have done nought but mourn Emilia since I arrived in your house.'

'No. It is not the same. Thinking, and writing – these are inadequate. I try to bring the wheel full circle. As if, by recounting the past, I can make her live again. But it is the path to madness, Helena. I need to hear that day spoken of once again. If I could revisit it, once more, perhaps I might be able to let her rest. To accept what has passed.'

'To begin again, Vermilion, is that your meaning? Would you learn to live again?'

'I cannot say. It is impossible. But speak to me of that day, Helena! If you do not, I shall never believe her truly dead.'

'Now is not the time, Vermilion. There is another matter I wish to speak of. I wish to convey some other news.'

'No! It must wait, I tell you. I need to hear it now.'

And knowing then that I would not, else, be satisfied, Helena finally began to speak.

'It was a quiet occasion, Vermilion,' she said. 'Emilia's life, once she had left the Temple, was simple. She had few friends, except myself. She said she did not wish for more human company, for she had found, through experience, that there were few people in whom one could place one's trust. The world was hollow, she used to say.'

I thought how strange it was that we should finally speak of her here, in the garden which could have been her own. I might have spent evenings here, with her by my side. We might have sniffed this air together, or watched the swans, now, as they twisted their pliant necks about, and buried them in their plumage, preparing to sleep.

'I have told you before, Vermilion, there were only two guests at her funeral, myself, and our son, Marcus. She was buried without ceremony, according to her own request. Vermilion, the funeral she had was not fitting for one so truly beloved as her. She had imagined that you would attend. She thought about it often. She thought you would bring flowers. Would weep false tears for her, as she did for her father.'

'Helena! I would have been there! But you did not tell me of date or place.'

'Come, Vermilion. For three years, you neither saw nor spoke to her. You communicated with her only twice. Once, a mocking note, to say that you would write her biography. Then to send a gift so cruel, I am certain her death was hastened by it. And you question that you were not invited to her funeral? I tell you, sir, I would not have thus offended her memory for all the world.'

'If I could take it back . . .'

'There is no going back, Vermilion. For three years, I cared for her. I was her only friend. *Three years*. Did you not, during that period, have time to regret? Was it necessary that she should die, so that Vermilion might feel remorse?'

As she spoke, a dark cloud began to creep across the moon. Helena's words stung me to the very core. I knew I had hurt Emilia, not once, but three times. Once, upon the Celestial Bed, once by leaving her when most she needed me, and once again, only a few months before her death, by sending her a gift to rub salt upon her wounded soul. I despise you, Emilia, was the unwritten message, for your face and body are being destroyed by a filthy disease. I cannot love that which is so defiled as you.

Yet how is it, I wonder, that she should have suffered so, when I, who have fucked ten thousand times, have not been touched by it? Sure, the armour I wear upon my prick must play some part in this, yet in truth I think I have indeed been a favourite of the Devil to escape so unscathed from all my exploits. Yet it should have been me. I should have been a victim of this plague.

I never even saw her! The words keep ringing in my brain. I only heard she had the pox from the Doctor, when I returned, after several months, to find her again. Yes! Had I forgotten to tell you that? It took this vain and stupid Vermilion three months to return to the Temple, but return he did, in search of his love.

'Emilia is gone, Vermilion.'

I had never seen him so close to tears, which welled so soon after I mentioned her name.

'My Vestina was defiled. The Neapolitan sickness took her. She left of her own accord.'

Why did I send the mirror? After near three years of silence between us? Having bought it when the Doctor was forced to close his second Temple, I kept it with me several months before I sent it. And I sent it, just before I set off for a trip to Europe. It was a way, I think, of killing our love. For the pain within me was so deep, so unknown to me, yet so affecting everything I did, each movement that I made, I *had* to murder it thus. I had to kill her memory to avoid the life of the soul. The life of sentiment! And after that I fooled myself for ten more years and lived a life so shallow that I might as well have killed myself as well as her.

I was alone, last night, as I wept. Helena said nothing, nor did she touch me to comfort me. I felt as if my very entrails might heave into my mouth. As if the blood my heart had spilled within me might issue from my eyes. There was nothing manly remaining. And the empty night was filled with the sound of my agony.

Eventually I was silent.

'The sun shone, Vermilion,' I heard Helena say. 'The afternoon shadows stretched out across the field where we buried her. It was hot and sweet, a beautiful autumn day. Everything plump and full, and bursting with life. Pale sky and golden sun above. And us, below. Silent. Unable to believe that her eyes would never see another morning.'

Hearing her words, calmer now, I was almost glad I had not seen it. I believed it now. That was enough. For I know, had I been there, I would have thrown myself into her grave. A pitiable would-be Hamlet who has lost his love. I'd eat a crocodile if it would bring her back.

'No more, Helena. I pray you, no more.'

And then, finally, she took my hand, my gnarled and twisted hand, gently within her own. I cannot tell you the solace of it.

'The worst is finished now, Vermilion,' she said. 'I will not taunt you longer.'

'Yet you punish me still.'

'No more. I promise you. No more. I brought you here, in fact, to convey some good news, but it is getting late now, and you are exhausted. Come. I will push you back to the house.'

'First tell me,' I said. 'What is your news? I am in need of glad tidings.'

'I do not know if you will be pleased.'

'Then you may only find out through telling me.'

'Our son is coming here,' she said. 'Marcus Quinton is coming to Carmine Hall.'

44

EMILIA

WHEN I AWOKE, it was to see her face. Full of luminosity. Sorrowful. I had not all my senses about me, and I was not able to reason or think clearly.

'I had thought you were a Catholic,' I said, for my mind at that time was all confusion.

'Sweet Emilia. My friend.'

'Will they come here? Will they burn this house down? Why the blue ribbons outside? I had thought you were a Catholic.'

'I am a Catholic, Emilia, but we hung the blue ribbons so that they would not burn us. My husband is not eminent enough for all and sundry to know his faith.'

'I saw a woman. I saw her. Dead, Helena. She was dead.'

'Rest now, Emilia. You must rest.'

'No! No rest! We cannot rest. They will burn us. I am burning now!'

And then she leaned forward and did a thing I will never forget. Though I was quite delirious, still I remember this. Helena kissed me, upon my forehead. She kissed the blackish scabs that now had formed there. Her kiss spoke to my unquiet soul. I slept again.

The next time I awoke, I was alone in the room. This time I had my wits about me, and I smiled to know where I was. Lord Quinton's house. I had been dressed in one of my thin night-gowns.

How calm it was here. How perfectly ordered this room, with its pale, pinkish walls and long, creamy curtains. The bed in which I lay was fashioned from dark oak, and was draped in thick pink velvet. Little carved birds frolicked at my feet, and close by my side was a chest of drawers, upon which was a large spray of roses whose smell infused the air.

Yet it was not simply the room itself that soothed me. I realized that the window was open and perhaps it was the cool air which made me smile now, in spite of all that had passed. No! It was not the air itself, but rather the sounds beyond the window. Ordinary sounds. Hooves upon the pavement. The voices of pedlars and children. Dogs barking and horses neighing. The quiet chatter of summer afternoons. Was it over then, the rioting?

Slowly I pushed myself up from the bed and walked to the window. Though all seemed well below, though London life seemed almost as it had always been, still the ravages of what had passed remained. On the opposite side of the square, Lord Mansfield's house was a ruin. A charred and blackened shell. And seeing it reminded me of the truth of all that had passed. So cheerful did the people seem in the streets below, it was as if they had forgotten what had passed only yesterday.

I heard the handle of the door being twisted then, behind me, and turned to see Helena entering the room.

'I am sorry,' she said. 'I did not know that you were up. I would have knocked, Emilia.'

I had never thought that I could be so happy to see a person. So devoid had my life been of anyone in whom I could put my trust, that the sight of Helena standing there seemed miraculous. She was the same as she had always been. Tall and seeming almost untouchable; more a black swan than a peacock; or a lily in shade. Yet beneath the sombre beauty, I detected a stirring of the heart. I saw it in her eyes.

Then I looked down, and saw her belly. Barely a change was noticeable there. It was a little rounder perhaps; only a little. For a moment, I wondered if it was true that she was with child, yet then I saw her, noticing my regard, place her hand across that place, and I knew that Vermilion's baby was indeed within her.

She walked towards me, came close and, bending her knees, kissed my cheek. Then, after hesitating a moment, she placed her arms around me, and pulled me close to her. As she held me, silently, I felt her belly push against my ribs. And I knew that beneath the dark silks, beneath the petticoats, beneath the skin, beneath the muscle, beneath the blood, amongst the waters, deep waters, a little child was resting. I believed that I could hear the heartbeat, thud-thud against my bones. The hands, reaching out to touch me, caressed their father's other love.

'I am so sorry, Emilia. So sorry.'

And then she moved away from me, and I was empty again. We sat down together in the window-seat.

'Why are *you* sorry?' I asked. 'What have *you* done?'

'You know, Emilia, do you not, what is the matter with you? We had a physician attend whilst you were sleeping.'

'Yes. I know it is syphilis. There is no need for you to break the news.'

'Though he is the father of my child, I swear I wish him dead.'

'There is no need, Helena. It was not Vermilion who did this to me.'

In the hours that followed, I unfolded my story. I told her how Vermilion and I had planned to marry (which clearly pained her, so I wished I had not said it), and how Lord Smellie (who should have been dead) had lured me to Vauxhall and the dark walks. I told her how he had raped me in a place he called our bridal chamber, and how Vermilion, on discovering this, had refused to see me more. I spoke of the rash that appeared on my body, and how eventually I could not conceal it. I told her of the Doctor's rage on hearing the news, and of his sorrow also. I told her that I felt I had no choice but to leave the Temple, and that, though I was mightily sorry for it, I had no other place to go but here. Finally, I told her what I had seen. The carnage. The woman who had lost her brains. I could not believe that already, it seemed, calm had been restored. I could not think how it had happened so quickly.

Throughout my speaking, she remained very quiet. She held my hands within her own to give me courage to continue speaking, or kissed me, murmuring, 'Oh, Emilia' or 'Poor child, you poor child.' And silent tears ran down her cheeks. It was only when I had near finished speaking that she seemed to regain the strength to speak. When I mentioned my experiences in Bloomsbury Square, she stopped me.

'Yesterday? You said yesterday, Emilia?'

'Of course.'

'My friend, it was not yesterday that you came here. You have been sleeping three full days and nights – that is why all is calm again. The riots continued until Thursday. It is Saturday now. Order was finally restored two days ago. But until then, we lived in fear. Many other Catholic houses in this area were burned. I tell you, on Wednesday night, the sky flared all around with the fires. There were soldiers all about the place, but it seemed the mob would not be controlled.'

'I slept? Through all of this?'

'Emilia, I could hardly believe it myself. Often I watched over you, the room illuminated only by the glare of the fiery sky, but that near bright as daylight. It seemed that none should sleep while London was thus disturbed, yet you slept on. People were fleeing from their houses, carrying all their worldly goods with them. The sound of gunfire often pierced the air, and there was not a house in the square that did not have candles burning throughout the night. In the whole of Holborn, the whole of Bloomsbury, I think you were the only person who was capable of rest. I held your hand, and it kept me tranquil. The sky was so red, so full of smoke and flying particles, that it seemed to me the very moon and stars had been obliterated. And yet you remained still. I saw a smile flicker on your face. I told myself your resting was a sign that we would be safe. A kind of omen.'

'Three days, you say, and three nights?'

'Yes. And such happenings you missed. For we could well observe, from this house, the fire at Mr Langdale's. But there is no need for you to hear it.'

'You are wrong, Helena. There is a need. My curiosity demands it.'

'Very well,' she replied. 'But first you must take some hot broth. You must have nourishment, my dear. You are still the bony creature I remember.'

I did not understand, at the time, why I wished so desperately to hear about the events that had occurred whilst I had slept. Yet now I think I see my reasons clearly. There was so much that went unspoken between us two at that time. To speak of events that were outside all that bound us – this was our way of trying to forget our differences; our shame at how each of us had hurt the other.

And so she spoke of Langdale's. This was a tale which, once heard, is impossible to forget. For Mr Langdale is an eminent distiller, whose distillery was situated about a mile away, on Holborn Hill. When the mob attacked this place, however, with the intention, no doubt, of procuring as much liquor as they were able to drink, they did not consider how highly flammable were the spirits stored therein. And so it was that the fire that ensued was beyond all imagination. The inhabitants of dozens of neighbouring houses were forced to flee their homes. The rooms of houses more than a mile away glowed as if it were still stark day.

It was not the fire itself, however, that was the worst of it. According to Helena's servant, a whole stream of scorching spirit was released from the distillery by the mob. It poured down the gutters of the street, slipping easily between the stones, whilst below, a great horde of people began building a dam so as not to let the liquor vanish. In this they succeeded, and hundreds of people, young and old, some women with babies at their breasts, bent down to satisfy their appetite. So much did they drink that several, it was said, once their head was down, never looked up again, but drank until they were dead, whilst others leapt up and danced in a frenzy around the pool, before collapsing into the lethal liquid. There were men and women in the basement of the distillery, unaware of the ferocity of the fire that raged above. They too were supping heartily, but when the fire reached that part of the building, they had no time to escape before they themselves caught fire. Helena's servant witnessed a great crowd of them running out into the street, with all the appearance of being human bonfires. And, as they plunged towards the ever-increasing stream of liquor, thinking that it was water, not only did they combust themselves, but they set the stream aflame, and the fire then seemed to run down the street, engulfing all who sipped there. When it reached the pool at the end, every soul who took a drop from it was turned into a ball of flame. Even the babes at the breast perished there, at the mercy of that terrible liquid fire. Next morning, when, by the order of the King, the military were beginning to overcome the mob (an armed force of ten thousand men, she said, was required to stop the universal anarchy), the whole of Holborn Hill was littered with the charred corpses.

Now, however, London had been restored to order. I could not help but think, however, that night, when Helena was gone, of the blackened bodies that lay in the gutter, after the terrible events at Langdale's distillery. I lay there, in the darkness, running my fingers across the scabs upon my face. It felt, to me, very like the skin of one who has been burned. And I knew, in that moment, that I would die. Not immediately, perhaps, but long before the syphilis made me mad. Long before my teeth dropped out and my nose rotted away. This was not a desire for death, but rather a kind of premonition. When I closed my eyes, I saw a flurry of black moths, so thick I could see nothing beyond them. It seemed as if my eyelids were stuck down and I would drown in a sea of dark and fluttering wings. Soft they were, so soft, like black petals that would smother me and bring me a death so sweet-scented that I would welcome it.

45

VERMILION

WHY IS IT that when my tale is so near its end, when I am ready, like Emilia, to wait for an early death, Helena insists on bringing life to this place? I know she means no ill, and yet I cannot think why she wishes to bring the young Marcus Quinton to Carmine Hall. Does she truly think that by doing so she can stir me into a lust for living? That I will be overcome, all of a sudden, with fatherly love, and that we will form a pretty family here?

I am, in fact, devoid of fatherly emotions. The thought of the child brings me neither joy nor dread. I feel nothing. Nothing but the near-crippling pains in my hands, and the irritation of the noise that now permeates this house.

Indeed, it is more than I can bear. Not only am I impeded by the gout, but also by the sound of hammering in the ballroom above, and a whole horde of housemaids which Helena has brought in, to prepare Carmine Hall for her son. I write in the library now. As I am chair-bound and only able to mount the stairs with help from two servants (who carry my chair up also), I like to remain here during the day, so that I can be closer to my gardens, which, it is true, have given me some pleasure of late. Yet here there are constant interruptions from Helena. What should she do with the old and rotting sheets? Might she have permission to hire an extra cook for the occasion of her son's arrival? Could she be allowed to hang a number of paintings, which she has discovered beneath a bed? I am beginning to tire of it all, and once or twice I have raised my voice to her. Still, even my anger now seems to have no effect. She is changed, I am certain of it. She *smiles* again. She *hums* in a most annoying manner, as she moves about the house, and seems in her element, instructing the workers on the restoration, and ordering the maids to polish harder.

You will forgive me, I hope, for writing briefly. All I mean to tell you, truly, is that there is clearly some attempt by Helena to create a mood of excitement in the house. I sense, in her demeanour, some suppressed happiness. She tries, when in my presence, to remain glum and stern, as she is wont to be, yet in truth she is having little success. And still, always, I hear the banging overhead. I know the place where my parents met their death is being transformed into some pleasure-dome again. They will hang a new chandelier from the ceiling. And I am unable to stop it. For what point is there, I think, in objecting to these changes? I no longer have any regard for Carmine Hall, because soon it will cease to be mine. Soon, when I have completed this work, I, like Emilia, shall lose the will to live. I shall watch the arrival of my son, but if he arrives after my work is completed, I shall have no energy to woo him. I shall say, quite simply, 'Here, Marcus. All this is yours. Take it. And use it well.'

For though Helena says he is a bad child, I cannot think he will be worse than I, Vermilion, have been. As it seems to me that the Gods will have their will, no matter what passes, I can see no purpose in trying to teach the boy to do good. He will do, I suppose, only what he desires.

Be patient, my friends. Our story is nearly through. Marcus and Helena – they are no more than distractions for me. With all this noise around me, is it possible that we must face these final chapters of Emilia's life? That I must peruse the last words that she ever wrote? Knowing that when I reach that final page, there will be no more going back. Nor will there be excuses for all that I have done. Simply, you will experience her sorrow, as I have, and, if you have a heart, you will weep for her.

And I say now, though I am no more than a gouty, chair-bound shadow of a man – I say that I will never forget the woman that I loved. Though I misused her, her name is written on my heart. At the moment of my death, it will burst upon my tongue. The air will be the richer for her name. And you may smile, Helena. You may smile all you like. Smile and smile and still I cannot share your joy. For a stranger son is a poor thing, who will not compensate for my loss. I will be guilty always. And a child made of such metal as I is no cause for happiness.

46

EMILIA

I HAVE BEEN writing now for several hours. Dark hours they
have been, but I have not been lonely. No. When I write, it is as
though I enter some other sphere. A place where my body, my
physical self has no existence. This is why I have begun working
into the night. When I write thus, by the light of a single candle,
I find that nothing seems to exist beyond my mind, my hand,
my pen, the page beneath it. When I must dip my quill into the
well, I do it quickly, unthinkingly. Always my hand rushes back
to the paper, where it continues to move, forming shapes that
once drawn, become invisible.

The patterns of my existence are changing. It seems to me
that the nearer I come to death, the less I desire to experience
my corporeal being. I have stopped my habit of glancing at my
reflection each day, in that mirror that hangs above the fireplace.
The mirror that Vermilion sent. I wish to forget the sight that
frightens me there. The horrifying, most ghastly sight. So
unjust, it is, that I should appear thus. Indeed, once, when
regarding myself in that glass, I was seized with a sudden
sickness. My own reflection seemed so distorted that I felt the
bile rise in my throat and I vomited, there on the fireplace,
before I had a chance to move.

It was not always so. Once I had admired what I saw in that
mirror. I thought I was an Angel. Yes, I remember now how I
stood at the head of the Doctor's staircase beneath the dome.
How they gaped, the audience, as later they came closer to me!
How the men lifted their eyeglasses and peered at me, watching
the lantern-light pour through my shift, making it quite transparent! A perfect nipple that, is it not? And have you seen her
mound of Venus? Think what delights are hidden beneath that

little bush! Would the crowd would disappear, eh, sir? Would that this ranting quack before you would stop speaking so that you might be alone with the Goddess! How you throb and ache and ... oh ... how you long to push her back upon the Celestial Bed, her smooth, white thighs parting for you, to reveal her pretty pink cunt. How much would the Doctor take for it, you wonder? Fifty pounds for the Bed, another fifty for the Vestina? No, she would not be so expensive as that. No Goddess at all, just another whore.

Yet I would not be this. I would, if it were possible, absolve myself of the body. For whether fair or foul of face, I am not what I seem. There is more to Emilia than can be discerned through an eyeglass. And this is why I work in darkness now. At night I find that only the mind and the pen have life. The face has no significance, nor the breasts, nor the thighs.

Since I arrived at Helena's house, my life has been most simple. There is nothing much of note that has passed in these three years. I have changed – oh yes, my quiet life has afforded me much time for contemplation. But the routine of my days has been most ordinary.

Firstly, I must say that without my beloved Helena, I have no doubt I should have perished in the street. When she took me in, I was weak beyond imagination. I was so thin, I am certain that before long I would have starved. That is, if I had not been shot before then, by the soldiers, for the blue ribbons attached to my bonnet.

In spite of her kindness, however, it soon became clear to me that Helena would not be able to keep me long within her house. Lord Quinton did not wish to have me remain as a guest here, and within a few weeks, Helena procured for me these lodgings, close by in Bloomsbury, where I abide, even now.

I have told you, my room now is a simple one – bare-walled and sparsely furnished. It is the place where I work, sleep and eat. The landlady, Mrs Kiddle, brings me two meals a day, a breakfast in the early afternoon and my supper at around eight in the evening. She is discreet enough not to question the strange hours that I have begun to keep. And though, at first, she did attempt to mother me, showing concern that I seldom ventured out, telling me it was not healthy to remain so long indoors, now she has finished with such fussing.

My life, however, has not been as dull as you might think. For though I spend many hours on my own, there has been a constant source of joy in my life. A daily visitor, without whom I am certain I would have perished sooner.

Young Marcus Quinton it is, who has kept me from despair. A child so different in temperament from his father that it is impossible I should not love him. Indeed, this little boy, though he is no more than two years old, is a child of such sweetness of manners, such quickness of mind, that when I am in his company I am oblivious to my own sorrow. When he is here, in my room, he sits upon my lap and sings the childish songs which Helena has taught him. When he has finished, he looks up at me, his egg-shell eyes gazing directly into my own. Such trust I see there, such unquestioning trust, that I almost envy him his innocence. For I know his love is not based on such fragile premises as the appearance of my face, but rather upon the fact that I am human and therefore kin to him.

There is no doubt that this boy is Vermilion's child. His hair, of the same dark hue, already curls about his shoulders, and his face seems to me to be an almost perfect miniature of his father's. Already I see a little bump upon his nose, beginning to swell and change his childish look. I see the hue of his eyes, which no artist could have matched. And the precise curve of his lips, which in Marcus seems almost amusing, for it is clear that he experiences none of the arrogance that that expression seems to suggest.

In truth, however, though I love Marcus, though he is a source of great happiness, still I cannot look at him without thinking of his father. I cannot look at him without thinking of the child that might have been mine.

Only once was I able to transcend this weakness. And then it was in a dream that was, in all other respects, a most horrifying imagining. I dreamed I saw a field, which sloped down from the horizon. I could not see beyond that hillside, yet still I was dazzled by the sight of the grass, blown sideways by the wind, and the way the sunlight caught upon it, as it rippled. On the hill, there was a yew tree, a sturdy old evergreen, and at first I saw only its outline, for I seemed to watch it from way above. Then I noticed that, down below, several figures were standing, and as I moved closer (seemed to glide lower, like a bird), I understood what took place here. The figures were dressed in black and they stood around a freshly dug grave. These figures, besides the parson and the grave-digger, were those persons who have been most influential in my life. Vermilion, Helena, little Marcus and Dr Graham. All of them, except for Marcus, were weeping, as the earth was shovelled over a coffin. And I, also (if I had possessed eyes, which I did not), would have wept, had I not suddenly understood the reason for their sorrow. This was my funeral that they attended. It was me that they mourned. And yet there was no need! I realized, instantly, why it was that I watched them from above. I had become what, in all my days in the Temple, I desired to be. I was dissolved into the air. The purest most aetherial substance. I could not be seen, nor even touched. My spirit was as a fine mist; a million droplets. I had no scent, and yet I mingled with the smell of the rain, of the thick green grass, and the smell of the earth itself.

And then I see how Marcus is different to Vermilion. For whilst all look down towards the ground, to the place where my bones and rotting flesh did lie, only the child looks up, towards me. I know that he senses me, and I can sense him, also. Though, on waking, all these secrets that I learned of him in my dream seemed impossible to recall, I am certain that in that moment I learned more of him than I have ever known of one person. And soon I knew that he was no longer below, but floating with me upon the air. I hear his laughter. And I laugh with him. Only he and I know that my death is not to be mourned.

Beneath us, however, the mourning continues. I see the grave-digger shovel the final earth upon my coffin, and the Doctor begins to speak. He takes a handkerchief from his pocket and, having wiped the tears from his eyes, he declares, 'What have we been thinking, my friends? There is no sense in our despairing. How foolish I have been to think that death could defeat a medical genius such as myself. Come! Watch!'

And at this he pulls his jacket open, and there, as if from nowhere, he produces the Celestial Throne, complete with Chinese rail, and columns of glass; sparking furiously with electrical fire. Then he falls to his knees and begins shovelling the earth with his hands.

'Come! We will revive her before sundown!'

With horror I watch the spectacle. Only Marcus (who is not truly there) does not fall to his knees, scrabbling in the dirt. The others are all beside him, and with no regard to their smart black clothes, they are burrowing to reach my coffin. Finally, when, exhausted, they reach it, they struggle to lever the lid from it and eventually they see me, laid out in my Vestina's robes.

I see their faces as they catch the stink of me, and see the putrefaction of my face. My nose has begun to dissolve. My face is covered in scars. My teeth (those that remain) are black.

'Put her on the chair!' Vermilion shouts.

And the Doctor drags me, the half-rotten Vestina, and places me upon the Throne. Opening his mud-strewn jacket once again, he pulls the spinning globes of gold and silver from his pocket and tosses them into the air, like little worlds. Magical as they are, they hang above the Throne, astounding the onlookers with their beauty. Their eyes are entranced at first by the rich metals, by the jewels, the glass. They wonder at the fire that sparks in the air. How man has finally harnessed the elements. How we have created lightning, even on a summer's day. They have almost forgotten their first purpose.

By the time that they remember, it is too late. The body of Emilia Anne Beaumont is burned to cinders. Only her skeleton remains. The rest of her flesh has turned to a black ash that stains the velvet cushions of the Throne. And then, in my dream, these images vanish. My mind is filled with the vision of black snow. It falls upon the Thames and freezes as it meets the surface. I see the whole of London now, and these black flakes are suffocating the city. I no longer know what they are. Snow? Ash? Moths? Petals? And if they are ash, from whence does it come? Is it Emilia's ash that falls thus? Or the ash of a hundred drunken rioters who perish in violent flame?

These thoughts rushed through my mind on waking. These thoughts are with me now, again, as I contemplate the true death which is so close. But I am not afraid of dying. I die with the knowledge that I have been innocent of any crime. I have never been possessed by the Devil, nor have I caused any of the frightful events that I have witnessed in my life. Even the fires, the terrible fires, which seemed to me to spring from my very soul, were no fault of mine.

This much I know. The disease from which I suffered was forced upon me. My beauty was not a thing that I chose. I was not to blame for my mother's death, for Daniel's desertion, nor for Vermilion's heartlessness. I know, also, that the Doctor was not a villain, but merely a little mad. I know that I had one true friend and her name was Helena. I know there is a child who will miss me sorely, and who may never understand the reason why I have gone. If my young Marcus Quinton should grow to be the young man I hope he will become – then I wish that he will read this tale. I desire that he will never blame himself for my death (as I blamed myself for my mother's), nor will he become a man akin to his father.

Tomorrow I will wrap these journals up. These words are fragile things and must be carefully stored. I would have them wrapped in cloth of gold, if I could, but, lacking such richness, I have decided to wrap them in the silken robes that once I wore in the Temple. They have been lying useless now for near three years, and I will be glad for them to serve a purpose once again.

I cannot be certain, of course, how soon my death will come, but I know I will not be kept waiting. I have courted the black fellow for too long now. I cannot think that he will let me down. And you must not think, dear Reader, that I will be sad to leave this earth. I have suffered too deeply and too long to wish to remain here now. Already my soul has begun to coil away from me. I struggle to concentrate my thoughts upon the page, for I can feel a kind of opening within my breast; a sense that something is being released there. It is spiralling up in a kind of vapour. Soon my body will be emptied of my self.

But whilst it still has life in it . . . before that last exhalation, what words remain within me to be written? Will my pen be used to pander to the desires of those that knew me? Shall I address my thoughts to Vermilion perhaps, and say that I forgive him now for what he did to me? No. If Vermilion should read these words, would I give him the satisfaction of such a pardon? Would I have him think that he can treat a woman in any way that he desires, that he can humiliate her, lie to her, break his promise of marriage, abandon her, and that still she will, upon her death-bed, say – you are forgiven. Only think how such a pardon would affect the rogue. Perhaps, he will conjecture, as the ladies seem to take his insults so politely, he could do worse, and still they will love him for it. Sure, he nearly raped Emilia once, yet afterwards she accepted his proposal of marriage. There is no telling how forgiveness would harm a man like Vermilion.

I write as if my words would have some impact on Vermilion's life, as if my judgement upon him might change his future. The truth, however, is somewhat different. Vermilion will laugh upon my deliberations. They will have no meaning for him. Indeed, no doubt I am vain even to believe that he will read these documents. When he has not wished to see or to speak to me for three full years, why should he, once I am dead, desire to read my words?

To this I have no answer. I am sensible, now, of the fact that Vermilion does not care for me. I do not deny that my own dwelling upon his name and on his opinion betrays an interest in him which I should not have. But if you, my female Reader, should feel tempted to mock me for the attention that I continue to pay to him, then I ask you to remember that, besides Helena, Marcus and my landlady, I have seen barely a living soul in these three years. Perhaps it is only natural then that I should dwell thus in the past and seek to counter the lies that Vermilion may spread. For I have no other life but that which I lived in the Temple. I have no other thoughts but memories to occupy my mind.

I do not forgive you, Vermilion. Though I know you will not read these words, still I must write them, and act as if you do. Here alone will the truth be spoken. That when first you kissed me, Vermilion, you left an imprint upon my lips. It has not vanished, and I cannot speak without feeling you there; the shadow of your kiss, hovering about my mouth. When your tongue entered my mouth, Vermilion, I sucked the velvet breath from you; I felt I stole some little part of you, and I harbour it, even now, within the casket of my heart. It beats still, Vermilion, as I write. What a safe box this is, for keeping you. How it is jewelled with rubies; studded with the stars that are my hope. You are trapped within it. You have not come to claim yourself, and so, Vermilion, I will keep the part of you that I have taken. A rarity, hidden away. For this portion of you is not tainted. This portion of you that I stealthily obtained was snatched in a moment when you did love me. It is pure as water; sweet as wine. It is unsullied, Vermilion, and I will keep it, even when my body is in the grave.

Now, Vermilion, as you read my words, that heart has shrivelled. Have no fear: the part of you that dwelled within it is contained within the scent of the flower that swells around me, even now. Like me, it will not truly die. But you, being mortal still, will miss it. You will wish that you could place your hand upon my breast and feel the thudding of my love's organ beneath it. The flesh of my breast that is gone. The bones of my rib-cage that are rotting.

I do not forgive you, Vermilion. Remember that. My spirit is nearly free now. But still, I tell you, I do not forgive you.

47

VERMILION

I AM SEATED in the library, within my gout chair. The floor and
the shelves shine about me. Yes – all has been restored for the
visit of my son. Not a corner of Carmine Hall remains untouched. The pictures seem to leap from the walls, so full of
colour are they. Even the books are free of dust. Only Emilia's
journals will remain as they are. Thick with the smell of her.

Oh God! I swear I never meant to kill her! For surely it was
my indifference that caused her life to ebb away. The disease
should not have killed her so soon as that. And though she does
not mention the cause of her death, I have no doubt that she
died because she willed it.

Dear Reader, do you think, because I do not speak of it, that
I can bear this anguish? Do you think I am not moved by these
words that lately I have read, the last Emilia ever wrote? If you
knew how much pain it causes me, even to curl my fingers
around the pen, you would know that I am willing to die if that
is what is required to pay for what I have done. This pain is
worse than anything I have experienced in my lifetime. These
words are written with crippled hands. You read a sentence in
the time it takes me to form a single letter. My hands are more
useless than paws. They are gnarled like the knots upon a tree-
trunk. And it is hard to stop myself from screaming at the agony
of my task.

And yet I know that this is nothing. This is bliss compared to
the spiritual pain suffered by my poor Melia. Bliss indeed, yet I
would suffer torture if her spirit would forgive me. I would be
pulled upon the rack; burned at the stake. Only I know it will
not help me. Nothing can change these final words that she has
written. They are stains upon the page; stains upon my heart.

My heart, that will not keep anything within it. My heart, full of holes. Bleeding constantly. Made of dull flesh and muscle.

Outside, the leaves begin to tumble. There is still sunlight in the sky, and it illuminates the dying landscape. Soon it will be winter. All will be buried beneath the snow. I do not know how I shall pass my time then, for the child, no doubt, will be irksome, and my work will be completed. But think! We have made it, my friends! My gouty hands did not get the better of me. The tale has been told, and before long you and I will be parting company. In truth, I have no reason to delay you. There is no need for you to stay longer with me. It is Emilia's story, not my own, which I have tried to tell. And even if I wished to keep you longer, my hands would not allow it. I will force them simply to complete my work this day, and then there will be an end to our companionship.

The thought is most unpleasant. That I should lose this, my only comfort. The knowledge that my pen will speak! That I will be heard! I have said − I had thought, when I began this tale, that I could find some reasons to explain my actions. That I could find some pattern to the past which would soothe me. Which would justify all that I have done. But now I find there is no shape to it. And I am left, neither purified, nor vindicated. I am left only with the knowledge that there was a woman named Emilia whom I loved beyond all reason. I am left in the knowledge that I betrayed her. I killed her because I could not see beyond what I saw. I wanted to take possession of her flesh, but did not learn that the source of my longing went deeper than mere matter. The source of my longing was neither face, nor breasts, nor the softness I found between her thighs. Nor was it her voice that I loved, nor her gestures. What I loved was her immortal soul.

In truth, there is no more to say. Only, I must conclude my tale with a warning. A warning to the masculine sex, to be precise, for though you perhaps began to read believing this to be a most immoral work, in fact that is far from the case. You were, no doubt, drawn into the story, believing that a male

377

narrator can always be trusted to deliver a licentious tale of whoring and deception, a story of a woman who faces great adversity but in the end succumbs to the wiles of the rakish villain who pursues her. And indeed, I hope that you were fooled by this; that you were enticed by my promises. But, more than this, I hope that this tale has taught you to weep. That you have no need, now, of my warning, which is this. Do not listen to your friends, Gentlemen. Do not regard a woman for the plumpness of her bosom, nor the perfection of her face. Do not look, Gentlemen, at the parts of her sex that will decay, but rather listen to her words. When she kisses you, think not of your prick, bursting against your breeches, but rather try to find if that woman steals your soul from your lips. If you concentrate, you will find the sensation impossible to miss. For now I think of it, I remember it well. A sense that I was surely dissolving into her. You will know, my friends, when she has you in the casket of her heart. You will know it, and I tell you, you must learn to cherish her for keeping you there.

But wait! I am disturbed . . .

Reader, some hours have passed since these last words were written. It was Helena who knocked upon the library door and I was furious, of course, that she should interrupt me thus, when I was so near to finishing my tale. What she has told me, however, changes everything. I can barely believe the news she brings. My heart is full of joy and trepidation. I tremble. I fear that she lies. My eyes are full of tears and you must know that our tale is not yet over.

48

VERMILION

I HAVE HAD some hours now, alone, to contemplate what Helena has told me. But still I cannot really believe that it is true. Though she has reassured me a hundred times this is no trick to make me suffer, still I cannot help suspecting some such thing. And yet . . . she has sworn it. And I trust her.

There is no easy way to break the news. You too will think it is some mockery. In spite of this, I will tell you straight what I have heard. It is this. Emilia Anne Beaumont is alive. She says my Melia lives!

The fact will prompt a hundred questions. This I know, for I have asked them all, and received my answers. All of them seem to follow a certain kind of logic, yet still the thought of it is too much to comprehend. I am joyous and afraid. For if it is true . . . If my love lives still, then I am happier than any other creature on this earth. Yet I know I will barely recognize her. After thirteen years, the disease will be far advanced in her. Many times I have thought of her as she must have looked before she died. No doubt I exaggerated the horrors of it. The scars left upon her skin. The rotting of her nose. All I know is that her face was spoiled enough to make her fear to look at herself. The very fact that she did not describe her changed appearance must surely mean that the damage done was by no means meagre.

But what do I care if she is rotting? I care only in that she will be in pain; she will be suffering. Now, after thirteen years, she is sure to be infirm. Now it is very likely her nose has gone. Her bones will be decaying. Like me, she may be bound within a chair. But what of it? She lives. She lives! I would embrace her, if her face were covered in ulcers, if her skin were red and flaking as an old man's elbow. Beneath, there will be beauty. Oh God, if there be a hole in the centre of her face, I know I will love her still. I had thought that her journal was the sole remaining expression of her. I have read it, over and again, thinking that she would never again speak to me. But to think her mouth has life! To think more words are waiting there.

I am like a child now. I cannot remain still, but have been wheeling the chair about the house like a madman. Forgetting, somehow, the pain in my hands, I have been turning my little handle at such a speed that I have become almost dizzy with it. I am reeling now, from the sight of this restoration that Helena has commanded. In the dining-room, the portraits of my parents have been uncovered, and the frames polished to perfection. The table gleams and the chairs are being reupholstered. Not for her son! (Our son, I should say.) No – all this, she says, is for Emilia. Emilia is coming to Carmine Hall.

Calm yourself, Vermilion. Calm yourself, and pass the rest of this afternoon by penning all that has passed. For she does not come until tomorrow. She brings the young Marcus with her. Calm yourself. Explain what you have been told.

Helena has said that Emilia did not die. And, when I think upon it, I know this is most plausible. For how else did I know of her death, but from Helena herself? Helena, who once led me to Emilia's lonely chamber. Who said that she would leave me there, an hour or two, so that I might remember my love, and think on what I had done to her. To think that when I found the journals, I thought I had made some great discovery! Yet Helena had left them there, for me to see. And Emilia, also, had been persuaded by her, to let me find them.

How strange to have spent what seems a lifetime dreaming of a love one thinks is dead. And then to be told it is not true. Simply, Helena says, Emilia believed that she was dying. When she laid down her pen, after writing that final entry, Helena says she wrapped the diaries up in silk and lay down in her bed, truly believing that now her task was over, and that she would not see another morning. She thought that Death took pity on such souls as her. She thought she had simply to will it, and her life would be over.

But Death was not so kind. He only takes those who are not ready. The fit and the well he takes with a sudden fair swoop. Those like ourselves, half in the grave already, he lets live on.

The following afternoon, Emilia woke up and saw that the world around her (her little room) was just as it had always been. She thought perhaps she would have to wait another night, but when Helena came, with the child, she spoke to her friend of her surprise that she still lived. My Melia's morbid thoughts came as a shock to Helena. She blamed herself for allowing Emilia to withdraw so from life. For not encouraging her friend to lead a more sociable existence. Yet Emilia insisted this was not what she desired. She told Helena about her journal. How now it was complete, she saw no purpose to her life.

I do not know, entirely, what happened next. It is clear that there has been some strong attachment between young Marcus and Emilia, and that Emilia has been leading, these last ten years, a better life than any that she knew before. I know, also (*if* the Lady Quinton is to be believed), that between them Helena and Emilia hatched the plot that I should find the journals. Finding herself still alive, Emilia did not feel they could yet be published, and, as she desired me to know how my actions had affected her, she agreed that they should be left where I would find them. It was not to punish me, Helena said, but rather in the hope that I might see my faults. That from her agony, some good might come. If a single rake could be reformed, Helena said, then there might be some hope left in the world. Only, in order for their plan to be successful, it was necessary that I should believe Emilia dead. Only then might I repent. On this, Helena was most insistent.

What was it then, I asked, that led her to tell the truth now? When she has been here several months, why has she waited so long to speak of this? Or rather, why has she told me at all? Even as I asked the question, however, I began to suspect that some deeper plotting was afoot here. Even before she told me the answer, I began to guess at what soon she confirmed to be the case. When they heard that I had returned from France, both women were curious. Helena had not seen me since the day that first I took the journals, and since then, the two of them had lived in a strange state of expectation. They had no idea how the reading might have affected me. They assumed (as Helena had not heard from me) that it had not changed me in the slightest. Emilia regretted that she had ever allowed them to fall into my hands, for there were times when she wished she had the journals once again in her possession, so that, upon her death, they might still be published.

That my arrival back in England came so soon after the death of Lord Quinton was a fortunate coincidence. This event allowed Helena to spin her yarn that she had been disinherited by her husband. Her fictional 'sister' who took care of the child was none other than Emilia herself. And Helena, far from being left poor, now held both Lord Quinton's town house in Bloomsbury Square and his country residence in trust for Marcus.

It seems, from what I had gathered, that Helena's mission was simply to see if I had changed. She did not think, when first she arrived here, that she would stay long. Only until she knew enough to return to Emilia and report on my current state of mind. In spite of recovering some peace of mind then, Emilia thought about me still. Though she had not forgiven me, neither had she forgotten her one short experience of love.

When Helena arrived, however, she said she was shocked to see the changes in me. She had thought that I would be no different – a little older, perhaps, but still as vain, still as heartless. What she discovered, however, was a broken man. A man who indeed continued to display a certain arrogance, but who, it was clear, was suffering. At first she tried not to be affected by it. She tried not to be touched by my deterioration, by the sorrow she sensed in me. But when she learned that I was working on these journals, she could not but be moved. She began to think that I was indeed a different man, and she longed to read what I had written, so that her suspicions might be confirmed.

One night, though she knew that it was wrong, she entered my study after I had gone to bed. Carefully noting the exact position of my work, she lifted it and took it to the library, where, by candle-light, she read, the whole night long, replacing it before I awoke. This she repeated for a second night, and when she had finished reading, she felt certain that Emilia must return. She did not know if she could persuade her, but having carried out a secret correspondence (aided, I was shocked to hear, by my faithful servant John), Emilia finally agreed.

And that, dear Reader (if ever there will be a reader of this tale, for if Emilia is indeed alive, I cannot tell if I shall ever wish to publish this precious document), is all that your Vermilion knows. It seems ridiculous, does it not, that I have spent so many months writing a kind of elegy for my dear Emilia, only to find she is not dead. It is impossible, I think, to tell you how the world has changed for me this day. How the orange light of evening seems more perfect than it has ever been. How I long to wheel myself along the path towards the fountain, so that I might drink in the strength of that sun, and learn, for the first time in many years, what it means to live in the present tense. And though I cannot think what I have done to be so favoured by the Gods, I know only that I must embrace this happiness. I know that a man who is given a second chance, has a gift, more precious than the pearl Othello once discarded.

49

VERMILION

STILL MY MELIA has not arrived. The carriage is not late. It is
not due to come here until midday. But I am impatient for it.
I feel I cannot wait that long. And though it still pains me
to write, I find this is the only occupation that can help distract
me.

This morning I rose early, at sunrise, and I ordered John to
prepare me a bath. This he did, and I removed my stinking
garments, and soaked a while in the hot water. I'll be damned, I
thought, if I'll open the windows today, and splash my vital
parts with icy-cold liquid. I am quite certain I shall not soon be
needing my precious machine, so what good would it do to
shock it with such actions? Why is it, though, that even as I
defied him, still I heard the Doctor's lilting Scots voice, resound-
ing in my ear?

And looking down at myself, thinking of the Doctor, most
surely mad as any man has been, still I mourned the fact that I
had lost him. That all the glory that once was his, now had
vanished. He was no better than any other travelling quack who
flaunts his wares upon the road. He had lost two Temples and
even his earth-baths on Panton Street. Now he was the Servant
of the Lord (Oh Wonderful Love), and the man that was my
friend was gone. Yet in spite of the change in him, I could not
help but imagine what his reaction would be to my ugly, gout-
ridden flesh. He would be disappointed in his Vermilion. Emilia
would be disappointed.

Oh God, what an ugly team the two of us will make! Indeed,
though I have thought upon her likely deformities, I have not,
till now, considered what will be her reactions to my own. For
this morning, once I had bathed, for the first time in many

months, I sat myself down before a mirror. This is a thing I have not been willing to face. The very treatment that I inflicted once upon my love. And I realized, in the instant that I saw myself, just how cruel I had been. For to witness one's own decay is a terrible thing. And what I saw, in the mirror, was a man whose appearance is beyond repair. You would not think that thirteen years could so transform the man, but here I am, balding, greying, wrinkling, fading. My hair (what is left of it) is brittle and wiry. My eyes are bloodshot; my lips, dry and mean-looking. Look what has become of Lord Vermilion! His skin is like chicken flesh! Only the fine line of his nose reminds us that this is he.

I spent nigh on two hours in front of that mirror, my gouty hands making even the simplest task seem near impossible. Shaving my bristles. Curling my periwig; powdering it thickly; positioning it to my best advantage. I would not, like Lord Smellie, paint my face with the dreaded ceruse, but I carefully plucked the stray hairs from my nose, and applied a pomade to my eyebrows, which I then coaxed into shape. Just a little rouge upon my cheeks was enough to lift their colour (without it being plain that I was painted), and the same upon my lips also, along with a touch more of that pomade to moisten them. What I achieved was barely satisfactory. I had the look of a corpse, held together by most unnatural means.

And so I am now. Dressed in my customary coat of red velvet, I am, none the less, only a pale reflection of the man that was Vermilion. In the end, Emilia despised even him. It is impossible that she will love me. However long I speak to her, admit my faults, I cannot think that she will let me in. Perhaps she comes here only to increase my suffering.

But I must stop! Already I hear the sound of hooves approaching my home. I am not ready for her! My body is prepared, but my mind is not yet ready.

I will tell you now, all that has passed this day. I vow I will not stop writing until I reach the end. A cursed habit, this scribbling is, for one whom it hurts so. But I will finish this story. If I am forced to place the quill in my mouth, I swear I'll finish it.

Remembering well, then, Helena's arrival, and her vision of me, ghost-like, at the window, I had screwed my courage to meet Emilia. On seeing the carriage approach Carmine Hall, two of the servants carried me and my chair down into the entrance hall. I am growing accustomed to this most undignified method of transport, yet today I found myself more bad-tempered than usual, afraid that Emilia might reach the door before they had put me down. My fears were not realized, however, and I was in good time to see the vehicle draw up.

Helena stood by my side. She placed her hand, reassuringly, upon my shoulder, but there was nothing could stop the rapid beating of my heart. The sense that I was about to die from too much expectation. Love me, Emilia, I thought. Only love me.

Though the sky was grey today, I barely noticed the dullness about me. All my attention was focused upon those carriage doors. Nor had I forgotten that another part of me was behind them. My son. Yet I could not imagine him. Still, as the coach driver opened the doors, it was he I saw first. A little dark-haired fellow, who skipped towards his mother. But though, in any other circumstances, I would have longed to approach him, look at him, today I could not. My eyes were fixed on some other point. A figure who emerged from the gloom within. My Emilia. Though she was dressed entirely in black, with a black veil across her face and a hat above this, I recognized the very tilt of her head; the line of her shoulders. Whatever ugliness was hidden by her veil, this was my love that moved towards us. She walked with dignity and with grace to Helena first, and put her arms about her, and her veiled cheek close to her face. Still I could not see what lay beneath the thick netting, yet I felt certain that she could see me better. She bent down a little then, so as better to greet me. Still she remained invisible, but now she spoke.

'My Lord Vermilion,' she said (never has there been a sweeter voice than this). 'How do you, sir?'

I could barely reply, so certain now was I that this was indeed Emilia.

'If this be magic,' I whispered, 'let it be an art, lawful as eating.' But if my words confused her, she did not show it. Merely, she said, 'I see you are much changed, sir. I confess I am surprised to see you so.'

'I am aged indeed,' I replied.

'No, no. I speak not of your age, Vermilion.'

And then she said no more, for she was interrupted by the child, pulling at her dress, and my eyes were drawn to him, and began to swell with brine. For here was a further joy, which I had not anticipated. This child of twelve years was the very image of my former self. When I had thought of my son, I had imagined him as a thing apart – a being quite separate from me. But now I saw the living proof that this boy was flesh of my flesh. His very being was entwined with mine. And yet he avoided looking at this stranger, bound to a wooden chair, until Emilia said, 'Marcus – you must say good-day to your uncle here – the Lord Vermilion.'

The child looked up at her, a pained expression on his face, and then he looked at me, and I saw his eyes – there was no doubting it.

'Good-day, sir,' he said, and averted his glance once again.

The next few moments passed as in a dream. I turned my chair about and wheeled myself into the entrance hall, and was followed by Helena, Emilia and Marcus, whilst several servants went out to collect their luggage. Helena announced that she would show our guests to their rooms, and as she had told me earlier that I should not expect to speak to Emilia immediately, I did not raise any objections to this. The whole scene seemed magical. Impossible to believe that this was not some reverie. My love, so close to me, yet hiding beneath veil and gloves, and barely speaking; my son, not brattish as I had been told, but shy and seeming sweet-tempered. He trotted up the stairs behind Emilia, so eagerly, as if he knew this place should be his home.

When they were gone, I asked to be carried to the top of the staircase, and I wheeled myself into my study. There, staring from the window, out at the folly, my parents' tower, I willed myself to be calm. I watched the heavy, grey clouds that seemed to shift above it. The garden seemed engulfed by their gloom. Still, in spite of this, I wished, at that moment, that I had legs that served me better. Then I would have run out there into the garden; I would have danced upon the lawns; I would have danced, even in the rain. I longed to feel the elements about me; the cold, vital air; the fresh water run down my cheeks. I regretted, instantly, my decision to be brought upstairs, for I felt the dust that hung in the air, catch my throat. This was the only room that the servants had not cleaned. I had ordered that they leave my private chamber alone. For this room has been a kind of haven for me in the months that have passed. This afternoon, however, it was a prison.

I must wait at least an hour, Helena had said, to give Emilia time to recover from the journey. I knew there was some sense in this, yet still it seemed the greatest cruelty that my love should be so near to me, yet out of reach. I could not help thinking of the words that she had said to me. 'I see you are much changed, sir.' If she did not speak of my age, to what did she refer? To my gout, perhaps? To my swollen belly? Or something else?

Just a single hour. It should not seem so long. And after that – I knew I should not have hoped it, yet I could not help it – perhaps she might always remain here. I knew that Emilia might not learn to love me, yet still I desired that she would stay. Her presence was enough. I hoped that she would find more happiness here than she has yet known. If she ever leaves me again, I know that I will die.

Unable to bear the seclusion within my study, I decided, after half of that first hour had passed, that I would take a look about my house. I had not yet gathered the courage to look at the restoration of the ballroom. I felt the very action of restoring it was a kind of insult to my parents. And yet I was curious. And I knew that to examine it would pass the time.

I wheeled myself, slowly, along the corridor, but when I was half-way along, I stopped, suddenly. For there, just inside the open door to the ballroom, stood Emilia. She must have been in a kind of daze, for in spite of the noise these little wheels made against the marble, she did not turn. Her back was towards me, and I could just see the edge of her face. It seemed she did not wear the veil.

Strange – in a sense I knew I was not ready to see her. Neither did I think that she would be prepared for me to look upon her damaged face. The moment for that revelation must be chosen carefully. First I must reacquaint myself with her. Reassure her that it was not her outer form that made me love her. And I must steel myself for what I would see, so that none of the horror I felt would be expressed upon my face. I must prepare myself for the hole, where the nose should be. I must prepare myself for the very worst of scars.

Still, I was afraid to return to my study. Though I did not wish to surprise her like this, I knew the very noise of my attempts to turn my chair about would disturb her. I was trapped in indecision; afraid to move a muscle lest it would make her sense my presence.

For several minutes I was motionless. I knew that at any moment she might turn and see me, yet I was drawn in by her stillness. She must have been entranced by the room, for I did not see even a flicker of movement about her. I was drawn, also, by her presence. By the very knowledge that she was here, alive, and close to me. Once we met again, once we spoke, perhaps I might offend her. Now, it was as if time had momentarily stopped. As if I were being blessed by this opportunity of proximity to her. Still it seemed to me as if all that had happened was impossible. That she could not truly be standing here. That she was a ghost indeed.

All of a sudden I knew that I must go. For no reason that I could discern, I felt as if the spell were broken, and I must do my best to turn and leave without distracting her. But this was in vain. The moment I began to twist the handle of my chair, she stirred. She turned around, swiftly, and saw that I had been watching her. And then I was certain that she was indeed a ghost, for the startled woman facing me was indeed my Melia, but a Melia whose face seemed barely to have changed since the very last day that I saw her. The nose was intact; there were no obvious blemishes. She looked at me, as if afraid that I had seen her. And I felt myself begin to tremble. I thought that I had become quite mad. But then she began walking towards me, and though it seemed impossible, I knew it to be true. She had even aged a little. It was the most beautiful sight that ever I had seen.

'Yes, Vermilion,' she said as she came to my side, and leaned towards me. 'Your eyes do not deceive you.'

I saw then that her skin was indeed a little scarred. A handful of imperfections scattered across her face. And I could not help but put my hand out to touch hers, needing to be certain that her flesh was warm.

'I had thought . . .' I began, and then faltered, as I found she was indeed no phantom.

'That the disease would be advanced?'

'In your journals, you said as much.'

'I think not, Vermilion. Read them again. Read my words.'

'Forgive me, Emilia,' I said. 'I find it difficult to speak. I am not myself.'

'I am sorry,' she replied. 'I had not intended so to shock you with my appearance.'

And then I began to weep. I was racked both with happiness and with remorse. I could not control the convulsions that swept my body. And seeing my reaction, she took my poor hand, so lightly within her own, and held it, I do not know how long, until I stopped.

'I had thought you dead, my Melia,' I whimpered. 'I had thought you dead, my love.'

'Indeed, I wished to die,' she replied.

'But the disease . . . I do not understand.'

'My syphilis did not go beyond the second stage, Vermilion. Once I was safe at Helena's house, the pustules began to heal. Only these little scars remain.'

'And yet you deceived me,' I said, desperation in my voice.

'You wrote that you could not bear to look at yourself. A horrifying, most ghastly sight, you said. The bile rose in your throat on seeing it. You vomited at your own reflection. Think – think how the thought affected me.'

'Vermilion,' she said, the pity suddenly having vanished from her voice. 'I know that is what you wanted me to see. When you sent the mirror, you desired me to hate myself. But I hated myself for a different reason.'

'A different reason?'

'Come. We cannot speak here. Is there some room where we may better speak? Where is that room from whence you came?'

'My study. But it is not fit for . . .'

'Come, Vermilion. Let me turn you about and take you there.'

And, not heeding my protests, Emilia pushed me in my chair towards my study, and though she coughed a little on opening the door, she simply wheeled me to the window, and pulled up a chair beside me.

'Is this how you look after yourself, Vermilion?' she asked.

'I admit I have become somewhat slovenly,' I replied.

After that, she said no more upon the subject. Indeed, she seemed entranced by the garden beyond the window, and I was again aware of the intense pleasure of simply being near to her. I had not thought that I would see her again. I did not deserve such happiness.

So many impressions had formed upon my mind in these few minutes. First, I had to accustom myself to the image of her. I had expected horror, but the changes were subtle. These tiny scars that peppered her skin in places, were not enough to spoil her physical beauty. Yet it was a different beauty from that I had known before. The features remained unchanged, her generous lips, her pale, pale eyes, and near-invisible lashes. I had near forgotten the power of them. Her thick, golden hair was coiled neatly upon her head, and seemed as lustrous as it had always been. Thirteen years had not truly changed her face. It was a little plumper, perhaps, which was a mercy as she had always been too thin. A few lines had appeared; a few creases around the eyes. But though this ageing gave her a certain distinction, it was not this that I noticed most of all. The real change ran far deeper than the skin. Though I could not, exactly, discern what the difference was I can only say it was a sense that the essence of my Melia had intensified. The looks that she shot me were stronger, bolder, than any I remember in the past. She was no longer afraid of me.

As she did not speak then, for several minutes, it was I who broke the silence.

'Emilia,' I said. 'There are so many questions that I desire to ask. So much I wish to say to you.'

'There will be time enough for that, Vermilion,' she replied, in a voice that seemed to lack compassion.

'I wish you would not hate me, Melia.'

'Do not call me by that name, Vermilion. That was never more than a ruse.'

'No, my love' (I did not dare to touch her now). 'I tell you, I loved you indeed. Love you indeed.'

'Indeed! Now you know my face is still intact. I should have known better than to leave my room without a veil.'

I knew her meaning instantly.

'You wished me to prove my love first? Before I saw your face?'

To this she did not reply.

'You thought I loved you only for your face, and so you wrote lies in your journals. You feigned your own death!'

'No, Vermilion!' she cried, impassioned now. 'That is not so.'

'Then explain to me,' I said, 'how I have misread your journals. Tell me how I was so mistaken.'

'Vermilion, I do not think you will understand it.'

'I can understand anything but your lying to me, Emilia.' And then, finally, she agreed to tell her story.

'When I looked into that mirror that you sent me,' she said, 'as I have told you, I saw no syphilitic's face. No, rather I saw a face that, in spite of everything, continued to be beautiful. A face that seemed to mock me with its radiance. I see from your expression, Vermilion, that you can make no sense of this.'

'But I am listening, Emilia. And I am trying to understand you.'

'Vermilion – you have read my journals. You know the agony that I have experienced. And yet it seemed to me, my face did not express this. A few small scars are not enough to show it. I *should* have been deformed, Vermilion – do you see? I *felt* defiled, spoiled. And I tell you – to see this beauty in a glass – it was always so painful to me. This face. This face it is that has ruined me. For why else did Lord Smellie wish to marry me? Why else did he wish to possess me? Why did the Doctor make me his Goddess, Vermilion? And why did you pretend to love me?'

'I never pretended, Emilia!'

'Oh Vermilion. You fell in love with my face, Vermilion, and my body. You did not love me.'

'I learned to love more than your face, Emilia. If only you will read my journals, also, you will know that it is true. Simply I learned it too late, my love.'

'That may be so. How can I tell, Vermilion? All I know is that what I saw in your most cruelly-given glass was an image that tortured me. Beauty is silent, Vermilion, inexpressive. When men see beauty, they do not seek to analyse it. They wish to possess it. My brother – who wished to sell me to the highest bidder; the Doctor – who wished to display me as his own, untouchable virgin; Lord Smellie – who first wished to have me be *his* wife, and when he could not, then wished to be first to defile me.'

'And I?'

'And you, Vermilion – you were worst of all. You wished to take my virginity before a crowd. The vital proof that I was yours indeed. And after that . . .'

'After that, when I had asked to be forgiven for my cruelty, I wished to marry you. But not to possess you, Emilia.'

'Yes – to possess me. For why else did you run away, once you knew Lord Smellie had raped me? Why else, Vermilion?

Because my beauty, having been possessed already, became suddenly worthless. Oh Vermilion – you were most cruel of all. Because I loved you, Vermilion. I truly loved you.'

'And I you, my Melia,' I replied. 'And I you. Only I was too stupid to know the meaning of it.'

And then, for the first time since I had seen her, this new Emilia looked me straight in the eye, as if she would detect the truth there. I say 'this new Emilia' because there was no doubt that she had changed. All her naïveté, all her superstition, seemed to have vanished.

'How changed you are, Vermilion,' she said, for a second time, echoing my thoughts about her own transformation.

'What do you mean by that?' I asked.

'Oh – when first I saw you today, I knew that a new spirit had entered you. Now I myself am to blame for regarding the outer self.'

'I am not quite so dashing as I was?'

'You are ill, Vermilion. It pains me to see it.'

Perhaps she did not know what pleasure that little phrase gave to me. Not all hope was dead then. Some stars yet sparkled in that casket-heart of hers. Some part of Vermilion remained enclosed there, still.

'Can you see beyond my illness, Emilia?' I wanted to ask, yet could not find the courage to be so honest. The words ran through my mind as the rain finally began to fall upon the garden.

But then she stood up, and said, 'I must rest now, Vermilion. It is an excitement for us both, this meeting. I would not tire you overmuch.'

'No! Stay!' (I longed to cry). 'There is no need to go yet!'

Yet instead, I nodded, meekly, and found I could not counter her wish. She was near the door when finally I overcame my new timidity. I had scooped up my manuscripts on to my lap, and began furiously to twist the handle of my chair so that I might approach her. She turned, on hearing the noise.

'Take these,' I said. 'I cannot think, on the instant, if my words will please you. I barely remember what I have written.

Still, it is a true testament of my emotion, Emilia. I hope that you will read it.'

She smiled at this, and raised an eyebrow. Again I felt the wonder of this occasion. My Melia, still flesh and blood.

'I will read it, Vermilion,' she said, taking the papers from me. 'If that is what you desire.'

And with that, she departed, leaving me alone to contemplate the life that lay ahead of me.

EMILIA

NEVER DID I think that I would see the day when I awoke, in Carmine Hall, to see the sun rise beyond the white tower, and to feel some emotion stirring within me that might be the blossoming of happiness. I chide myself, even to see those words written down. For I have been fooled before by Vermilion. Once I allowed myself to believe in his love, and then I was deceived. Should I allow him, once more, to enter my heart, when it is he that has been the instrument of my greatest misery?

What is it about the man, I wonder, that affects me so? Three days ago, when first I arrived here, I was quite shocked by the change in his appearance. Helena had warned me I would notice a difference in him, and yet I had been unable to imagine it. For I realize now that in some senses I have been guilty as he. It was Vermilion's beauty that first attracted me; the intensity of his gaze; the strength of his features; the loveliness of his dark hair. Even his arrogance made me love him, for it made me think, weak as I was, that I could follow him, and he would always lead me in the right direction. Yet suddenly, when I arrived here, I had to remake my picture of Vermilion. My Vermilion had grown grey and somewhat fat. A gouty invalid, a little too large for his chair. Yet with this physical change, the worst of him seems to have evaporated. Though I do not know how he has been affected by his experiences in France, I know, having read his journals, that he has spent the last few months thinking only of me.

I have not seen him since our meeting in his study. What a horrible room that was! The air stinks of dust, leather and port wine. The portraits on the walls are in need of attention, and the upholstery on the chairs is rotting. I do not know how

Vermilion manoeuvres his gout chair about that room, for the floor is littered with rubbish: paper and bottles are strewn about, and I doubt if it has been cleaned since first he returned from France.

Still, what do I care for all this? I speak of it only because it surprises me. It shows that the man who seemed once so in control of his life has now allowed himself to sink into despair. It seems, to me, that he has come to hate himself for his past actions. He is in great pain yet he refuses to see a physician and aggravates his condition by continuous drinking. And indeed, I believe his claims that he desired only to finish the journals, and then to die.

So many changes do I see in Vermilion, that he is barely the same man with whom once I fell in love. Yet still I trembled when I saw him. Still the look from his eyes made me quiver. When we were alone together in his study, I left him quickly, because I knew that soon I would be unable to hide my true feelings. And this time, I will not have him triumph over me. If I will return to him, he must learn to treat me as his equal. He must not think that he has merely to glance in my direction and I will submit to his will.

In spite of this, there is no doubt I remain attracted to him. It is many years since I have felt the surge of love in my veins, yet how easily it has resurfaced. I had thought that I no longer knew how to feel such passion, yet it had been dormant all along, not dead. In his eyes, I saw the essence of my Vermilion. And I remembered the power of physical desire.

I have not written yet, of course, of my reactions to his journals. Perhaps it is because the power of his words is so great that I can think of no way to describe my joy at their discovery. I know this is no hoax. When Vermilion wrote the words, he thought that I was dead. When he began writing, it is true, he still kept up the façade which was his rakish self, but how soon that began to dissolve. How complex a man he has discovered himself to be. I have not wished to see him, whilst I read his words. I wished to finish them first, and I am glad that he has not attempted to see me. For I needed time to adjust to the man he has become

Yes, how strange it has been to read of his suffering. For so many years I have thought that he remained indifferent to me. I have lived my quiet life, and convinced myself that I have found a kind of happiness. For when Helena said her son was most unpleasant, and like his would-be father, Lord Quinton, in fact she lied to prevent Vermilion from mourning his loss. Marcus is a charming child, and when he was three years old, Lord Quinton, recognizing that my syphilis was indeed gone, yielded to his wife's fondness for me and allowed me to be his son's governess. I have spent my time since then between Bloomsbury and Yorkshire, and I have found some peace in this quiet existence. I have learned to suppress the love that never truly died.

And now! To find my love has been returned. It is an unhoped-for gift. Yet still, I must not hope too much. For though his words express a love as deep as my own, I cannot be sure that his actions will match his words. And I refuse to be subservient to his will. I am not the Melia that once he knew. My mind is full of different thoughts to those that used to occupy it. Now I have no fears of being possessed by the Devil. Now my vanity has fled, and my self-pity also. Rather, I have been reading the newspapers. I am surprised, indeed, how little Vermilion has written about France, for there is much afoot there that must not be ignored. Not a mention of Marat's murder! Not a word of the fear which made him flee! It seems, to me, that Vermilion has been living in a dream-world here. He has isolated himself from the world. Whilst the great Revolution Debate is all the rage in London, to Vermilion it is nothing. He has wanted, it seems, to leave all life behind him.

I cannot verily tell what will be the outcome of all this. Helena, it appears, having observed Vermilion for several months, now wishes that the two of us should be reunited. She says that whilst she cares for him still, she no longer harbours any desire for the man. I do believe my friend, and yet I doubt Vermilion. Though sometimes I have thought our lives were bound to be entwined, other times I fear the union. And yet already I find myself caring for him. Though Helena has told me he has refused to see a physician, I have arranged for one to come today, for I have heard gout can be cured, if the patient will only do as the doctors ask. Even in the few moments I was with Vermilion, I perceived his agony. And if he would have me love him, then first I shall insist he learns, once again, to love himself.

Already, I see, the sun is higher in the sky. The greyness of my first day here has departed, and now the autumn sun illumines the grounds. How beautiful it is here. I had never realized it would be quite so beautiful. In the last few minutes, Vermilion has emerged into the garden, accompanied by young Marcus. My window is open and I can hear them laughing together, Vermilion and his son. The boy is running ahead, eager to explore, but Vermilion's chair has stuck upon the path, and now Marcus runs back and pushes the father, whom he does not know to be his father, along. And I know, on seeing this, I must not leave. For this is no place for a man alone. If Helena had not come here, I dread to think how Vermilion would be now. And if we were to leave, all of us, tomorrow, the thought of him wheeling himself around in that chair, with no friends to keep him company – that is intolerable. I cannot think that he would survive very long.

No. Perhaps I had decided this the very moment I stepped from my coach. Or even before that, when I saw the gateway in the distance. Perhaps there is a part of us that can recognize what is home, and has no need to reason it. Already, it is clear: I shall remain at Carmine Hall.

VERMILION

SUCH AN ORDEAL I have had this morning. Emilia has sent a doctor to me, and Helena told me that if I refused to see him, my Melia would refuse to see me! To make matters worse, even, having seen this wretched fellow, and agreed to follow his regimen, I now discover that Emilia has left the house. She has gone to explore the gardens with young Marcus. How much longer will she keep me waiting?

This was a *serious* doctor. He did not come brandishing Aetherial Balsam, nor did he advocate a week buried to my neck in mud! No! This doctor was dressed from head to toe in black, a slow-moving and stern-looking fellow, whose wig had not a hair out of place, and whose tight lips seemed incapable of emitting the bellowing voice that escaped from them. This was a man who seemed, to me, completely without humour, and yet, though I have decided (for Emilia's sake) to take some notice of his words, I could not help but wish to laugh at nearly every sentence he uttered.

'Lord Vermilion, my first advice to a gouty man such as yourself is to avoid eating meat that is over-cooked. I do not mean, by this, sir,' he said, 'to recommend the customs of Cannibals and Tartars, who eat raw flesh; or beasts of prey, that devour animals alive. (But it may be observed, that the first are free from diseases, and the other, amazingly strong and vigorous.) Lord Vermilion, when we pickle, preserve, pot and smoke our meats, we destroy their ability to be easily dissolved within our bodies. They keep for years, like mummies!

'And to these instructions I would add this, which is even more important: the stomach wants wine no more than the nose wants snuff! For when we drink overmuch, nature, like a true female, cries out at the first violence, but submits in time, is reconciled, and grows fond of the ravisher. The worst offenders, Lord Vermilion, I tell you, are Madeira and port, which instead of dissolving, harden everything within the stomach, and thus leave a crapulary, crude, sour load of yesterday, to ferment, fret, and irritate the stomach and bowels every day.'

'But what, doctor,' I replied, finally managing to interrupt his monologue, 'what relevance are these things to my gouty condition?'

'Sir,' he said, 'the gout is caused by over-indulgence!'

'And may it be cured, by temperance?' I asked.

'The popular opinion, which no doubt you have heard before, is that it cannot! They say it is an incurable disease, yet I tell you, though you are too far gone to make a complete recovery, that by following my advice, I assure you your fits of gout will become less frequent, far shorter, and less violent. Your joints, though they will never be perfectly straightened, should indeed reduce in size. You need not be such an invalid as you are.'

'And tell me, doctor,' I said, still doubtful as to the possibility of this, 'what must I do to achieve this type of recovery? Must I starve myself, perhaps? Or worse, avoid the drinking of wine?'

'Indeed no, sir. For you may eat any meat, so long as it is not preserved by any of the methods that I have mentioned, and you may eat plentifully of fresh vegetables and fruit. You may eat bread also.'

'Doctor, I have heard this before, from one Dr James Graham, of the Adelphi Temple!'

'Indeed,' the man replied, 'and though he was most certainly a quack he did not always spout electrical rubbish. I advise you to follow his dietary advice.'

This doctor concluded his advice by saying that in addition to Temperance he would also advocate Activity and Peace of Mind. As soon as I felt ready for it I must walk a little each day, even if I could only manage two or three minutes at first. He also prescribed a soft and slowly operating laxative, and a daily rub with flannels or flannel gloves, fumigated with gums and

401

spices, which should brace and strengthen my nerves and fibres and move my blood about without any fatigue to myself.

And that, I suppose, would have been the end of it, had I not offered him some coffee before he left. We sat together in my bedroom, sipping from little cups, with a small fire burning in the grate. At first I continued to ask him about his gout-cures, at which he furnished me with several tales of Gentlemen such as myself, who had found great relief by following his methods. After a few minutes, however, when there was a pause in the conversation between us, I sensed that the doctor had something that he wished to say to me.

'Lord Vermilion,' he began. 'When first I came here today, I felt that your name was familiar to me.'

'And why is that, sir?' I asked, intrigued.

'There was a man I tended once, around two years ago,' he said, 'in Colchester. I tended him upon his death-bed, and he used, in his delirium, to utter strange words which I could make no sense of.'

'What did he say?'

'I cannot remember his exact words, sir, but I do recall that he claimed that like the cat, he had nine lives! When I asked him what he meant by this, he said that he had died once already, the first time by Vermilion's hand, and that this second death was not the end of him.'

'Tell me more, doctor,' I said. 'Tell me more.'

'Yes. It is all coming back to me now. He used to utter nonsense that in his third life he would be stronger. More than that, I cannot say.'

'I believe you are concealing something, doctor,' I said.

'Indeed sir, for if it is you that he spoke of, I would not frighten you with a dead man's curses.'

'Come, doctor! I am not frightened by such things. What did he say?'

'Well – since you insist on it. He said that when he lived again, he'd be certain to kill the Vermilion fellow.'

'And yet two years have passed, and I am not dead yet.'

'No, sir, I am glad to witness it.'

'Nor am I afraid of the curses of this man. For I know of only one person who might have lived in Colchester. And it is true I thought that I had killed him once. You speak of Lord Smellie, do you not?'

'The very man, sir. Yet tell me this. He said that you had shot him dead, and that he sprang to life again. I remember this nonsense. There was not a bullet mark upon him.'

'No, nor would there be. Yet I will not tell you the meaning of this secret, until you tell me more about his death. It was syphilis, I presume?'

'Oh no, sir. No. For though I tended him whilst he had the pox, he never went beyond the second stage of that disease.'

I was sorry to hear this. I had always hoped that Smellie would die a most ghastly death.

'What was it, then, that killed the man so young?'

'A terrible thing, Lord Vermilion, that I would not even wish upon an enemy.'

'Nothing can be too terrible for *him*, doctor. I hope that you will tell me that his death was slow and agonizing.'

'He must have been a villain indeed, to have deserved this. He died of lead-poisoning.'

'*Lead-poisoning?*'

'Indeed. From wearing too much of that ceruse upon his face. From the time that he was a young boy, he painted his face with a compound of white lead. His desire for the perfect complexion, sir, not only deformed him, but killed him in the end.'

And then I could not help but laugh. It was strange. It was not exactly mirth that I was feeling. The very mention of the man had made my blood boil with indignation. Yet how apt that he should die of this! That his very vanity should have killed him! Lead-poisoning. I should have guessed it. My laughter bubbled in my chest. It spilled over and its sound filled the room.

'Tell me more, doctor,' I said, when I was finally able to catch my breath. 'I pray you – tell me more.'

'It is not my business, sir,' he said, stern as ever, 'to speak of a man's illness as if it were a joke.'

'Oh pish, doctor. The man was evil. He ruined two lives. And I'll treble your fee if you will tell me of his suffering.'

I do not think this doctor cared if Smellie were evil or not, but the mention of the fee made him forget his reluctance to speak. However, I will admit that when I heard his tale, I found it was impossible to continue laughing. To say that he died from over-painting his face is a funny thought! But to know the whole of it – that is something else.

The doctor told me that Lord Smellie, like myself, was stubborn and ignored his symptoms for some time before consulting a physician. Had Emilia or I (or indeed Smellie) known the first thing about medicine, we would have realized, on first spying that blue line etched upon his gums, what was his ailment. For that, the doctor told me, together with the constipation that he complained of, and the pains in his stomach, were amongst the surest early symptoms of the poisoning.

According to the doctor, by the time that his illness was diagnosed, Lord Smellie was too affected by the poison to avoid his certain fate. The constant use of the ceruse had not only poisoned him but discoloured his face yellow and black. Whilst the boy Smellie began by desiring to hide a few freckles and small blemishes, the man ended by painting ceruse across a complexion destroyed by the very agent that he used to disguise it.

Thus it was that our Macaroni jester killed himself. Soon after Lord Smellie ran away from London, the doctor said his hair would have begun to drop. His appetite would have been very small. He would have been listless, clumsy, tired, nauseous. And he would have been covered in the pox that had affected my Emilia. Indeed, as this doctor had prescribed mercury for Smellie's syphilis (which made me, suddenly, somewhat distrustful of him), Smellie's teeth turned quite black, and eventually he lost almost all of them.

How strange it was to think of this. That the fate which I feared had befallen my Emilia had instead overtaken the very character who truly deserved it. The primping, preening Macaroni had turned into a freakish monster. The doctor told me his wrists had dropped, so that he had very little strength in his hands. His speech became slow and he suffered from the constant taste of metal in his mouth. As he became more and more infirm, he was confined to his bed, but still he insisted that his servant paint his face each day, and that a hair-dresser attend him to curl his periwig. Though he seldom had visitors, he said that he could not live with his ugliness exposed to the world.

What a pitiful sight Lord Smellie must have been in those last years. How horrible those symptoms from which he finally died. His memory was much disturbed, the doctor said, he suffered unbearable abdominal pain, and frequently vomited (with great difficulty) a thin green liquid bile. Eventually, Smellie began to suffer convulsions also. First he lost the use of one half of his face, then his right arm and then his leg. The doctor was there as my enemy died. 'Paint my face when I am in my coffin and ensure my lips are cherry red!' These were his final words.

EMILIA

WHEN, EVENTUALLY, I came in from the garden, Helena joyfully told me that Vermilion had indeed seen the doctor I had sent. She said that she had peeped in upon him since, and, seeing that he was busy with his pen, she had left him alone.

I, however, felt that I could wait no longer until I saw him. When we were out of doors, Marcus had told me that in spite of the fact that he was an invalid, Lord Vermilion was the kindest fellow he had ever met, and when I laughed at the description Marcus looked at me, bewildered.

I knocked upon Vermilion's door. He bade me enter, and when I did so, he looked up from his book, and darted such a glance at me, that I felt obliged to look away. Then, knowing this was no good, I looked at him again. Our eyes met, and for a moment neither of us spoke. I knew, in that moment, that there would be no separating us. The man before me in a gout chair was not the Vermilion I once had known. We were bound together, I felt, by invisible threads. Spirits danced about us, spinning hair-thin ties around our mortal forms. There was no world beyond us.

It was Vermilion who spoke first.

'I am glad you are here,' he said. 'Come. Sit by me.'

And I joined him, close to the fire. I felt the flames flush my cheeks.

'I have read your journals, Vermilion,' I said.

He seemed somewhat embarrassed at this as he replied.

'Oh – they are not well written.'

'On the contrary, sir. I had not expected such eloquence.'

'No doubt I say many things which will make you uncertain of me.'

'No such thing. I am convinced that you have changed, Vermilion.'

'A pity then,' he said, 'that I was not able to change whilst I was still handsome.'

'Perhaps your very handsomeness might have prevented the change.'

'I hope not, Emilia,' he said. 'I hope not.'

We were silent again then, each of us feeling, I think, that it might be too soon to speak the words that waited on our tongues. Instead of voicing my love then, I asked him about the doctor.

'You had a visit from the physician this morning, Vermilion, did you not?'

'Indeed I did,' he said. 'And I am most hopeful that my condition may improve.'

'Has he prescribed some medicine for you?'

'He has. But chiefly, he says that I must cure myself. I must abstain from alcohol and from all meats except those cooked very plainly.'

'He sounds very like Dr Graham!'

It was the first time that his name had been mentioned

between us, and to say it served as a kind of release, I think, for both of us.

'Yes!' he laughed. 'It will be very like being in the Temple again!'

'Have you heard from the Doctor, Vermilion?'

'Indeed I have,' he said, 'and it is to my shame that I did not reply. He is, I think, quite mad. He has styled himself the Servant of the Lord, Oh Wonderful Love, and he has repented of his use of electricity. Now he bathes up to his mouth in mud for hours on end, and vows he can live for many days without any nourishment whatsoever.'

'Then what I have read is true indeed. I have seen it in the newspapers, Vermilion. And I have heard it said that he claims he will live to the age of one hundred and fifty.'

'Yes. I have heard that also.'

'Do you think it is possible?'

'I do not know, Emilia. The Doctor has always been able to surprise us.'

'Indeed. I remember when I entered the Temple for the very first time. I was so angry at my brother . . .'

'Your brother Daniel! Do you still see him, Emilia?'

'No, Vermilion. I have not seen him since the day when you threatened my honour before him and Lord Smellie. I have heard that he left the Adelphi on the day of your duel. Also, I have been told that the house on the Terrace has been sold, but I have never, since that day, set eyes upon my brother.'

I saw the pity then, on Vermilion's face, and the sorrow also.

'Have you never tried to find him?'

'No. I have thought about it often. Sometimes I remember the brother that I loved. The one who taught me how a pearl is formed from a grain of sand. The one who talked to me of Descartes. The clumsy brother. The brother who could not keep his curls in place. I loved him, Vermilion. But on that day when he told Lord Smellie that I could be tamed, he ceased to be a relation of mine.'

'And yet after that day, you found it possible to forgive me. Why not him?'

'It was his duty to protect me, Vermilion. He was bound to me by blood. And he betrayed me.'

'And so you have no family remaining.'

'No family but Helena, and Marcus. But in truth they are your family, Vermilion, not mine.'

'Helena no longer loves me, Emilia. You know that. She only desires that you and I might find some happiness.'

'Helena has been most kind to me. I would do much to please her.'

'I hope you will not love me simply to please Helena.'

He took my hand then, even though I saw it pained him, and I found I could not remove it, nor could I deny that I did indeed love him still.

'Now that I have read your words, Vermilion, I do not doubt the strength of your love. Only – I have been so long alone . . .'

'Marry me, Emilia,' he said, 'and I will be more than husband to you. I will be father and brother and sister and son. My love will encircle you, wherever you might walk. If you fall, Emilia, I will be there to catch you. You will not utter a word, but that it will be treasured.'

'You have been reading too much poetry, Vermilion!'

'And what if I have! I'd crack the poet's skull in two if I knew I could find words there that would win you.'

'Words are not enough, Vermilion. You know that by now.'

'Do you need more proof of my devotion? Emilia, since the month of June I have done nothing but think of you. I have done nothing but devote myself to your memory.'

'And it is that which makes me love you now, Vermilion,' I said, wondering if I might regret my words. 'In truth, Vermilion, I wished for no further proof than a simple kiss.'

At which my love took my hand and I moved towards him, and felt his arm encircle my waist. I bent down by his side, and felt the warmth of his breath, close to me. And indeed, there are no words to speak of this. This home-coming. This long-forgotten feeling spreading through me. Warm blood. I bit his lips and tasted his sweet blood. Blood in my throat and in my veins. No difference between them. Blood between my teeth.

Blood on my tongue. I heard him gasp then. Or was it I that could not catch my breath? Two mouths, but which of them was mine? The one that spoke. The one that uttered words between the kisses.

'Yes, Vermilion. I will marry you.'

And then, again, I lost the sense of being separate.

52

VERMILION

TOMORROW IS OUR wedding day. Two months have passed since either of us has set pen to paper. Oh – we began with good intentions. We wished to chronicle the progress of our love. And yet, when one is happy, how dull the prospect of sitting at a desk! How dull the thought of an hour's scribbling, when that time could be spent in the company of one's love.

So it is that we have neglected our tale. Instead, we have been busy, reacquainting ourselves with one another, and I, also, have spent much time with my young son. He is a delightful child, more headstrong than at first I thought him, very quick to learn, and sometimes suspicious. I think he is still somewhat confused by this sudden change of circumstances. Though he was not, apparently, very close to Lord Quinton, he has been affected by the loss of him, and cannot be expected to recover quickly from this, nor from the long absence that his mother has so recently inflicted on him. We have decided that it is best he thinks of me as an uncle. I am told there is enough gossip in the village about our household, without disclosing the truth. For this reason, I shall make arrangements to prevent the publication of this document until after Marcus's own death. If he should guess at my identity (for the strong resemblance between us is most marked) then we will be honest. Otherwise, we all agree, this knowledge is best kept secret. He will be my adopted son, and I will do all I can to be a father to him. To speak the truth would be, I feel, a selfish act.

I do not know if ever this document will be read. Still, we feel, it is essential to complete it. To have come so far and leave the tale unfinished would seem most foolish.

Let me tell you, then, that in these past two months Emilia

and I have reached an understanding of one another that I never thought could be possible between two human beings. Though it seems, perhaps, that when she arrived she forgave me very quickly, do not doubt that she has expressed much anger since then. Many times I have thought that she would change her mind and not marry me at all, for her memories of my betrayal are so painful to her, and, when she thinks upon it, she feels she cannot trust me again. At times like that, I have found that nothing will pacify her anger and her resentment, which seem directed not only at me, but all mankind. I have no defence, of course, in this, but to admit my guilt and to speak of my regret and my love. I try to remain with her when she rails, for I know that I deserve the words she fires at me. Sometimes it is several hours before she will forgive me, but that forgiveness, when it comes, is so precious to me that I would endure far fiercer onslaughts if I knew that such sweetness would eventually be my reward.

Only in the past few weeks have Emilia's emotions begun to settle. Now I know that she loves me indeed. And I love her, this new Emilia, this different Emilia. Once she was so innocent, so naïve, so weak. I loved the spirit that inhabited her then, but now it has developed and is stronger, more knowledgeable, more confident, and this I love yet more. She has read, on Helena's prompting, *A Vindication of the Rights of Woman*, and has been influenced by what she has found there. Indeed, so impressed have I been by the lines she has read me from this book that I have been forced to reassess my opinion of the author, and I have read it myself. Though I cannot think it is quite possible to live as Wollstonecraft would have us live (indeed, from what I have heard, she does not even live by her principles herself), there is much sense in what she writes. And, having read it, I know that Emilia's indecision about marrying me (for do not doubt, there have been times when she has regretted her hasty acceptance) has stemmed from the fear that she has been too sentimental; that she is spurred by lust and by emotion, and not by sober judgement. Only constant discussion between us has assured her that our marriage will be based on more than mere passion. That what connects us is our new-found friendship, also. Though Wollstonecraft would have it that love and friendship cannot subsist within the same breast, there I do strongly oppose her views.

Perhaps you think it strange that Emilia still expresses her passion for me. Do you think it is based on a mere memory of what I was, and that when she leans to kiss me, she closes her eyes and thinks of the face of a younger Vermilion? How could she, after all (you say), desire an invalid? Well, it is not for me to reason this, yet I will say that I believe she loves me now, more than she ever has. I have seen her face light up on seeing me. I have seen her look upon *my* face, and trace each feature with a love I could never have imagined. Also, I should tell you that I am recovering from my illness. In spite of my scepticism, I have been following the physician's regime. I have not touched a drop of alcohol since the day that he visited me, nor have I put a spoon in the pickle pot, or eaten any preserved meats. To my surprise, I have found I am experiencing a reduction in the swelling of my joints. I have been walking a little also, increasing the amount of time I spend out of my chair each day. Sometimes I walk alone in the gardens with Emilia (or hobble, rather, I should say), and sometimes we go together, all four of us, and I speak with Helena whilst Emilia looks after Marcus. There is no jealousy or resentment. Helena's love for me died long ago, and she seems happy to live here with her son and her friends.

Whilst I recover, however, I cannot help but think what might have been my fate had I remained in France. Since Emilia has returned, I have begun to take an interest once again in the world beyond Carmine Hall, and what I have heard has distressed me much. The Queen of France, Marie Antoinette, was executed on the very day Emilia returned to me. Whilst I was experiencing such joy, that noble lady dressed herself in white for the occasion of her murder. They cut off her hair that morning as she left her tiny cell. She was bound and put upon a cart, which took her to her place of execution. It is said that as she ascended the scaffold, she trod heavily on the foot of the executioner, and the very last words she spoke were, 'I beg your pardon. I did not do it on purpose.'

Nothing but silence is adequate to express my sorrow at this deed. Nor can I find it in me truly to believe what is happening in Paris. The Duc d'Orléans, Madame Roland, Bailly, Barnave – all of them have died beneath the guillotine. I do not know where this will end. It seems the whole world has been changing, whilst I, Vermilion, have done nothing but dwell upon my memories.

But come! Today has been too joyful to think upon this now. For I woke, this morning, shivering with cold, to see icicles hanging from my window-sill. Winter has come again then. Suddenly, and without warning. It is December now. There will be no roses nor no cornflowers for our wedding. Instead, I will gather holly for my Melia. I will bind the branches together, so that she will not prick her fingers upon the thorns.

Once I was dressed this morning I walked over to my window and saw a sight I have not seen for many years. The grounds of Carmine Hall were swathed in white. A snow had fallen in the night, and my garden was quite transformed by it. No one had yet set foot outside the house, so there was not a blemish on the surface of the earth.

Instantly I thought of my childhood. When I was a boy, I had always loved this weather most. My parents' folly, the white tower, never seemed more perfect, more a part of the landscape, than at times like this, when the whole world was white as it. This was a child's paradise, and I opened my window to sense it fully. My eyes ached; were dazzled by all this brightness. The fountains were frozen over. The entrance to the grotto was now invisible.

I knew when I saw it what I would do today. For tomorrow our nuptials will be taking place. Love has returned to Carmine Hall. I rang for John and he fetched me coats and boots and rugs, and wheeled me to Emilia's room. She was already dressed, and when I advised her of our excursion, she was glad to come with me. I was carried downstairs, and Emilia pushed my chair out into the garden. The little wheels soon became stuck in the snow, however, so I took my stick and said stubbornly that I would walk.

In truth, I barely felt any pain at all this morning, in spite of my exertion. We kept to the path, crisp beneath our feet, and Emilia held my hand to help me, as we walked along the row of limes, heavy with clumps of snow. Once or twice I stumbled, but always she supported me, and eventually we reached the foot of the tower.

Then, as I had seen my father do, on wintry mornings long ago, I took a large key from my pocket and went to insert it in the lock. It was all frozen over, but I persevered and eventually I was able to turn the key.

As the door opened before us, I was overcome with the memories that greeted me. The smell of the place, which had been contained there for countless years, now spilled out into the icy air. The smell of old stone, and moss and cobwebs. In spite of the cold, they were all there. The smell of small animals. The smell of two people, long dead now: my dear parents. I had thought that there was nothing left of them, yet it seemed their spirits lingered here.

I like to think that Emilia sensed them too this morning. When that door opened (of its own accord, almost, it seemed), she looked at me as if she understood everything, even though I had told her nothing of this place. A love monument. She knew it. It did not need to be spoken. She was so beautiful at that moment. There! I have tried not to say it, yet it spills out, in spite of myself. Will I be believed, perhaps, if I say that the beauty was in her expression, not in her features alone? It was her happiness that moved me. The animation that I saw there. I knew that finally she trusted me.

Together, we ascended the spiral staircase. I, before her, with my stick, slowly, determined I would not stumble. She was patient behind me, not questioning my ability to climb. She would not hurt my pride in such a way. As I walked, I remembered the last time that I had ascended these stairs. How I leapt up them, a boy, like young Marcus. I'd bring him here too, before long, and show him the sight that had always so astounded me when I was young.

Now, of course, this task was arduous to me. Only the sure knowledge of the gift that it would bring me enabled me to continue. Round and round we walked, step after step, the two of us, together in this tower of stone. The walls rose high above us, smooth and white as the snow. The tip-tap of my stick and of our steps echoed all around.

Eventually I felt a cold breeze against my face. I knew then that we were nearly there. Just a dozen more steps. And then we reached the summit. I climbed through the little doorway at the top, and then I helped Emilia through, and watched as she walked forward to edge of the parapet. I saw her gasp: the swift intake of breath and the look of incredulity that crossed her face. Then I moved forward to join her and saw it too. The whole of the snow-covered metropolis, spread out before us.

For me, who for six months had seen nothing beyond the gates of Carmine Hall, it was a revelation. My world had become so narrow of late, so very enclosed, and I felt a liberation on seeing this. This frozen city. Fields and fields of whiteness and, beyond that, the icy roof-tops.

'Look – I can see St Paul's!' Emilia said.

And indeed, it was just possible to make out that distant pale dome.

'And can you see Ranelagh?' I asked.

'Where?'

'Over there – you see – you can see the gardens around it.'

We could not see everything from there, but we spent some time trying to trace the places which we had known so well.

'That must be the Strand,' Emilia said.

'Yes. And St James's Park, a little further along.'

I held her hand then, for I realized that we were surveying our past here. The river was plain to see, yet for a moment we did not speak of it, nor did we seek to point to that place where the Adelphi nestled behind roof-tops. Even so, I knew where Emilia's eyes had come to rest. I knew what went through her mind. She was looking to see whether the boats were moving. Trying to discover whether the Thames had frozen.

'I have seen that city burn, Vermilion,' she said suddenly. 'I have been besmirched by that city.'

She was silent a while, and when I did not respond, she continued to speak.

'When I first came to know the metropolis, there was a frost, just like this one. I thought it was a kind of new beginning for me. Of all that passed before that time, I was ignorant. And I regret all that has passed since. But it is over now – do you understand? The ice cleanses London. We *may* begin again.'

I kissed her then, to mark that new beginning. I kissed my Melia, knowing that tomorrow she would be my wife. And then I took her hand, and together we walked around the parapet. There was a statue I wanted to show her. One my father had commissioned when the tower was first built.

'Look,' I said, as we approached the small figure. 'Do you recognize him?'

She laughed.

'Of course,' she replied.

It was a marble statue of a young man of extraordinary beauty. He was crowned with flowers and he held a torch in his hand. But his torch was dripping icicles, and the flowers were topped with snow.

'It is Hymen, is it not?'

'Indeed it is.'

'They say no marriage will endure if his spirit is not present at the nuptials.'

'And do you believe that, Emilia? Do we have need of such superstition?'

'I think not,' she replied, suddenly sure of her purpose. 'Hymen has had his day.'

Together we turned then from the statue, not looking back, but moving once again around the parapet. When we reached the other side, we stood quietly for a while, our fingers entwined. The glare of the frost brought tears to my eyes. And it seemed, for a moment, to suspend the city. For beneath us, London was still. London was silent. Only the breath of my lover echoed in my ear.

53

EMILIA

VERMILION HAS SAID it should be I that write the final words which will conclude this tale. He tells me that all he has thought, he has entered already in these pages. He says he has no desire to try to close the story, for he says it has no end. It is continuous.

And indeed, I believe this to be true, for I tell you, Reader, a change has come about. For here, in this sea-shell womb of mine, a pearl is forming. I feel it, already, though it is very small. I cherish it. I place my hand upon my abdomen, and imagine the beating heart of my new child.

Six months have passed now, since our nuptials, and there has been much joy and laughter at Carmine Hall. The new ballroom is completed. Vermilion, still, has not been brave enough to enter it, and yet I believe that he will. I think that he is ready to accept the death of his parents. I think that he is ready to live again.

Before long, then, the ballroom will be used once more. The sound of a hundred voices will echo along the corridors. And I should tell you that Vermilion, also, may be dancing there. His health is much improved. By changing his habits, he has begun to transform himself. Love and the physicians have made him new. And though he has not discarded his stick, he no longer has need of his chair. Now whole days pass by when he feels no pain at all. And even when the attacks of the gout do return, they are less frequent than before, and less intense.

In truth, I would say that our happiness was quite complete. Through the long thirteen years when I was without my love, I could never have imagined that this would come to pass. That he loved me all along. That he would one day marry me. That I would bear his child. Indeed, our joy has been marred only by the news which we have heard, just two days ago. It came to us in a letter, addressed to Vermilion, dated the twenty-fourth of June.

Dear Sir,
I regret to inform you of the sudden death of one who I know was once a friend to you. My brother-in-law, Dr James Graham, died yesterday, at his house opposite the Archers' Hall, Edinburgh. He was forty-nine years old.
Should you wish to attend his funeral, I shall be forwarding the details presently.
Sincerely yours,
Dr Thomas Arnold

It is strange, perhaps, that both of us should be so moved by this event. When he had read the letter, Vermilion began to tremble. He sat down as I approached him, and he handed it to me, unable to speak. I, too, was overcome by the words that I saw written. It seemed impossible to me that this had come to pass. Some freakish event of nature that was most unnatural. For how *could* he have died? Had he not vowed he would live till he was one hundred and fifty? Did not his extraordinary medicines have the power to achieve at least a longer life than this? Though I did not summon it, I heard a strain of music, inside my head. And the words that accompanied it.

Hail! Vital Air – Ætherial! – Magnetic Magic – Hail!
Thine Iron Arm – thy bracing sinewy Arm! – is everlasting Strength!
And thou, celestial Fire! – Thou, FIRE ELECTRIC – GREAT
    RENOVATOR–
THE LIFE OF ALL THINGS! Hail!
Come, then, ah come! O sacred HEALTH!
The Monarch's Bliss! – the Beggar's Wealth;
Root of the soft and rosy Face!
The vivid Puffe – each charm, each Grace!
The Spirits when they gayest shine;
Youth, Beauty, Pleasure – all are THINE!

Vermilion looked at me then, his eyes brimming over. I realized that I had been quietly singing, and I stopped abruptly. So struck with sorrow was I that I barely knew what was happening to me. I could *see* the Doctor, ascending the staircase in a blaze of whiteness. I could hear his voice – sand in an hourglass. *Remember, my Vestina. Here you shall know nothing but calm and serenity. In my Temple, your soul will be cleansed.* Whatever he had done to me, I knew that he, like Vermilion, had loved me. I remembered the night when the Gordon Riots were just beginning, when he had slept by my side. Just thinking of it, I could smell him. The overpowering scent of jasmine. I remember how he cried and how his salt-water tears fell upon me. Yes, it seemed impossible that he was gone. .

Only this morning, I have been reading about the Doctor in the newspaper. They write that towards the end of his life he would madden himself with opium, rush out into the streets, and strip himself to clothe the first beggar he met. But I cannot believe these words. I will not believe that he was so deranged. Even if it were true, I will never remember him thus.

We have decided not to attend the Doctor's funeral. Vermilion thinks that the journey would be too arduous for one in my condition. And indeed, I know the Doctor himself would not wish to risk the life of a child thus. Helena, however, will be attending, and she has said that she will scatter flowers on his grave on our behalf. White roses, she says; she can think of no fitter blossom.

Now, I have no more to tell. My story is indeed beginning, and the thought of this is a source of strength to me. I do not fear beginnings any longer. I know that the child, within me, is no Devil Child. I know there is no curse that hangs over me.

Indeed, what lies ahead is likely to be ordinary. In Carmine Hall there will be no miracles. No cripples fully cured. No blind men made to see. In Carmine Hall, there will be no Macaronis with painted faces, no Quack Doctors promising what is impossible. No. And though in France, heads are rolling, a terror reigns, I can only hope that here, in England, we will see no such thing. We will sleep in beds made of wood. We shall no longer witness electricity leaping across the room, but rather shall watch it in the heavens, and be glad that it remains there.